In the dark hallway outside the silent bedroom, Carey stared. Her flashlight beam glinted off something on the hall carpet.

She touched it gingerly. It was wet. And sticky.

She flung the bedroom door open, dashing for her friend's bed.

The dead face stared up at her, a silent shriek contorting its dessicated inhuman features.

A muted creak penetrated her consciousness.

She turned and fled, desperate to outrun the sounds behind her.

But they were following her. . . .

DARIELLE KEITH

Dark Union

A DELL/EMERALD BOOK

Published by
Dell Publishing Co., Inc.
1 Dag Hammarskjold Plaza
New York, New York, 10017

Dell TM 681510, Dell Publishing Co., Inc.

ISBN: 0-440-01694-0

Printed in the United States of America

First printing—September 1983

For my husband, John
And especially for
String Bean, from Tomato

Like to the apples on the Dead Sea's shore,
All ashes to the taste.

. . . in the dark union of insensate dust.

—Lord Byron

1

Carey Hunter, brown eyes narrowed to slits against the glare of the late-afternoon sun on the waters of the bay, wheeled sharply to the left, off the narrow paved road onto the dirt driveway that widened almost immediately into the ferry parking lot. She had heard the rhythmic chug of the little boat's diesel engine from some distance up the county road, before she'd been able to see the dock through the pine trees hemming in the road between the town of South Bay and Archie's ferry. The six-o'clock ferry was the last out to the bay islands until the next morning.

The driveway and parking lot were rutted and scored with tire tracks, and Carey came dangerously close to losing control of the borrowed bike and taking a nosedive as she braked to a stop at the edge of the wooden dock.

"Archie!" she shouted. "Wait for me! I just have to put your bike back in the barn, okay?"

Archie English was loosening the bowline at the far end of the dock. He straightened up, holding the line taut against the pull of the outgoing tide, his bright blue eyes squinting at her out of his weather-beaten face despite the fact that the descending sun was over his right shoulder. With almost the full length of the old dock separating them, he looked to Carey even smaller than he was.

"Good enough where she is," he called back, the enigmatic smile crisping the corners of his surprisingly full lips plain to hear in his voice. "Put her away myself when I get back. Just set her up against that stump there . . ."

"Thanks, Archie," Carey yelled into the stiff offshore

7

breeze. She hurried the bike across the parking lot. "I'm sorry I'm late."

She made sure the bike was steady against the rotting pine stump, then raced back across the lot, out onto the dock, and clambered down into the stern of the old half-decked motor launch. The polished oak planks set below the gunnels port and starboard and across the stern formed a U-shaped open passenger-and-cargo compartment, the deck of which was crowded with cardboard cartons and wooden crates bursting with summer fruits and vegetables.

The only other passengers were four teenagers seated along the port rail. Carey smiled fleetingly at them and began to struggle out of her loaded knapsack. Archie tossed the bowline aboard, raced down the dock, loosed the sternline, and flung it on the board. He leaped into the stern beside Carey and strode forward to the wheel. He had the ferry under way before she sat down.

As she was shoving her knapsack under the seat, Carey felt she was being watched. She glanced up. The four teenagers were eyeing her closely; their faces betrayed no expression.

"Hi," Carey smiled at them, a little uncomfortably. "Are you going to Fustin's? Island?" she added, in case they were new to the bay area. When they did not acknowledge that she had spoken, she went on compulsively, "You'll love it. It's beautiful. All the islands are," she continued quickly, in case Fustin's wasn't their destination. "Each one seems to be prettier than the one before—whether you're coming or going." She stopped abruptly, thinking, God, I sound awful, like some stupid travelogue. The typical New Yorker vacationing in the wilds. She felt herself flush with embarrassment.

There was no reply. The four simply continued to stare at her expressionlessly.

Maybe they don't speak English, Carey tried to console herself. Maybe they're foreign tourists.

The instant she thought it she knew it was ridiculous. The teenagers looked as American as apple pie, from their rock-star–stenciled T-shirts right down to their beat-up

joggers. Even the fact that their gender was indeterminate—
Carey leaned toward assuming they were all girls; she
could not detect any sign of even adolescent down on their
faces—marked them as indisputably, if outdatedly,
American.

They were a slightly scruffy-looking lot, with their faded
T-shirts and ragged, all but colorless jeans. Without knowing why, she felt sure their tatterdemalion look was not so
much deliberate as inescapable. They must come from a
very poor family, she decided, then realized that she did
think they all came from one family, were probably sisters.
There was no outstanding resemblance; they did not all
have carrot-red hair or hooked noses or anything as obvious
as that. Yet it was difficult to tell one face from another.
Their hair color varied from dirty blond to light brown; as
far as Carey could determine, all of them had hazel—or
were they green?—eyes. But they were each small and
slender, delicately boned, and it was this body resemblance as much as anything else that bespoke blood
relationship.

But they can't all be sisters, she thought suddenly,
unless they're quadruplets. Maybe they're cousins or
something.

Embarrassed by their silence and irritated by the inso-
lence of their prolonged scrutiny, Carey began to think
they intended to discomfit her. And try though she did to
deny them that satisfaction, she knew they had already
succeeded.

For the zillionth time in the almost ten years she had
been sharing a dormitory room or an apartment with Margie Packer, Carey wished fervently she had her roommate's
fast mouth and Dorothy-Parkeresque ability to handle any
situation with an untoppable quip. Margie would have put
these scruffy-looking little monsters in their place, but quick.
They'd all be staring at the deck now, instead of at her,
and with red faces, too. Carey had never known anyone to
get the better of Margie Packer.

She sighed, wishing Margie would hurry up and get
there. She had to come soon. The summer was already

more than half-over, and Margie's job required that she take her vacation before the middle of September. Maybe there'd be a letter from her at the general store and post office on Fustin's Island, telling when she was coming.

Carey wondered if Mrs. Mitchell, the storekeeper and postmistress, would consent to give it to her, even if there were one. Mrs. Mitchell had rules that were never broken—at least, not for the summer tourists, whom she held in contempt as mere "city folk"—and one of them was that on Saturdays her post office closed at noon. It was already almost six-thirty; it would be after seven, Mrs. Mitchell's closing time, when the ferry docked. Carey clung to the knowledge that the middle-aged woman would not lock the door until after Archie had delivered her stock.

Carey turned sideways on the starboard plank and stared northeast across the bay, searching for something on which to focus her eyes. For this first half of the ride, all the islands were on the port side of the ferry route; to starboard there was nothing but the water.

The bay rippled under the stiff wind blowing off the Atlantic, a wind that grew increasingly more forceful as the ferry coursed farther and farther from the lee of the shore. The crests of baby waves sparkled in the afternoon sunlight. As they subsided—they were not big enough to break—they took with them their flickers of gold, wave and sunlight both swallowed up by the bay.

Carey wondered what happened to that captured light; did it really sink into the dark blue of South Bay, never to shine again? If so, where was it? Down there in the depths, a shimmering, liquid buried treasure of light waiting for eyes sensitive enough to see it? Or was it already changing, breaking down into molecules of—no longer light but something else—some even more elemental substance? Or did light and wave never couple at all but only seem to, creating an illusion or, even less, the reflection of an illusion? Water blink—was that it?

She thought a moment and shook her head. Water blink was something else; what, she couldn't remember. She sighed, wishing, as she often did nowadays, she had paid more attention to physics in college. There was so much she wanted to understand, and she lacked even the rudiments necessary to begin.

She sighed again and raised her eyes to the horizon. Was that the ocean out there, or was the bay so large she was still seeing only it? She didn't know that either and, frustrated at her inability just to enjoy the wide expanse of riffling, glittering sea without coming face to face with her own shortcomings, she considered going forward and standing beside Archie. But she knew, after six weeks of riding his ferry, that it was impossible to get a word out of him while he was at the wheel. She was damned if she'd give those rotten kids on the port plank the satisfaction of seeing her ignored by Archie as well.

So she sat still, smarting from their rejection, and unwillingly recalled another—this one far more meaningful and so more painful to her. Try as she had during all the weeks since then, she still didn't know what had started the ugly fight between her and Nick two nights before she had been due to leave for Maine. Nor what she had said that was terrible enough to have caused him finally to jump out of bed, yank on his clothes, and storm out, yelling, "That's it, okay, that's it, Carey, we've had it. We're finished. Goodbye."

She had waited for him to call until the evening before she was to leave for Maine. Then she had called him—or tried to. There was no answer the entire evening. Knowing he could get her address from Margie if he wanted it, she had held off writing to him for a month. Two weeks ago she'd broken down and written him a short note. In it she'd tried to maintain her self-respect and at the same time soothe his apparently wounded Italian macho pride. As she was only guessing at the cause of his anger—he had picked the fight, not she; of that she was sure—she didn't know if she had succeeded in either effort. Nick was a difficult, temperamental man; after a year-long affair, she was equally sure of that. If she didn't get a letter from him soon, she knew, she'd have to face the fact that it was all

over, that they had indeed had it. She was no more knowl-
edgeable about how she would feel about that than she was
was of the real cause of their breakup—or where the
sunlight really went after South Bay swallowed it.

She shook her head and tried to put Nick out of her
mind. Barren Island was coming up off the starboard bow.
A little hunk of bare rock where only one lone, wind-bent
tree had managed to grow. It appeared to Carey that it
could well have been the rock to which the fisherman
chained Gregorius in Thomas Mann's *Holy Sinner*. Yet
there was a small house on it, built in a series of levels,
almost like a staircase, up the leeward side from a small
wooden dock. There could not have been more than one
room at each level, so narrow was the structure. Carey
longed to know who had built the house and when, and
who—if anyone—still lived there. She had asked and been
told, variously, that "nobody knows anymore," "Letty
Greeble's father after her mother run off and left them,"
"old Doc Parter since he went funny in the head," "some
artist from New York; nobody here'd build a thing like
that and call it a house and live in it," "Sarah McKinley,
onct her folks was killed down Sartsport way, in that
funny business." She had also received blank stares and
no answer at all. All she knew for certain was that Archie's
ferry did not stop there. A small dinghy with an outboard
motor was moored to the dock, as it had been each time
she'd ridden the ferry.

As Barren Island fell astern, Carey twisted around on
her seat to study the strange climbing house as long as she
could. As always, every window was shuttered, and she
tried to imagine someone in there watching the ferry go by
as she herself was watching the island go by. There had to
be somebody living there, else why the dinghy with its
outboard? The outboard was shiny and scrubbed-looking,
even if the house was not. The house was stark—as stark
as the rock to which it clung—and desolate, unpainted,
looking like nothing so much as wind- and seaswept
driftwood. It had a run-down air about it, but that would
not have counted for much on the bay were not the win-

dows always shuttered, imparting a sense of hidden, frightened eyes peering out, unwilling to be seen themselves. It struck Carey as strange that, in such a little-trafficked, lonely place, anyone would feel the need to shutter the windows in order further to keep out the world, and she was never able to pass Barren Island without experiencing a sadness, without wondering what terrible grief or unbearable pain had caused someone to take up a life of such utter isolation.

As the details of the house became indistinguishable in the distance, she shook herself and swung around on the plank seat. Four pairs of hazel-green eyes were still staring at her.

When the ferry docked at Fustin's Island, it was just after seven o'clock. The four girls sat like lumps, unmoving. Carey struggled into her knapsack straps while waiting for Archie to gather a load of supplies destined for Mrs. Mitchell's general store. When he was finished, there was one crate more than he could manage sitting on the dock.

"I'll carry that for you, Archie," Carey offered, squatting down beside it, "if it's not too heavy for me."

"Will be," Archie grunted, his small, wiry body all but obscured behind a towering load of crates and boxes.

"What's in it?"

"Crockery. Thanks just the same."

Carey tested the weight of the crate, trying to lift one end. She couldn't budge it. She stood up.

"Sorry."

"No matter." Archie started up the dock at a near-trot.

Carey caught up with him on the path leading up the hill to the store. Maybe if she arrived with Archie, Mrs. Mitchell would relax one of her hard-and-fast rules and—if not let her buy some food—at least give her her mail. She felt certain there would be a letter from Margie and prayed there would also be one from Nick.

"Where are those kids going?" she asked as she scurried after him.

"Dunno," he muttered. "Didn't say."

"Are you going out to Tallwater tonight?" Carey asked,

falling behind as the hill steepened. Tallwater Island was almost as large as Fustin's and also harbored a community. It was about five miles due northeast up the bay. She wondered if the four teenagers were going there.

"Nope." Archie had not slackened his pace. "Tallwater's Tuesdays and Thursdays. Less'n I get a call." He trotted on in silence for several yards. "Didn't get no call today."

Carey found his lack of curiosity about the people he ferried back and forth on the bay inconceivable. "They're strange kids, aren't they?" she puffed, out of breath now. "Dunno."

For a few moments Carey thought that was all he was going to say, but after a few more yards he spoke again.

"Didn't hardly have time to notice 'em." He trotted a few more steps, then added, "Leastways, they was quiet."

They arrived at Mrs. Mitchell's in silence. Carey had learned weeks ago when it was time to give up in South Bay.

A light was on inside the small, two-story, clapboard building, but the porch light was not. Set as it was amid a dense growth of towering pines, twilight had already descended on the little general store, and the darkened bare bulb in the fixture over the door said plainly business was finished until Monday morning.

They found Mrs. Mitchell standing, arms akimbo, just inside the screen door at the front of the center aisle. Behind her, in the dim light cast by the one 40-watt bulb burning over her ancient cash register, the interior of the little store loomed indistinct and mysterious, a place of shadows and indeterminate shapes, dim spaces, dark images, and even darker corners. Carey felt foolishly glad that Archie was not only with her, but in front of her, and would step in ahead of her.

Mrs. Mitchell was plainly in no mood to break her rule about the store's hours. After seven P.M. she would sell beverages for as long as she felt like it—"Not about to see anybody go thirsty all night," was how she explained her arbitrary decision—but nothing else. Carey suspected the rule did not apply to the locals, unless they happened to arrive when a summer tourist was in the store, but only to vacationers like herself. This night, however, Carey would not have been surprised to see it applied to God, had He chosen to walk in and ask for something. Mrs. Mitchell was in a high dudgeon.

"You're late," she barked at Archie as he trotted through the doorway after Carey had opened the screen door.

"B'lieve we are," Archie grunted as he kept up his same pace down the aisle to the rear of the store, where he deposited his crates and cartons on the floor.

Carey was not deluded into thinking he included her in his statement; she had come to know that Archie, when confronted, invariably resorted to the royal "we."

"It's Saturday." Mrs. Mitchell scowled at him.

"B'lieve 'tis," Archie agreed noncommittally.

"Saturday is Saturday."

"Always has been." Archie carefully dusted off his trousers. "Reckon it always will be."

In the brief silence that followed Archie's observation, Carey thought it might be a standoff. She underestimated Mrs. Mitchell.

"You know it's Saturday, Archie English," she snapped.

"Reckon as how I do, Miz Mitchell."

"Then why're you late?" she demanded loudly.

"Dunno." Archie scratched his head. "Them extra passengers, mebbe."

Carey experienced a thrill. She had not expected this. It was her fault the ferry was late, yet Archie was covering for her. She felt a rush of affection for him; he must actually like her. She hadn't thought anybody in South Bay would ever let himself like an outsider. Suddenly she felt less intimidated by Mrs. Mitchell. She wouldn't ask to shop, but she would try asking for her mail.

"What extra passengers?" Mrs. Mitchell's eyes were alight with curiosity, though her voice did not betray it.

"Dunno. Buncha kids."

"They comin' here?"

"Doubtful. Didn't leave the ferry."

"Where they goin'?"

"Dunno. Back t' the mainland, less'n they're off'n the boat when I get back."

"Who are they?"

"Dunno. Look like mebbe Pine Woods folk. Got that funny look."

"Don't see them folk down here much." Mrs. Mitchell seemed to have forgotten her anger.

"That be a fact."

"Well." Mrs. Mitchell gazed through the screen door thoughtfully for a moment. "Well. You bring that crockery I ordered?"

"Ayup." Archie started back down the store aisle for the door.

"Folks breakin' a lotta dishes this year," Mrs. Mitchell announced as he went by her.

"Ayup."

"Them kids pay you?" She asked brusquely as he opened the door.

"They will," Archie said over his shoulder just before the door banged shut behind him.

Carey remembered she had not paid him at the same moment she realized she was now alone in the store with Mrs. Mitchell. She took a deep breath and opened her mouth to ask for her mail.

"You see them kids?" Mrs. Mitchell demanded before she could speak.

"Yes, I did, Mrs. Mitchell," Carey heard herself replying. It was the first question, outside of her purchases and the state of her landlady Mrs. Rambeau's health, that the storekeeper had ever directed to her. "There were four of them," she offered quickly.

"What'd they look like?"

"Like teenagers." Carey was surprised again. Pine Woods inhabitants must occupy some special place in the bay-area mind, she decided, if the possibility of their appearance could provoke Mrs. Mitchell into gossiping with a nonlocal. "They had on jeans and T-shirts. Nothing special."

"Kinda dirty-lookin'?"

"I guess so." Carey thought a moment. "More like

unkempt, or scruffy-looking, I think, than actually dirty. But, maybe.''

"Girls or boys?"

"Girls, I think." Carey smiled. "It was hard to tell, Mrs. Mitchell. They really had the sixties unisex look. I decided they were girls, but I don't really know.''

"They be from Pine Woods, by gory." Mrs. Mitchell nodded her head energetically. "All them Pine Woods folk got that same look. Can't tell the boys from the girls—nor the men from the women, hardly." She paused frowning. "Can't hardly tell one from the other whichever they are 'n' that's a fact.''

"Where is Pine Woods, Mrs. Mitchell?" Carey interjected hastily, while Mrs. Mitchell was shaking her head and clucking her tongue disapprovingly.

"Be up north a ways. A good ways. Near two hundred miles." Mrs. Mitchell seemed to be searching her mind for more explicit directions, to locate Pine Woods exactly for Carey. "Past the Shin Pond and White Horse Lake, 'n' a bit over t' the west of Cut Lake. But this side of Spoon Mountain. T'other side of Grand Lake Seboeis, though," she added quickly, as if Carey were about to undertake the trip and must not get lost. "Ain't Down Easters. Just woods folk. Don't like it when they come 'round here, don't like it a'tall. Ought t' stay in their own place." Her voice had become agitated.

"Well, they didn't do anything, Mrs. Mitchell," Carey said reassuringly. "They were very quiet.''

"They talk t' you?"

Mrs. Mitchell asked the question so suddenly that Carey felt as if the woman had pounced upon her.

"No, not a word. I tried to talk to them, but they wouldn't answer—wouldn't talk to me. They just stared at me the whole trip," she heard herself conclude. She hadn't meant to mention that.

"That's them!" Mrs. Mitchell now warmed to what was obviously one of her pet peeves. "By gory, don't it get you! That is surely them. Are the strangest lot I ever laid eyes on. Never say a word. None of 'em. Just look at

everybody else like they ain't never seen people before—'n'
mebbe they ain't, for all I know. But it's a caution all the
same—very queer potatoes. 'Nough to give a body the
jimjams. Don't like those folk,'' she went on adamantly,
'' 'n' don't trust 'em neither. Somebody ought t' build
a wall around Pine Woods, that's what they should do.''

''You've seen them, then?'' Carey asked, astonished at
what was, for Mrs. Mitchell, a flood of words. ''Do they
come to Fustin's Island often?''

''Onct before. That be enough.''

Mrs. Mitchell did not continue. Carey was unsure whether
her first or second question had been answered. But she
sensed it was all the answer she was going to get, for the
large woman was now peering down at her over her
half-glasses.

''Be wantin' your mail, I s'pose?'' Mrs. Mitchell's
voice had taken on an aggrieved tone.

''Well, I certainly would appreciate it, Mrs. Mitchell.''
Once again, Carey was stunned. She decided it must be
that Mrs. Mitchell felt obliged to her for the information
about Archie's passengers and wanted to pay off the debt
promptly in order to feel free to treat her as an outsider—
city folk—again as soon as possible. She didn't care, as
long as it got her her mail. She smiled at the storekeeper as
nicely as she could.

''Post office closed at noon.''

''I know, Mrs. Mitchell.''

''Every post office in this country closes noon on
Saturday. It's the law.''

''Yes, I understand.''

''Won't open again till Monday mornin', eight o'clock
sharp.''

''I know. I wasn't going to ask you—'' Carey started to lie.

''You been on the mainland all day?''

''Yes, I have. I had some shopping—''

''Well, just this onct.'' Mrs. Mitchell picked up the
enormous keyring that hung on a dark metal chain against
her ample bosom. She selected a large brass key out of the
multitude chained around her thick neck. ''Don't go thinkin'

you can come in here every Saturday 'n' ask for your mail
after closin' time. This may be a country post office, but
it's a reg'lar post office all the same. I'm just doin' you a
favor, just this onct. Understand?''

"I certainly do, Mrs. Mitchell. And I'm very grateful."

"Happen t' know," Mrs. Mitchell came out from behind
the counter and crossed the store to the wire-mesh door
fronting a small cubicle built against the far wall, "you got
a letter t'day. No sense it takin' up my space till Monday."

She fitted the key into the lock and turned it. The door
opened inward, and Mrs. Mitchell followed it into the tiny
cubicle. Carey marveled that the storekeeper and the door
could both fit inside Fustin's post office, given Mrs.
Mitchell's size, but she kept her face both grave and grateful.

"There," Mrs. Mitchell said, emerging from the post
office and locking the door again. She crossed the store
back to Carey, holding out the envelope to her. "I shouldn'ta
done that, remember. That's fed'ral property in there."

"I really appreciate it, Mrs. Mitchell." Carey smiled
her very best smile at her. "It was very nice of you."

"Try t' be of help in the world, when I'm able."

Carey saw that Mrs. Mitchell was watching her closely,
and decided it must be that she wanted to know something
about the letter or at least observe Carey's reaction to it.
Carey felt she now owed Mrs. Mitchell this pleasure.

In the six weeks she had been on Outer Island, coming
to Fustin's twice weekly to pick up her mail and buy
groceries for herself and Mrs. Rambeau, Mrs. Mitchell
had never exhibited the slightest trace of interest in her
mail—or in her, for that matter. Carey felt almost one of
the natives for the first time, and so great was her pleasure
in this acceptance she would, had the letter been from her
mother or even Margie, have been tempted to read it to the
storekeeper. But it wasn't from her mother, nor from
Margie. It was from Nick.

Still, she felt she must do something. She studied the
"N. Pocetto" in the upper left-hand corner a moment,
then looked up with a big smile.

"Oh, thanks, Mrs. Mitchell," she said, keeping the big

smile on her face and praying Mrs. Mitchell would not detect her ambivalent feelings; the letter could make her happy or break her heart, after all, when she read it. "Thanks. I've been waiting for this one for a week and a half. It's from my boyfriend. Really, thank you so much."

"What kinda name's that 'Pocetto'?" Mrs. Mitchell asked briskly. "Italian?"

"Yes. Italian."

"Thought so." Mrs. Mitchell turned away, walked down the aisle to the end of the counter, and went behind it. "Store's closed, you know. It's Saturday. Always close early on Saturday."

"I know." It was over, Carey did know—the conversation, her brief period of acceptance, all sense of sociability. She was once again an outsider, to be tolerated only, not included. She sighed a little. "Thanks again for the letter, Mrs. Mitchell, I really am very grateful. I'll say hello to Mrs. Rambeau for you—if you'd like."

"Might 's well. No sense in not, if you're goin' t' be seein' her." Mrs. Mitchell's face had set itself apart from, if not exactly against, the likes of Carey Hunter once again.

"I will be. I bought her a little present in South Bay, something I thought she'd like. I'll be taking it up to her as soon as I get back to Outer Island."

"That so."

"Anyway, I go up to see her at least every morning and every evening, just to make sure she's all right and see if she needs anything."

"Ayup."

"So I'll tell her you said hello when I go up to see her tonight. And thanks once again."

"Whenever, be all the same t' me."

"See you Monday, Mrs. Mitchell. Have a nice weekend."

"Till Monday, then."

And all because you're a damned Italian, you bastard, Carey thought affectionately, feeling the letter in her right hand as she closed the screen door of the store with her left. Not only have you cost me my peace of my mind for almost seven weeks and damn near wrecked my vacation, now you've cost me the first real conversation I've had with anybody up here. You son-of-a-bitch, it better be worth it. She squeezed the letter gently, then folded it and shoved it into the front pocket of her jeans, and started down the path to the dock.

She met Archie coming up with the crate of crockery just around the first twist of the footpath.

"Archie, I have to pay you—"

"Can't stop now. Getcha down t' the dock," he grunted, trotting by her at his usual fast clip.

"But—" She didn't want to hang around the dock with the Pine Woods kids still on the ferry.

"Down t' the dock," Archie repeated, disappearing around the bend into the thick growth of pine trees.

Carey stood for a minute looking at the trees, then turned and started down the path. She walked slowly, loitering here and there to lift a heavy, dropping pine branch and inhale the crisp scent of the needles. It was almost chilly in the deepening shade of the tall trees, although the sun was still quite high in the evening sky, but Carey felt no desire to hurry. One of the things she had grown to love best about the Maine coast was the frosted air. Even during the hottest part of the hottest day, she had discovered, she could step into the shade and almost need a sweater. Archie came up beside her just as she was stepping onto the boards of the little pier. In his taciturn, Down East way, he made no comment on her obviously dilatory descent from the store, but Carey felt certain he knew she had been waiting for him to catch up with her before subjecting herself to the scrutiny of his passengers. As she expected, they were watching the two of them from the ferry.

Carey pulled some bills out of the other pocket of her jeans and thumbed through them, then pulled one out and extended it to Archie.

"A five's the smallest I've got, Archie. Sorry."

"Got the change." Archie took the five, and dragged a shabby leather purse from a trouser pocket and opened it.

He stuffed Carey's bill into one compartment and counted out her change from another, then counted it again before handing it to her.

"Thanks, Archie. And thanks for before—back at the store."

Archie shrugged and nodded, grinning ever so slightly at her. "More bark than bite up there," he said cryptically.

They walked along the dock to where she had moored Mrs. Rambeau's dinghy.

"See you soon, Archie. Probably Monday."

"Just loosen them lines for ya," Archie offered, stepping over to the piling around which Carey had tied the bowline. "Tide'll take her head," he offered by way of explaining his choice of which line to let go first; it was an outgoing tide, " 'n' she won't swing back. Get aboard."

"Thanks, Archie."

Carey could hear the surprise ringing in her voice. Archie had never extended himself like this for her before, and she had never credited his taciturn exterior with even a minimal sensitivity to the feelings of others; weeks ago she'd assumed he had none of his own. She climbed down into the dinghy feeling ashamed of herself, slid out of her knapsack, and set the oars.

Archie coiled and dropped the line down into the dinghy's bow in almost the same movement. The little boat nosed away from the dock into the bay as he stepped to the sternline and loosed that.

"Tide's with ya'," he called down to her, dropping the rope neatly onto the stern thwart. "Wind's against ya', but 'tain't strong enough t' matter much with this tide. Got a good hour or more before sundown. Be out t' Outer long b'fore she sets. Regards t' Miz Rambeau, now."

"Will do. Thanks, Archie. And thanks again for the loan of the bike."

Archie waved and nodded, watching the dinghy clear the dock.

You condescending snob, she said to herself, of herself. You really are city folk, Hunter. She smiled warmly up at Archie.

She stretched the oars forward, behind her, and took a long stroke with them. The dinghy was already almost past the end of the dock. As the prow of the ferry to her left slipped astern of her, Carey realized she was hardly going to have to row at all. The outgoing tide would carry the little dinghy straight to Outer Island. All she would really have to do was steer.

She rested on the oars and turned her head to see if her knapsack was lying in any water. It was dry. She gazed back at the ferry. The four teenagers were now at the starboard rail, watching her drift out across the bay. After a few seconds she bent over the oars and, outgoing tide or not, rowed energetically for Outer Island.

By the time she had moored the dinghy to Outer Island's little dock and climbed the wooded path to the Berries, her rented house, Carey could think of nothing but Nick's unopened letter. She slung her knapsack onto one of the old wooden kitchen chairs and dashed for the bay window in the living room—her favorite place—where the last of the sun would allow her to read it without lighting a kerosene lamp. Mrs. Rambeau's house, the big house on Outer Island, had gas-fed wall fixtures, but the Berries had gas only for its refrigerator. All lighting was by mantle and hurricane lamps.

Curled up in the overstuffed armchair, with late sun-beams highlighting her streaky blond hair and falling without heat on her face and hands, Carey tore open Nick's letter. For a second she held the single page without unfolding it, her heart beating very fast inside her chest. She knew she stood just as good a chance of reading that he wanted to end things with her as that he wanted her back. When she couldn't stand not knowing any longer, she unfolded the sheet of paper and read the few handwritten lines.

"Carey, got your letter the other day. Don't know what to say. I guess we're just in different spaces. I don't think we want the same things anymore—maybe we never did and were just too turned on to each other to know it. You want to be liberated and independent and I want a girl''—Carey grimaced with anger in spite of the gathering tears in her eyes—''who enjoys being a real woman. Where do we go from there? You tell me. Nick.''

She sat for a while looking out the bay window at the sunset, fighting not to cry. Even at however many hundred miles away, she was determined not to give him the satisfaction of making her cry. She felt she'd humbled herself enough for one day already.

''Damn you,'' she snapped finally, and slammed the letter down on the lamp table beside her chair. ''You macho asshole. 'A *girl* who enjoys being a *woman*,' huh? You don't know what you want, Mr. Pocetto. You just want what you want, that's what you want. Whether it makes any sense or not.'' She jumped up and stormed toward the kitchen. ''Well, life isn't that way, Mr. Big Man, life isn't that way.'' She ripped the straps of her knapsack open and flung back the flap, then yanked parcels and paper bags out of it, scattering them across the surface of the kitchen table. ''You want me, then you take me as I am. A person. I am a person. I am not here just to be an appendage to you. I am not some mindless body for you to screw, who'll sit in a corner until you feel like screwing again. I have a brain, and I don't need you to tell me what to do and what not to do. You want me—or don't want me! Don't take me if you can't take me as I am. I don't care. That's just fine with me. Because I am not a 'girl,' Nick Pocetto. I'm a woman. A 'real woman.' Something you know nothing about. You can go to hell. You can just go to hell, for all I care.''

She grabbed the package for Mrs. Rambeau and stomped out of the house, snatching her navy sweater from the row of pegs by the kitchen door as she went. She was halfway up the path to Mrs. Rambeau's house before she realized Nick hadn't said he wanted to end their relationship.

She had a rotten evening, and a fretted Sunday, anyway. For the first time since she arrived on Outer Island, Carey was bored and didn't know what to do with herself. Even her elderly landlady's scolding pleasure in the cotton cardigan sweater Carey had bought for her didn't lighten her state of mind. She wrote Nick seven letters of reply and burned them all in the Berries' woodstove. She walked the path around Outer Island three times and saw nothing that interested her. She made four trips, instead of her usual two, up to the big house, had four teas with Mrs. Rambeau, and came away from each not knowing what they had talked about. She cooked herself two dinners and ate neither of them. She tried to read but couldn't concentrate. She was furious with Margie for not being there to cheer her up. She had a terrible time.

When she went to bed Sunday night, her feelings toward Nick were less clear to her than ever. All she could determine was that she desperately wanted to hurt him as much as he was hurting her—and just as desperately wanted to make love with him. The latter feeling infuriated her.

2

Very early Monday morning, Archie English sat bolt upright in his bed at the sound of a piercing scream.

Which did not stop, but went on and on, on one shrill note, at one inhuman pitch. Archie, after a moment's shock, leaped from his bed to his bedroom window in one movement.

"Tarnation Christ," he whispered unconciously as he peered out. He could see nothing but the double row of majestic pine trees separating the side yard of the house from the ferry parking lot. His great-grandfather had left them standing when he cleared the land, to mitigate the odors of the dung dropped by the carriage and wagon animals which had delivered the passengers and supplies headed for the bay islands a century ago. Archie English was the fourth-generation captain-owner of South Bay's only ferry service. "Holy Mother of God."

The scream now abruptly changed. A staccato of short, strangling sounds came one on top of the other, so rapidly that it sounded like one voice screaming two screams simultaneously.

Archie was covered with gooseflesh as he tore off his pajamas and yanked on his corduroys and turtleneck. He raced from his bedroom barefoot, still struggling with his belt buckle.

As he forced his way through the ground-sweeping, interlaced boughs of the pine trees, he saw Ellen Dobbler standing in the parking lot beside an unfamiliar car. A small carton lay tilted in one of the ruts near her feet. From it, a shallow stream of golden-yellow yolk and translucent albumen seeped slowly along the bottom of the rut, glistening in the early-morning sunlight. Something else—a small heap of clothes, perhaps—was lying on the ground between Mrs. Dobbler and the car.

"Miz Dobbler?" Archie shouted as he sped across the empty lot. "Miz Dobbler!" He reached her, grabbed her arm, and pulled her to him. "What's goin' on? What're ya doin'?"

Terrible, gargling shrieks continued to issue out of the middle-aged woman's throat. Archie shook her. Her voice suddenly seemed to scream three screams at once. He had never heard anything even faintly like it in all of his fifty-six years. Her eyes stared crazily into his. Her right hand flailed wildly at the ground. Archie glanced down. There was the strange heap of clothes almost at their feet. It wasn't quite flat enough to be only clothes; it wasn't filled out enough to hold a human body.

Archie half squatted down and looked closer. His face abruptly drained of all color.

"Oh, m'God," he breathed, his eyes widening and bulging from their sockets. "Lord God a'mighty."

* * *

"Thin' else?" Mrs. Mitchell eyed Carey over her glasses.

"That's all for today, thanks, Mrs. Mitchell." Carey smiled at her automatically. The cumulative effects of not eating and sleeping only fitfully for two nights and a day and a half had left her almost beyond the reach of Mrs. Mitchell's intimidation. She was still focused, body and mind, on Nick. Or herself. She had not yet separated the two.

Mrs. Mitchell did not return her smile. "Ayup." She continued to stare at Carey.

"Well, I could take some coffee, too, I suppose." Mrs. Mitchell's unblinking gaze began to pressure her slightly; if she owed the storekeeper a larger purchase today for having given her Nick's letter Saturday, Carey was willing to give it to her.

"Don't hold with too much stockin' up." Mrs. Mitchell did not move to get the coffee; her gaze did not waver. "Might not be here long enough to use it all up. Never can tell. Only the good Lord knows when. Just wasted money, is all stockin' up is. Ayup."

"But then," Carey rummaged amid all the debris of the past year with Nick that was cluttering her mind for an appropriately neighborly answer, "not using up all your money would be just as wasteful, wouldn't it, Mrs. Mitchell?"

"City folk'd think thataway. Don't make it right."

Early in her stay, Carey had learned that the landed bay islanders considered all non-islanders—with the one exception of Archie English—foreigners to one degree or another. They might, like old Mrs. Rambeau who owned Outer Island and both the houses on it, rent out their second houses or empty rooms to summer tourists, but they didn't accept them in their hearts as fully human. And, of all the seasonal tourists, city folk were definitely the lowest-degree creatures on the bay islanders' scale.

Fustin's Island, small as it was, with fewer than thirty houses on it, had an unwritten community rule about property sales. No Fustin's Islander could sell a house or piece of property without the consent of every other Fustin's

Islander. In the last forty years, no outsider had won that unanimous approval. Ex-islanders, who had been forced to sell for financial reasons, had been bought out by the other islanders. No one owned a piece of Fustin's Island today whose family had not been there since the early part of the century. Fustin's was a closed community.

"You want the coffee?" Mrs. Mitchell challenged her.

"Uh, no. No." Carey felt as boggled by the storekeeper as she did by Nick. Everyone was expecting her to make the compromises, come up with the answers. She didn't have any answers. "I'll take your advice and get it next time."

"Don't do t' make extra trips." Mrs. Mitchell finally looked away in order to total Carey's bill on a brown paper bag. "Don't hold with wastin' time, neither."

Carey decided to remain silent. As with Nick, she knew that, whatever she might say, Mrs. Mitchell would find a way to disapprove of it. She felt very tired.

"That'll be eighteen seventy-three." Mrs. Mitchell made no attempt to bag Carey's purchases while she waited for her money.

Carcy took a twenty-dollar bill out of her jeans and handed it to her. Mrs. Mitchell studied it front and back, snapped it smartly three times, then rang up the sale on her ancient cash register and carefully counted out Carey's change from the open drawer. Then she closed the drawer and just as carefully recounted it into Carey's hand.

"Thank you." Carey smiled again, weakly. But now that her money was good, Mrs. Mitchell was busy bagging her groceries and neither saw nor returned it.

"You seen Miz Rambeau of late?" Mrs. Mitchell's voice accused her of dereliction.

"Just before I rowed over." Carey felt her mouth twitching with a real smile this time. This exact same exchange had occurred twice weekly for the past six weeks. Mrs. Mitchen knew her routine on Outer Island as well as she herself did. "The potatoes, bread, flour, dried peas, and bacon are her groceries. I see her at least twice every day; yesterday I went up four times. I always go up to the big house every morning as soon as I get up to make sure she's all right, and the same every evening after dinner.''

"Not an invalid. Or baby. Peggy Rambeau don't need a bandog. Been takin' care of herself just fine long before she had t' rent out t' city folk summers.''

"Well, but she's quite old, Mrs. Mitchell, and seems awfully frail to me to be living alone on that deserted island like that. I always feel worried about her.''

"Born on that island, bore 'n' buried her children on that island, 'n' Mr. Rambeau as well, 'n' she'll die on that island.'' The righteousness in Mrs. Mitchell's voice did not quite cover up a note of relief.

"She still is awfully old to be living all alone out there, so far away from help if she ever needs it.'' It was the strongest statement Carey had made in a day and a half; her concern for her landlady was genuine. Even Mrs. Mitchell couldn't intimidate her on the subject of Mrs. Rambeau. She had grown very fond of the old woman over the last weeks, in spite of Mrs. Rambeau's unconcealed contempt for city folk, and she knew Mrs. Rambeau had come to depend upon her as well. "I'll check on her at least twice a day for as long as I'm here.''

"Born alone 'n' we die alone. The way God made the world. Ain't nothin' you can do about it. Better t' die in your own bed than some city folk-run hospital. Don't expect you city folk understand that, though.'' Mrs. Mitchell pushed the two packed bags across the counter. "That be all till Thursday, then.'' She took two envelopes from the top of the register and slipped them into one of the bags. "Mail's on the side.''

Carey knew from experience she wouldn't get another word out of Mrs. Mitchell until Thursday, not even if she told her Outer Island had sunk to the bottom of the bay. "Thank you, Mrs. Mitchell. See you Thursday.''

Archie's ferry was approaching from the mainland as Carey made her way out on the dock to where she'd moored the dinghy. A sharp offshore wind had sprung up while she'd been in the store; it made it difficult to get the heavy bags stowed safely under the stern thwart. By the time she was ready to loose her mooring lines, the ferry had docked.

Carey waved to Archie. He nodded grimly back at her. Usually he waved back, and Carey felt a small twinge of rejection as she called out, "Do I have any mail, Archie?" She'd learned during her third week on the bay, through a slip of the tongue by Archie, that he checked through the mailbag before bringing it out to Mrs. Mitchell's post office. Once she had made it plain, circuitously, that she believed what Fustin's Island's postmistress didn't know couldn't possibly hurt her, Archie had not been adverse to letting Carey know, on Mondays and Thursdays, if she had any letters to wait for. She timed her twice-weekly shopping trips to coincide with the noon ferry, which carried the mails, for this reason.

"Can't tell," he shouted back at her. "Ain't looked t'day." He seemed distracted, not really paying attention to her.

Carey wondered if she'd said or done something on Saturday that had made her even more of an outsider than she already was, if such an extreme were possible. She stood on the dock for a few minutes, watching Archie unload the ferry, then climbed down into the dinghy and retrieved the two letters from the side of the shopping bag where Mrs. Mitchell had stuck them. One was from her mother, and the other, happily, from Margie.

She realized, as she looked at them, that they had to have been delivered to the post office on Saturday. Monday's mail was either still on the ferry or lying on the dock somewhere amid the growing pile of crates and cartons Archie was unloading. She felt irritated and amused at once.

"So that's what my information about those kids was worth to you, Mrs. Mitchell," she muttered aloud. "One out of three. You old witch."

She expelled a breath in a sudden huff, tore Margie's letter open, and read it.

Margie would be arriving Monday morning on Fustin's Island on the first ferry. She was going to spend the first weekend of her vacation with Jeff at his house in Connecticut, and would leave from there Sunday afternoon for Maine. She'd decided to rent a car, rather than hassle with all the plane and bus connections necessary to meet the South Bay ferry schedule, so would be on "adorable Archie's"—a quote from one of Carey's letters to her about the bay residents—first ferry from the mainland bright and early Monday morning. And Carey better be there on Fustin's Island to meet her, or she'd never hear the end of it. Love, love, and by the way, she better not get eaten by a bear or any other wild animal, or Carey would never hear the end of that either. She was a city person and was only doing this because Carey had talked her into it with sworn promises of how much she would love "the wilds" if she would only try them once. Would she indeed? She better, and it was on Carey's head if she didn't and lost her mind with all that uncivilized peace and quiet. Was there anything approaching a disco in that godforsaken place? Should she bring her passport? Ha-ha. Did Carey know what her idea of a vacation was? Well, it was two weeks at the Plaza, right in the heart of old New York. Two wonderful, luxurious weeks at the Plaza, being waited on hand and foot, with breakfast in bed and after-theater dinners and champagne at midnight and discoing till dawn and sleeping till two and having Margaritas by the pool. By the way, does the Plaza have a pool? She didn't know, she'd never been there—*yet*—but it must have a pool. The Plaza has everything. Everything Margie Packer wants, sigh. And just for Carey's information, *that* was where they were spending their vacations next year. At the Plaza. Turnabout was fair play, after all. This year the pits, next year the Plaza. Believe it. *If* she survived the wilds of South Bay, that is. If not, Carey was to bring her back home in a box—a mahogany box, by the way, no cheap knotty pine—and bury her in Shubert Alley right outside the stage door of the Booth Theater, which, with her talent, was where she should be working, not in Hovsepian's office typing up the contracts of lesser talents. Oh, God, there was no justice in the world, which had to be why she was coming to Maine instead of the Plaza where she belonged. Wasn't Carey bananas with all the peace and quiet yet? Had she heard from Nick? Till Monday, Margie. (After that, who knew?)

Carey grinned and refolded Margie's letter, put it back in its envelope, and shoved both it and her mother's letter—which she was saving to read back at The Berries—into a pocket of her jeans. Only a week to wait, and then Margie would be there. She felt greatly cheered up and was climbing back onto the dock when Archie came hurrying by, at a somewhat faster than usual clip.

"Archie—?" she began.

"In a hurry t'day," he grunted, behind his load of crates, and hurried on down the dock.

Carey watched him until he had disappeared up the path into the pine trees, then loosed the dinghy's sternline. The offshore wind was blowing up harder now, and the tide was changing. She was going to have row the three-quarters of a mile against both the wind and an incoming tide. She half loosed the bowline and climbed back down the vertical wooden rungs as fast as she could to grab and slip the line before it slipped by itself and the dinghy drifted under the dock. She had to grab the oars and row with all her strength to keep from being swept against the pilings.

It was a rough trip to Outer Island in the little dinghy. The wind strengthened by the moment, or so it seemed to Carey as she bent over the oars, rowing directly into a northeast wind. The closer she got to Outer Island, which lay a full three-quarters of a mile closer to the mouth of the bay—and open ocean—than Fustin's, the harder she had to work and the slower her progress became. The water grew increasingly choppy as she neared the Atlantic; one particularly bad wave caught the dinghy broadside and almost overturned it. She was drenched by spray and noted, without being able to do anything about it, Mrs. Mitchell's brown paper bags disintegrating under the stern thwart. By the time she made the tiny dock on Outer Island, her groceries were awash in the bottom of the little boat.

The sky was heavy with dark, threatening clouds. Fearing a storm, Carey dragged the dinghy into the small boathouse. She rescued the most perishable of her purchases—Mrs. Rambeau's flour was a lump of paste, and her dried peas were bursting out of their soggy cardboard box—and pushed her way into the now howling wind sweeping across Outer Island. The winding path that led to the Berries seemed endless.

"Must be a real northeaster coming," she muttered as she finally gained the kitchen and dumped her wet parcels on the table.

Finding nothing suitable in which to carry the rest of her purchases, she grabbed her knapsack from one of the pegs by the kitchen door and the lobster pot from under the sink, and started back down to the dock.

It was a fast trip going down, with the wind at her back. After she had unloaded the dinghy into her knapsack and the huge pot, she closed the boathouse doors and lay in place the heavy two-by-fours that served to bolt them. She felt certain the bay was in for a real storm.

Her arms were shaking from the weight of her waterlogged burdens as she kicked the kitchen door of the Berries shut behind her. She dumped her knapsack on a chair and plunked the lobster pot down on the table. The crunch and crack of eggshells told her she had set it on a carton of eggs.

"Oh, damn." She moved the pot to one side and snatched the dishtowel from the side of the cast-iron sink as five of the twelve eggs spread their contents across the table.

After she had cleaned up the mess, sorted and separated out Mrs. Rambeau's groceries from her own, dried off what could be dried off, and found other containers for those that couldn't, she put a kettle on to boil. Then she dashed upstairs and changed into dry jeans, a T-shirt, and warm sweater. She retrieved her letters from the pocket of her wet jeans; they had survived the ride intact, except for some smearing of the ink on the envelopes. Carey toweldried her short, curly hair quickly and went back downstairs to make her tea.

Settled down in the big armchair in the bay window overlooking the blackberry patch for which the house had been given its name, and beyond that the expanse of the bay, Carey sipped at the hot tea and read her mother's letter.

Her parents were both well, the garden was getting enough rain for a change, her father's firm was thinking of relocating in Arizona, and they both thought that, with Carey on her own and her younger sister, Anne, away at college, it might be a nice change to a milder climate at their time of life. Her father was furious with the President over the Social Security business, as anyone his age would be. Her mother still thought cutting the size of school lunches for growing children was criminal—and bespoke a mean man. But what could you expect from a government of men who refused to ban baby formulas that caused malnutrition? What men needed was to bear children, and what the government needed was more women in it. Had Carey thought of going into politics, now that she had decided to change careers? Her sister was already complaining about having to take trigonometry in the fall, since she wasn't a math or science major. All was well. They loved her. Mother.

Carey lightly kissed her mother's signature at the bottom of the letter and put it back into its envelope. She took another swallow of hot tea and picked up Margie's letter, thinking unkind thoughts about Mrs. Mitchell, and reread it. Only one more week to wait, and then Margie would be there with her. Then she'd have an ally against Mrs. Mitchell's arbitrary sorties. And someone who would put all the Down East rejections she kept getting in their proper perspective, which was: not worth taking personally. She'd have company and someone to talk to. And not just someone, but Margie—funny, fuming, wild, wonderful Margie, who loved being alive and had something witty to say about even the most painful experience. Carey felt better just having her letter—nothing ever seemed so bad to her since she'd had Margie around to make her laugh about it—and read it again. Then she put it down and drank the rest of her tea, looking out at the stormy bay and the lowering sky.

She was about to get up when she realized something was wrong. This *was* Monday. She snatched up the letter and read it one more time. Monday. Damn, why hadn't Margie put a date on it, instead of just a day? Carey grabbed the envelope and peered at the postmark. Ink from the address had run into it, and it was impossible to read. She started to read the letter once again and noticed that the day, in the upper left-hand corner, had been written on top of something else. By holding the letter up to the window, she finally made out a date underneath. Margie had written the letter a week ago Thursday. Over a week and a half ago. And probably forgotten to mail it, Carey realized. A week ago last Thursday. She was arriving— had arrived, or should have arrived—this morning.

But she hadn't. There had been no passengers on Archie's ferry when it docked at Fustin's. Carey had been there. So where was Margie? Carey read her letter again, slowly and carefully. It became obvious Margie had meant that this past weekend would be spent in Connecticut with Jeff, and this Monday—today—would be the day she would arrive. But she hadn't.

The crash of an unfastened shutter startled Carey. She jumped up and dashed out onto the porch. One of the living-room shutters was crashing back and forth in the roaring wind.

Remembering Mrs. Rambeau's admonition to close all the shutters in the event of a northeaster, Carey circled the first floor of the house, closing and fastening each of them. It made the house quite dark, despite it's being midafternoon, when she got back inside.

"My God, it's gloomy," she complained aloud. "Damn you, Margie, why didn't you come when you said you would?" She had almost decided Margie was spending an extra night or two with Jeff before joining her on Outer Island. She knew Margie was not bursting with eagerness to spend her vacation away from what she considered civilization. As she made her way upstairs to close the

second-story shutters, Carey couldn't help feeling a touch
of jealousy—toward both Margie and Jeff. She wished
simultaneously that either she had Nick or that Margie
didn't have Jeff. Either circumstance would have les-
sened her feeling of aloneness.

When she came back downstairs, she knew she should
take Mrs. Rambeau's groceries up to her so the elderly
woman wouldn't worry about her having swamped or sunk
the dinghy. She shed her cardigan and took her navy
sweater from its peg by the door and pulled it on. She
packed what remained of Mrs. Rambeau's groceries into
her knapsack and left the house. She had to set the knapsack down on the small, covered back stoop and use both
hands to pull, then push, the two doors to against the
wind. As she started toward the path that led uphill to the big
house, she had a clear view of the bay from the backyard. It
was covered with whitecaps, much too rough to take out
the dinghy. If the water got much rougher, even the ferry
wouldn't run. Margie was on her own until the storm was
over.

"Serves you right, Miss Undependable Packer," she
muttered, working the knapsack straps over her shoulders.
"You're late, you wait. Your choice, not mine."

Though uphill, the trek to Mrs. Rambeau's house was
easier than those from the dock to the Berries, for now the
wind was at her back.

Getting back's going to be something else, though, she
said to herself.

Sternfirst, where Mrs. Rambeau lived, was built on the
highest point of land on the small island. It had been
named, she had told Carey, by her great-great-grandfather,
whose sailing ship had been flung upon the island stern
first during one of the worst storms in the bay area's
history, sometime around 1830. Mrs. Rambeau's ancestor
had claimed the island, built his house largely from the
wreck of his wooden vessel, and then named it for the
direction by which he had inadvertently made his landing
on it.

Carey didn't know whether to believe the story or not, but thought it was a good one. And had finally decided the house's name was so improbable that the story no doubt was true. Feeling the force of the wind at her back now, she was even more inclined to believe it. She had also seen, on her first visit there, that Sternfirst was shaped like a ship, had been built from very old ship's timbers, and had unnaturally low ceilings and doorways. The windows had mostly been added at a later date, using much newer wood. It was furnished with a great deal of antique ship's gear, and a great iron anchor rested in the middle of the front yard.

"Saw you coming along." Mrs. Rambeau had the kitchen door open before Carey could knock. "Get in out'n that wind."

Carey stepped into the warm kitchen and slid her knapsack backward onto the kitchen table.

"I'd better fasten your shutters before I come in, Mrs. Rambeau," she said, hurrying back out again. "It's really blowing up. There are your groceries—what's left of them. I'm sorry but the flour got soaked on the row back, and I think the peas and bread are ruined too. It was awfully rough. I'll be right back."

"That's all right. Thank you, dear," Mrs. Rambeau called after her.

The rain hit in a driving sheet before Carey had fastened the last of Sternfirst's shutters. She was soaked to the skin when she got back inside the house again.

"Stay right there, dear, where you can't hurt the floor." Mrs. Rambeau's order brooked no disobedience. "There's towels 'n' a robe on the chair there." She pointed, and turned back to her stove.

Carey stripped to the skin and toweled herself vigorously. She was shivering with the cold. The woolen man's bathrobe was hard and threadbare; it smelled stale with age. Carey thought it must have been Mr. Rambeau's, and wondered how many years it had been hanging, unworn, in some musty closet. It felt harsh and abrasive against her skin.

"This'll take the chill out'n your bones." Mrs. Rambeau poured a dollop of liquid from a dusty, unlabeled bottle into Carey's cup of hot tea. A pungent odor of fruit rose from the steaming cup. "My blackberry brandy. From the berry patch down t' the other house." She gestured vaguely with the bottle. "Nobody t' drink it up since John went t' meet his Maker, God rest his soul." She closed her eyes while offering the blessing.

"Smells wonderful." Carey inhaled deeply. "Thank you."

"Don't burn yourself. Tea's practically still on the boil." Mrs. Rambeau was rearranging Carey's clothes to her own satisfaction on the extra chair, which Carey had dragged close to the woodstove, hoping to dry them quickly. "Wouldn't do t' let you catch a chill. Never know where such things lead to."

"I'll be all right, Mrs. Rambeau. Really. Don't worry about me."

"Wasn't. Don't see anything t' worry about. 'N' don't intend to."

Carey repressed a smile and tried to sip her tea.

"These clothes won't be dry till tomorrow, maybe not then less'n the rain lets up, which it won't. Three days, that'll be it. Regular nor'easter, that's what it is. A mite early, but it's about the time. You'll have t' stay here tonight." Mrs. Rambeau seated herself across the table from Carey and, picking up her teacup, blew on the steaming contents.

Carey started to protest but caught herself. She didn't want to stay, but she could not leave the old woman alone in such a storm in the event some accident happened to the house, or to her. And since there was no way she could get to Fustin's Island to see if Margie had arrived until the storm blew itself out, there was no reason not to stay.

"I think so," she agreed, smiling. "And thanks, Mrs. Rambeau. That's very kind of you."

The old woman gave no sign of having heard her. She was busy cooling her tea, or pondering it. Carey wasn't sure which. There was a long silence during which both of them paid attention only to their cups.

"Appreciate your fastening up the shutters," Mrs. Rambeau said at last. "Some things get awful hard t' do when a body's got on in life. Used to be I'd love t' see a good nor'easter blowing down the bay 'n' hearing John out and about, latching them shutters up tight 'n' slapping a tarp over the woodpile on the porch 'n' dropping four stones on it so's not t' lose it 'n' wet the wood. John always kept four big stones aside the woodpile year-round, just for nor'easter time. And blizzards," she added musingly.

Carey could think of no suitable comment. The old woman's reverie, so wistfully delivered, touched her. Her impulse was to reach across the table and hold the frail, almost transparent, blue-veined hands in her own and insist, "It's all right, it's all right, everything will be all right," until the widow's face shed, somehow, its ravaging griefs. She did not dare act upon such an impulse. Further, she knew she would be lying; nothing would ever be all right for Peggy Rambeau, ever again.

"I'd keep a kettle on the boil the livelong day 'n' my blackberry brandy right handy on the table 'n' a big pot of chowder steaming on the stove for him. Secret of life's having something t' do 'n' somebody t' do it for." Mrs. Rambeau fell silent again.

Carey thought of Nick, and his letter, crumpled and smoothed out again, back at the Berries. She wondered if she felt that way about him; had he, for her, been a somebody to do things for? Her feelings about him and their year together were a maze in which she found no easy answer. Nor did she know if she had been such a somebody for him, either. She began to wonder if she even knew who Nick was; indeed, if they knew each other. She found it disconcerting to suspect they might simply have been objects to each other, not somebodies at all. She suddenly envied Mrs. Rambeau the simplicity of her feelings, and felt very blue.

" 'Tain't so much fun anymore." Mrs. Rambeau finally took a swallow of her tea. "Not anymore."

Carey's desperation to say the right thing rose up again like a tidal wave within her. Nothing occurred to her. Mrs. Rambeau was old; her husband was dead, her children buried young after an influenza epidemic in which all four had died within weeks of each other. Mrs. Rambeau's griefs could not be comforted. They would be with her until she died. Helplessly, Carey began to cry, not entirely for Mrs. Rambeau.

"Landsakes, child, whatever is the matter? What's upset you?" Mrs. Rambeau rose brittlely from her chair, and came around the table to pat Carey's head and shoulder with butterfly fingers that spoke more of embarrassed disapproval than comfort. "Are you sick already?"

"No. No. It's just that you're—" Carey fought back her tears and her reason for them. "I know you're . . . I just think . . . I'm upset about something. I'm sorry."

A long silence followed, during which Carey came to feel first embarrassed, then guilty, as she realized she had breached one of the bay area's most sacred rules of social conduct. The islanders were not demonstrative people, she'd learned. Feelings were something they expected people to keep to themselves, and from which the rest of the world deserved to be spared. Carey knew Mrs. Rambeau must be inwardly shaking her head at her lack of propriety even while she politely refrained from criticizing her aloud.

"Ayup," the old woman muttered at last. "Ayup." She picked up the barely sipped-at teacups from the table and carried them to the sink. "Best I fix up some dinner. Must be way past time."

Carey glanced up at the old pendulum clock ticking comfortably away on the kitchen wall. The hands said four fifty-two.

Carey wiped her face and nose with her hands, which were all that was available to her. "What can I do to help?"

"Nothing." Mrs. Rambeau spoke too quickly. "Just go

make yourself t' home in the parlor. Two women in one kitchen makes a mess, not a meal.''

Banished, Carey moved with uncomfortable self-consciousness toward the door leading to the rest of the house. She paused in the doorway.

''I'm sorry if I''—she searched for a way of putting what she felt that would be acceptable to her hostess—''embarrassed you just now, Mrs. Rambeau. I'm just—''

''City folk got different ways from people,'' Mrs. Rambeau cut her off kindly but quickly. '' 'S nothing against you. You can't help it. It's the way you were taught. It just ain't our way.''

Feeling everything was against her in this place where she was the foreigner, Carey turned and walked into the large, old-fashioned dining room.

''You'll feel different when you've got some food in you,'' Mrs. Rambeau called after her. ''Empty stomachs make for weak characters.''

Alone in the dining room, Carey winced at this final judgment upon her, while knowing Mrs. Rambeau was trying to comfort her. But it was impossible. The old woman was right. Their ways were too different, and only Carey—the city folk—was flexible enough to bend, change, and make the effort. Mrs. Rambeau would go on judging her, no matter what she said or did, even when she believed in her heart she wasn't judging. For deeper than such a belief, Carey knew, was another unshakable belief that her way was the only right way. Mrs. Rambeau couldn't help it, either. It was the way she had been taught.

Carey found her way through the house—she had never been invited out of the kitchen before—to the second floor, looking for the bathroom. There was none. Puzzled, she came back downstairs and discovered, at the foot of the stairs, opposite the main parlor, an enormous bathroom with ancient fixtures and a footed cast-iron tub. If it had ever been layered with porcelain, it showed no signs of it today. Carey wondered how Mrs. Rambeau, barely five feet tall to begin with, got into the high tub at her age. Or if she did.

She washed her face and, finding no tissues in the bathroom, blew her nose into a wad of the stiff, hard toilet paper until it felt clear again. Then she returned to the parlor and waited, helplessly, for a very early dinner.

The northeaster, true to form, lasted three days. Carey's clothes did not dry for two of them, and Mrs. Rambeau, true to form, would not hear of Carey putting them on again while so much as one-quarter of one inch of one seam remained even vaguely damp.

"I won't have you getting sick in my house. By gory, whatever would folks think of me! You may wear your clothes as wet as you please when you're in the city, but you'll wear them dry or not at all when you're in my house. Ain't that robe comfortable for you? Was John's favorite robe he ever had. He always said, 'Margaret'—he never would call me Peggy like other folks do—'Margaret, this is my favoritest robe I ever had, it's just so comfortable.' Ain't it comfortable for you? You got no place t' go. Wet clothes'll give you the ague for sure. Leave them clothes on the chair, ain't none of them dry as yet."

It was not all said at any one time, but it was all said many times over until, on Thursday morning, Carey woke well before what would have been dawn in better weather, tiptoed downstairs to the kitchen, and all but leaped into her jeans, T-shirt, and sweater.

"Them things all dried out?" Mrs. Rambeau appeared behind her like an apparition.

Carey started, noticeably.

"Nothing like damp garments t' give you the ague." Mrs. Rambeau was exploring the seams, underarms, and wristbands of Carey's clothes with detective fingers.

"Yes, yes," Carey couldn't get the words out fast enough. "They're totally, completely dry, Mrs. Rambeau. Really. Thank you."

"Ayup," Mrs. Rambeau said at last, her fragile old fingers lingering on Carey's sleeve. "Reckon you're right, they seem to be.'' A defeated sadness had crept into her voice.

It dawned on Carey that the old woman didn't want her clothes to be dry, didn't want her to be able to leave her alone with only her memories again. Stifling her longing to embrace Mrs. Rambeau, Carey gestured toward the windowed kitchen door.

''Boy, it's still raining cats and dogs, Mrs. Rambeau,'' she commented carefully. ''You could get drowned out there.''

''Then stay in a warm house, if you've got one around you,'' was as far as Mrs. Rambeau went in confirming Carey's suspicions.

Carey stayed until mid-morning, when the rain let up almost as suddenly as it had begun on Monday. Since this was the other day of the week she always took the dinghy across the bay to Fustin's to do the shopping for both of them, she felt it would be the least painful point to make her move back to the Berries. She also resolved to spend more time at Sternfirst during the remaining weeks of her vacation.

''My roommate, Margie Packer, was supposed to come Monday on Archie's ferry,'' Carey explained to Mrs. Rambeau as she stuffed the woman's shopping list into a pocket of her jeans. ''I want to get over there and see where she is. She must have gotten stuck somewhere because of the storm, but she's sure to arrive today. Margie will think she came to the wrong island in the wrong bay if she doesn't see me right there to meet her. She's not the independent type.''

''Ayup.'' Mrs. Rambeau spoke after a brief pause. ''Won't be seeing so much of you, now your friend's come, I don't suppose.''

Carey experienced, once again, a rush of helpless feelings.

''Oh, Mrs. Rambeau, that's not true! You'll see more—of both of us. I've written Margie so much about you, she's dying to meet you. As soon as we get back, we'll both come up with your groceries. And, if you're not sick and tired of my company, why don't you have dinner with us tonight down at the Berries? Please. We'd love to have you. Oh, please, do come.''

Mrs. Rambeau eyed her quizzically.

''You're not just saying that because you feel sorry for a lonesome old lady that's lived too long, are you?''

Carey threw caution to the winds and flung her arms around Mrs. Rambeau, hugging her as hard as she dared. The elderly woman felt fragile in her arms.

''No! How dare you even suspect a thing like that!'' Carey kissed her faded, wrinkled cheek. ''You're wonderful company and I really enjoy you. And Margie said in her letter''—Carey invented this on the spur of the moment but felt it a perfectly acceptable lie—''she wants to hear all about your great-great-grandfather's sailing days and how your house got its name and all your other stories for herself and can't wait to meet you. Now, will you come to dinner with us tonight?''

As Carey stepped back, releasing the old woman, she saw tears in her eyes.

''I was just spoofing you,'' Mrs. Rambeau mumbled, her voice a trifle hoarse. ''My, you city folk surely do let yourselves get carried away.''

''Will you come to dinner with us tonight?'' Carey insisted.

''Nope.'' Mrs. Rambeau grinned like the proverbial Cheshire cat. ''You two young folks come here. Give me something t' do all day,'' she added quickly before Carey could protest. ''Nice t' have somebody t' do for again. For a while.''

''I accept.'' Carey kissed her cheek again, lightly. ''Thank you. We'll be back as soon as the ferry gets in. Sure this is all you need?'' She stuck a finger in her pocket where the list was tucked.

''You might bring a nice pot roast as well,'' Mrs. Rambeau answered. ''Big enough for three, 'n' a bit over for me for a couple more bites tomorrow. Ayup, let me get you some more money for it.'' She turned toward the cupboard.

''No, that's all right. Margie and I will bring the roast

since you'll be doing the cooking—and, anyway, it'll make up for your things I lost on Monday rowing back.''

"No guest of mine ever had t' sing for his supper in my house," Mrs. Rambeau announced archly, taking a cracked china cream pitcher off the top shelf of her cupboard. " 'N' that blow wasn't your fault. 'Tain't the first time the bay took my supper or the next day's bread." She fished around in the cream pitcher with her stiffened fingers and finally handed Carey a ten-dollar bill. "Now you buy a real nice, good-sized one, 'n' don't embarrass me in front of your friend with your city ways, Carey Hunter."

Carey smiled and took the money.

"All right, Mrs. Rambeau, I won't. I promise."

" 'N' get a mite more potatoes, too, long 's you're there. Your friend'll be hungry after that long trip."

"Okay." Carey stuffed the bill into her pocket. "See you later, Mrs. Rambeau."

"Now you just wait right there one-half of a minute." Mrs. Rambeau shook her finger at her. "Happens t' be I got somethin' for you." She hurried out of the kitchen and hurried back in before Carey could think what she was up to. "Here." She held out a hand to Carey; in it was a piece of scrimshaw. "This's for you. It's the piece you said you liked so much t'other night when I was showin' you John's collection. In return for the nice sweater you brought me Saturday."

"Oh, Mrs. Rambeau——" Carey started to protest.

"Now, you just take it, Carey Hunter," the old woman ordered. " 'Tain't much, but you said you liked it, 'n' I don't get out 'n' about off'n the island anymore like I used to, t' buy you somethin'. So you just take this from me in return." Her faded old eyes were snapping with insistence.

Carey took the small piece of scrimshaw carefully in her hand and looked down at it. It was whale ivory, carved in the shape of a mermaid, with the facial features, hair, nipples, and tail scales heightened by engraving. She knew, because Mrs. Rambeau had told her, that it was over one hundred and fifty years old, having been carved by the

same Great-great-grandfather Whittier who had first settled
on Outer Island. Carey suspected Mrs. Rambeau was unaware that it was very, very valuable.

"I don't know what to say—" she began.

"Then don't say it. Just pleasure me by acceptin' it 'n'
go for them groceries, so's we can eat before midnight
t'night."

"But, Mrs. Rambeau, this is very valuable. As an
antique. It must be worth a great deal of—"

"It's mine t' give away if I chose to," the frail woman
said stoutly, " 'n' I chose to. It's yours, 'n' that's an end
to it."

"Well, gee, thank you, Mrs. Rambeau." Carey looked
up at her, knowing there were tears in her eyes, plain for
the old woman to see. "Thank you very much. I'll treasure it. Really, thank you."

"Yes, well, ayup, just glad you like it. Now, you be
careful with that dinghy. Bay's always tricky with currents
after a nor'easter, child. I want you should get back safe,
now, with your friend." Mrs. Rambeau stepped forward
and opened the kitchen door.

Carey paused at the Berries only long enough to grab
her wallet and slicker jacket. Mrs. Rambeau had been
right; the bay was choppy with middling whitecaps, and
unfamiliar currents swung the little dinghy broadside into
the incoming tide's rough water the instant she lifted her
oars to start the next stroke. She had to row hard to keep
from drifting sideways down the bay, right past Fustin's
Island, and couldn't risk a glance to see if the ferry was
coming until after the dinghy was safely moored.

The ferry was not coming. It was nowhere in sight.
Carey felt both frustrated and relieved; eager as she was to
see Margie, she was glad to have arrived before her. She
decided to get the shopping over with and stowed in the
dinghy, so she and Margie could leave immediately for
Outer Island and be alone to talk. Margie could best Mrs.
Mitchell for her on Monday.

Carey was stowing her grocery bags in the dinghy when

she heard the throbbing of Archie's diesel engine. She
rammed the last bag snugly under the stern thwart with her
foot and climbed back up on the dock. It seemed hours
before she could make out that no one was aboard the ferry
but Achie himself.

"Don't you have any passengers?" she shouted at him
as soon as the small boat was within hailing distance.

Archie shook his head. He did not wave. He was
unsmiling.

"Archie," words came tumbling out of Carey's mouth
in a rush as the ferry captain threw his bowline to one of
the men hanging about the dock, "have you had any
passengers this week—since Monday?" She scrambled
over the rail onto the ferry as Archie was racing astern for
the other mooring line. "I'm expecting my friend, my
roommate, from New York. She was supposed to be here
Monday—last Monday, when the storm started." She was
following Archie out on the afterdeck when she realized he
was already halfway back amidships. "Listen, she wrote
me she'd be here Monday, and even if she stayed longer
with her"—Carey changed her course just in time—"with
friends in Connecticut or got held up somewhere by the
northeaster, she should be here today. Didn't you see
anybody on shore? I asked Mrs. Mitchell, and she said
nobody new had come to Fustin's all week, that the ferry
didn't run during the storm, so she must still be on the
mainland, so you must have seen her over there. She has
to be in South Bay by now. Wasn't she there at the
ferry?" She stood still for a second or two as Archie
swung himself over the rail of the ferry onto the dock, then
climbed hurriedly after him. "Even Margie would get here
by now. Archie, haven't you seen her? She's got to be
here somewhere."

Archie was quiet for a few moments, gazing down at
her hand tugging at his sleeve.

"Ain't seen nobody," he said at last, not looking at her
face, "nobody don't b'long in these parts. Nobody come
over this mornin', only the mail I been holdin' 'n' Miz

Mitchell's stock.'' He was silent again briefly, then added, ''What's your friend's name?''

''Margie. Margie Packer. Marjory Packer. Why?''

''Best you come back to the mainland with me after I get everything delivered up t' Miz Mitchell's. Howie''—he turned to the man who'd secured his lines—''you gimme a hand here? Got three days' supplies t' get up t' the store, with that nor'easter.''

The three men on the dock nodded without speaking. Two of them clambered aboard the ferry and began lifting crates, cartons, and mail sacks over the side to the one who stayed on the dock.

''What's your friend's name, did you say?'' Archie turned back to Carey before she had chance to speak again.

''Marjory Packer, but—''

''Ain't seen her that I know of. Just you wait for me here, 'n' I'll take you back over with me. No charge,'' he added flatly.

''Why? Why do you want me to go into South Bay? What for?'' It flew through Carey's mind that Margie had written she was renting a car and driving up. ''There hasn't been an accident, Archie? Margie wasn't in an accident, was she?''

''No accident 'round here that I know of. Just you wait right here till I'm through.'' He turned again to the men unloading the ferry. ''Mind you don't put out the mail for Tallwater, Howie. Bags with a *T* on 'em. Nor them crates over t' stabbard. All for Tallwater.'' He walked over to the growing pile of supplies littering the end of the dock, squatted down, and began to stack a load for himself.

The two men on the ferry nodded solemnly at him and went on with their work.

''Archie.'' After a moment's surprise, Carey hopped after him and stood over him. ''Do you know something you're not telling me about Margie?''

''Don't know nothin' t' tell.'' Archie still did not look at her. '' 'Bout nobody. Got t' make my deliveries. Just you wait here.''

Carey did not wait there but followed him, pelting him with questions, back and forth on his several trips up to Mrs. Mitchell's store. She grew increasingly annoyed with Archie's taciturn answers, if they could be called even that. They answered none of her questions.

"Just best you come over t' the mainland for a spell. I'll bring you back this afternoon's ferry," was as much as she could pry from him.

Carey abandoned him to Mrs. Mitchell's stock-toting and turned her anxiety upon the storekeeper, in hopes there would be a letter from Margie explaining her delay somewhere in the three-day accumulation of mail for the bay islanders and their summer guests. To her surprise, Mrs. Mitchell acquiesced, putting down the green composition book in which she recorded her inventory and skillfully thumbing through stack after stack of envelopes, whipping them out of the mailbags with a practiced hand.

"Nope," Mrs. Mitchell said with finality, setting aside the last stack. " 'Tain't nothin' here for you."

"Thank you, Mrs. Mitchell," she said quietly, after a moment. She felt sure the woman had flipped through the bundles of envelopes too fast to really be certain, but she felt momentarily defeated by the reserve of the strangers around her. "I appreciate it. I'm sorry if I've taken up your time."

"I seen you're upset," Mrs. Mitchell forgave her, and picked up her composition book and went back to her inventory.

Before the ferry could return to the mainland, it had to make its regular Thursday run to Tallwater Island. It was a long ride, a full five miles up the bay, and Carey had made it only once before, to sightsee, in her now almost seven weeks on Outer Island. But it didn't interest her this day; it seemed only long and boring. Every small island they passed looked like nothing more to her than the one before; the glare of the sun on the water hurt her eyes; the chug of the ferry's engine, usually so pleasant to her ears, seemed deafening and as irritating as the roar of New York rush-hour traffic.

She did not leave the ferry while it was docked at Tallwater. She sat still on the starboard plank in the stern and watched Archie unload the rest of the cartons, crates, and mailbags from the ferry. It took far less time than at Fustin's, as Archie did not here have to deliver the island's supplies to some other place. A blond boy of around fourteen or fifteen inventoried the deliveries on the dock and signed Archie's black notebook. Before the ferry had pulled away from the Tallwater Island dock, the boy had disappeared with a load of cartons along a path twisting through a dense growth of pine trees and underbrush.

Carey did not enjoy the ride to South Bay, she endured it. Neither she nor Archie had spoken since before leaving Fustin's Island; when they at last drew near it again, Carey experienced a few minutes of anger as Archie slowed the ferry and steered it in close to the dock to check for possible passengers. There were none and, with a quick wave to the one man still hanging about the little wooden pier, Archie increased the speed again. The ferry soon left Fustin's far behind. They rode the remainder of the trip, too, in silence, while the bay stretched out ahead of Carey as if it were eternity.

"You've got to tell me," Carey demanded as she followed Archie along his own dock and across the parking lot, "what's happened to Margie, to my friend? Why am I coming with you here?"

"I'll take you over t' th ... take you over in the pickup." He strode rapidly toward his battered old pickup truck, parked at the far end of the lot.

Carey had to run to keep up with him.

"Take me where?" She veered around a green Corvette that was sloppily parked, jumped into the truck, and slammed the door. "Where are we going?"

" 'Preciate you don't slam them doors like that. Pickup's so old they're liable t' fall right off." Archie turned the key in the ignition and stomped the gas pedal several times. "Gettin' so she don't start right up no more neither."

"Archie," Carey said carefully, controlling her anger, "are you going to tell me anything, or—"

"Nope," he answered expressionlessly. The truck started up with a grinding noise, and he backed it out of its spot. "Don't know nothin' t' tell. Just some people better see you. Prob'ly nothin' a'tall."

"What people? Why? Why do they want to see me? I don't know anybody up here."

"Nope." Archie swung the pickup onto the road leading into the town center of South Bay. "True enough, I reckon."

Carey stared at the side of his face. She hated him. And his bay-folk, Down East ways. And the bay. And Maine. And all New England. She wished she'd never come here, never talked Margie into joining her up here. Margie was right. They should have gone someplace civilized. Someplace where people had some feelings and treated other people as if they did as well. Because they did. She did. She had feelings, and right then they were very clear cut: anxiety about Margie and fury toward Archie English.

The jolting ride along the potholed county road, washed out in low spots by the recent northeaster, kept her thoughts in a state of flux, tossed back and forth between speculation on Margie's whereabouts and well-being, and what to grab onto to keep herself from being jounced through the roof of the pickup's cab. At either extreme, her anger toward Archie increased. When he finally turned into a driveway and pulled behind the adjacent house, he did it so abruptly that Carey was hurled against the cab door and saw neither the old tin mailbox on a post beside the road nor the small sign reading SHERIFF atop it. She let out a sharp cry of pain. Archie paid no attention.

"Stay in the truck," he barked at her. "Got t' stop by here along t' where we're goin'."

He climbed out of the truck and crossed the graveled drive to the back door of the house.

"Miz McCannister?" Carey heard him shout through the door. Then he disappeared inside.

Cursing his delay as well as his driving, Carey gingerly massaged her sore spots and told herself Margie was fine, probably even pacing the ferry dock by now, and that Archie's insistence on creating a mystery about her was some dumb South Bay way of torturing the rest of America. He was punishing her for being one of the vacationers who made him rich every summer. Before she had time to convince herself of this new train of thought, Archie was back.

"Not there," he said cryptically as he swung himself into the driver's seat.

"Are you trying to kill me or your pickup with turns like that?" Carey asked sarcastically, bracing herself for their exit from the driveway.

Archie said nothing. The mailbox was on his side of the driveway now, and he made the turn just fast enough to keep her busy hanging on.

They were into the slightly more populated center of the tiny town of South Bay when Archie suddenly shouted, "Mind the turn now!" and spun the wheel of the truck.

Carey's full attention went to something to hold on to. She saw neither Archie's quick, sideways glance at her face nor the large, black-lettered sign, suspended between two posts set in the lawn in front of a big white house, that read: DOBBLER'S FUNERAL HOME. Archie drove down the driveway and into the parking lot behind the house at top speed. When he parked, the entire large Victorian house was between Carey and the sign.

"Better come in here," he ordered her as he got out of the truck.

Carey climbed down out of the cab and followed him to the kitchen door at the back of the house. Archie opened it without knocking and stepped inside.

"Mornin', Miz Dobbler," he nodded grimly at the middle-aged woman standing at the sink. "George about?"

"Ayup." Mrs. Dobbler nodded back at him. "He's in the—"

"I'll find him," Archie cut her off, too quickly. "This here's Miss Hunter from New York." He emphasized the

words "New York" so heavily Carey felt momentarily
uncomfortable, sure he was deliberately warning the woman
that she was city folk, a foreigner, an outsider, and
therefore to beware. "Been staying out t' old Miz Rambeau's
The Berries for the summer."

Mrs. Dobbler looked stricken, as she nodded at Carey.
Carey felt too confused by a sense of secrets on their part
to do more than politely nod back at her. She followed
Archie silently out of the kitchen, down a short hall,
through a door to the right, and down another hall, a long
one.

Archie stopped before a closed door. Carey stopped
behind him. There was a noticeable pause before he spoke.

"Ayup." His lowered voice held a terrible finality.
"We're here." He reached for the doorknob.

Carey experienced a sudden sense of dread. Half-
expecting—absurdly—to find a mad scientist and his
monster on the other side of the door, she took a step back
as Archie pushed it open and stepped inside. But when she
looked, there were only two ordinary men seated inside,
one on either side of an old wooden desk. The one behind
the desk was tall and thin and middle-aged, and wore a
long white cotton coat or smock. The other, the one in
front of the desk, was older—or looked it—and grossly
overweight; he was in his shirtsleeves. They looked up
with unhappy faces.

"George." Archie stuck out his right hand.

The white-coated man rose from behind his desk and
shook it.

"Archie," he said.

"Polly." Archie turned so that his still-extended hand
now pointed at the fat man's enormous belly.

"Archie." The fat man struggled up from his chair and
pumped Archie's hand with excessive heartiness.

"Stopped over t' your house a bit ago." Archie's voice
was flat, conveying nothing. "Missus said you wasn't t'
home."

"Nope," Polly McCannister concurred.

"Told me," Archie continued after a lengthy pause, "I'd most likely find you t' here. All things considered."

"Ayup." The fat man looked serious, frowning down at his broad belly.

"This here lady with me," Archie said at last, after another prolonged silence, nodding his head sideways and over his right shoulder, "is from New York City."

Again Carey noted the exaggerated emphasis with which Archie's voice uttered the words "New York City," as if they were a code or a clue or, again, a warning. This time, the second time in less than five minutes, she did not experience it as a personal condemnation of herself or a warning against her so much as to her. An alarm rang throughout her nervous system.

"An' she's been stayin' the summer out t' old Miz Rambeau's, on Outer Island, in The Berries." He stopped.

An interminable pause now occurred, during which the two men studied her, the fronts of their clothes, their hands, each other, and Archie. Carey thought they were possibly considering what Archie had said about her; possibly they were not. She looked from one to other of them and waited. She sensed that she really didn't want them to speak, that she might be better off not knowing what this meeting was all about. She was also beginning to feel that if somebody didn't soon tell her just that, she would scream.

"Ayup," came from the fat man, Polly, at last.

"Ayup," instantly followed like an echo from George Dobbler.

Archie took a deep breath. "She was expectin' her friend from New York City—"

For the third time Carey registered his ridiculously obvious emphasis on geography. Her body accelerated immediately into a state of alarm so extreme she felt paralyzed by tension.

"—t' be on the mornin' ferry." Archie took another pause. " 'Cept she wasn't. So I brung her over t' check with you." He paused again, frowning. "Thought it best," he finished, and stepped to one side.

Carey was dimly aware Archie had just completed some, for him, monumentally difficult task, that he had done what he'd felt he had to do. It was apparent to her that he had nothing else to say and was greatly relieved by this fact. She looked at the other two men expectantly, silently urging them to speak while simultaneously hoping they would never answer.

For a considerable time it seemed they would not, that she would get half her wish. But finally the fat man struggled again up out of his chair, one hand straying to his shirt collar and yanking at the open sides when it could find no necktie to tug. He cleared his throat.

"Well, now, ma'am . . . miss," his speech started slow and proceeded to lose momentum as it went on, "I'm Sheriff McCannister. Sheriff of South Bay. And the islands. Whole area. Ayup." He cleared his throat again. "And this here's George Dobbler. He's . . . a local." His face flamed. "And I reckon you know Archie?"

He waited, so Carey nodded once.

"Ayup." Sheriff McCannister looked more unhappy by the moment. "Well, now, miss—? Miss—?"

"Hunter. My name is Carey Hunter."

"Ayup." The sheriff paused, seeming to ruminate on Carey's name. "Best I write that down." He began a prolonged struggle with his various pockets, finally producing a small black notebook and a ballpoint pen. "Hunter, Carey," he said aloud, very slowly, as he wrote just as slowly. "With a *e?*" He looked up at her questioningly.

"With an *e*."

"Ayup. Got that." He scratched his chin. "From?"

Carey looked at him blankly.

"Where you from, Miss"—he checked his notebook—"Hunter?"

"My God." Anger was plain in Carey's tone. "New York. New York City. He already said so." She jerked her left elbow in the direction of Archie. "Three times."

Archie nodded impassively in agreement.

"New York City." The ballpoint pen moved carefully across the narrow page. "Street address?" Sheriff

McCanniser's voice revealed nothing. If he had a reaction to Carey's outburst, it was not detectable by her.

"Three forty-seven West Seventy-sixth Street. Apartment Four B." Carey's voice cracked like a whip. "Zip one zero zero two three."

"Ayup," the sheriff said when his hand at last stopped moving. "Got it."

The ensuing pause was so long, Carey began to crack in spite of herself.

"Please, sombeody's got"—her voice broke on the word—"to tell me why I'm here. I'm very worried. If you know something about Margie—about my friend—for God's sake tell me. You're all killing me." She felt her face flushed, her body sticky with perspiration.

The three men appeared highly uncomfortable. Their eyes looked away from her, scanning walls, windows, their own shoes, or, in the case of Sheriff Polly McCannister, the circumference of his stomach, below which, for him, his shoes were invisible. Finally Dobbler gestured vaguely to McCannister when their eyes accidentally met during their separate scannings, and the sheriff cleared his throat once more.

"Well, Miss . . . Hunter, seems we've got a bit of a problem here. Can you give me your friend's name, please?" Notebook and pen poised in midair, he waited.

"Margie Packer. Marjory Packer, in full. Same address as mine," she anticipated him. "We're roommates."

"Dern things never write when you need 'em to," Sheriff McCannister finally said in exasperation after a long battle with his pen. "George? You got a pen?"

"Ayup. Minute." Dobbler pulled open the center drawer of his desk and rummaged through its contents.

"You're doing this on purpose," Carey burst out.

No one in the room paid the slightest attention to her. It was exactly as if she had not spoken, indeed, as if she were not even there.

"There y'are, Polly," Dobbler said at last, handing a pen across the desk.

"Thankee, George." The sheriff took it. "Now, miss, could you gimme them facts again."

Carey repeated what she had said, her voice a little shrill. She was feeling with increasing certainty that something terrible had happened to Margie.

"Got it," McCannister said at last. "Well." He paused again, studying the point of the pen he was now using for what seemed to Carey a deliberately long time before going on. "How old w—is your friend?"

"Twenty-seven."

"Hair?"

"Auburn. Coppery-colored. Wavy. About to her shoulders. She has beautiful hair."

"Eyes?"

"Green. Real green, not hazel."

"Height?"

"I don't know. Average. About five foot six or so, I guess."

"Weight?"

"God, I don't know. I don't know. She's slender. She has a nice figure, a really nice figure. She's just right for her height. She's very pretty—a lot of people think she's beautiful. I think she's beautiful. She's got a mole on her left wrist. She worries so much about getting cancer from it she wears her watch on her right arm, even though she's right-handed. But she won't have it removed because she's terrified of being cut—of surgery. What else in God's name do you want to know? Her shoe size? I don't know it. Glove size? Hat size? Her medical history? I don't know them either. She's got pierced ears," Carey finished in a small voice, tears in her eyes. Through them she noticed George Dobbler reading a piece of paper on his desk and nodding his head as he did so. "She's all right, isn't she? Margie's all right? Isn't she?"

Sheriff McCannister's shirt was darkening with sweat despite the chilly air. He dragged a huge, dirty handkerchief from a trouser pocket and mopped his head and face.

"Well, now, miss, we don't rightly know that yet."

"Is she here? Is Margie here?"

"Might not be her after all. Stranger things have happened." The sheriff's face belied his last statement.

"If Margie's here, I want to see her. Now," Carey confronted him. "This minute."

"First off, we don't know for sure if it's her—your friend. Hard t' tell. We do have a body here. Might fit the description you gave. Might not. Hard t' tell." Sheriff McCannister's manner and speech rhythm had altered markedly, as if he were now suddenly in a great rush to get whatever it was that lay before him over with as quickly as possible. "I'm gonna have to ask you, unfortunately, t' identify it—if you can, miss."

"Of course I can," Carey snapped. "I know Margie as well as I know myself—better, probably."

"It's . . ." The sheriff looked extremely uneasy. "It's . . . not in such good shape."

Carey lost her breath as surely as if he had punched her in the solar plexus. This was a new unknown. What had they—or who?—done to Margie? She had not even begun to take in the import of the sheriff's word "body"; still, she was trembling.

"Oh," she said. Her voice sounded breathless. My God, I sound like Marilyn Monroe doing a love scene, she thought, horrified at her inappropriateness. Her reaction to this thought was, inexplicably to her, to giggle. "Well, let's get it over with, then," she forced herself to add through giggles she could not control.

Polly McCannister and George Dobbler raised eyebrows and exchanged glances. Archie English's small body shrank a bit inside his clothing.

"Think you best sit down, young lady," Sheriff McCannister gently propelled Carey to the vacated chair and more gently pushed her down onto it. "George?" He looked up at his friend. "I think Miss Hunter here could use a little snort of somethin'."

"Ayup." Dobbler's voice was inaudible, though his lips moved. He opened another drawer in his ancient desk and produced a bottle.

"Ellen's best," he said, sounding as inappropriate as Carey felt. He pushed the bottle across the desk.

"Got a glass?" A decided note of irritation had crept into the sheriff's voice.

Dobbler flushed. He bent over the desk drawer again.

"Cup do?" He straightened up and handed a white china cup across the desk to McCannister.

The sheriff snatched it without answering. He set it down, opened the bottle, poured out some of its contents, and stuck the cup under Carey's nose.

"Drink this," he ordered her, adding, "wish t' Christ ol' Doc Burry'd hurry up 'n' get here."

Carey obediently took the cup, tilted it against her lips, and swallowed its contents in one gulp. She neither tasted the liquid nor felt it going down her throat.

"Goin' into shock." Polly McCannister made his announcement as an accusation of George Dobbler, glaring at him.

Dobbler shrugged helplessly and looked guilty.

"No. No, I'm not." The drink was working in spite of Carey's dulled sense of it. She put the cup down and stood up. "I'm fine. I just want to see Margie."

"Hold on there one little half of a minute please." The sheriff pushed her firmly back down onto the chair and cleared his throat. "First things first. 'N' first thing is, this—uh, body—may not be your Margie. Can't know that for sure 'less you can identify her." He paused a second. "And you mayn't be able t' do that."

A new note of alarm struck Carey's nervous system. These were stronger words than the sheriff had used before. She stared into his face blankly, not knowing what to say. She still did not think of the body she was to identify as a *dead* body; her mind refused to consider that aspect of the situation.

"You see," Sheriff McCannister continued, " 's somethin' mighty strange about this here body we got. Somethin' we can't figger out. It—uh—just ain't normal, you see. No violence," he inserted hastily, "it wasn't done no violence. No, sirree, nothin' like that. Not a mark on it.

However this . . . body . . . met its end, we know it didn't suffer none. Leastways, not much,'' he added lamely.

"I want to see . . . it." Carey stood up.

"Yes, ma'am, we'll get t' that. But I'm thinkin' I best prepare you a little. Venture to say it's gonna be a shock, whether it's your friend or not." Polly McCannister placed a mammoth hand on Carey's shoulder but did not try to force her to sit again. "You see, Miss Hunter, this here body we got here died some way we don't know nothin' about." Again he cleared his throat.

"Well?" Carey stared at him uncomprehendingly.

"It's . . . completely dry." McCannister was not; he was sweating profusely, and mopped his head and face again with his soiled handkerchief. He took his other hand from Carey's shoulder and reached for the bottle of Ellen's best. He poured himself a drink and drank it, with a nod to Dobbler, who nodded back.

"I don't understand." Very little of what was being said now was reaching Carey's intelligence. "I just want to see Margie. I've been expecting her since Monday."

The sheriff shook his head anxiously. "This body's completely dry," he repeated himself. "De-hy-drated." He stressed the first and third syllables. "Ain't no moistures left in it a'tall."

"So?" Carey still stared at him.

"So it looks awful, for God's sake," Sheriff McCannister burst out. "Jesus. Like some Egyptian mummy from out'n one of them pyramids. Looks a thousand years old, by gory. Only it ain't. 'Bout fainted m'self when I took a look at it." His manner softened. "It's . . . pretty bad, miss. It's bad. 'S gonna be a shock, even if ain't your friend. Had t' tell you 'fore you went in. Bad. 'S bad. Real bad." He patted Carey's shoulder absently. "I'd never let someone like you see it if it wasn't that you're missin' somebody." He sighed. "You want another snort afore—?"

"No." Carey carefully smoothed down her jeans and slicker jacket, then fluffed her curly hair. She was unaware of doing this. "I'd like to go . . . see now."

*   *   *

George Dobbler accompanied Sheriff McCannister and Carey farther down the long hall to another door, as did Archie English. This door was marked KEEP OUT in hand-painted red letters. As Dobbler turned the knob, Carey stopped and confronted the sheriff.

"I'd like to go in alone, please." She could not put into words the sense of violation the three of them represented to her. That they were male made what she was feeling all the more unendurable. "I don't want anyone—"

"Well, now," McCannister interrupted her, "I'm sorry, miss. I just can't permit that. I got t' go in with you. 'S the law. Crime's been committed—maybe. Must be. I'm sorry."

"Well not them, then," Carey's voice rose harshly.

"Well, miss, now George here, he's South Bay's, uh, mortician. Always 'companies me on cases like this—cases that got t' be investigated, that is. I know how you must be feelin', but I'm sorry."

"Well, at least Archie docsn't!" Carey shouted, although he was the one she would have chosen to be with her, had she had a choice.

The sheriff nodded solemnly. "Be true," he said softly. "Arch, y'mind? The young lady here prefers   "

"What is my friend—a sideshow? A freak?" Carey's voice was shrill with outrage. "Are you charging admission? I'm going to report this to somebody. I warn you. Get him out of here."

Archie had already backed down the hall. Now he disappeared hastily into George Dobbler's office.

"He's gone," Polly McCannister said soothingly. "I'm real sorry, miss. You're upset, I know. I understand. Archie, he was only tryin' t' help. I'm sorry."

Carey swept past him through the doorway as Dobbler opened the door and strode to the table in the center of the white-walled room.

"Wait, miss, here now, wait, you mustn't—" Sheriff McCannister's order came too late, his enormous body moved too slowly.

Carey swept the white sheet covering the small body onto the floor.

For a split second, she saw only clothes, laid out as if to feign a body: a pair of old, faded Levi's and a well-worn, embroidered Western work shirt. Then she realized there was a body in them—a tiny, shrunken body, smaller than a pygmy's. Its hands and face, all that were exposed to view, Carey could not have identified as ever having been human. Shrunken smaller than an infant's, they were grotesquely twisted and distorted. The hands seemed to have been frozen while they were frenziedly clawing at something; nails with garish splotches of polish much too big for them were jagged and broken.

Carey fainted before she saw more than the scream contorting the tiny, sere face.

3

"That looks like it might be it," Vergil O'Malley, the younger of the two young officers assigned to the case, sang out, pointing to a large, white Victorian house up ahead on the left, "fits the description, sir. Got a big sign on the lawn, too, though I can't make it out yet. Sir," he added emphatically.

Lieutenant Paul Tilley glanced sideways at the young man behind the wheel, his blue eyes a mixture of amusement and irritation. "One 'sir' per paragraph is enough, O'Malley," he grumbled. "This isn't the army."

"Yes, sir. Sorry, sir—" O'Malley flushed a bright red and bit his lip. "I mean—"

"Skip it, O'Malley." Tilley crumpled the styrofoam

coffee container in his hand and dropped it on the floor of the car. "Just pull in if that's the place."

"Yes, sir."

Tilley stared through the windshield at the large sign on the lawn of the house they were approaching. The angle of the road was still not right for him to be able to read the lettering on it. He knew he'd been a son-of-a-bitch to both O'Malley and Skeet Coggins, the other officer Chief Skillin had assigned to him, ever since they'd left Bangor, and that neither of the young men had done anything to deserve it. It wasn't they with whom he was really angry, it was his chief.

He was furious with Skillin for refusing to give him more experienced men, for insisting he take the two newest, greenest officers on the force "in order to let them get some experience under their belts." Tilley snorted inwardly at the recall of his chief's words. He had other ideas about how new recruits ought to be broken in. Moreover, he'd had a strong feeling, from the moment he'd heard the local sheriff's voice on the phone that afternoon, that something genuinely bizarre had occurred down in quiet little South Bay.

Damn the nor'easter, too, he said to himself as the road straightened out and the sign slid into full view. If the lines hadn't been knocked out Down East, I'd have gotten that call on Monday—when I should have had it—and Jim would have been available. He felt a real need for Sergeant Jim Crowley, his regular partner, not only for the man's years of experience on the force but for the familiarity between them and the unspoken ease with which they worked together. He and Crowley were a team—a good, effective team. His intuition told him he had never been in more need of that kind of support than he was going to be today.

"This is it, sir," O'Malley said, half a question in his voice. "I'm pulling in."

"Right," Tilley muttered.

Lt. Tilley, with O'Malley and Coggins behind him, had barely stepped into the front vestibule of the house when

Archie English leaped to his feet in the parlor just beyond, shouting, "M' God! The six-o'clock ferry! I clean forgot! Dang bust it." Before anyone else could think to speak, he added philosophically, his voice and manner suddenly imperturbable, "Well, by gory, she's just gonna be some late, that's what she's gonna be. Like it or lump it."

"Who is that man?" Tilley asked Polly McCannister, who had met him at the door, looking past him into the parlor.

"I'm going with you." Carey announced in a flat, expressionless voice, before McCannister had a chance to reply to Tilley's question. She got to her feet and stood unsteadily. "Margie will be there. I have to meet Margie. She'll be waiting for me. . . ."

"You ain't goin' nowheres in your condition," Polly McCannister growled authoritatively, lumbering toward her. "Not so long as I'm in charge here."

Tilley's eyebrows shot up, and a little smile quirked the corners of his mouth. He thought of three deliciously sardonic ways of enlightening the lardy local sheriff as to the extent of his authority now that he, Tilley, had arrived, but verbalized none of them. For the moment he contented himself with sticking his dark head into the parlor and concurring in a voice far more commanding than his comfortable face, he knew, had led McCannister to expect.

Lt. Paul Tilley of the Bangor Police Force carried an unprepossessing air about him. Of average height, lean, his black hair salted with gray at the temples and back of his neck, he blended inconspicuously into his surroundings—until he either spoke or looked directly into someone's eyes. His voice was as deeply baritone as his eyes were blue, and either gave instant notice that their owner was in full possession of himself and of the situation. People did not often argue with Paul Tilley.

"As you're my only means of immediate identification, Miss"—he glanced questioningly at Polly McCannister, who hastily supplied Carey's full name—"Miss Hunter," he finished gently but adamantly, "I must insist that you remain here." He looked into her brown eyes and thought,

This young woman's in deep shock. What the hell happened to her?

"It's not Margie," Carey came back at him tonelessly. "I've told them—it's not Margie. It's not her."

"She's already viewed the body?" Tilley squinted at McCannister, his blue eyes cold as steel.

"Well, ayup, yeah, ayup," the sheriff mumbled uncomfortably, shifting his weight from one foot to the other and pushing Carey back down onto the sofa with a fleshy hand. "Ayup, she did."

"Jesus," Tilley swore softly under his breath.

"Well, but—she insisted—" McCannister began, his face reddening.

"It isn't even her hair." Carey stood up again suddenly, bumping her head into the sheriff's protruding belly. McCannister tilted backward, away from her, and did a little dance to keep from losing his balance. "I know Margie," Carey went on, seemingly blind to McCannister's sudden jig, "and that isn't Margie. It isn't. It can't be," she finished dully.

"I suggest you fill me in on what's already gone down here, ostensibly by way of investigation." Tilley did not attempt to hide his sarcasm.

"Be glad to, glad to." McCannister again dragged his enormous soiled handkerchief from his trouser pocket and mopped his sweating face, "Lieutenant—Captain?—"

Paul Tilley stifled the rush of contempt he experienced and simply shrugged, ignoring the plea in the local sheriff's baggy eyes.

"I swear I'll come right back fast as I can if her friend's on the dock," Archie English jumped into the sudden silence in the room, nodding his head vigorously at everyone there. "I swear. May God strike me dead if I don't." His deeply tanned face darkened instantly, taking on a look of consternation. "Ayup, I will," he added lamely, and started for the back door.

"One moment please." Lt. Tilley did not raise his voice.

Archie stopped dead in his tracks.

"I must insist that you also remain. For questioning. Everyone in this house is to remain here for the time being."

Archie turned back and looked at him dumbfounded. Then he looked at his watch and looked up again, this time at Polly McCannister. There was a stricken expression on his face. He opened his mouth, but no words came out.

"Now see here," Polly McCannister did not meet Tilley's icy eyes as he huffed and puffed his way uneasily through his protest, "Arch English here's got a ferry t' run that's late already. Shoulda left at six o'clock. People be standin' on docks all over the bay worryin' themselves about him. Man's got a right—"

"Then they'll just have to worry themselves a little longer, won't they, sheriff?" Tilley gave him a withering look and waited for an answer.

"Ayup, guess so," McCannister finally stammered. "Guess so. Ayup."

"Right." Tilley looked away from him and strode farther into the parlor, pausing by the sofa to gaze down at Carey's face a moment. Then he walked to where Archie was standing. "I'll make this as brief as possible, Mr. English, so you can get on about your business. But I'll expect you back after your run for further questioning." He took Archie's arm, and walked him out of the parlor and down the hallway.

When he returned, alone, a few minutes later, he found an elderly, white-haired man with a stethoscope dangling from his ears preparing to take Carey Hunter's blood pressure. He waited until the old man had finished, then stepped forward.

"I'm Lieutenant Paul Tilley, Bangor Police. And you are—?"

"This here is Doc Burry," Polly McCannister hurried in. "Doc t' all South Bay. 'Course he ain't actually from the bay hisself, y'understand, he hails from Mealeyville." McCannister gestured broadly toward the west wall of the house. "All the same—"

"That's some thirty miles or so from here, isn't it, doctor?" Tilley asked.

"That's correct, Lieutenant Tilley," Dr. Burry said, dropping his stethoscope in his black bag, open on the floor beside the straight chair he, or someone, had pulled up beside the sofa. "I came as soon as I could after Polly's—Sheriff McCannister's call early this afternoon. Was setting a broken arm at the time."

"Then you haven't yet examined the body." Tilley turned and eyed McCannister. "You do have a body here somewhere, sheriff?"

"Ayup. We do that. It's—"

"Has your local doctor examined it? Has he been called in?"

"Doc Burry is our doctor," McCannister answered, his voice a bit on the defensive. "Nobody else t' call in. Ain't got another doctor in the whole bay area, not for miles around."

"I see." Tilley turned back to Dr. Burry. "Then you haven't yet examined the body?"

"No, sir, I have not." Dr. Burry snapped his black bag shut and stood up. "This young woman here is in shock. There's nothing to be done for her until she comes out of it and reacts to whatever happened to her." He glanced from Tilley to McCannister. "What did happen to her, Polly?"

"She took a look at the body we got back there," McCannister replied in a grim voice, jerking his thumb over his right shoulder.

A brief, apprehensive silence followed. Tilley felt a small shiver race down his spine and looked again, frowning, into Carey's blank brown eyes. What the hell? he again asked himself. Then, abruptly, he shook himself and straightened up.

"We'd better take a look at your body now, sheriff," he said quietly. "Doctor," he glanced at the man, "would you accompany us, please. Is there someone who can stay here with Miss Hunter and keep an eye on her? I'll want my officers to come with us." He looked now from McCannister to Dobbler. "And you two, of course. Am I correct in assuming you're George Dobbler, the local mortician?''

"I am," Dobbler replied.

"I'm staying here," Ellen Dobbler who had come into the room unnoticed, suddenly spoke up in a trembling, pleading voice. "I can look after Miss Hunter."

"Yes, of course," the policeman nodded at her. "You'll be here. I didn't mean to overlook you, ma'am. Thank you. Coggins, O'Malley. Sheriff?''

Polly McCannister led Lt. Tilley, the two police officers, and Dr. Burry out of the parlor and down the long hall. George Dobbler followed them as far as the door to his embalming room, then suddenly excused himself.

"Reckon it best if you do your own examination, doctor," he muttered to Dr. Burry. "We can compare notes later. Be in my office, gentlemen." He turned and walked quickly back down the hall.

Tilley knew his repugnance had communicated itself to the rest of them. The four men for whom this was to be a first viewing hesitated outside the closed door; the red-lettered KEEP OUT seemed excellent advice as Sheriff McCannister turned the knob and pushed open the door without moving from his spot in the hall. Tilley felt his skin crawl slightly, and glanced at the faces of his officers and the old doctor. The sheriff's revulsion could also be felt. It was several seconds before Paul Tilley, the man, conquered his paralyzing reaction to the presentiment of imminent horror pervading him and walked forward, officer of the law, into the still, white room.

Halfway to the sheet-draped table, he was aware of hearing only his own footsteps. He stopped and turned back.

"Gentlemen," he said caustically, "follow me, please."

Carey Hunter sat on the sofa in the parlor staring blindly into space. In her mind she watched Margie waiting excitedly on Archie's dock, growing impatient because the ferry was late, introducing herself in her rushed, vibrant way to Archie when he arrived. There the scene suddenly froze and hung motionless inside her head for a few moments, with Margie's green eyes caught in midsparkle, her sculptured lips curved in the dazzling, generous smile Carey knew so well, enjoyed so much.

Then it was gone, replaced by Margie losing her temper, stamping a Gucci-booted foot and shouting at Archie about his ferry not being on schedule after her long drive from Connecticut. This new scene was vastly more reassuring, volatile Margie having a small tantrum when things didn't go the way she expected them to, not namby-pambying about with a smile on her face like some Goody Two Shoes. Not the explosively exuberant Marjory Packer she had lived with for ten years. And if Margie was losing her temper, she must be alive. And well. And safe.

Carey's fantasy continued as if the entire afternoon had never happened. Archie and Margie boarded the ferry, Margie still feisty about his unpunctuality. She watched Margie crouch down and pat the deck of the passenger section aft with a manicured hand to be certain her soft-sided luggage was not sitting in a puddle of seawater. Then, as Archie stepped up to the wheel, Carey allowed Margie to calm down and become her other self, charming and witty, during the run out to Fustin's. Margie would not be subdued by Archie English's refusal to utter even a grunt while at his helm. Margie would get answers out of him. Archie would talk at the wheel in spite of himself. Margie Packer, when she wanted to be, was irresistible.

She indulged Margie in a fresh temper when Carey was not waiting for her on the dock at Fustin's Island, hearing in her mind every fuming four-letter word Margie would let go with about having only two weeks—not the whole summer, like Carey—and every second being precious, as the empty dock grew larger and larger with the ferry's approach.

The fantasy went into minute detail. Margie had on her old, faded, laundered-soft Levi's—her favorites: "I hate designer jeans," she would shout while dressing for a night of discoing at Les mouches with Jeff. "What human body can dance in these things? They're a fucking straightjacket!'' And her hand-embroidered Western work shirt—''every mother stitch done by these lily-white hands themselves,'' she almost never failed to remind Carey when she wore it. ''This is the real me, Hunter.''

No, not that shirt. Why had her mind pictured that shirt? Margie never wore that shirt anymore except around the apartment. ''Embroidery is out,'' she had announced not long ago when Carey had suggested she wear it to travel in for a weekend trip with Jeff, in hopes of arresting Margie's tantrum over not having anything new and interesting to wear. ''You want me to look like one of the natives when we stop for coffee? I wouldn't travel to my own funeral in embroidery anymore, Hunter. Remember that—in case you have to bury me some day!''

No, it wouldn't be that shirt. Why had she put that shirt on Margie? Margie would be wearing—yes, that's it—her pink shirred made-in-Turkey blouse she'd gotten in Aspen in February. ''My Lois Nettleton top,'' Margie called it.

Margie had seen Lois Nettleton getting into a taxi on West End Avenue one evening the previous summer wearing a pink shirred blouse and jeans. A few months later she saw the actress on ''Pyramid'' wearing the same blouse and became passionately excited. ''It's the same damn blouse, Hunter. I am telling you I saw her live, on the street, in that same exact blouse! I love it! I've got to get me one like it, I've got to!'' Margie hadn't rested until she had found a top, not really like it at all but at least pink and shirred, during a ski weekend. ''It's close, it's close,'' she had raved, modeling it back home in the apartment for Carey. ''Maybe I should shorten the sleeves and use the cut-offs to make them fuller. Like Lois'.''

But she hadn't, not yet anyway. Margie Packer was one of the world's great procrastinators. ''Next week. Next week I'm going to do it,'' she had said once in answer to Carey's innocent: ''I thought you were going to fix those sleeves to look like Lois Nettleton's.''

Another time, standing in front of the full-length mirror on the living-room closet door contemplating the effect of the blouse's sleeves rolled up, Margie had offered a deeper explanation for not having gotten around to changing them: "My arms aren't as pretty as Lois Nettleton's. Maybe I'll just leave them alone." She resignedly rolled the sleeves back down again.

Lois Nettleton was Margie's all-time favorite actress and most beautiful woman in the world. "Oh, God!" she would moan in her low moods, "Why couldn't I have been born with a face like that? Jesus, that woman looks like an angel." She couldn't sit through a television program or film of Lois Nettleton's without keeping up a running dissertation about the actress' being "even more exquisite in person, Hunter—I know. I'm telling you she is even so much more gorgeous in person you wouldn't believe it. Believe me, when I saw her that night on West End Avenue I nearly fainted. You think she's beautiful on TV? You should just see her in person. Out of this world. That lady's face is absolutely out of this world. I'm not kidding you. She's perfect." Adding, after a few minutes, in an exaggeratedly despairing voice, "And then there's me and you, babe. Oh, well." And grinning when Carey stuck out her tongue at her.

Margie, an actress herself who had ended up, at least for the present, working as assistant to a small-time personal manager, further considered Lois Nettleton the world's greatest actress. She never missed anything the actress did and read TV Guide— hawkeyed for her name—the way some people read the Bible.

"She's like Duse, she can do anything, be anyone, create any age. She doesn't need makeup or wigs or costumes or anything. She's got that gift—that great gift that hardly any actor today has, really has—for creating an inner life and sustaining it so strongly she actually can change her physical self. She does more than sustain it, she lives it. She doesn't just act on a stage, she lives on a stage—or in front of a camera. She's incredible. And we waste her. Look at what she's doing. This country doesn't deserve a talent like Lois Nettleton. She should be on a stage every day of her life. I should have been a producer, Hunter, that's what I should be doing. Talent like that should be used. Seen. In what-was-that-play-that-closed, you know, with what's-his-name, I can't stand him, she played an entire love scene with just her right arm—her right arm; no other part of her moved—and left you so weak you couldn't get out of your seat. You didn't know whether to rush home and make love or sit there and weep because your heart was broken for her. With her right arm. You tell me who else in the business today can do that?''

Margie was definitely a Lois Nettleton superfan. She would have been wearing her pink shirred Lois Nettleton top with the unfixed sleeves.

And she would have noticed the spoke missing from the ferry's wheel: Margie had a fine eye for detail. Carey's fantasy, switching from present to past to present again, now had her friend haranguing Archie about what had happened to it. This was something Carey herself had wanted to do on her first trip across the bay but had been too embarrassed to, lest Archie think she was implying his boat wasn't seaworthy. Margie would have no such reluctance about satisfying her curiosity.

As the ferry neared Fustin's Island, Carey's viewpoint shifted and she saw, as if from the dock, Margie waving wildly to her from the stern. Margie was here!

"Margie! Margie! Hi!"

The ferry drew still closer. As it did, Carey saw her friend change with lightning speed. Margie's face—her entire head—dried up and shrank. Her skin leaped back from outsized teeth, exposed in a gruesome grimace. Her eyeballs bulged forward, then reversed, almost imploded, into her brain and shriveled instantly to lurid, leaden, wrinkled little concavities—without eyes in them, so total was the loss of iris color—ghoulishly staring out from under dessicated, warped eyelids.

Her fantasy was out of Carey's control. It was, in fact, a fantasy no longer. It had become a living memory.

Seconds after Lt. Tilley had pulled back the sheet covering the stainless-steel examining table in George Dobbler's embalming room and exposed the macabre anhydride, Officer O'Malley vomited into the sink on the side wall. Officer Coggins fainted.

Dr. Burry, white as the sheet Tilley had removed, knelt beside him and broke an ammonia capsule under his nose. With Coggins coughing and still ashen, the elderly doctor helped him to his feet.

"Get out of here," Tilley growled, then turned on the green-about-the-gills O'Malley. "You better get out of here, too. You're no good to me like that." Tilley himself was gray-faced under his tan.

The young officers nodded weakly and fled from the room.

"Will they live, doctor?" Tilley asked sarcastically, not expecting an answer. He was furious all over again with Chief Skillin for refusing to give him two more experienced men.

"They're in shock, same as the young woman in there," Dr. Burry replied in a flattened voice. "Same as us."

The two men stood still, looking at each other, unable to bring themselves to do what they were there to do.

"Why is this body dressed?" Tilley finally snapped. "Hasn't there even been a preliminary examination yet? Who's responsible for this?"

"I arrived here after you did, Mr. Tilley." Dr. Burry reminded him evenly, "So I'm afraid I can't answer that."

"Goddamn amateur police. Playing around with things they don't know a damn thing about. I hate cases like this." Tilley hardly knew what he meant. He'd never seen a case like this before. Rage was close to overwhelming him, and he needed a scapegoat. His experience with the local sheriffs and police chiefs outside of Bangor had given him small cause to hold them in any notable regard.

"Perhaps we should get out of here for a few minutes," Dr. Burry said after a pause, in the same pancaked voice. "Come back a mite later. Give ourselves time to get adjusted to . . . it . . . a little, Mr. Tilley."

"I doubt we'll ever adjust to that"—Tilley paused ever so briefly—"thing, doctor. I suggest we get on with it."

*   *   *

"Margie!" Like a broken record, her friend's name shrieked out of Carey Hunter's throat, over and over and over.

Ellen Dobbler, not at all recovered herself from her discovery of the ghoulish cadaver only three days earlier, patted at Carey's flailing hands gingerly and whispered, "My dear," again and again.

George Dobbler got to the parlor first, followed not quite immediately by Officer Coggins.

"Jesus," Coggins exclaimed as he stepped into the parlor.

Dobbler stepped backward into the hallway, colliding with him.

"Christ, man," he barked at the young officer, then shoved him clear across the hall, shouting, "Doc! Dr. Burry!" He bolted forward into the parlor again. "Out of the way, Mother," he growled at his wife, who had never, in fact, been a mother, and, taking her place beside Carey on the sofa, attempted to restrain her thrashing arms.

Carey was vibrating from head to toe. Her teeth chattered against each other with such force the sound rattled around the room at a level just below her screams. Every muscle in her body had taken on a separate life of its own, the purpose of which seemed to be to tear itself free from every other. The mortician found it impossible to keep a grasp on her.

Ellen Dobbler had moved away from them and was now weeping, her face pressed hard against one of the parlor walls. Her tears made dark splotches that ran like rain down the faded, once-flowered wallpaper, streaking it.

"Help me, you goddamn fool!" Dobbler shouted at the staring, immobile Coggins.

"Margie!"

At the sound of the first earsplitting shriek, Paul Tilley started with such violence that his right hand struck the head of the tiny carcass as hard as if he had deliberately thrown a punch at it. Having no structural flexibility, the dehydrated remains simply spun on the slick metal table, waving nearly empty sleeves and jeans legs like flags.

The miniature, stick-stiff legs struck Dr. Burry's left hip while he was still in midstart himself. A sound of revulsion escaped from his throat as he leaped away from their loathsome touch.

Lt. Tilley caught the shrunken, boardlike body before it fell and straightened it lengthwise on the table again, then automatically, quickly, covered it with the sheet.

"Christ, we're acting like a couple of schoolgirls," he muttered. There was more horror than self-reproach in his voice.

The piercing shriek had seemed to come from the hideously protracted mouth of the corpse, already grimacing in a silent scream. It took him a moment to realize it had not, and another moment to realize the screaming had not stopped.

"That young woman!" Dr. Burry ran for the parlor.

Tilley followed on his heels, angry at himself for feeling grateful for anything that took him out of that room of such inexplicable and abominable death.

Here he's got a symptom he knows how to cope with, Tilley thought as watched the doctor order the ineffectual Dobbler away from Carey and shout at him to move lamps and vases out of her reach.

"Help me," the doctor now shouted at Tilley, snatching an afghan from an old easy chair near the sofa. "Wrap her in this. Not tight, not tight, let her get it out—just enough to keep her from hurting herself."

Tilley grabbed one of the crossed ends of Mrs. Dobbler's handiwork, and together he and the doctor controlled Carey until at last she subsided into heartbroken sobs and tolerable shivering.

So, he thought compassionately, it is your friend after all, poor kid. He put his arms around her and held her firmly.

"I'll give her a shot now." Dr. Burry stood up, looking around for his bag.

"No." Carey lifted her swollen, tear-washed face from Tilley's stomach. "I don't want a shot."

"You need rest now," Dr. Burry protested. "Been through quite a ordeal, young lady. Be over in a second. . . ."

"I won't take it. You can't make me." She looked up at Tilley for support. "He can't make me take it."

"She's right, doctor," Tilley said quietly. "It's her choice."

Dr. Burry opened his mouth to protest again, his face flushed with anger. Tilley knew it was directed more against him than Carey.

"Have it your way then," the old doctor sputtered. "Can't force her. I won't take responsibility, though, anything happens to her."

For a moment Tilly felt sorry for the old man. He could see the doctor's face aging right before his eyes. Now he feels thoroughly useless, Tilley thought. I've taken away from him the only thing he knows how to do here.

But he did not regret his action. Now that Carey had come out of shock, he wanted her to make a positive identification of the thing in the back room, so he could get on with his work. You're a ruthless son of a bitch, Paul Tilley, he told himself. That's why I'm good at my job, he answered himself.

"I want to see Margie," Carey was saying. "I just want to see Margie."

Tilley looked down at her. Underneath the tear-stained face, swollen eyes, and reddened nose, he could see there was a very attractive young woman, perhaps even a slightly beautiful one when she was happy. He knew he didn't give a damn, however; that to him all Carey Hunter was, was a means to an end: the identification of a probable homicide victim. If she was that, if she could positively identify the body—what remained of it—then she represented a saving of as much as three days of his time, maybe considerably more. His time was important to him; one more New York vacationer was not. Tilley got a bellyful of New York vacationers every summer.

They had not endeared themselves to him. He heartily wished they would all stay in New York where they belonged and spare his beloved Maine their careless, littering, destructive ways. Their city ways. He still remembered very clearly the campsite keeper's wife up at Duck Lake, years ago, saying to him, after a bunch of New York kids had all but razed the campsite to the ground "just for fun," and he'd been sent up to investigate the damage and find the kids, "City folk got city ways."

Indeed, Paul Tilley felt, they did. And they weren't his ways. All he wanted from Carey Hunter was that she serve his purpose as quickly as he could force her to and go back where she came from. Back where she belonged. Until that time, she was just one more piece of the puzzle he'd been handed to put together. He felt relieved that she was a small piece, to be early and easily used, and dispensed with. He felt sorry for her; he was not a heartless man. But his sorrow for others did not often go very deep. He couldn't afford to let it.

George Dobbler appeared from somewhere with a wet washrag and put it into Carey's hands. She pressed it to her face for a few seconds, then wiped her face and hands with it, and stood up, shaking Tilley's arm from around her shoulders as she did so. He saw that she was unsteady on her feet, and took her arm gently.

"Easy does it now," he said quietly.

"I want to see Margie."

"Absolutely not." Dr. Burry sounded tired, and very, very old. "I'll have no part of this."

"I'm going to see Margie."

Atta girl, Carey Hunter, Tilley thought to himself. You stick to your guns.

"Now let's not rush things here." Sheriff McCannister appeared in the doorway and shuffled a few steps forward into the parlor.

Tilley blistered him with a look of contempt. "I'm in charge here now, sheriff. We'll do it my way. The sooner she gets it over with, the better it'll be for her."

"That young woman's still in shock," Dr. Burry said,

sounding weakly horrified. "What you're doing is inhuman. I won't take responsibility for this."

"I will." Tilley's voice held a reprimand. He loathed country cases where he was surrounded by well-meaning fools and armchair experts. He knew that the longer Carey waited before viewing the body again, the more anxiety she would build up. "Sure you feel up to this now, Miss Hunter?"

"At least you could let her get some rest first—" Dr. Burry began.

"I can't rest till I know."

"She can't rest till she knows," Tilley said in unison with her. He looked down at her, a touch of admiration in his eyes. Here was a New Yorker who at least was not a fool—and not pretending to be an expert, either. He felt an unexpected burst of anger that, of all the people in the room, it had to be she who was suffering the loss. Tilley had long ago given up hope that there was any justice to be found in the world, but he had never lost his sense of outrage over the absence of it. "Ready to go?" he asked her gently.

"I won't take part in jeopardizing a patient's health, maybe her life," Dr. Burry shrilled. "I warn you, sir, I'll be no part of this."

"You don't have to be," Tilley answered curtly. "You can do your job later."

"I won't be bullied by some big-city policeman!" Dr. Burry was red in the face. "I demand that I be taken off this case—"

"I wasn't aware that you were on it," Tilley interrupted him caustically. He felt sorry to humiliate the old man in front of his friends, but he wanted him to shut up so he himself could get on with his job before Carey changed her mind and complicated things for both of them.

"I—I—"

Tilley looked back at Dr. Burry. He felt he was witnessing the last of the old man's energies draining out of him.

"I'm sorry, doctor," he said. "But I know my job."

"I have a right to—"

"You have a job to do," Tilley snapped, his patience at an end, gesturing toward Mrs. Dobbler who was still weeping against the wall. "Do it. And let me do mine." He turned to Carey at his side. "You okay?"

"I can't stand not knowing."

"I know." He squeezed her arm understandingly.

As he started to lead Carey from the room, he sensed that no one else was moving.

"The rest of you can wait here," he said acidly, over his shoulder.

George Dobbler started forward. "I'll come with you, Lieutenant Tilley. In case you need . . . anything."

Tilley nodded and kept walking.

At the door to the embalming room, Tilley stopped and turned to face Carey.

"Are you sure you feel up to this?" The doddering old fool of a doctor could, after all, make a report—and probably would if something happened to Carey Hunter, if only to absolve himself. Tilley suspected Dr. Burry might want to save some face out of this godawful situation as well.

"I'm all right now."

"Bad sight in there."

"I've already seen it."

Tilley shrugged and pushed open the door.

Carey advanced slowly but determinedly to the table. She did not lean on him, but Tilley kept a firm grip on her arm all the same. She stopped beside the table and took a deep breath.

"Ready?" Tilley prayed he was not making a terrible mistake, rushing things as he always did. "Sure?"

Carey nodded grimly. As he carefully folded down the sheet to expose only the face of the dehumanized cadaver, Tilley noticed her eyes were closed. He was about to flip the sheet up again and call off the whole business when her eyes opened and she looked down at the horrifying mask of death on the table. She winced and a small moan of anguish escaped from her throat, but she did not look away and she did not faint.

I was right, Tilley thought with relief. Thank God. He looked at Carey closely, his admiration for her growing. You've got real guts, lady.

"It looks like Margie's hair," Carey said in a small voice, after a few seconds. "At least, I think it does. It's hard to tell. I think it is—maybe. But Margie's hair is . . . alive. It's auburn, all full of coppery highlights, and wavy. Really wavy. And soft, not like . . . And it's brighter, much brighter. This doesn't have any color or life to it at all. I don't think it can be her. It doesn't look like . . . anything. I can't tell. I'm sorry. I can't tell. Margie's only twenty-seven," she finished, with shocked emphasis on her friend's age.

Tilley fought down an impulse to rush her out of the room, away from the mummified little corpse, and asked softly, "Did your friend have any identifying scars, or marks of any kind?"

"She has a raised mole on her left wrist. And one on her—" Carey's hushed voice died in her throat.

"Yes?" Tilley prodded her.

Carey shook her head and bent over the unrecognizable face. Then she straightened up again.

"What is that?" She pointed to a small, dark mark on the dried-up face, at the outer point of the left cheekbone.

Tilley bent down and peered at the spot.

"Mr. Dobbler?" He was thinking that the damnfool old doctor might have come in handy after all. "Did you examine this?" He pointed at the mark.

George Dobbler moved forward to peer at the spot Tilley was pointing to.

"It's a mole, I think." He straightened up and exhaled distastefully. "Hard to tell without a tissue test. Condition's just—well, never seen anything like this before. My outside best guess is a mole."

Tilley looked at Carey. Her face was expressionless.

"May I see the left wrist?"

Tilley turned back the edge of the sheet carefully to expose only as much as necessary and pushed up a denim sleeve until a tiny, prunelike hand was visible. Carey bent down again.

"And this?" she asked Dobbler as she straightened up, pointing to the wrist. "Do you guess this is a mole, too?"

Dobbler bent down for a moment, studied the mark on the left wrist, then stood erect quickly. " 'Pears to be, yes. But only a tissue test will tell." He stepped back.

Carey looked up at Tilley, her face still a blank. "May I see the other wrist?"

Tilley carefully uncovered the right wrist. Carey walked around the table and looked at it.

"Was there a watch?" she asked softly.

Dobbler nodded. "Sheriff found it beside the body. He has it, with a few other things he found."

After a moment Carey bent over the awful face. She remained there a long time—too long, as far as Tilley was concerned. He had seen more than one bereaved person develop a morbid fascination with corruption. He was about to ease her back, away from the table, when she suddenly lowered her head even farther and kissed the hideous face.

"Oh, Margie," she whispered, her voice breaking, "Margie. What did they do to you? What?"

Tilley was stunned. He stared at Carey with disgust, all his former admiration for her fallen away from him. She stood up at that moment and looked at him, catching his expression. Her eyes hardened.

"She's my friend," she told him, the contempt in her voice matching the disgust on his face. "I love her."

Tilley flushed, a thing he rarely did. The slight young woman from New York was right, of course, and he was wrong. Still he felt his skin crawl at what she had done. He attempted to berate himself for being incapable of such love, but he knew he didn't set much store anymore by love. What Paul Tilley was ashamed of was that he had allowed his face to betray a feeling.

"I understand, Miss Hunter," he said, in his most professional voice.

"I doubt that you do, Lieutenant Tilley," Carey replied icily.

Bitch, he thought, feeling himself flush afresh. He knew she was right, and he could easily live with that. What he found irritating to live with was that she also knew it. New York bitch. His public tactic, however, was to get back to business immediately. "It's your friend, then? Your friend Margie? You can positively identify this"—he gestured vaguely at the table—". . . her as your friend?"

"This is my friend, Lieutenant Tilley."

Tilley heard Dobbler sigh, a poignant, small sound.

"I'm sorry, Miss Hunter." Tilley had a sudden—and absurd, to his mind—impulse to put an arm around Carey Hunter's shoulders, but at that moment they were straighter and stiffer than his own. He found himself turned right around once again thinking, I could get to really dislike you, lady. He decided to dispense with Carey Hunter with all possible dispatch. "Can you tell me how you made the identification, Miss Hunter?"

"I just made it. I know. I just know." Carey's eyes blazed with a defiant superiority that made Tilley wince inwardly. "And that's her earring," she added scornfully, gesturing toward the side of the wizened head. "She designed them herself, and had them made for her in the Village."

"I see. Thank you, Miss Hunter. I think we're finished here for the time—"

"I'd like a few minutes alone with my friend. She was . . . my best friend." Before Tilley could protest, Carey added, "I have that right."

"Not in the event of a homicide, Miss Hunter, I regret to say."

"Are you saying Margie was murdered, Lieutenant Tilley?"

"No, I'm not saying that, Miss Hunter. I'm saying *in the event* it turns out to be—"

"Then you don't have any proof?"

"I don't have anything, Miss Hunter, except another case." Tilley did not say that he also had a very educated guess that Margie Packer had not dyhydrated herself.

"Then I have a right to a few minutes alone with my best friend." Carey's defiance had built to the point of cracking her composure.

Tilley recognized the signs, made a snap decision, and, as was his way, shrugged. He knew it would be easier to give her what she wanted than have her create a scene into which the doctor might be forced to intercede. He didn't need another black mark against him in the country doctor's report; the files of the cases he'd handled were full of them already. The only reason he kept his job was that his cases were, to the letter, filed under "Solved." He had no illusions about solving the case of Margie Packer easily or quickly. Best to avoid all the black marks he could on this one.

"As you wish, Miss Hunter."

He turned, took George Dobbler's arm, and ushered him out of the room, closing the door behind him.

Then he waited, right outside the door, furious at the delay this tourist from New York was causing him.

In the parlor, Dr. Burry was recommending a sedative for Mrs. Dobbler, whom he had finally convinced to leave the wall and sit in the armchair.

"Would you get my bag, please, officer," he asked Coggins, who was still fidgeting by the hall door. "Believe I left it in the . . . in Dobbler's room down there." He jerked his thumb in the direction of the embalming room. "I need it to treat Mrs. Dobbler here." He turned back to his patient, patting her shoulder, murmuring, "There. There, there. There now. There. Now, now."

Coggins paled and hesitated. Dr. Burry looked around at him.

"Well, go on, young man. What're you waiting for? Get my bag, I said."

Coggins moved out of the parlor as if his body were being pummeled through the doorway and dragged, protesting, behind his sense of duty down the hall. When he got to George Dobbler's office, he stopped.

O'Malley was sitting with his head on his arms, which were crossed on George Dobbler's desk. Coggins stepped briskly inside.

"The doc wants his bag. 'S in . . . there—in that other room. I'm busy, so you gotta go get it for him. He's in the parlor with the old lady."

O'Malley merely groaned.

"Come on, man," Coggins spat at him. "Get your act together. Tilley's gonna bust your ass when we get home if you don't shape up."

O'Malley still did not move.

"Goddamn it O'Malley! The old lady's sick, and the doc needs his bag. Get your Irish ass off that chair and go get it."

O'Malley looked up at him with an ugly, retching sound and grabbed for muck-green metal wastebasket in front of his chair.

"Shit. I wish to God I'd picked the Fire Department instead." Coggins stomped out of the room.

Tilley motioned him to be quiet as he reached the embalming room, whispering, "Can't you walk without stomping like that, Coggins? You sound like Paul Bunyan, for chrissake."

"Doc needs his bag," Coggins whispered back. "Says it's in there."

"Not now," Tilley hissed. "Shut up and be quiet."

"The old lady's—" Coggins caught himself as he noticed George Dobbler. "The older woman down there can't stop crying, and the doc wants to give her something. Told me get his bag."

"Not now," Tilley repeated in an emphatic whisper. "I said shut up."

George Dobbler took a step forward and opened his mouth to speak. Tilley whipped a finger against his own as his tongue, with no help from him, made a *ssst* against his teeth. Dobbler took a step backward and stuffed his hands in the pockets of his long white coat, and looked worried.

Inside the embalming room, Carey was unable to formulate her thoughts or reasons for staying by Margie's side. Buried somewhere in her mind was the feeling that this was what people did when someone they loved had died: spend a few private moments alone with the lifeless body. She had no thought as to how those moments should be spent.

She stood by the table staring at Margie's hideous face. Dimly she felt that, if Margie had had to suffer so shockingly, the least she could do was make herself suffer too. Perhaps, in some unknown way Margie would know, and know then she hadn't suffered entirely alone. It was a dim, small hope, barely perceived by Carey, and soon dulled into oblivion by deepening bewilderment before a mystery her mind could not grasp.

Nobody died this way. People were killed in accidents; people were murdered. But not this way. She'd never heard of anybody looking like this, no matter how brutally they'd been slain. She couldn't understand it, couldn't even begin to imagine what could have happened to Margie. So she simply continued to stand beside her friend, with all her thought processes stopped.

Minutes went by.

"Jesus," Tilley breathed, looking at his watch. "How the hell long has she been in there?"

Coggins shook his head dumbly. Dobbler looked at his own watch.

"Don't rightly know," he finally whispered back. "Can't rightly tell now."

"Jesus," the detective breathed again, realizing that neither of them had thought to check their watches when they had left the room. This was excusable in a country mortician who rarely handled murder victims, but not in himself. He was thoroughly irritated at his own ineffectuality. This wasn't like Paul Tilley. He began to realize he hated this case.

More minutes went by.

Polly McCannister, after a useless "Mind if I use your phone, Ellen, t' call my office?" to the still softly weeping Mrs. Dobbler, went to the kitchen and telephoned his wife to see if any other business had come up that called for his immediate attention.

None had. His wife asked if he was all right, if everything was all right.

"Right 's it can be with a mess like this on my hands," he replied irritably. "Be home whenever. Whenever this big-city big-shot detective takes it off'n my hands. Which he ain't officially done yet," he offered by way of explanation, adding, "though he was quick enough t' take over soon 's he come through the door."

When he had nothing else to say, Polly McCannister simply hung up the phone. He did not say goodbye to his wife.

"Sheriff," Dr. Burry fired at him crustily as soon as he reentered the parlor, "this woman"—Dr. Burry had brought Ellen Dobbler into the world and was family doctor to both the Dobblers and the McCannisters—"needs medication. I don't know where that fool officer got himself to this time. Go see if you can get my bag from . . . Dobbler's room."

He could not know the appellation would spread throughout the bay area, to imply a horror not only unspeakable but incomprehensible. The human mind could conceive of "Dobbler's room." It could not conceive of what was today in it.

McCannister glared at the old man a moment, then continued across the parlor and into the hall.

" 'M not the gol-danged errand boy," he muttered angrily as he marched down the hall, fingering the tarnished metal badge that hung limply from his shirt pocket. "Things around here gotten mighty outa hand since them city cops arrived. Might 's well've bought this here thing in the five-and-ten-cent store. 'N' they can't figure nothin' out anymore'n I can." His step grew suddenly lighter.

Tilley put a finger to his lips as soon as he saw the sheriff striding purposefully down the hall. McCannister did not slacken his pace.

"What the hell's goin' on here?" the sheriff whispered. "Doc Burry's gotta have his bag." He glared accusingly at Officer Coggins

"She asked for a few minutes alone with her friend—friend's body, that is," Tilley whispered back. "That's her right."

"Christ," McCannister blurted out, "the i.d. was right then. It is—"

"What i.d.?" Tilley hissed at him, eyes flashing. "What goddamn i.d.?"

McCannister flushed. It started on his nose and spread rapidly over his fleshy face, then over his sparsely haired scalp and down the back of his neck. His head soon took on the look of a giant red balloon. The flush simultaneously spread down his throat and onto his chest, visible in the V of his open shirt. Then he went from shamed red to angry purple, resembling nothing so much as a rutting gobbler, with purple folds of fat twitching nervously under his chin as he struggled to speak.

"You have i.d.?" Tilley's voice was lethal.

"Handbag." The sheriff was puffing as if he had just run the quarter mile. "Lady's purse. I—"

"And where did you get that?"

"Out'n the car. I reported the car on the phone when I—"

"But not a purse." The contempt in Tilley's voice cut through the sheriff's feeble defense of himself like an ax.

"—reported the rest of it," he finished, in a barely audible murmur.

"Except a purse." Tilley's following silence demanded an admission of guilt.

"Except . . . the purse."

Tilley didn't have to say anything else and knew it. He had only to stare, which he did with devastating effect, at the dissolving local sheriff.

At long last, as if he were talking to a hysteric who must be kept calm in order to draw information out of him, Tilley said, too slowly and too carefully, "And where, exactly, did you find this purse—where in the car, that is?"

"On the front seat," McCannister muttered.

"Which front seat?"

"The death . . . the right one. The one on the right-hand side."

"And have you opened it?"

"Ayup."

"And did you examine the contents?"

"Ayup. A' course." McCannister's voice could barely be heard.

"And the name on the i.d. you forgot to mention you found—do you remember what it was, sheriff?" Tilley allowed all the contempt he felt for the local officer to be summed up in the word "sheriff." He had the distinct satisfaction of seeing McCannister wince and flush brightly again as fresh sweat broke out all over his face and dripped off his several chins onto his shirt.

"I remember all right." A sullen note, Tilley realized, was creeping into the sheriff's humiliated tone. "I just forgot about it, 's all."

Tilley was on top of him again before his last syllable finished sounding.

"You just said you remembered. Which is it? You remembered? Or you forgot?"

He watched McCannister struggle to subdue his anger and found the scene oddly satisfying, yet dissatisfying at the same time. Much as he despised incompetence, he realized his real anger was with whoever had killed Carey Hunter's friend and left her in a state so terrible as to be beyond comprehension. Still, he had not that party to take it out on—yet.

"The name was Marjory Packer."

"I can't hear you, sheriff."

McCannister cleared his throat. "I said," just a little louder, "the name was Marjory Packer."

Tilley stared him in silence.

"You'd have had," McCannister offered at last, "'t' have her identify the body even if I'd—"

"Shut up, sheriff." Tilley's voice contained so much anger that everyone started slightly.

He suddenly remembered Carey, in the room with the body, and looked at his watch. He felt irritation at and concern for her, but also a strong constraint at the idea of interrupting her prayers or tears or goodbyes, whatever it was she was doing in there. He decided to let her have a minute more—a minute he could use to destroy completely what was left of the bumbling, rednecked, so-called sheriff trembling before him.

"Tell me, sheriff, do you remember if you managed to discover and make note of anything else you've forgotten to tell me about?"

McCannister glanced at Dobbler, who now flushed and began to sweat slightly. Tilley thought he had seldom seen two men look so guiltily conspiratorial, and knew he had hit home.

"Well, sheriff?"

"Well, uh, there was . . . is . . . oh, God," McCannister dug out his dirty handkerchief and mopped his dripping face. "Can't talk about that in front of—"

"In front of what?"

" 'S just a kid," the sheriff gestured feebly at Officer Coggins.

"He's a police officer," Tilley said tartly, then added, even more tartly, "where the term has some meaning."

The instant he said it, he regretted it. Neither of his officers, this day, had acted much like being in uniform meant anything at all. Looking into Sheriff McCannister's rheumy brown eyes, the detective could see just how ill advised his words had been: the local law officer now wore a distinctly contemptuous, triumphant look. Tilley kept silent and merely outstared him.

"Well, George here'll tell you. 'S more his department than mine anyway." McCannister took a small backward step and shut his mouth.

Tilley gave him a withering look and turned to Dobbler. He was surprised to catch the mortician giving his friend a look of stark hatred and wondered what it was the two of them still had up their sleeves about this baffling case.

"Well, Mr. Dobbler?"

"It might be best spoken of in more privacy," Dobbler replied with obvious unease.

"We'll speak of it now."

George Dobbler took a deep breath. "If that's what you want, Lieutenant Tilley." He took another deep breath, and when he spoke next his manner was brisk and professional. "During my examination of the body, I found the nipples and aureola of both breasts badly damaged. Can't be certain of the nature of the damage or what could possibly have caused such damage. Tissue's far too dehydrated t' tell without a more sophisticated examination of tissue samples than I got the kind of equipment t' do here. But my guess is, judging from what I can estimate about this damage, that you're going t' find the lactiferous ducts severely ruptured. On forensic autopsy, that is. Sounds real strange, but it came t' me that maybe—just maybe— all that dehydration took place, somehow, through the nipples." He paused, and Tilley noted he gave the sheriff another uncharitable glance. "I discussed this in detail with Sheriff McCannister here after I did my examination and apprised him of everything I've just told you. And it's in my report—my written report—of course." He stopped, and Tilley again saw him cast his friend a hostile look.

Tilley was no longer particularly surprised. Not only was he far more taken up with the undertaker's bizzare report, but he had seen the best of relationships break down over the issue of responsibility too many times during investigations to do more than note it.

"Never saw anything like it in my life," Dobbler was finishing in a removed voice.

Tilley understood that, too. He himself had seen things

he could not have survived with his sanity intact had he
not had the ability to separate himself emotionally from
their impact on his sensibilities.

McCannister was now magenta and not merely twitching,
but bobbling. The look he leveled at Dobbler told Tilley
their friendship was finished, at least for a very long time.
Officer Coggins stood, slack-jawed and white-faced, gaping at the undertaker. His face held an expression of
horrified disbelief that bordered on noncomprehension.

Tilley had no such delicate reaction. In fact, he had no
reaction at all except to move to protect Carey Hunter.

"My God," he said, almost loudly, the moment Dobbler
stopped talking, jumping for the embalming-room door.
"If she sees that—"

He was inside the room before the words were quite out
of his mouth.

4

Mrs. Rambeau woke slowly from her nap in the old,
cushioned rocker. She had been dreaming, as always now,
of her earlier life; this afternoon she had been crossing a
horizonless desert with her father when Herbert Hoover's
face appeared in the sky, nearly as big as the sky, all but
filling it.

"Citizens of this great nation," his voice did not simply
proceed from his mouth, but arrived at little Peggy Whittier's
ears from a 360-degree stereophonic atmosphere as the
light faded theatrically, leaving only President Hoover's
face spotlighted in a black mystery. "I am doing all I can
for you. Look. See. Watch. Observe what Herbert Hoover
can do."

Hoover's face faded into the blackness. Little Peggy slipped her hand into the safety of her father's to dissolve the fear she felt in the pitch-darkness. She could feel her father's presence, but could not see him. His hand kept her mostly safe.

Suddenly the sky burst into piercing points of light with a majestic fireworks display, brilliant, beautiful, and breathtaking. Peggy felt her mouth drop open with wonder. Her mind was dazzled beyond thought. Then it was over, with dripping rainbow-colored and gold and silver lights leaking down the sky as they faded out.

She felt her father's hand disengage from hers. But it was all right now; the dark held marvels, not terrors, for her tonight.

"You think that's so great, Herbie," her father's voice boomed out, filling the universe just like the President's had done. "Just look what Eddie can do."

His left hand plunged into his jacket pocket and then hurled things she could not see, in the dark, skyward. Instantly the sky was filled with exploding lights in intricate and fantastic patterns—so fantastic they made Hoover's display seem primitive. Next, her father's right hand flung from his other jacket pocket another invisible handful heavenward, and these lights were even more spectacular than his first ones.

The spectrum of colors was beyond anything Peggy Whittier had ever seen or imagined. There were hundreds, even thousands of colors to the lights, none of which she had ever seen before. And not just tints or degrees of known colors, but totally new colors, colors she had never suspected existed. Spectrum after spectrum, as her father's hands continued to fling from his bottomless pockets colored lights that burst in the sky in ever new and different, more brilliant patterns.

"What do you think of that, Herbie Hoover!" her father shouted as the last of his creations faded into the black sky.

Peggy Rambeau changed realities in a daze. It took her

several minutes to familiarize herself with her parlor, her present self, her expectations for this day.

Then she remembered. She carefully folded back the wool afghan covering her lap and legs, and rose, slowly and stiffly, from the chair. The late-afternoon sun was tipping the choppy waters of the bay with shimmering, blinding gold. She shook her head, bending carefully forward to peer through the rain-washed windowpanes.

"Can't be," she muttered to herself and made her slow way to the kitchen. The clock on the wall confirmed that it indeed was. Bitter disappointment swept through her.

" 'Tis," she said aloud finally in a soft, sad voice. She felt now very, very old, as if her age had doubled since first waking from her nap.

With painful slowness, Mrs. Rambeau filled her kettle, set it on the ancient woodstove, and stoked up the fire, always burning, beneath it. With stiff fingers she pried open an old tin tea can and carefully dropped a pinch of tea leaves into a clean cup she took from the dish drain. She glanced frequently at the old wall clock, and just as frequently through the glass panes of the upper half of the kitchen door and down the path leading to the Berries. The silence of the death-emptied house grew louder and louder in her ears.

"Young folks got more excitin' things t' do with themselves than spend their time with an old woman like you, Peggy Rambeau," she scolded herself. "Don't mean nothin', now."

But by the time her tea was ready, she had lost her taste for it. The ticking of the clock had become rhythmic hammer blows against her skull; her head ached painfully.

Peggy Rambeau heard the sound of her slippered footfalls on the bare wood floor deafeningly loud as she left the kitchen. The house was emptier than it had ever been. A grief more profound than those she had known she suffered at the deaths of her children and husband overflowed her heart and spread to her toes and fingertips, stole like a thief into her spirit. She could not confront it, but it confronted her—and overwhelmed her.

Stiffly she dragged her aching body up the old wooden stairs to her vacant bedroom. She lay down on the ancient brass bed that had supported her in love, in births, and in weeping grief at deaths, and tried to cover herself with the faded patchwork quilt folded at the foot of the bed. But the bed did not support her in this loss that made all her other losses newly real. Exhausted by the effort, she gave up and lay mostly uncovered in the chilling sunset air. She was too tired, and too sad, to bother longer. She felt very old, deeply fatigued, and utterly useless. There was no one left on earth who had the slightest need of her.

After several minutes she managed to rouse her arms again and, drawing them up, neatly folded her veined, gnarled hands across her thin, fallen breasts. She closed her eyes.

"Sweet Lord," her mind and lips silently prayed, "have mercy on me, a sinner. I know I'm just filled with wickedness 'n' not deservin', but if it can be Your will, merciful God, take the cup out'n my hands. Don't mean t' be complainin', but it's awful bitter, Lord, awful bitter now." Tears trickled out of the corners of the old eyes, down the flakey, wrinkled face. "I'm sorry, Lord, I know you give me more blessin's than I ever earned. I shouldn't be talkin' t' you like this, but it's hard, so hard. Well, Thy will be done. Amen. Forgive me, Lord, I know I should bear any burden you give me gladlike, for Jesus' sake. But I . . ." Her mind gave up the prayer.

Her heart, broken in too many pieces for her now to acknowledge, prayed more eloquently: I've outlived my usefulness. Don't mean nothing t' nobody no more. Nobody needs me. I got nothing t' do 'n' nobody t' do it for. Let me die. Surely that ain't askin' too much at my age, if You're as merciful as they told me You was. God? Can't You see I ain't even any use t' You anymore? Or have You forgot me too?

Peggy Whittier Rambeau was wounded beyond repair. This thrust of the knife was not the mortal one, but it was the one that cut away all defenses and pretensions, making her aware of the pain of the others. There were no pyrotechnic grandeurs left in the pockets of her soul.

5

Carey was standing where he had left her, beside the examining table. Tilley couldn't immediately determine exactly what she might have seen; he could see only that the sheet had been folded down neatly to expose the faded jeans and denim shirt holding the little anhydride. As he stepped up beside Carey he saw instantly that the embroidered shirt was still buttoned up to the collar.

"Are you finished now, Miss Hunter?" he asked quietly, reaching for the sheet and rolling it back up over the remains with deft movements. "I've allowed you quite a long time. I really think you should let this go now." He paused, sheet in hand, then covered the face and head. "Better to remember your friend as you knew her. Try and forget you ever saw this."

Carey turned her head and looked up at him with enormous, bewildered eyes. Tilley knew she would never forget. He felt superficial. He also knew there wasn't much else he could have said.

"I'm very sorry."

Carey continued to stare at him for almost half a minute. Finally, Tilley took her arm.

"It's best we go now," he said, almost in a whisper.

"Margie wouldn't have been wearing that shirt."

"What?" Tilley had expected any one of a thousand

grief-stricken statements, or none at all, but not a comment on the deceased's outfit.

"Margie wouldn't have been wearing that shirt."

Tilley made a fast mental note to requestion Archie English about the clothes he'd found on the body Monday morning. He was on alert as he tried to ease Carey out of the room.

"What would she have been wearing?" he asked, taking her arm.

"Embroidery is out in the eighties," Carey said without emotion. "Margie hasn't worn that shirt outside the apartment in three years."

"I see."

"Especially not for traveling. Arriving places."

"I understand."

"I know she wouldn't have worn that shirt."

"I'll check into it, Miss Hunter."

"Not to come up here."

"I'm sure you're right." Tilley tried to guide her away from the table, but Carey wasn't moving.

"She would have been wearing her pink shirred Lois Nettleton blouse."

"I'm glad you told me."

"The label says 'Made in Turkey.' "

"We'll check it out very carefully, Miss Hunter."

"I know she would. I know Margie."

"I understand."

"So there's something wrong about her being dressed like this."

"Thank you for telling me. Little details are sometimes the most important of all in solving a case."

"The jeans are right, but that shirt isn't."

"I'll remember that." He felt Carey start to turn away from the table under the insistent pressure of his hand.

"Margie was a big fan of Lois Nettleton's."

"So am I," Tilley said lightly, forcing a tight smile. He was glad of any chance to change the subject before Carey, like so many New Yorkers he'd encountered, decided to investigate what she obviously felt to be an impor-

tant detail herself. "Really admired her in 'Centennial.'
You a fan of hers, too?"

"Margie would never have roomed with me if I hadn't
been."

"A real superfan, eh?"

"It was more than that. Margie's an actress too, so
she understood what Lois Nettleton was doing when she
saw her work."

"From the inside, I guess."

"She understood. I just appreciated."

"Mmmm." Tilley nodded his head unconsciously. Now
he knew exactly what she was talking about.

"There's a difference."

"I know that, Miss Hunter."

"You do?" Carey looked at him ingenuously.

For a moment Tilley could see her as she had been when
a child. It touched him, and that made him uncomfortable.

"There's an inside appreciation in every field. Not just
in the arts. You must know that yourself."

"I never thought about it."

Tilley let out a deep breath as he walked her into the
hall. "Well, think about it sometime."

"Margie made theater seem like the only important
thing in the world."

"I'm sure she did," Tilley said soothingly, then told
himself he was being patronizing. He shrugged; all that
mattered to him was getting Carey Hunter as far away as
possible from the embroidered shirt. "Coggins," he said,
"I want you to take Miss Hunter back to the parlor and
stay with her there. Tell Dr. Burry I need him here. And
you," he turned to the others, "Mr. Dobbler and Mr.
McCannister. I need you two here as well."

"The doc wanted his bag," Officer Coggins mumbled.

"Then get it, man, get it. And be quick about it."

"Yes, sir." Coggins paled, but marched into the examining room without hesitating.

"Am I free to go now?" Carey looked up at the detective.

"Almost. If you'll wait in the parlor for a little while, I
have just a few questions to ask you. Then you can go."

Tilley smiled slightly at her. "You've been very helpful, Miss Hunter. Thank you. I know how hard it was for you."

Officer Coggins emerged from the examining room with Dr. Burry's black bag gripped in one hand. As he and Carey started down the hallway, she looked back over her shoulder and asked in a small voice, "You'll tell me about the shirt, won't you?"

"Just as soon as I know anything. Promise."

Lt. Tilley knew he would do no such thing. He'd hope she would forget about it, remain certain she never would be able to, think of a good lie to tell her if she ever managed to get hold of him again, and pray to God she never found out the truth. He didn't hold out any real hope of that, once the story leaked out to the press. But he did feel he could expect that Carey Hunter by then would be back in New York where she belonged, and any contact between the two of them finished once and for all.

"No reason, Howie," Archie English lied cryptically— and transparently—to the question put to him as he secured the bowline of Mrs. Rambeau's dinghy to the stern of the ferry late that night. " 'N' no passengers neither," he added, glancing at the curious crowd gathered on Fustin's quay, staring inquisitively first at him, then at Carey huddled on the far side of the otherwise empty passenger–cargo compartment, then back at him again. " 'M just helpin' out so Peggy Rambeau don't worry all night about her dinghy."

"Anythin' I can do helps Peggy Rambeau," the man came back eagerly, "be more'n glad t' do, Archie." He started forward.

"Nice a' you t' offer, Howie." Archie swung himself over the ferry's rail. " 'Preciate you let go with the bowline, then."

The man named Howie did not look pleased, but he loosed the line and tossed it aboard. Mrs. Mitchell had already stepped forward, elbowing three eager boys aside, and was loosing the sternline as the ferry's prow swung away from the dock.

"Let go astern," Archie called out.

She did, and hurled the heavy line aboard.

"Ferry won't be stoppin' return trip, folks," Archie let them know over the starting chug of the boat's engine.

No one on the pier moved. More than half the population of Fustin's Island watched the little ferryboat disappear into the sloe-black of the starless, moonless Maine night. They remained there, in the murky glim cast by the pier's lone worklight, even after the ferry's running lights had been swallowed up by the dark and the distance. They would stay until they saw her lights approaching again, had watched them go by and be swallowed up again in the direction of the mainland. Archie's ferry had not made a night trip in thirteen summers.

"Sure you're all right, now?" Archie, his ferry riding at sea anchor about two hundred yards out from the Outer Island dock, was tightly coiling the dinghy's bowline over a thumb and under an elbow. "Dock if I could, 'n' come up with ya." He made oblique apology for the ferry's draw. "Been tellin' Peggy Rambeau for years that dock got t' be extended."

"It's all right, Archie." Carey secured the oars in place and looked up at him from the center thwart. "Thanks for bringing me back. I'm sorry to have been so much trouble to you all day."

"No trouble," he assured her quickly, "no trouble a'tall. No, sir. None at all. You take care, now." He dropped the coiled line down into the dinghy's bow. "This'll pass. All things do, Carey." It was the first time he had called her by name.

Carey continued to look up at him, using the dinghy's oars just enough not to be carried astern of the ferry with the tide. "Thank you." She could think of nothing else to say.

"Ayup. I'll keep the Spartan on ya till I see you're safe ashore." He went to the wheel and adjusted the small searchlight slightly so that its beam fell across the dinghy's bow. ''You get some rest now.''

''Thanks again, Archie.''

''Right. G'night now.''

''Good night, Archie.''

When the dinghy was securely moored, Carey straightened up and waved into the searchlight's beam. She could not see Archie behind it, but the beam of light dipped twice before swinging off her. A moment or two later, the ferry's engine started up, and her running lights were shortly mere red and green pinpoints in the distance.

Carey made her way stumblingly up the path to The Berries. She found herself alternating between numbness and near-panic. The path, which she knew so well, was suddenly foreign to her in the darkness of this particular night; The Berries itself was fraught with invisible apparitions and blind terrors. Her heart was pounding against her ribs, and her mouth grew desert-dry before she located the big flashlight in the top right-hand drawer of the old Hoosier cabinet against the far wall of the kitchen.

With trembling hands she lighted every hurricane and mantle lamp upstairs and down, before she remembered Mrs. Rambeau would be waiting, worried, for her. For her and Margie. She owed it to the old woman to go up to Sternfirst and tell her why they had not come for dinner.

Dinner. Dinner was still stowed under the stern thwart of the dinghy, down at the dock, Carey realized. It would have to stay there till morning. She knew she could not make herself tread that path again by night; it would take all her courage just to get up to Sternfirst. Much as she wanted to be alone, she prayed Mrs. Rambeau would insist she stay the night in the big house. She no longer wanted to be alone on Outer Island—or anywhere in Maine—and doubted she would find the courage to come back down to The Berries before full daylight.

She left all the lamps burning, not because she intended to come back that night, but because she couldn't bear to be in the house even for a second alone in the dark. The powerful flashlight made the path up to Sternfirst easier to walk but no less terrifying than the one from the dock to The Berries. Once again her heart was pounding and her mouth dry when she opened Sternfirst's unlocked kitchen door.

Sternfirst, too, was in darkness. Carey found the matches for the kitchen stove and lit the gas wall fixtures in the room, turning the wicks up as far as they would go without smoking. She decided Mrs. Rambeau must be sleeping, but knew from her stay during the northeaster—it seemed to her a hundred years ago—that the old woman slept lightly and woke frequently through the night, often coming downstairs to use the bathroom or make herself a cup of tea. Carey would sit at the kitchen table and wait until she heard her. After twenty minutes or so, she crossed her arms on the table in front of her and rested her head upon them. She felt terribly, unendurably tired.

She woke with a start—how much later she didn't know— and looked at the clock on the wall. It was after one. She had no idea now what time it had been when she got to Sternfirst—or indeed anyplace else that day, that yesterday. Undecided whether to stay in the kitchen, make herself more comfortable in the parlor, or tiptoe upstairs to Mrs. Rambeau's door, Carey stood up. A wave of grief and loss overwhelmed her, surging up in every part of her so that even her fingers and toes seemed to be weeping and in pain. She sat back down and cried for a long time.

By two o'clock she decided she would go upstairs and listen at Mrs. Rambeau's door. She washed her face in the iron sink, dried herself on a kitchen towel, and took the flashlight.

The house beyond the kitchen was dark and still, unsafe. The flashlight beam threw changing pools of light and shadow all around her, and she could hear her heart clamoring frantically against the walls of her chest.

"I must not think," she whispered to herself as she tiptoed up the stairs. "I must not think. I must not think."

She wished she were anywhere on earth but Outer Island, South Bay, Maine.

She stood a considerable time in the hall outside Peggy Rambeau's bedroom, listening carefully. Not a sound came from behind the closed door. Careful to keep the flashlight aimed away from the door, Carey found herself turning constantly to flash it up and down the unlighted hallway. Her breathing was loud and shallow; she began to regret ever leaving the comparative security of The Berries.

In one of her turns, the beam of light glinted off something on the hall carpet near her feet. She swung the light back and looked down. The carpet reflected pinpricks of light, as if it were wet. Squatting down, Carey touched it gingerly with her free hand. It was wet. And sticky. She turned the light on her fingertips.

They were smeared with a mucinous semifluid that appeared, by flashlight, to be randomly and messily striated with blood. Carey stared at it uncomprehendingly for a few seconds.

"Mrs. Rambeau!" She leaped up and flung the bedroom door open, dashing for the old woman's bed. "Mrs. Rambeau—?"

There was an enormous something—a comforter or an overstuffed eiderdown—heaped on top of the bed. Carey dropped the flashlight and tugged at it, unable to see what it was. It was extremely heavy, so she tried to shove it away, but that was harder. She finally got a grip on something that felt like a leather strap and dragged the thing off the bed. It dropped with an ominous thud on the rag rug beside the fourposter, half obscuring the flashlight. Carey reached down and found the handle and yanked the light free.

"Mrs. Rambeau—?"

She shone the beam of the flashlight on the bed.

The last face of Margie Packer stared up at her, the same silent shriek contorting its dessicated, inhuman features.

"Well, can you tell me anything, Dr. Maker?" Tilley asked the young pathologist who had been sent in the absence of Dr. MacKay Logan, the chief medical examiner, to examine Margie Packer's body before removing it to

Eastern Maine Medical Center for autopsy. "Anything at all?"

"I'm afraid not, Lieutenant Tilley." Dr. Maker straightened up and swallowed. He looked sick, his face greenish-gray, and utterly confused. "I've never seen anything like this in my life. I'm at a loss—"

"I need something to go on, doctor," Tilley pleaded tiredly. "I've got nothing, except a shrunken corpse. What do I go looking for—a witch doctor? Some jungle savage? Come on, Dr. Maker. Give me something, for chrissake."

"I'm sorry."

"Well, what about the breasts—the nipples? You must have some idea what could cause that kind of damage?"

"I don't. Maybe if the body wasn't so . . . shrunken and . . . dessicated. . . . But I honestly can't tell a thing. It just looks like they were . . . torn off, almost, by some powerful suction." Dr. Maker rubbed his face with his hands.

"Well, that's something, doctor. What kind of suction? I mean, what could suck with sufficient force to tear the nipples off a woman's breasts?"

The young doctor shuddered. "Nothing—nothing I know of. I don't know, Lieutenant Tilley, I just don't know."

"A machine of some kind?"

"I don't know. I can't imagine what kind of machine it could be."

"Some kind of do-it-yourself version of a milking machine?"

"I doubt it. I just don't think so."

"Why not?"

"Because a machine would have torn the entire breasts to shreds—maybe right off, for all I know. And that isn't what happened." The young man thought a moment. "No machine could have sucked every bit of moisture from a human body—even from the bones—and done, actually, so little damage to the breasts. I'm speaking in relation to the complete dehydration when I say that, Lieutenant Tilley."

"Mmm." Tilley now thought a moment. "Well, that's two somethings, Dr. Maker. Probable: suction force beyond our understanding. And not probable: a homicidal, woman-hating genius with a new invention. Anything else?''

Dr. Maker shook his head.

''Right. When will Kay—Dr. Logan—be back?''

''Tomorrow morning.''

''Good.'' Tilley stretched his neck, then straightened his tie. ''I don't want this body touched by anyone else, understand? This is a job for MacKay Logan, and I want him doing it.''

''I couldn't agree with you more, Lieutenant Tilley.''

Tilley noted that the young man looked decidedly relieved. ''Fine. Then you make sure that's what happens to it. In fact, I don't want anybody else even to see this thing. There'll be all hell to pay if the media get wind of this before we've caught the killer. You do think Marjory Packer was murdered, Dr. Maker?''

Dr. Maker looked stunned. ''She had to have been. She sure as hell didn't do this to herself.''

''Right. And that's our third something.'' Tilley sighed. ''I've had some stingy cases, but nothing like this. Even with three somethings, I still have nothing to go on. Well,'' he yawned and stretched, ''it's after two. You must be tired. Tell my boys how you want her wrapped up for the trip—they've already been briefed on the necessity for confidentiality. A panic at the height of the tourist season—the number of highway accidents alone would be staggering.''

He yawned again. ''I'm going back down to the ferry landing to see if anything new's been turned up in or near the car before I head back to Bangor.'' He stared down at the remains of Marjory Packer for a few moments. With the clothing removed, it was even harder to believe this shriveled, ghoulish little thing had a few days ago been a normal, healthy, attractive young woman like—Tilley couldn't stop himself from finishing his thought—like Carey Hunter. Irritated, he looked up at Dr. Maker again. ''I hope it's clear to you, Dr. Maker, that I'll hold you fully responsible if anyone other than MacKay Logan touches—or even looks at—this body?''

"Yes, it is, Lieutenant Tilley. Very clear."

"You sit up all night with it if you have to. I'm not kidding, Maker, believe me."

"That won't be necessary, Lieutenant Tilley."

"I think it will, now that I've thought of it. I'll assign somebody to do just that. Then you can get your beauty sleep." Tilley grinned at him. "And I can get mine—if there's any night left to get it in by the time I get back to Bangor. Well, thank you for your help, Dr. Maker. Appreciate it. By the way," he added as he started to leave George Dobbler's embalming room, "is your name really Noble? Noble Maker?"

"Yes, it is, lieutenant. That's what's on my birth certificate, and that's what I was christened," the young man said defensively.

"Good God," Tilley shook his head and chuckled. "Why the hell don't you change it?"

Carey stood frozen to the spot. She wanted to run—to fly—out of the room, but she could not. She wanted to close her eyes and not see—have never seen—the grotesque, petrifying visage in dried miniature before her, but she could not do that, either. She did not know if she was dreaming or awake, hallucinating or clear-witted; her mind accepted neither explanation and was doing its best to eject the entire day and night from her experience. This couldn't be real. This had already been real once before. It couldn't be real twice. It was real again. This couldn't be happening to her. It was happening to her. It had happened to her once and was happening to her again. She'd wake any moment and the whole thing would have been a mad dream. She was wide awake and it was all too real.

As if an irresistible force outside herself controlled her, she found herself looking at Mrs. Rambeau's exposed chest. Like frames of a badly spliced movie, she saw, in speed-of-light succession: a tiny, withered breast; torn edges of print fabric; a miniature mutilated nipple—or no nipple but the dried, open end of a breast after an avulsion had occurred; jagged flanges of white cotton; another mummified little breast, its mangled, nippleless end just like the first one; a pearl button; a dehydrated breast; a tuft of white thread; a hideously missing nipple; torn edges of fabric; a torn, nippleless, ragged-edged breast; a silent, shrunken shriek; splotches of bloody mucus; a torn breast; pearl button; nippleless breast. . . .

A muted creak penetrated her consciousness. She whirled around, almost tripping over the thing she had dragged off the bed, and fled from the room scarcely knowing she was doing so. Explosions of light bounced from wall to wall, ceiling to floor, stair rail to step as she raced downstairs, the flashlight jolting in her hand.

All the way down the long pine-hemmed path leading to the dock, she heard racing footsteps behind her, felt hot breath on the back of her neck. She fought with the dinghy's mooring lines, breaking her fingernails and lacerating her hands. They were full of splinters by the time she got both lines loosed, but she felt no pain. She jumped off the dock feet first into the dinghy, almost scuttling it. In trying to set the oarlocks in place in the gunnels, she broke the blade of the starboard oar in half as the outgoing tide carried the dinghy half under the dock into a piling.

Frantic and confused, Carey tried to drag the dinghy back out from under the dock by the two-by-fours studding the pilings. The tide was too strong for her and carried the little boat on under the dock, sweeping it almost out from under her. The flashlight, which she had dropped when she jumped into the dinghy, rolled around on the bottom of the boat, throwing its beam of light everywhere except where it might have helped Carey to get a firm grip on something.

She lost her grip on a wet two-by-four. The dinghy was lifted by a swell. Her head struck another two-by-four, and she was knocked to her hands and knees between the center and stern thwarts. The flashlight rolled, shining directly into her eyes, blinding her. She grabbed it and straightened up, kneeling erect on the bottom of the boat as the bow drifted out from under the far side of the dock. A hand grabbed at her hair.

"Give me your hand! Give me your hand! Quick!" a husky, boyish voice with a distinctive catch in it yelled.

Carey swung the flashlight up. Its beam caught a face, glaringly white in the powerful light and, for an instant, not more than inches from her own. A familiar face. Carey blinked, trying through her panic to remember where she'd seen the face before. The focused light reflected its own image in two bright, greenish eyes, and then it struck her.

It was the face of the silent teenagers who had stared at her so insolently on Archie's ferry the past Saturday evening. Not the face of just one but all of them, as if their four faces had melted into each other, becoming one, aged just a little in the process.

It was the last face in the world Carey wanted to see staring down at her at this moment. She swung back the large flashlight and with all her strength struck at the hand clawing for a grip on her hair.

"Prouty?" Tilley hailed a middle-aged sergeant as he climbed wearily out of his car. He had parked it on the county road outside the ferry parking lot, the entrance to which was blocked off, according to his instructions, by two Bangor squad cars. He strode past them and across the dirt lot. "Prouty! Anything new?"

Sergeant Prouty turned toward them. "Afraid not, lieutenant. Sorry."

"Damn." Tilley stopped in front of him. "What about tire treads, footprints, anything?"

"We've taken casts of everything, sir," Prouty replied. "But I wouldn't count on anything turning up. Mr. English admits he drove his pickup in and out of here several times, and that local sheriff"—he gestured toward McCannister, who was standing near the green Corvette with New York license plates listening to three police officers deep in discussion—"what's his name?—anyway, he owns up to having driven his car in here when he answered Mr.

English's call, and then coming back with the undertaker. They both drove in, right up to the Corvette. The undertaker in his hearse and what's-his-name in his car again. If there was a vehicle that drove in here sometime Sunday night or Monday morning, it's unlikely any impressions would have survived that much traffic—even if there hadn't been a nor'easter. As it is, well, lieutenant, frankly the men are pretty riled up about this. They feel it's a waste of time.''

"So do I." Tilley eyed him speculatively. "But I've got to grasp at straws—I've got absolutely nothing else to go on. What about the car?''

"The registration and rental agreement were in the glove compartment. It was rented by a Marjory Packer all right. The whole interior's been dusted for prints and then gone over with a fine-tooth comb. Nothing. We won't know about the prints, of course, until they've been checked out.''

"Of course." Tilley felt impatient. He already knew all this.

"Other than that, there doesn't seem to be a thing. Of course, when we get the car up to Bangor and tear it apart, maybe something will turn up.''

"But you doubt it.''

"Yes, sir, I doubt it.''

"So do I.''

"I think whatever happened, it happened outside the car.''

"So do I—unfortunately for us.''

"Then with three days of hard rain and high winds—''

"I know, I know, Prouty," Tilley said wearily. "There's unlikely to be even a chance in a million of the slightest shred of anything still being here. I know.'' He sighed. "Nevertheless, I want this lot kept blocked off. I want two men posted here all night. And I don't want that car towed out of here until after you've made a daylight search of the whole area first thing tomorrow.'' He looked at his watch and grimaced. "This morning. Understand?''

"Yes, sir.''

"See to it, Prouty."

"Yes, sir."

Tilley turned away from him and strode over to the three officers near the Corvette. He ignored McCannister, who backed off uneasily as he approached, and directed himself to his officers.

"Find anything?"

"Nothing, lieutenant," one of the men spoke up. "Car's clean as a whistle. Not even any luggage in it."

"Don't remind me," Tilley muttered sarcastically, glancing contemptuously at McCannister. "So. That's about it, then, eh? Think anything might turn up in daylight?"

The three officers glanced at each other uncomfortably.

"Not really, sir," the man who had spoken before finally answered. "We've given it a pretty good going-over, lieutenant."

"I'm sure you have." Tilley managed a tight smile. "And I appreciate it, Meacock. But give it another one just the same, in the morning, before it's towed off. Just in case."

"Yes, sir."

Tilley looked from one to the other for a moment.

"I know how you're all feeling, men," he said quietly, "and I don't blame you. But so far we've got absolutely nothing to go on in this case. We have to come up with something—anything, I don't care how small. A violent—and very bizzare—murder was committed, right over there." He took the torch Prouty was holding and shone it on the muddy area marked off by a ring of stones near the side of the car. "I want that area—and a good five feet around it—dug up tomorrow morning and combed through. For anything—even a fingernail, a hair, a thread—anything that isn't mud and stone. Understand? And then I want it sent to Eastern for lab tests. Including the mud. That clear, Meacock?"

"Yes, sir," Officer Meacock replied, a touch of animosity coloring his voice.

"You don't have to like it, Meacock, or understand it,"

Tilley commented darkly, looking the officer directly in the eye, "but you do have to do it. Understood?"

"Yes, sir." The animosity was gone from the officer's voice.

"In the morning, then." Tilley turned away and walked over to McCannister. "Sheriff McCannister, I'm leaving my team here to go over everything again in the morning, as soon as it's light." He glanced at his watch. "That's in a couple of hours. Sergeant Prouty will be in charge. You'll take orders from him, and report to him before you do anything or go anywhere. Is that understood? This case is under the jurisdiction of the Bangor police, and no independent actions are to be undertaken. By you or anyone else. Do I make myself clear?"

"Clear as crystal, Lieutenant Tilley," McCannister answered sullenly.

"Excellent."

Tilley turned and looked around the parking lot, lighted unevenly by flashlights and squad-car searchlights, until he spotted Archie English standing near the pine trees on the far side. He walked over to him.

"Mr. English I think you'd better not plan on making any runs out to the islands tomorrow morning. My men will be working here some part of the day—possibly a good part of the morning—finishing up their search. Your parking lot will have to stay blocked off until they're done. I'm sorry if this inconveniences you, or anyone on the islands, but I'm certain you understand the necessity of all this."

"Ayup," Archie nodded at him, "I do."

"Thank you, Mr. English. You've been extremely cooperative, and I'm very grateful. I hope we can wrap this up in time for you to make your noon run. I'll ask Sergeant Prouty to do his best."

"Ayup. 'Preciate if you do that, Lieutenant Tilley," Archie said gravely. "Always like t' get the mail delivered on time."

"We'll do our best, Mr. English."

Tilley turned away and headed back to Sergeant Prouty,

who was now sitting in one of the squad cars blocking the entrance to the parking lot, writing in a small notebook.

"Prouty?" Tilley asked, leaning against the open car door. "Think you can wrap up here by noon tomorrow?"

"Christ, I hope so, sir." Prouty looked up at him with tired eyes. "Actually, I don't see why we shouldn't be all through by nine or ten, if we start at first light. Unless the tow truck's delayed," he added.

"I'll see that it damn well isn't," Tilley growled, then grinned at him. "Thanks, Prouty. And keep your eye on old what's-his-name, the local bumbler. He's mad as a wet hen about all this and probably itching to redeem himself, so watch out for him. Don't let him screw up anything else."

Prouty smiled. "I won't, lieutenant. Don't worry."

"Don't ask the impossible," Tilley gave the man a wry smile in return, "not the way this case is going. Well, keep me informed. And stop by my office as soon as you get back tomorrow—today," he corrected himself, looking at his watch again. "Christ, I hope I have time to shave when I get back. Remember, keep me informed. Even of nothing."

"I will, sir."

"Right. And good luck, Prouty."

"Thanks, lieutenant. We need it."

Tilley walked off toward his car, wishing Sgt. Prouty hadn't reminded him of the blank wall he was up against on the case. When he reached his car, he stood for a moment gazing out over the dark waters of the bay. Somewhere out there Carey Hunter was . . . doing what? Sleeping, he hoped, by now. Or crying into her pillow for her dead friend. He shrugged. There was nothing he could do about it, except his best to find Marjory Packer's murderer. Carey Hunter would just have to bear her pain like all the other friends and families of murder victims. He shrugged again and slid behind the wheel of his car, pulling the door to with a slam. Damn it, why did the woman keep popping into his head? He was finished with her. If she and her roommate had stayed where they belonged, the roommate would still be alive.

He started the car, then paused with his foot on the brake pedal and stared again out over the bay through the open window. Was she all right out there, alone on that deserted little island? Of course she was. The old woman, Mrs.— Mrs.— Mrs. Rambeau, that was it—was there. Carey Hunter was probably with her. Anyway, it wasn't the people on the islands who were in danger, in all probability; it was the people right here in South Bay and the surrounding areas. If there even was any further danger— but Tilley felt intuitively there was. Experience had taught him that psychopathological killers—and he had no other explanation for what he had seen in the last ten hours or so—once started, didn't stop until somebody stopped them, with either bars or bullets.

He shifted uneasily on the car seat. All the more reason he should get going and start to work on his report. Something that had gotten by him in the telling might stand out when he studied his notes in the comparative quiet of his office. Carey Hunter—damn her for continuing to recur to his mind—would be all right. Suffering now, but in time she would be all right.

He stepped on the gas, pulled the car forward, then stopped it again. Nobody else had ever had to go through quite what Carey Hunter had gone through—was still going through, undoubtedly. Well, there was nothing he could do about that part of it, he reminded himself. He pulled ahead to Archie English's private driveway and turned his car around. But when he got back to the ferry parking lot he stopped again, yanked up the emergency brake, and got out to stare once more across the bay. He couldn't shake the feeling that something wasn't right with Carey Hunter.

"Well, of course something isn't right with her, you damn fool," he muttered to himself, forcing himself to get back into the car. "Nothing is right with her right now. Get your ass out of here and go do your job."

He drove off up the county road toward South Bay and Route 1, disconcertingly aware that for the second time in his life he was unwillingly receiving strong impressions of the feelings and experience of another human being. The first time, the impressions had been those of his wife, when she was dying. He refused to let himself dwell on that. He had loved Thea, adored her. He loved her still. They had been as close as two people could possibly be. It didn't surprise him that some kind of psychic communication had developed between them at a time of crisis.

But Carey Hunter? A New York tourist he'd never known existed before yesterday and would forget by tomorrow—or at least the tomorrow after the day he closed this case. It was ridiculous. In fact, it was impossible. He was just tired. A good strong cup of black coffee would set him right and elute any lingering impressions of that blond-haired, brown-eyed New Yorker from his brain cells.

Tilley stepped on the gas pedal and took off up the road at breakneck speed.

6

"Yeah. . . . Yeah. . . . What?" Lt. Tilley suddenly came alive at the Bangor end of the telephone connection. "The dinghy's missing, too?"

"Ayup," Polly McCannister's voice worried its way into his ear like a gnat. "It's missin', all right. Me 'n' Arch, we searched the whole dang bay in Howie Rucker's speedboat. That dinghy ain't in South Bay, 'n' if ain't in South Bay—"

"What about the old lady, her landlady?" Tilley was rifling hurriedly through his notes. "Mrs.— Mrs.—"

"Peggy Rambeau didn't take the dinghy," came over the phone, followed by an ominous pause.

"How do you know that, sheriff?"

" 'Cause Peggy Rambeau's dead." The sheriff's voice sounded as dead as the word itself. "Was just gettin' t' that part." He sighed loudly. "Me 'n' Arch, we found her up t' Sternfirst."

"To what?" Tilley barked.

"T' her house. Not the one she rents out. The one she lives in. 'S called Sternfirst."

"Go on, go on."

"Well, me 'n' Arch, we found her there, dead in her bed."

"She die of natural causes, it look like?"

"No, sir." McCannister's voice came less strongly through the receiver. "She looks . . . she looks . . ."

Tilley waited a moment, then realized the local sheriff was unable to go on.

"Bloody hell, sheriff, are you trying to tell me . . ." Paul Tilley discovered he, too, found it hard to go on.

"Ayup."

"Jesus."

They were silent a moment, on either end of the connection. Then Tilley shook himself and got down to business.

"All right, sheriff. I'll be down there as soon as possible. Where is the body now?"

"Right where we found it."

"Mr. Dobbler or Dr. Burry examine it?"

"George went out there. Old Doc Burry, he refused t' go. Said you—"

"Never mind, never mind. Can you have a boat ready for us?"

"Arch'll take ya. On the ferry."

"Tell him two hours at the outside."

"Ayup."

"How soon can you organize search parties in your area and get going? I want every island, every inch of woods, every building and vehicle—everything—searched with a fine-tooth comb. I want that young woman found. Understand?"

"Easier said than done, Lieutenant Tilley." McCannister's voice sounded disgruntled now.

"Do it anyway. As fast as possible. I'll expect to see searches in full swing by the time we get there."

"Carey Hunter ain't rowin' that dinghy on land, Lieutenant Tilley, if ya don't mind me sayin' so. Was a—"

"We don't know she's in the dinghy, sheriff. We don't know she was ever in the dinghy last night, after Mr. English brought her back. Now get going."

"—outgoin' tide last night."

"What?"

"Was a outgoin' tide last night. Crested around seventhirty this mornin' or so."

"God." Tilley ran his free hand through his hair. "All right. I'm calling the Coast Guard in on this. But I want those search parties out anyway, McCannister. You understand?"

Tilley heard an irritated "ayup."

"Good. Get going. We'll be there inside of two hours. You say all the lamps had been lit at the . . . in Miss Hunter's house?"

"Ayup. A couple of 'em was still sputtering when Arch 'n' me got there."

"Any sign of her having been at the other house?"

"Her—or somebody 'sides Peggy Rambeau. The kitchen lamps was burnin', high. They's wall fixtures. Gas-fed. Woulda burned till her tank was empty. Oh, 'n' Peggy's door was open. Her bedroom door."

"What do you make of it, McCannister?"

"Well, wouldn't s'prise me if Miss Hunter went up there—Miz Mitchell t' the general store on Fustin's, says she goes up there reg'lar like, t' check on the old lady— 'pears t' me she went up there last night after Arch brought her back, saw Peg—saw the . . . saw what happened 'n' wanted t' get off the island fast as she could. 'Pears t' be blood on a coupla the pilings down t' the dock. 'Bout far enough apart t' be the ones she used t' moor the dinghy."

"Why," Tilley asked when McCannister had finished

speaking, "did you and Mr. English decide to go out there? What prompted you?"

"Arch called me when he saw the dinghy was missin'."

"I don't understand." Again Tilley was rifling through his notes, looking for his interview of Archibald English. "Outer Island's almost a mile farther out in the bay than Fustin's, and not a regular stop on the ferry route. He couldn't have seen a missing dinghy a mile away."

"Nope. He went out there special, after his first run t' Fustin's—the first one he got t' make after your men cleared out, that is. He was gonna use the horn t' signal Miss Hunter till she come down t' the dock 'n' told him everythin' was all right. That's when he seen the dinghy was missin'."

"Did he signal her?"

"Ayup. She never come down."

"Why did he feel this was necessary? Did he say?"

"Nope. Just said he had a funny feelin'."

"I see. And then he went back to Fustin's and called you on Mrs. Mitchell's phone?"

"Ayup. 'N' I come out with my outboard, 'n' since Howie—Howie Rucker—was down t' the dock when I got there, he gave us a loan of his speedboat. 'S faster'n my old put-put. Arch missed another run, helpin' me search the bay," the sheriff added in a voice that told Tilley he felt the ferryman deserved a word of praise.

"Is there anything else, Mr. McCannister?"

"Nope. Don't think so. Rest you better see for yourself. We ain't touched a thing," McCannister added in a defensive tone.

"Good. Can you get a man posted on the dock at Outer Island to make sure nobody does? Someone reliable? We can't risk any tourists stopping there and nosing around, sheriff."

"Already done that, Lieutenant Tilley." The local sheriff's voice traveled over the telephone wires puffed with pride. "Miz Mitchell's out there. Closed her store 'n' went out there in her outboard."

"Mrs. Mitchell? You let a woman go out there?"

"Peggy Rambeau's her oldest friend. Marian Mitchell's right fond a' Peggy Rambeau. Nobody'll get past Marian Mitchell, Lieutenant Tilley. Promise you that."

"Will she stay away from the houses? Stay down on the dock?"

"Better'n a jiggerman 'n' a bandog rolled up together. Don't worry 'bout Marian Mitchell."

Tilley did worry, anyway, all the time he was putting out an APB on Carey Hunter, asking the Coast Guard for a sea search, and organizing an investigation team to accompany him to South Bay. That he, this time, received almost the full cooperation of his chief in selecting the men he wanted did little to mitigate his wrath at having not only a country case, but a country case that was not going to be easily solved or kept much longer from the media, and a ferryman for an investigator, and a storekeeper—a woman—for a guard. As for the local sheriff, well, he already had his mind made up about him. Still, the man hadn't done so badly this time. Except for not calling Bangor before he searched the bay and permitting a middle-aged woman, however ferocious, to go out to a deserted island and play sentinel in what just might be only the beginning of a string of the most bizarre and baffling murders—Tilley no longer had any question in his mind but that they were murders—in the history of the human race. Tilley brought his thoughts up short. Hell, what else was there? The man was a damn fool. A yokel playing at being a policeman and full of self-importance. There was obviously a maniac loose in South Bay—and a brilliant maniac at that, to have devised a way to kill by dehydration through the breasts. Some sexual freak the likes of which had never been known before. He shuddered, then shrugged. It had happened—twice now, apparently—and he had to work with it, however inconceivable it seemed. And before it happened again, he had to get to South Bay and take charge of things.

Tilley's one bitch was that his chief had refused to let him call in the state police to close the bay area. Chief Skillin worried about the media getting wind of things and the resultant loss of millions of dollars in tourist business to the state for the rest of the summer. Or so he said. Tilley suspected he was equally, if not more, worried about his job. It was no secret around the station house that Ho—behind his back, on the force under his command, his nickname was lengthened to Hoho—Skillin had friends in Augusta. And it was generally believed that, without those friends, Chief Hosea Skillin would still be, if not exactly pounding a beat, certainly well down the line in the hierarchy of the Bangor Police Force.

Tilley held his own private view of the matter, and it was that, while Hoho Skillin was a good administrator, he was a lousy cop; there were at least five men Tilley would have preferred to see in the chief's chair. Skillin was fine as long as there was nothing more serious than parking tickets and a few burglaries. Tilley had no illusions about the demands his chief would make on him in his handling of the Mummy Murder, as the case had been dubbed by the lab technicians at the Medical Center, nor of the security, now, of his own job. But that wasn't what worried him.

What worried Tilley was the next victim. Already there had been two in four days. This said obsession to Tilley, lifelong controls broken down and a demented mind on the rampage.

He was drawn as tightly as an overtuned fiddle string, and a very unhappy man, when he hurried out of the Bangor station house to catch up with his team, already on their way to South Bay.

"What's going on, lieutenant?" Jack Hoyt, newsman for WABI-TV, accosted him as he headed for his car. "What's up?"

"Nothing, nothing at all, Jack," Tilley said matter-of-factly. "Just the chief's way of seeing to it we earn our pay."

"Come on, Tilley," Hoyt came back at him. "Don't bullshit a bullshitter. I know a big one when I see it."

"Not this time, Jack. Sorry. Your nose for news is way out of joint this time." Tilley opened the door of his car and slid in beside Sergeant Crowley.

"You want it kept under wraps, I'll keep it under. Until you say so. But let me in on it, Tilley."

"There's nothing to let you in on, Jack." Tilley kept his voice affable. "Believe me. Let's go, Jim," he said to Crowley.

"Bullshit," Hoyt said. "Look, Tilley, you've got no choice. If you let me in, I'll keep quiet about it as long as—"

Tilley smiled at him. "Jack, you never kept quiet about anything in your life."

The car was moving now, backing out of its parking place.

"The hell you say." The newsman was striding beside the car, his hands gripping the open window. "And if you don't, Tilley, I'll get it anyway and no holds barred. So what—"

"Never threaten me, Hoyt. Never." Tilley rolled up the window, forcing the man's hands off the car.

"All right, you son-of-a-bitch," Hoyt called after him as the car rolled away. "You asked for it."

"Step on it, Crowley," Tilley growled irritably. "Before I get out and deck that bastard."

"Well, Howie Rucker 'n' some of the boys're searchin' Fustin's, 'n' Pete Todd's gettin' a couple gangs together t' take care a' the back a' the bay." Polly McCannister was huffing and puffing from his trot across the parking lot, and trying to shout over the noise and bustle of the Bangor police boarding Archie's ferry. " 'N' Colly Robb 'n' his son're takin' care a' South Bay here"—he coughed and wiped sweat from his forehead with a hand—" 'n' I still gotta call—"

"All right," Tilley cut him off, "go call them. I'll check with you when I get back here." He turned and started to walk up the dock.

"You mean I ain't t' go? With you? Out t' Outer?"

"Your work is here," Tilley tossed over his shoulder.

"But—"

"Get on it, sheriff. Before it's too late."

"Son-of-a-bitch."

Tilley heard the muttered curse behind him. He ignored it and, one hand on the ferry's starboard rail, swung himself over the side into the passenger compartment.

"Everybody aboard?" he demanded of Crowley.

"Yes, sir."

"Let's go, Mr. English," he shouted to Archie.

When the ferry was well away from the dock, Tilley began his briefing in a soft monotone. He had learned a long time ago it was a waste of his energies to shout for an audience's attention; when he wanted to be heard, he whispered. By his third word the only sounds were his voice, the chug of the ferry's engine, the slap of the water against her hull, and the occasional scream of a gull overhead. Before Archie dropped his sea anchor off Outer Island, every man aboard knew exactly what he was to do and how fast Tilley expected him to do it. Further, it was patently clear to everyone that the case was an extremely sensitive one and that not a word was to leak out about it until it was solved, or heads would roll.

Howie Rucker's speedboat, Archie's seldom-used dinghy, and Polly McCannister's outboard, which had all been in tow, were brought alongside. Tilley, Crowley, Chief Medical Examiner MacKay Logan, the forensic unit, and the police photographer crowded into the speedboat and took off, with Crowley at the helm, for the dock. Mrs. Mitchell met them and caught their bowline and secured it, a loaded shotgun broken over her forearm.

Jesus Christ, Tilley said to himself, just wait till I get my hands on that jackass McCannister.

"You the detective from Bangor Polly McCannister said was comin' out here?" Mrs. Mitchell challenged him, unsmiling.

Tilley nodded, not trusting himself to speak.

"You mighta signaled. Good thing for you ya came over on the ferry. Been a boat I didn't know, I'da sunk the lot a' ya—mebbe hurt somebody." Mrs. Mitchell was plainly put out.

"My thought exactly," Tilley leveled his most com-

manding stare at her. "So now that I'm here, and in
charge, and you know who I am, I want you to unload that
shotgun, get into your boat," he gestured slightly toward
the outboarded dinghy moored ahead of the speedboat,
"go out to the ferry, and stay there. Is that clear?"

It wasn't. "Polly McCannister told me t' guard Peggy
Rambeau's dock, 'n' he's sheriff down here. So this is
where I stay till he tells me t' go." Mrs. Mitchell's face
was red with outrage.

Arms akimbo, shotgun dangling down one ample hip
and thigh, she blocked exit off the narrow dock as effec-
tively as an armed—and angered—bear. Tilley could feel
his men piled up behind him on the boards. He had to do
something before she made a fool of him in front of them.

"Sheriff McCannister is not in charge of this case, Mrs.
Mitchell." Silently he thanked God for bringing her name
to his mind. "I am. And Outer Island is now under the
jurisdiction of the Bangor police and off-limits to unautho-
rized personnel. I don't mean to be abrupt, but I must
insist that you leave. We have barely two hours till sundown and a great deal to do. And unload that gun
immediately."

"Don't feel I should leave here till Polly McCannister
tells me to. 'N' I ain't unloadin' m' gun. Had a funny
feelin' ever since I heard 'bout them Pine Woods folk."

"What folk?"

"The four teenagers who come on the ferry last
Saturday. Carey Hunter told me they was there. Pine
Woods folk. Queer folk."

"Carey Hunter met them?" Tilley pursued.

"Not t' say met. They never talk t' nobody. But they
was on the same ferry. Queer folk."

"Lieutenant Tilley?" Crowley called from the speedboat.
"You want me to make another trip? The rest of the
guys'll never fit into those two little dinghies without
sinking them."

Tilley had an inspiration. "Mrs. Mitchell, can you handle a speedboat?"

"That 'n' anythin' else that floats."

"You would be of great help to us, in that case, if you would make a trip or two with the speedboat and get the rest of my men ashore. As you can see," he turned and pointed at the two dinghies making their way to Outer Island, McCannister's, with its outboard, only a short distance ahead of Archie English's rowboat, "we're losing a lot of time. Not to mention tying up my assistant here. I'd be very grateful if—"

"Out'n there, young fella." Mrs. Mitchell suddenly slipped past him with the ease of a dancer and addressed herself to Crowley. Before Tilley had finished, she was halfway into the cockpit.

"Lieutenant?" Crowley gazed up at Paul helplessly.

"Get out, get out, Crowley. You heard the lady. Besides, you're needed more ashore. Thank you, Mrs. Mitchell."

Crowley climbed onto the dock. Mrs. Mitchell had the boat maneuvering neatly out from the dock almost before Tilley freed the speedboat's line, and he had to hurl it at the bow. It struck the forward hull and slid into the water. Mrs. Mitchell glanced up him, an expression of immense satisfaction on her face.

"Shit," Tilley muttered under his breath. Then he remembered the shotgun. He was about to hail her and remind her—ask her, this time—to unload it, but he stopped himself. She probably could handle that as well as she could a boat. Which, he hated to admit, was very well indeed. He took a deep breath and exhaled. "Well, what the hell are you all waiting for?" he barked at his men. "Get on with it."

MacKay Logan, standing beside Peggy Rambeau's bed, shook his head and made a brief note in his notebook.

"Any idea how long she's been dead, Kay?" Tilley, behind him, asked.

"How about five hundred years? I can't say, Paul. It's totally dessicated. Can't estimate any degree of rigor mortis with a body in this condition. This whole business is unbelievable." He attempted to examine the neck for ligature marks, but again the shrunken rigidity of the remains defeated him. He made another note in his notebook and automatically tried to check the whites of the eyes for any traces of petechial hemorrhage. The whites were not white but lead-colored; the eyeballs were tightly wrinkled into hardened little bits of gray tissue, no longer convex but concave, as if some incredible force had sucked them back against the brain. He could determine nothing. He made one more useless note and reexamined the torn breasts again. Here, at least, he could tell something definite, if only as a result of having examined, that morning, another body in the same condition, which had suffered the same damage. He made some more notes, stuffed his notebook and pen into the inside pocket of his jacket, and stood up.

"Well?"

"Can't you tell anything you don't already know from what I've been able to tell you about the other one, Paul. Sorry. Just the obvious—same condition, same apparent cause of death, same breast damage." He glanced down at the tiny form on the bed. "Wait a minute." He bent down and carefully studied first one shriveled hand, then the other. Then he stood up. "Have them bag the hands when they wrap it up. I want to examine the fingernails when I get it. I think she may have put up a fight." He thought a minute. "Well, we'll see. It's all yours, Paul. Call me when you're finished. Don't forget I want the mattress as well as the bedclothes. Somebody bled something a lot of something—on this bed. And it certainly wasn't that." He jerked his thumb at Peggy Rambeau's corpse and left the room.

Tilley nodded. The photographer moved in and for several minutes the tiny, mummified figure of Margaret Whittier Rambeau was again bombarded with explosions of light. Two lab technicians with the forensic unit waited with shocked faces a few moments after the photographer was finished before preparing the cadaver for removal.

"Holy shit," one of them murmured as he bent over the bizarre anhydride.

The rest of the unit was already at work dusting surfaces

for fingerprints and searching the house for minutiae. The light was fading, but Tilley would allow no lamps to be lit.

"Just hurry up and do what you can. We'll come back first thing in the morning." Damn McCannister. If only the fat fool had called him before he went speeding around the bay, playing at searching for the dinghy.

The dinghy. With a start, Tilley thought of Carey Hunter. He was extremely concerned about her and refused to speculate whether she was wandering in the deep woods around South Bay, at sea in a rowboat, or already the next victim. He would go down to the dock and get on the walkie-talkie and check if there had been any reports on her. He was about to turn away from the bed when a large, dark stain on the rag rug at his feet caught his eye.

"Crowley?" he barked. "What do you make of this?"

He squatted to examine it and was touching the edges of it gingerly with his fingertips when Crowley joined him.

"Whatever it is, it's already dried," he commented. "Get me a flashlight." He stayed hunkered there, gazing at the stain.

Crowley returned with a flashlight and turned it on the rug. A technician came and squatted down beside them.

"Have to run tests on it, Lieutenant Tilley," the technician said. "Looks like blood, but a lot of things do." He tested the stain here and there with his fingertips. "It's completely dried, whatever it is."

Tilley stood up. "Roll up this rug and bag it. Take it back to the lab. I want a report on that stain first thing in the morning."

"Right, sir."

"Wait a minute." Tilley's trained eye noted a darkened, dried stream running away from the far edge of the stain toward the door of the bedroom. He followed it to the door, where the edge of the rug touched the hall carpet, and out into the hall. He squatted again, called for the flashlight, and studied it a moment before getting up. "Cut this piece out of the hall carpet here as well and take it back for testing." He was certain it was blood, and certain it would match the stains on the bedcovers and mattress.

What he wasn't certain about was how it had managed to run so far—unless the old woman had seriously wounded her attacker, who had then managed to stagger from the room. But then . . . He squatted down once more and searched the hall carpet, inching along on the balls of his feet, all the way to the stairs. He found nothing. He stood up and walked back in the other direction, past the bedroom door, to the porthole set in the outside wall at the end of the hall. Again, he found nothing, except right outside the door. He was baffled.

"Doyle," he ordered the technician, "don't cut this carpet. Mark it for the doors, the stairs, and the ends of the hall, and roll it up and take it along."

"Right, Lieutenant Tilley."

After giving Crowley his instructions and informing him he would send up two men to remain in the house that night, Tilley made his way down the wooded path to the dock. The appointed officer and Mrs. Mitchell were there, not engaged in conversation. Her shotgun was still hanging, broken, over her right arm. Tilley shrugged and got on his officer's walkie-talkie. There were no reports on Carey Hunter or an abandoned dinghy.

He took the path to the right leading off the dock and made his way to the Berries. As he opened the screen door to the kitchen, Tilley realized he was extremely curious about where, and how, Carey Hunter had been spending her summer. It annoyed him.

"Any signs of anything?" he asked Ned Lyons, the officer in charge.

"No, sir," Lyons replied. "Just normal day-to-day living. We've dusted 'n' all, but I don't think anything will turn up. We're about finished. Found these," he handed Tilley several letters carefully sealed in marked plastic bags. "Most of 'em were in a bureau drawer in the bedroom she'd been using." He gestured to one bag, which contained four or five letters. "Those two," he pointed to another of the bags, "were on a side table in the living room. In their envelopes, just like that. Must've gotten wet, 'cause you can't read the addresses on 'em. This one,'' he gestured at the next to the last of the plastic bags, ''wasn't with its envelope. It looks like it got crumpled up to throw out, then she changed her mind. Reads like it's from her boyfriend. And that's—''

Tilley read what he could make out of the letter through the plastic as Lyons finished his report.

''—the envelope. We found it on the floor in the living room. Under a chair. Nothing else but clothes, books, and makeup. You know, the usual.''

Tilley finished the letter and looked up.

''Leave two of your men to stay the night when you're through. And send two up to the other house to do the same thing. They're to sleep in the downstairs parlor and touch as little as possible. I've radioed Perkins to send sandwiches and coffee over, if he can reach that ass of a sheriff. If not, I'll send somebody back with them as soon as I can. I'll be down at the dock.''

He walked out of the kitchen and made a quick but thorough tour of the house, checking every room, Carey's suitcases—open on the bedroom floor—and bureau drawers. He poked through her makeup in the bathroom before making his way back downstairs. His hand strayed to his pocket, feeling the plastic bags inside. So Carey Hunter had—or had had—a lover named Nick. And it was his job to find her for him. He was in a very sour mood by the time he got back to the dock.

7

It was barely quarter to five the following morning when Tilley and Crowley pulled into Archie's parking lot. A team of sleepy, disgruntled policemen was huddled in the passenger compartment of the ferry; Archie was on the dock, ready to loose the stern mooring line.

"You sure you don't want me to drive you?" Crowley asked as he got out from behind the wheel. " 'S a good two hundred and some miles up there. Yunker or Prouty could take charge of—"

"No," Tilley said firmly, sliding over into the driver's seat. "I want you in charge. And as soon as you finish up with the old lady's house, send a man straight to Eastern with whatever you've got for the lab—the chief's already on the ragged edge about this case leaking out before it's solved. I need every man I can get right here, and, Jim, I want that damn island gone over inch by inch. There's got to be something there. So find it. Anything turns up, leave word for me at the station. I'll be checking in as often as I can find a phone."

"Right."

"Keep on top of the Coast Guard and McCannister. I want to know the minute somebody finds that girl. Or the dinghy," he added unhappily.

"Will do."

"Here." Tilley half turned, reaching over the back of the front seat, and hefted an enormous plastic bag off the rear seat. "For God's sake, don't let me drive off with these. Tell the guys I'm sorry it's just sandwiches and oranges, but at four A.M. I was lucky to get anything."

Crowley took the bag, grinning. "Don't worry, boss. I can handle their guff."

"Yeah, well, they deserve better." Tilley slammed the door shut. "They won't get it, though. Not as long as they stay policemen. Don't tell them I said that," he added quickly, with a grim smile. "Not today, anyway. I'll try to round up something decent for them tonight." Tilley had no illusions that his case was going to be solved in time to appease his chief's frayed nerves. "Oh, and Jim, tell Perkins there's about five gallons of coffee coming for the eight-o'clock boat and not to let English leave without it. Hope it's at least lukewarm by the time you guys get it out there."

"Right. Thanks, Paul."

"For what?" Tilley started to back the car around, then braked. "I'll be back as soon as I can. Expect me out there before sundown. Tell English, if I don't make his six-o'clock boat I'll want him to take me out there when I do get back. Do your damnedest, Jim."

He was off before Crowley could answer.

Tilley took Route 1 as far as Cherryfield, then turned onto 193 to cut over to Route 9. He was extremely irritated about having to leave the search area; he respected Jim Crowley as much as he did any man on the force, but Paul Tilley never quite trusted anybody to do anything totally right except himself. He already knew he'd go over the whole damn island again the next day, no matter what Crowley turned up. And that irritated him, too—with himself, for not being able to delegate responsibility with a free mind.

Even more, he was worried sick about Carey Hunter. Where the hell had the damn girl gotten herself to? Not that he would have expected—or wanted—her to sweat out the night on Outer Island after discovering Mrs. Rambeau's body, certainly not when it was just as likely as not that the murderer had still been on the island when Archie English brought her back night before last. Indeed, he was grateful and relieved that Carey had fled—*if* she had fled, alone and of her own volition, if she hadn't been taken by force, and the dinghy simply set adrift to confuse the police and tie them up searching for her. He didn't want even to consider the latter alternative, but he couldn't permit himself not to. It made him sweaty with apprehension to acknowledge it was as real a probability as anything else at this point. All he knew was that Carey Hunter and the dinghy were both missing, not necessarily together.

He should have listened to his intuition Thursday night and had English ferry him out there. He'd been kicking himself about that for so many hours his butt was sore. But damn it, why hadn't he done just that? Why had he insisted to himself that what he was sensing was only her grief about her friend? He'd really known better—or would have, if he had stopped, for one minute, being so goddamn irascible about her worming her way into his feelings.

So she'd gotten to him, turned him on a little. It was only a little. She'd go back to New York soon—as soon as he found her, and he *would* find her. And that would be that. He shouldn't have jeopardized her life because his own feelings for her made him uncomfortable.

Well, come on, now, he couldn't take that much on himself. He'd had work to do. How in hell would he have explained a two A.M. sightseeing tour of South Bay to old Hoho if she'd been all right? But she hadn't been all right. He knew that then and he knew it now. And his conscience refused to let him alone.

In Veazie he caught 178 for a few miles, crossing the Penobscot at Old Town to pick up 95—with misgivings— all the way to Sherman Mills. The misgivings weren't the result of the Interstate but of the sounds his car was already making. Damn and double-damn. Why hadn't he taken it into the shop last week, before all this happened? He'd known for three months he needed a new carburetor, just hadn't wanted to take the time. So now, when he needed every second he could squeeze out of every day, he'd have to take the time, make the time, lose the time if it came to that. Triple-damn. Well, the damn thing just better not quit on him today. It better get him where he was going and back again. If it would just do that, it could die in peace forever on Archie English's parking lot, for all he cared.

"If you go before then," he muttered grimly, aloud, "I may just get out and beat you to death right here on Interstate 95. I guarantee you won't go in peace if you konk out on me before we're back in South Bay, baby."

At Sherman Mills he took Route 11 into Sherman. He had to do three things: call the station, call the Coast Guard, and get a container of coffee. All three turned out not to his liking. Crowley had not been in touch with the station. The sea search, resumed at first light, had turned up nothing so far. And the coffee, after he tore a triangular piece out of the plastic lid and sipped at it, was weak.

"Goddamn it," he growled.

He set the container on the dashboard, started the car, and headed north on 11 toward Patten, where he could pick up 159.

He hated weak coffee. Weak coffee always reminded him of his wife, and the less he thought about her, the better he got through the day. It had been more than eight years since Thea died, and nearly nine since she'd first been taken ill, and, except for having stopped drinking before his drinking stopped him, Tilley felt he'd taken little more than baby steps out of his grief. And none out of his anger. He was still in a rage with God and with life for having taken Thea from him.

Pericarditis. Who the hell ever heard of pericarditis? It was so rare the doctors had scarcely known what to do for his wife. She'd spent months in the hospital, every second filled with excrutiating pain. Tilley had spent those months snatching every spare moment he could from work to be with her, raging inside that she was being made to suffer so much, while maintaining as cheerful and positive a front as if she were suffering no more than heartburn or indigestion.

Neither his inner rage nor outer blithesomeness affected the inevitable course of his wife's illness. She worsened, little by little, as the months went by, and one morning, after Tilley had spent the night at her bedside, she died.

For reasons he did not clearly understand, Tilley had never been able to come to terms with the cause of his wife's death. An inflammation of the pericardium? Nobody died of an inflammation. He felt Thea had been stolen from him and forgave no one—doctors, nurses, the hospital, the specialists he'd called in from Boston, the Lord, or life itself. Even Thea, to some extent, he had been unable to forgive for deserting him. In the secret places of his heart he'd never quite shaken the terrible feeling that if she'd wanted to live, to stay with him, loved him a little more, she could and would have gotten better.

He knew it was utterly unreasonable, but he continued to feel it no matter how he argued with himself.

Initially, immediately after she was gone, Tilley had begun to drink to ease the agony of his loss and blunt the razor edge of his fury. An intense man, it required stupendous amounts of alcohol to numb the pain he suffered. For almost seven months he'd begun every day by reaching for a drink, straight from the bottle, even before he turned off his alarm clock. He'd ended those days lying in a stupor, drunk and disheveled, usually still half-dressed, on the fourposter he and Thea had shared for three and a half wonderful years. A few times he had picked up a woman in a bar somewhere and gone home with her, intending at least to obtain relief from the sexual frustration he suffered. Inevitably he'd ended up across her bed, much too drunk to complete the act he had come to perform. It was a time terrible for him, and it had not ended until he woke one morning in a strange woman's unfamiliar apartment.

He had reached for the bottle he knew had to be there, somewhere near the bed, and found it empty. He'd dragged himself off the bed and searched the room. All he found was dirt and disorder—dirty sheets, soiled blankets, filth matted into the carpet, layers of thick dust on all the surfaces. He'd stumbled into the bathroom to urinate and found his stomach turning at the blurred sight of a filth-encrusted toilet, sink, tub, and floor. The living room, when he managed to get there, was no cleaner. Eventually he'd staggered his way into the kitchen.

In the midst of grime and slop and the ubiquitous odor of rotting garbage, he had found a no longer young woman who looked, to his blurred vision, as dirty as her surroundings. She was seated at a dirt-encrusted table, drinking coffee out of a long-unwashed mug. Above all, what stood out in his mind were the black lines of old dirt etching the folds of fat on her neck.

"There a goddamn drink in this place?" he had slurred angrily.

"You kiddin'?" she'd sneered at him over the edge of her mug. "With you about?"

He had stared at her.

"Whyn't ya git yer ass outa here?" she'd demanded, putting the mug down loudly on a dirty plate. "If'n I had one, I wouldn't give it t' you. I din't know you was such a pig when I invited ya home with me last night. I thought you was a gentleman—ha-ha."

When Tilley continued to stare at her in disbelief, she had added, "Can't stand lushes. Can't stand 'em. Just git yer ass outa my place, will ya, huh?"

At the door, after shuffling along behind him in her battered, soiled slippers as he searched for his hat, overcoat, and jacket, and making no secret of the fact that she didn't trust him not to take "her things," the woman had taunted him, "You wasn't even any good for what I brung ya home fer. Never knew a lush that was. 'S why I can't stand the whole lousy lot 'a ya. 'N' don't never come back, neither, buster. Don't need you messin' about with me and my place again."

The directive had been superfluous. Tilley had no intention of messing around with her or her place—or any other pickup—ever again. He also had no intention of ever drinking another drop of alcohol as long as he lived. He'd felt ashamed to the marrow of his bones. Worse, he'd been consumed with guilt about Thea. After what they had had together, he could scarcely believe he had debased her memory by sinking to such depths. They had had no children. She would live only so long as his memory of her survived. And to have taken her living memory into such a place, before such a creature . . . He'd sworn to God—his anger was not gone but it was more bearable to him then than his guilt—that he would never show himself so unworthy of the life and the love he had shared with Thea again.

He had gone home, phoned his chief—then a man named Art Urquhart, for whom Tilley had had the greatest respect and admiration—and asked for two weeks' sick leave.

"But, I warn you, Paul, the pressure's on me to kick

you off the force," Urquhart had let him know after granting his request. "You know I don't want to do it. You're one helluva cop—or you used to be. But I can't hold out forever against City Hall. Your drinking's no secret in town, you know that."

"Chief, if a different man doesn't walk through your door in two weeks, I'll quit myself and save you the trouble. And if I *am* drunk then and forget I said this, please do kick me out. On my ass."

Two weeks later a different man had walked through the doors of the Bangor police station. Tilley was not the man he once had been, by any means, but he was also not the man he'd become since his wife's death. He had not had a single drink in the eight years since then.

Except for his coffee. He was aware that the strong, black coffee he drank too much of was a substitute for him for liquor, that it sometimes rattled his nerves and frequently gave him sleepless nights. He could even go so far as to admit to himself that he was now as addicted to coffee as he had once been to alcohol. But he viewed it as an infinitely preferable addiction and told himself that someday he'd give that up too. But not quite yet. Certainly not this day.

He reached for the container of coffee on the dashboard and took another sip of the dishwater-weak brew the little counter restaurant had given him. He smiled wryly. Not quite as bad as Thea used to make, but bad enough. It was a curious kind of relief to him to be able to think of his wife these days without being engulfed by rage and self-pity, to find his love for her still alive inside him. Thea Runnells had been the only woman he had ever loved, and he'd loved her with a passion. The passion slumbered now, finally, but the love remained. He didn't expect ever to love again as he'd loved Thea, and he was grateful he'd gotten hold of himself before he'd lost the feeling completely. It was all, he was sure, he was ever going to know of real love.

Curious, he mused, that he should be thinking so much about Thea today. Though the thought crossed his mind that, as he was now greatly concerned—oh, surely very anxious, but not emotional—about whether that New Yorker, Carey Hunter, was going to live or die, that might have something to do with it. But he refused to dwell on it. He might be suffering a minor, temporary attraction to her, but Carey Hunter meant nothing to him. The most he could say for her was that she was obviously a young woman capable of genuine love. That was apparent in her affection for the all but unidentifiable remains of her friend. But . . .

He thought of the letter he had read in the plastic bag, signed "Nick." The weak coffee suddenly tasted worse to him, and he plunked the container back on the dashboard. Damn. He really hated weak coffee. He'd throw it out in Patten and get a fresh container.

He did, and also called the station house and the Coast Guard again. The coffee was better, but the results of his calls just as fruitless. No word from Crowley, and no sign of Carey Hunter or the dinghy.

He took Route 159 from Patten to Shin Pond, and stopped again for another container of coffee and a grilled cheese to go. He phoned the Bangor station house and the Coast Guard while his order was being prepared. There were still no new developments. Irritated, he paid for his order, snatched the paper bag off the counter, and hurried back to his car.

The last fifteen or twenty miles of road were unpaved, and Tilley's eyes flashed back and forth between his wrist-watch and the deep ruts and gaping potholes ahead of him. He was forced to keep the car under twenty miles per hour and was cursing aloud at the loss of time miles before he finally reached his destination, feeling he should have extracted from Archie English a revelation about the four teenagers on the ferry last Saturday in his first questioning of the ferryman. The whole case was a bummer, as far as Tilley was concerned, and he included his own handling of it in that estimation.

The look of the little town of Pine Woods did nothing to improve his mood as he drove down the dirt main

street. The houses were run-down, faded paint peeling off
the exteriors. Shutters hung awry from broken hinges beside dirty windows; front steps were broken or missing;
porch roofs, where the original supports had cracked or
broken with time, were buttressed haphazardly with
unfinished tree trunks bearing jagged stumps of limbs
hastily chopped off. Here and there an ancient trailer listed
drunkenly on makeshift blocks. The whole town wore
a crazy, slounched air, as if at any moment it might all fall
down on top of itself.

"Jesus," Tilley breathed softly, gazing around. He had
heard occasional stories about Pine Woods but had never
been there before. He did not permit himself the amateur-
ishness of thinking it was exactly the kind of place that
could breed a homicidal maniac, though he was tempted
to.

He pulled up in front of the general store and post
office, turned off the ignition, and got out. One of the five
steps leading up to the porch was missing, and he tested
each of them cautiously before trusting his full one hundred and thirty-two pounds to it. The screening from the
bottom half of the door was torn in a deep, right-angle tear
and bent outward. Tilley was careful to stay clear of the
wire barbs as he opened the door and stepped into the
store.

"How do," he said blandly to the small, slender, brown-
haired man behind the counter, near the register. "Got any
coffee?"

"Over there." The man pointed across and on up the
store aisle. He did not smile back, despite Tilley treating
him to his friendliest public grin.

Tilley turned and looked. "No, sorry." He turned back
and deliberately grinned sheepishly. "I should have make
myself clear. I mean hot coffee, already brewed, to go. In
containers."

"Nope."

"Do you make sandwiches?"

"Nope."

"Well, how about some fruit? Got any apples?"

"Up front."

"Thanks." Tilley walked back to the front of the store, aware of the man's eyes on his back as he went.

The store was as dirty and disheveled inside as it was out. Tilley was surprised—and relieved—to find a bushel basket, though encrusted with years of dirt and badly battered itself, filled with a fresh pick of shiny green Grannies below the front window. He particularly liked the tart, biting taste of Grannies and selected three of them, each with an enticing splash of rosy pink on it.

"Nice batch of Grannies," he complimented the store-keeper as he plunked his three down on the counter. "From around here?"

"That mean you're takin' 'em?" The man's face had yet to change its expression.

"Yes, please."

"Them be all?"

"Afraid so." Tilley smile. again. "What I really want is a cup of coffee. Anyplace in town I can get one?"

"Nope." The man placed the apples on his counter scale and weighed them. "You gonna eat 'em now, or you want 'em bagged?"

"Bagged, please."

"That'll be fifty-seven cents." The storekeeper did not move to bag the apples.

Tilley pulled a handful of change out of his pocket and counted out sixty cents. The man took it, turned the two quarters and dime over several times, studying them keenly, then rang the sale up on his register, carefully counted out three pennies, and slapped them down on the counter. As he bent down to retrieve a brown paper bag from under the counter, Tilley asked his next question.

"Is there a gas station in town? I need gas."

The man stood up, shook open the little bag, and dropped the apples into it before he spoke. All the while he studied Tilley's face.

"Pump's right outside. Have t' 'bout step lively not t' walk slam int' 'er comin' in the store."

Tilley cursed himself for not having noticed the gas

pump. What the hell had he been doing anyway? Sight-seeing? That damn girl. If she hadn't gone and gotten herself lost, his mind wouldn't be split down the middle like it was.

"Guess I'm tireder than I thought. Never noticed it," he said aloud. He yawned, covering his mouth with his hand. "Been on the road since before sunup. Would you mind filling her up? Got a long drive back when I'm through here."

As the man got near the door of the store, Tilley called out, "There a phone in here I can use?"

"Nope." The man let the ragged door slam shut behind him.

"Damn," Tilley muttered. He snatched his apples off the counter and left the store, again careful not to catch his trousers on the torn screen.

"That take me to Squa Pan?" he asked, standing across the car from the storekeeper and gesturing down the dirt road.

"Nope." The man now kept his eyes down, apparently on the pump handle in his hand.

"Well, will it take me somewhere where I can pick up 11 again?"

"Nope."

"Where will it take me?"

"Nowheres."

"It must go somewhere." Tilley knew full well it need not.

"Don't. Ends outa town two–three miles."

"Well, where's your police station? I need some help."

"Ain't got none."

"There a sheriff here?"

"Ayup." The man removed the pump handle from the car's tank, replaced the cap, and walked behind the car to hang the hose back on the gas pump again. He peered at the dirty window. "Took less'n five gallons," he said loudly in his husky contralto voice. "Be six ninety-three."

Tilley pulled his wallet out of a rear pocket and handed him a ten-dollar bill.

"Where do I find your sheriff?"

"Hard t' say." The man took the money and headed toward the store.

"Well, where's his office?"

The man went up his front steps as if they were all there and disappeared into the store without answering. He stayed inside so long Tilley was on the point of following him in for his change, when he at last appeared again.

"T' his house," the man answered as if no time had elapsed since Tilley's question, counting his change carefully into his hand. "Fourth on the left, on up the road." He gestured slightly in the direction Tilley's car's was headed.

"Thanks."

The man looked at him, still studying his face, for a few moments, then turned on his heel and headed back toward the store. "Funny 'bout ya sayin' ya didn't see that pump," he said distinctly, not looking over his shoulder. "Car's parked near on top of 'er."

Tilley tossed his bag of Grannies through the open window, strode around the vehicle, and slid in behind the wheel.

"Funnier yet, I really didn't see it," he muttered as he started the car up. "And that's one you don't know."

He pulled back onto the dirt road and drove slowly, counting the houses on his left aloud. He parked across the road from the fourth house and got out of the car again, looking at it.

It was not quite as old and run-down as everything else in Pine Woods; the paint was less grayed and peeling, the windows actually clean. But like all the other houses, an enormous, shiny TV antenna dominated a roof that looked in need of repair. In the yard beside this house were two junked car hulks, tireless, their wheel rims sunk almost to the fenders in the earth. The doors were missing and the interiors gutted. The hood of one stood upright; the other had none. Both were rusted beyond ever telling what color they had once been.

Engines probably torn out, too, Tilley mused as he crossed the road. Really a growing community, Pine Woods.

He glanced from the cars to the house and thought he saw a curtain—a torn curtain—shift slightly at one of the front windows. Well, he thought, they're bound not to get too many strangers passing through. Yet he wondered if the storekeeper had phoned ahead on his nonexistent telephone, if that was what had kept the man so long getting his change.

Tilley shrugged. So what if he had? Even if the man he was looking for actually did come from Pine Woods, the whole town couldn't be in on the crime. Besides, the case was still under wraps. Not a word had yet leaked out— even to Jack Hoyt. The only story that was out was that Carey Hunter, summer vacationer from New York, was missing and believed to be somewhere at sea in a dinghy.

He found himself suddenly very grateful for the good weather since the northeaster. "Just let it stay that way, for chrissake," he muttered, somewhere between a prayer and a curse, "just till we find her."

"Hi." The door opened and a mere slip of a girl, to Tilley's way of thinking, stood just inside it, smiling.

"Hi, yourself." He grinned back at her.

"You here to see my father?"

"Is he in?"

"No." Her expression grew more serious. "He's over to Mayor Farley's, in a meeting." She glanced across the road at Tilley's car. "You're not from around here."

"No. I'm not."

"Well, come on in. If you want to wait for him. I don't know when he'll be back. Big doings," she exaggerated the words, laughing aloud, "in little old Pine Woods. Want some coffee?"

"I'd love some." For an instant Tilley let himself feel the girl was an answer to a prayer. "What 'big doings'?" he asked casually.

"I don't know." She shrugged, and Tilley was stopped for a moment, confronted by a reflection of himself in the mannerism. "You'll have to ask my dad. He doesn't tell me anything. Says I'm too young to be trusted." She laughed, but there was a note of pain in the sound.

"Are you?"

"No. I'm eighteen." She faced him a little defiantly.

"Atta girl." He studied her face for a moment. "I'd be inclined to trust you if you were eight." Few people, Tilley knew, were better sources of information—reliable information—than rebellious teenagers.

The girl laughed again. "Not if you lived in Pine Woods, you wouldn't."

"Oh? Why not?"

"No reason. Come on in. I'll make you some coffee." She turned and led the way into the house. "I'm not very popular in Pine Woods, that's all," she finished, stepping lightly and quickly down the center hallway toward the rear of the house.

Tilley followed her, his curiosity piqued. She led him into the kitchen, where she rummaged around in a cabinet until she found a coffeepot and a can of coffee. Tilley was struck by the odd, unused look of the room. It was clean, to his surprise—spanking clean, in fact. He had the distinct impression the room had never been used for the preparation of food. As he watched the girl reading the side of the coffee can carefully, the impression grew stronger.

"Want me to make it?" he asked gently.

"Gee, yeah. Would you?" She looked up at him, blushing. "My dad always makes the coffee. And drinks it," she added quickly. "That's another thing I'm too young for."

"Not in my book." He looked down at her flushed face, set off prettily by soft, brown, straight hair that fell to her shoulders. Her hazel-green eyes were sparkling with excitement, making him think of Cinderella entering the ballroom. "Will you join me?" He took the coffeepot from her hand and gestured with it sweepingly. He was very curious to get a look inside it.

"No," she answered quickly. Then, "Yes. Why not?" more quickly.

She's lying to me, Tilley's senses told him. She isn't going to drink a drop. I'll bet on it.

Puzzled, he lifted the lid of the coffeepot and peered in. The pot had been used, but not very often. Well, maybe it was new. It didn't look new, however. It looked unused. Old, but unused. He turned on the water, rinsed the pot out several times, then filled it to the four-cup line. The coffee can, when he reached for it, had never been opened. He glanced up at her.

"Got an open can?" he asked innocently. "This one's new."

"No, no, that's okay." She sounded flustered. "Open it." She pointed to an old-model wall can opener, protruding from the side of the kitchen cabinet beside the window over the sink. "My dad probably finished the other can this morning. He drinks gallons of coffee."

Not out of this pot, he doesn't, Tilley thought. He wondered why the girl suddenly sounded so rattled. And why in the world she was lying about her father's coffee consumption. It made no sense, but he felt certain she was lying.

"By the way," he said, turning the handle of the can opener, "what's your name?"

"Patti. With an *i*. Patti Welles." Her face relaxed a little. "What's yours?"

"Paul. Paul Tilley. With an *e-y*," he teased her. "Patti with an *i*, short for Patricia?"

"No."

"Hmmm." He spooned the fragrant coffee into the basket of the percolator, feeling his mouth water. "Short for—short for—for Patience?" He clapped the lid on the pot.

"No. Here, we better use the hotplate. The stove's out, and it takes too long to get it going." She took the pot from him, set it on an old-fashioned, single-coil hotplate that rested on a small square of tin at the end of the kitchen counter, and plugged the cord into an outlet in the wall. "It'll be ready in no time. Have a seat."

Tilley wandered over to the old woodstove against the far wall.

"A real old-timer, huh?" He looked around at her. "Haven't seen one of these since I was a kid. Boy, sure brings back memories." He lifted one of the fire covers and peered in. The inside of the stove was scrubbed clean and empty—no kindling, no ashes, no sign of recent use.

"We don't use it in the summer," Patti said quickly, nervous and disconcerted again. "Why don't you sit down? I'll mind the coffee."

"I will. Thanks," Tilley said easily. He replaced the circle of cast iron over the hole in the top of the stove and eased himself down onto one of the wooden chairs at the table. To distract her, he took up the matter of her full name again. "Patti with an *i*. Short for . . . for what? I give up. Tell me."

"No." She turned her head away. "I hate my name. It's stupid. Don't ask, okay?"

"Okay." He watched her a few moments. "Why don't you come and sit down with me? Coffee takes quite a while to perk."

"Sure. Okay." She sat on the edge of the chair at the far end of the table from him. "Where you from?"

"Bangor," he answered.

"What're you doing up here?"

"Came to talk with your father."

"Why?"

"Well, seems we've got a missing New Yorker down South Bay way—"

"Oh, I heard about that on the radio," Patti interrupted him excitedly. "Carey Hunter, right? Is that the one?"

"That's the one."

"Gee. Are you a policeman or something?"

"Or something." Tilley grinned. "I'm a detective."

"Wow." She stared at him, eyes wide. "But what're you doing up here, then?"

"Just checking out a report. Seems four young people—about your age, in fact—were down in South Bay last week. Rode on the ferry with her out to one of the islands.

I'm hoping to talk to them and see if they noticed anything about her that might help us. That's all." He watched Patti Welles's face without looking at her.

"Oh."

Tilley noted that her face, so open and excited when he first arrived, now closed completely. Damn it, he thought, this kid knows something. He said nothing, waiting. He knew that if he waited long enough, she would speak, out of discomfort, to cover the silence between them.

It took much longer than he expected, but finally Patti said, "I don't know anything about that. Nobody from Pine Woods gets down that way much."

Still Tilley waited.

"I haven't heard anybody from here was down there."

And waited.

"If I had, I'd sure tell you." A pause. Then, "Honest I would."

He knew she was lying. He would have bet his life on it. He nodded at her, unsmiling, then abruptly flashed her a big smile.

"Well, probably a false report. We get hundreds of them in cases like this."

"Yeah. I bet. Everybody trying to be helpful, huh?"

"You got it, Patti." He paused, then asked, "How's our coffee doing?"

Tilley had three cups of coffee with Patti Welles. As he had suspected, she drank none at all. Occasionally she put the cup to her mouth, pretending—Tilley could tell the liquid never quite touched her lips—to sip at it. During this time he found out Patti loved classical music, played the piano—very well, in her own estimation—by ear, and had taught herself to read music; that she had begged her father to let her at least apply to the Boston Conservatory of Music and that her father had refused. He further learned she had then applied on her own, secretly, in defiance of him and been refused, to her bitter disappointment. This she blamed on her schooling in Pine Woods, remaining convinced that if she had grown up in any other town in America—where, in her mind, the schools offered a "decent education in music''—she would have made it. It was obvious she carried a great anger toward Pine Woods inside her.

Then she had tried to convince her father to allow her to apply to the University of Maine, in Orono. This, too, he had refused to permit her to do, being unwilling to let her live away from home. She was to begin attending Aroostook State Teachers College, in Presque Isle, in September as a day student. It would mean a daily commute of almost one hundred miles each way, and she was angry and frustrated about not being able to study what she loved. Yet, she emanated an unmistakable delight at the prospect of getting out of Pine Woods—highly understandable to Tilley after less than an hour there—meeting new people, and learning anything at all, even if it could not be her first choice.

"Of course," she summed up her situation thoughtfully, as if she were talking to herself, "I'll have to teach here after I graduate. I can't live anyplace else."

"Why not? People don't live at home all their lives anymore. Once you can earn your own living, you can go anyplace you want."

The girl looked up at him. Tilley caught a look of panic in her eyes.

"Oh, no. No, I couldn't do that. Uh," she hesitated, "uh, there's such a need here. I'd have to stay here—I mean, I'll owe it to everybody to teach here."

"*Owe* it? Owe what? Why?"

She didn't answer him directly. "I wouldn't feel right not teaching here. And it's okay. It'll be good. I can do some good here. It'll be fine to teach here. Really. It'll be great. I'm real happy about it, Mr. Tilley."

It was the first time she had called him by name.

"Paul." He smiled at her warmly, feeling rather sorry for her. "Friends call each other by their first names, Patti."

"I wish you were my friend." She blurted it out, tears springing to her eyes. She turned her face away from him.

"So do I." Tilley got up, came around the table, and

sat on its edge next to her. He put a hand on her shoulder. "And I will be, if you'll let me. What's the matter, Patti? What's troubling you?"

"Nothing. Nothing." She got up and moved away from him. "You want to make another pot of coffee? I'm just being silly. Skip it."

"I don't think you're silly."

She laughed. "Well, I do. I've already said too much. My father would have a fit if he found out I'd talked to you like this. You won't tell him? When you see him? You won't tell him, will you? Again a look of panic darkened her hazel-green eyes.

"Of course not. Why should I?" Tilley smiled gently at her. "This is strictly between you and me."

"Promise?"

"I promise, Patti."

After a moment she heaved a big sigh. "You want some more coffee, Paul?"

"No, thanks, Patti." He chuckled, though he was not feeling amused, and looked at his watch. He felt certain Patti had given away as much as she was going to about herself and Pine Woods for one day. He knew, too, it was not as little, or insignificant, as it seemed. He looked at his watch. "I'm about coffeed out, as they say. And I've got to get back to South Bay before six o'clock. Do you suppose I could interrupt your father's meeting to talk to him for a few minutes? Where is it being held?"

"At Mayor Farley's house, but . . ." Patti bit her lip.

"But?"

"Well, he'll be mad if I tell you where—oh, crock," she added abruptly. "Let him be mad. I don't care. Hers is the next house down, across the street. They're so stupid and secretive about everything here. It's important you talk to him, isn't it? I mean, that girl's missing and you want to find her before something happens to her, don't you." Her hazel-green eyes gazed at him with the trust and innocence of a small child.

"Very much. Very, very much, Patti." He stood up and

realized his bladder was at the bursting point. "Would you mind if I used your bathroom before I go?"

Yet again Tilley noted panic in Patti's eyes. She flushed. Tilley was puzzled, though he kept his face bland. He could smell that he was on to something, that he'd hit a raw nerve, but it made no sense to him. He waited for the girl to answer him.

"Uh, no. Sure. Why not? Everybody's gotta go, right, when they gotta go?"

Her attempt at humor was so inappropriate that Tilley's mind was making notes at top speed—notes to which he couldn't begin to guess at the conclusions.

"Well, it's that way." She pointed to the kitchen door. "Out back. It's a . . . privy."

One of his notes now was that it wasn't embarrassment that caused her to hesitate, but a need to search her mind for a forgotten—no, a little-used—word. He was more puzzled.

"We don't have a bathroom. Indoors."

She was lying. Tilley knew it in his bones. What he couldn't figure out was why she would deny it, not allow him to use it. What the hell could be so secret about the Welles bathroom? Well, he certainly wasn't going to get a look at it today. That much was plain.

"Thanks. Appreciate it." He walked to the kitchen door and turned back. "I enjoyed talking with you, Patti. And thanks for the coffee. Listen," he reached into his inside pocket, pulled out his notebook and pen, and wrote his name and telephone number on a blank page, "if you ever feel like talking—if you need somebody to just listen— give me a call. Collect. I'd like to hear from you. Okay?" He tore the page out and held it out to her.

After a brief hesitation, she crossed the room and took it from him.

"Sure. Thanks. Maybe I will." Her voice was light; her face and eyes were dark. "Who knows? Always helps to have a friend, right? Thanks. Don't hold your breath, though," she added, forcing a laugh. "I'm pretty busy."

"If you feel like it. Thanks for the coffee, Patti. Be seeing you, maybe."

"Maybe," he heard her say to his back as he left the house.

He found the privy as immaculately clean, and as obviously seldom used, as the kitchen had been. It confirmed his certainty there was indeed an indoor bathroom. As he crossed the yard back to the road, he toyed with the idea that Patti Welles was simply neurotic, the victim of some extraordinarily Victorian toilet-training. He didn't believe it for a minute. He was at the mayor's front door before he had time to come up with a better theory to pursue.

"Is Sheriff Welles here?" he asked of the youngster who opened the door. "I'd like to see him if he is. It's important."

"Yeah." The child eyed him suspiciously. "Who're you?"

"Lieutenant Paul Tilley, Bangor Police."

The eyes before him widened.

"It's very important I see Sheriff Welles."

After a moment, the youngster—Tilley realized he couldn't tell if the child was a boy or a girl—bawled at top volume, "Ma! Man here wants t' see Sheriff Welles! Ma? Wait a minute, I'll fetch 'er for ya." The child slammed the door in his face, and Tilley could hear pounding footsteps racing toward the rear of the house.

In a few minutes the door opened again, and a woman with a pleasant but careful face confronted him. Tilley was struck by the fact that she was small and slender, her body and face showing no signs of age, despite some gray in her dirty-blond hair. She was just about the same size as the storekeeper and Patti Welles. And she, too, had hazel-green eyes. So did the child behind her, peering out at him with an intense curiosity.

"I'm sorry to keep you waiting," she said politely. "Who is it you want to see? My son here"—she half turned and rumpled the youngster's light brown hair—"is too excited to be coherent.'' She smiled. ''We don't get many strangers up our way. Won't you come in, please.''

''I'm here to see Sheriff Welles, ma'am,'' Tilley said as he followed her into the front parlor of the house. ''I'm Lieutenant Tilley, Bangor Police. Are you Mayor Farley?''

''Yes, I am. Can I help you?''

''Possibly. I'd appreciate talking with both of you, if you can spare me a few minutes.'' He smiled ingratiatingly at the woman.

''Certainly. Davey, run ask Sheriff Welles to come in here, like a good boy, please. Go on,'' she urged her son when he didn't budge from her hip, ''go on.''

Reluctantly the little boy took a couple of steps backward, then stopped.

''C'n I come back?''

''No,'' his mother replied firmly. ''You can go outside and play.''

''Aw, gee whiz, Ma.'' Davey Farley did not move.

''You heard me, Davey.'' His mother fixed him with an authoritative eye.

''Aw, gee whiz,'' the boy repeated and dragged himself, shuffling, out of the room.

Tilley smiled at the mayor. ''I seem to be an object of great curiosity,'' he said pleasantly.

''Well, as I said, we get very few strangers here. Pine Woods is far off all the major roads.'' She smiled back at him. ''You do have to look for us to find us.''

''I'll vouch for that,'' Tilley concurred with a chuckle.

''Well, what can we do for you, Lieutenant Tilley?'' Mayor Farley asked him.

''If you don't mind, I'll wait till Sheriff Welles joins us. That way I won't have to repeat myself.''

''As you wish.''

Tilley made small talk with the woman until Sheriff Welles entered the room and she had introduced them. His mind noted that the sheriff, too, was small and slim and of indeterminate adult age.

Doesn't anybody get old in Pine Woods? he asked himself. Or do they all die young? Tilley never dismissed anything that came to his attention, but he put this oddity aside for the time being in order to get on with his business.

After establishing that they were aware of the sea and land search in the South Bay area for Carey Hunter, he told them of the report that four Pine Woods teenagers had been on the bay's ferry the previous Saturday evening with the missing young woman. He made no mention of the two bizarre homicides.

"So, of course, I'd like to talk with them. Just to get their impressions of Miss Hunter. It probably won't lead anywhere, but you never can tell. Kids are sharp—they notice things we adults often overlook. They just might be able to tell me something that would help, even if it was just that she seemed upset, or not upset, or distracted, or whatever. At any rate, we've got to run down every lead. I'm sure you both understand that."

"Yes, yes, of course, lieutenant," Mayor Farley replied warmly.

Tilley was certain he read a false note in her voice and listened carefully.

"But none of our youngsters has been out of town recently. Not since the Fourth of July picnic at Scraggly Lake, and that's just a hop, skip, and a jump from here." The mayor smiled at him apologetically. "We're not traveling folk up here, Lieutenant Tilley. We tend to stay put."

Tilley's intuition told him again that she was lying. "I see." He turned to the sheriff. "What about you, sheriff? You know of any of your kids who took a trip to the coast, with or without their parents' permission?"

"Can't say as I do," Sheriff Welles replied, his eyes wide with innocence.

Damn, Tilley noticed with a start, he's got hazel-green eyes, too. Everybody I've seen in this town has hazel-green eyes. And is small and slender, almost the same size. They all even look like each other. Must be one hell of a lot of inbreeding up here.

Ordinarily he would not have found that worth pondering, in a small, removed, mountain community that had little contact with the outside world. But the fact that every single person he'd spoken with—albeit only four, discounting the boy—had lied to him made Tilley especially aware of every little detail.

"I see. Well, I wonder if I could talk with some of your teenagers, then? You know kids, if some of them slipped away when they weren't supposed to—"

"There's no 'not supposed to' here, Lieutenant Tilley," Mayor Farley said offhandedly with a smile. "We don't keep our youngsters prisoners, I assure you."

If she hadn't voiced it, Tilley would not have considered the possibility. Now, thinking back on Patti Welles's story of her disappointed hopes for a college education, he began to wonder.

"But if you want to talk to a few of them, you'll find them all over at the high school." The mayor looked at her watch. "In fact, they'll be getting out for lunch soon."

Tilley caught an exchange of glances between the mayor and the sheriff. The Welles's over-clean kitchen and empty, polished woodstove and barely stained coffeepot raced through his mind. What the hell was wrong in this town? Something was, but what? And what did it have to do with the school lunch hour—and an unused coffeepot? He was baffled.

"That would be very helpful, Mayor Farley. I'd like to get this over with and get back to South Bay as soon as possible. Appreciate your help."

"Anything we can do to help you find that young woman," she replied, "we're more than glad to do. Creighton," she turned to Sheriff Welles, "could you take Lieutenant Tilley over to the high school? They'll be out in twenty minutes, so you've plenty of time to catch them before they all run home for lunch. Would it help if you addressed an entire class or two, lieutenant? Sheriff Welles here can ask Miss Noonan, the principal, to hold the bell."

"Yes, that would help. A lot. Save me considerable time as well. Thanks very much. How long," Tilley looked at his watch, "will it take to drive out there?" He had a hunch and prayed there was enough time to act on it.

"Not more than five minutes."

"Well, that's good." Tilley nodded his head and smiled what he hoped was a boyish smile. "Could I use your bathroom before we go?"

"Certainly, Lieutenant Tilley," Mayor Farley answered, without a trace of anything unusual in her voice. "It's upstairs, last door on your left down the hall."

"Thank you."

Tilley strode from the room back into the front hallway and took the stairs two at a time. He felt disappointed, but still mildly curious about the bathroom. When he entered it, he could detect nothing the least bit unusual about it. In fact, it was quite modern and normally used-looking, two towels lumped together on the rod under the window, one washcloth barely wrung out and slowly dripping onto the tile floor. Undoubtedly used by a small boy, he thought wryly. He poked around for about a minute, then flushed the toilet and hurried back downstairs. Well, maybe Patti Welles had been subjected to a Victorian toilet-training after all. Or was simply embarrassed that her home didn't have indoor facilities. Certainly there was nothing out of the way about the Farleys' bathroom.

"Sorry to delay you, sheriff. And thanks again, Mayor Farley. Oh, by the way, is there a pay phone at the school? I'm way overdue to check in with my chief."

"I'm afraid not, Lieutenant Tilley." The mayor smiled sweetly at him. "But you're welcome to stop back by here and use mine."

"Well, thank you very much. That's very nice of you. See you in a little while, then." The mayor was standing at the screen door of her house, looking after them, when Tilley turned back and asked, "By the way, school opens early up here, doesn't it? Thought it wasn't till after Labor Day. And today's Saturday anyway."

"This is summer school, Mr. Tilley, and today's a make-up day, on account of the storm," she said through the screening. She sounded pleased with herself, a trifle superior perhaps.

"Ah. Forgot all about that. Luckily, as I saw it back then, I never had to go that route myself. Thanks again."

Tilley strode out ahead of Sheriff Welles to his car. The sheriff directed him to the high school. It was set well back from the road and seemed innocuous enough, not quite as dilapidated as everything else in Pine Woods. It didn't, at least, look like it was about to fall over.

They entered the small brick building by way of double front doors, and Tilley followed Sheriff Welles down the hall, around the corner, and down another hall to a door marked PRINCIPAL. Welles pushed it open and went in. Tilley was right behind him. He was determined to see as much of everything in this town as he could.

"Miss Noonan about?" the sheriff asked a young woman busy typing in the outer office.

Tilley looked at her. Light brown hair, hazel-green eyes, small, slim body. Pretty, as well, but then, they all were, in an inexplicable way. Even the men. At any rate, that made five.

"Oh, yes, Mr. Welles, she's in her office. Did you want to see her?"

With something of a start, Tilley realized that all the Pine Woods inhabitants he had been speaking with sounded alike, as well as bearing an uncanny physical resemblance to each other. Not so much in their speech patterns—the storekeeper had spoken more idiomatically than the others. It was, he realized, that they all sounded like deep-voiced women. The men didn't have lower voices. In fact, as he thought back over the morning, Mayor Farley had had, if anything, a slightly deeper voice than Sheriff Welles. He also recalled now that the sheriff had barely spoken to him in her presence; had, in fact, spoken only once after their introduction, and that in answer to a direct question. And his directions to the high-school had been mono-syllabic.

"Please." The sheriff looked at his watch. "And quick, before the noon bell rings."

The secretary cast a quick glance Tilley's way, he

observed, then exchanged an even quicker glance with Sheriff Welles.

"Just let me check with her a moment." The young woman got up and hurried to a door behind her, knocked, and went in, closing the door behind her.

No, wait a minute. It wasn't quite that they all sounded like women. What they all sounded like was adolescent boys, kids with frogs in their throats—or, maybe, girls with husky, whiskey voices. Whichever, Tilley was aware he hadn't heard a man's voice since arriving in Pine Woods. Maybe some genetic thing, if they were as inbred as they looked? He didn't know, but it seemed unlikely to him. He made a mental note to ponder this on the drive back, and looked forward, with suspended credulity, to checking out the color of Miss Noonan's eyes and her height, weight, and body type—and doing the same with each of her students.

8

Carey wakened, wet and chilled, stiff and sore, and badly sunburned despite her summer's tan, to a second brilliantly sunny morning in the dinghy. The Atlantic stretched away and merged with the horizon all around her. Nowhere could she detect anything but swelling waves of blue-gray, no matter how she squinted against the light glancing off the water.

She was scared, but not as scared as she had been the morning before. That had been the worst time, with her mind still numb from identifying the hideous miniature mummy that had once been Margie Packer; her senses newly shocked by having discovered the similar remains of

Mrs. Rambeau; her body exhausted, her shoulders and arms rigid with muscle spasms, and her hands blistered and bleeding from hours of frantic rowing. But this had not been all; there had been sheer panic at the memory of the startlingly white, familiar face on the dock above her, the extended hand (the fingers of which she could still feel clutching at her hair). The murderer's hand—she was certain—now after her. Forever after her, because she'd seen his—or was it her?—face. Even adrift, alone, in what appeared to be the middle of the Atlantic Ocean, she had not felt safe from that incomprehensible killer. She had been paralyzed by terror which, like a centrifugal force, whirled her, helpless, outward from the very center of herself. She had not been able to conceive that it would ever abate.

And when it finally, by agonizingly slow degrees, did, there had been the sun, the merciless, unrelenting sun, coming at her from above and below and around. God, what a sun. Carey Hunter had had no conception of the ferocity of the sun on a summer sea.

She'd tried to row, pulling her sweater sleeves down over her bleeding hands, but her arms would scarcely move, and her shoulders screamed in protest. After a few feeble strokes, she'd realized the dinghy was lazily turning in a circle. Lifting the oars from the water, she saw the starboard oar had but half a blade, and the crack of breaking wood, under the dock the night before, echoed in her ears. Dimly it came to her that all the hours of desperate rowing in the dark had been futile. All she had done was to keep the little dinghy turning in circles while the outgoing tide carried it out of the bay, away from land.

It was at this moment that Carey had realized she was lost at sea. The oars had slipped from her hands. She had sat motionless, staring with unblinking eyes at the vastness of the water all around her. Then, slowly, thoughtlessly, she had collapsed over her own knees and allowed the enormity of it all to engulf her.

The sun, however, had shortly proved stronger than her sense of hopelessness. To escape it, she'd tried lying face down in the water sloshing in the bottom of the dinghy, but found she couldn't stay there more than a second or two. Terror at the prospect of the killer even then bearing down upon her had her on her knees almost before she was prone, searching the wide waters for a sign of an approaching boat. She wasn't going to allow him, or her, to catch her unawares, as she felt certain the killer had to have caught Margie. Margie was a fighter; Carey knew her friend would have put up a hell of a battle if she'd had even a moment's awareness of violent intent. Well, so could she—so would she, she had determined. And she'd see to it she had more than just a moment's warning. The killer wasn't going to get to sneak up on her unawares.

It had come to her that there must be other boats in the North Atlantic besides hers and the killer's. She could be rescued before the killer ever reached her, if she could make whoever was on board see her. She had reached under her sweater to tear off her white T-shirt and tie it to the end of one of the oars when she realized that any passing boat she might see could be the killer, searching for her. She wouldn't know until it was too near to escape from.

"Well, then, I'll just fight," she had said aloud, sounding to herself much braver than she felt.

It had been well into the morning, almost noon, before she'd noticed the sacks of groceries stowed under the stern thwart. The meat had already become sour-smelling, and she'd started to throw it overboard when she suddenly thought of sharks. Did they come this far north? She had no idea. Hadn't she read somewhere they could smell blood in the sea from some incredible number of miles away—like thirty or something? Or three hundred? No, that had to be impossible. Still, she did not feel up to another encounter with anything, certainly not a shark, so she had stuck the roast up in the bow, as far away from herself as possible. In another couple of hours, in such sunlight, it would really be fetid.

The loaf of whole-wheat bread she'd bought looked like it had turned back into dough inside its wrapper. The dinghy had shipped a lot of water during her frantic, all-night escape efforts. She had torn open the wrapper, squeezed the excess salt water out of it, and set it in a lump on the stern thwart to bake dry in the sun. The eggs had been fine, though their carton was about to disintegrate. She'd cracked two of them, one at a time, and eaten them raw out of their shells. To save the remaining ten, she had reworked the soggy bread into a lumpy wreath and carefully set the eggs in the center of it, pushing the sodden remains this way and that to cushion each egg and keep it from rolling into the next each time the dinghy rolled and pitched with the gentle swells.

She had had no way to open the large can of V-8 juice among her purchases, so she'd left it where it was. The gallon of milk in its plastic jug, however, had been perfect—and would stay so until it soured in the heat. She had drunk as much of it as she wanted, thinking it was unlikely to last out the day.

Then she had had an idea. She had pulled in the sternline, left trailing overboard since the night before, and tied it securely around the plastic handle. She had tightened the cap as hard as she could and set the container on its side on the stern thwart, well away from the bread and the eggs. It was square, but she had put a foot up beside it anyway, to be sure it didn't slide into the eggs.

She had watched it while she ate some salty, sea-soaked raw broccoli and a raw potato. When she'd finished, the milk still hadn't leaked, so she had carefully lowered it over the side into the water. It had drifted down and away until the line was taut, and she had felt enormously pleased with herself. Now that, she had told herself, was being self-sufficient. And smart. And, a survivor. She had felt much better about her situation—and herself.

She'd picked through the rest of her own and Mrs. Rambeau's groceries, rescuing what was rescuable and chucking what wasn't up in the bow on top of the putrifying meat. She had set whatever else could be dried on the forward thwart, as a protection for the eggs. Realizing she was feeling much stronger since eating—she couldn't re-

member when last she'd eaten anything, let alone a meal—
she had decided to row again.

It had been near-agony to use her hands and arms again,
but she'd tried to maneuver the dinghy until the sun would
be on her face, and found she couldn't. It seemed to be
directly overhead. She had let go of the oars and allowed
them to ride on their oarlocks rather than try to ship them.
She then had looked at her hands. The palms were covered
with broken blisters and oozing watery blood. There were
multiple splinters in them, a very large one protruding from
the tip of her right index finger. She managed to get the end
of it between her teeth and draw it out. The rest were too
deeply inbedded to go after without a needle, so she had
dangled her hands over the side of the dinghy in the sea,
remembering vaguely from somewhere that salt healed. It
also stung, she discovered, and after a short while she had
withdrawn them and tried to sleep, hunched over on the center
thwart. She couldn't. She had found herself constantly
bobbing up to peer in all directions for either land or
another boat.

Occasionally she had heard the sound of jet engines overhead, and less occasionally spotted the brief gleam of silver
light where the sun's rays struck some part of a transatlantic
jetliner. These moments had made her feel very small, very
lost, and close to hopelessness again. Who was ever going
to find her on the whole huge Atlantic Ocean like that? She
and the dinghy together were no more than a matchstick.

Then she had hunched over again and tried to sleep,
with her arms crossed on her knees, her head on her arms.
Inside of a few minutes, she had found herself popping up
again to have another look.

"It's boring," she had said to herself aloud, after an
hour or so, "being lost at sea."

When the sun had finally begun to cast a small shadow
of her, this way and that, in the rolling, pitching dinghy,
she again took hold of the oars. Her hands were no longer
just tender, now they were on fire, but she persisted.

"You can heal later," she had said to her hands over
and over again, wincing as she struggled with the heavy oars.

Figuring she had to come ashore on land somewhere if she kept the afternoon sun at her back, she had rowed slowly and unevenly, struggling against the starboard oar to keep on a course, throughout the afternoon. Sometimes she'd stopped to trail her hands in the water, sometimes to fight off attacks of sheer panic, and sometimes to cry a little. For herself, for Magie, for Mrs. Rambeau. Sometimes she had sat still just to rest her arms and shoulders. Once she had eaten another raw egg, half-baked by the scorching rays of the sun, and another time dragged in the container of milk and drunk until it was barely half-full. The rope had been so painful to her hands she had not let it out again, but tightened the cap and shoved the container under the stern thwart, on its side, to lie awash in the cold water in the bottom of the dinghy.

She hadn't the faintest idea if she'd gotten any closer to land than she had been when she started, but, painful as it was, rowing gave her the feeling of doing something. Not just sitting and waiting helplessly for somebody else to do something—there was nobody else, anyway; it never occurred to her anyone other than the killer might be searching for her. Or simply to die. She had seen enough of death in the past twenty-four hours to last her forever. She wanted desperately to live. So she had rowed, sporadically, until the last of the light faded out of the western sky.

She had eaten sun-baked eggs and salty raw vegetables and bread crumbs by starlight, and drunk more milk by moonlight. It was still cool and fresh, so she had rationed herself, thinking of the next day and—who knew?—the days after that.

The sea was even calmer Saturday than it had been on Friday. Munching on another raw potato, Carey felt grateful for that. If only some big ship—that wouldn't be the killer, she felt certain—would come over the horizon, surely they would see her. She could make them see her on a sea as calm and flat as this.

She finished the potato and dragged the milk container out from under the stern thwart, gingerly unscrewed the top, and sniffed it. It still smelled good. She permitted herself three swallows.

Working the oars was even more painful than it had been the day before. Her palms were now as raw as ground meat and, smooth and worn as they were, the handgrips of the oars were sheer torture. The skin on the back of her hands, as on her face and neck, was badly sunburned in spite of her summer tan. Merely opening her hands to grip the oars wrinkled the parched skin beyond bearing, and closing them around the oargrips was worse, stretching the skin till the backs of her hands felt as if they would split open and driving the splinters like hot needles deeper into her flesh. Tears flooded her eyes with every movement, spilled down her cheeks with each stroke.

To try to keep the blazing morning sun off her blistered face, Carey kept her head tucked down as she attempted to row, judging her direction by the position of the shadows her legs cast. When they began to creep starboard toward the gunnels—which was constantly, due to the broken starboard oar—she rested the port oar for a few strokes until they slipped back into the water sloshing about in the bottom of the boat. Her strokes were very shallow and lacked real force; her hands could bear scarcely that, no matter how her will chided her. She was forced to seek relief from the pain by taking long pauses between each stroke. She knew she was getting nowhere, but kept repeating, Every little bit helps, even if it doesn't seem to. Without believing it.

As the sun rose steadily over the endless ocean she could feel her face burning anew on top of the previous day's burn. She felt helpless, victimized. There was nothing she could do but keep taking shallow, short strokes with the oars. She dared not let herself cry; the skin on her face was too taut and flaming with pain. The salty tears that persisted in dripping down her cheeks burned like molten lead and made her anxious about the body moisture she was losing. She couldn't stop them, however. She had never suffered anything as agonizing as the pain in her hands.

She worried, too, about the dwindling milk in the container. It was, by midmorning, more than half gone, and she had seen nothing—not land, not another boat, not even a gull. She now limited herself to one swallow at a time, but dimly sensed she was losing track of how much time had gone by since she had last reached for the container.

The water in the dinghy was rising. Of that she was certain. Yesterday it had been sloshing over her topsiders; today it was at her anklebones. It terrified her, and all she could think to do was to keep rowing, telling herself, Don't think about it. Just don't think about it. Consequently, she thought about it almost without ceasing.

What she hardly thought about now was the face she had seen. She did still suffer brief attacks of panic over reaching shore or hailing a boat, being rescued, thinking she was safe, and then suddenly being assaulted and mummified. These images would come to her as, head raised into the blinding sun, she searched the horizon for a sign of something—someone—other than herself. Screams then rose in her throat, and she would peer frenziedly, trying to spot something to row away from, not toward. At these times she forgot her splitting hands and searing face, even the agony of gripping the oars. She forgot to watch for the shadows of her legs and rowed frenetically for a time, until the pain in her hands fought its way into her consciousness. Then she would drop the oars with a cry and plunge her hands over the side into the sea. And cry again aloud at the fieriness of the salt water on her raw flesh.

She no longer connected the specter of her terror with Margie or her former landlady. When she thought of them, they flitted through her mind as still alive, reasons to keep rowing and save herself. Wait till I tell Margie about this number, her mind would say to her. Or, God, poor Mrs. Rambeau must be worried sick about her dinghy and the groceries.

Before the sun was directly overhead, Carey was spent. She could not make herself hold the oars, let alone try to take another stroke. She let the oars ride aimlessly in the water, and lay across the center thwart with her hands trailing over the starboard side. She was too exhausted to feel hungry, and while thirst plagued her, she was anxious to conserve every drop of the milk that was left and so determined not to take another swallow till sunset. The pain in her hands was excruciating. Her arms, shoulders, and back ached unbearably. Her face, neck, and ears felt as if they had been roasted over an open fire. Even her back, under her navy sweater, felt sunburned, as did her thighs under the denim of her jeans. She realized that the longer she lay inert, the less motivation she had ever to move again, to try any longer to save herself. But she found herself overwhelmed by an enervating ennui. It was simply easier to lie there than it was to try to do what was obviously hopeless. Maybe later. Yes, she'd row again in a little while. But not right now.

She dozed fitfully through the early afternoon, slipping in and out of good dreams and bad. Dreams of her mother, her childhood, and Margie turned into nightmares filled with monsters and madmen. Pastel illusions permeated with sweet security fragmented into garish, blood-red, blind alleys of pursuit down which she was chased interminably, never caught, never able to escape. Family picnics in the summer fields of her girlhood, were invaded by demons and death's-heads. A Christmas tree, sparkling with colored lights and the antique glass ornaments so lovingly treasured by her mother year after year, lured her to come nearer, take a closer look; she found it hung with grimacing death masks and leering gargoyles. Under it, as under the bridge in the fairy tale once read to her, lurked hundreds, maybe thousands, of tiny, dried-up trolls desperate to devour her. Her thirteenth-birthday party moldered before her eyes into a desolate graveyard where shifting, sliding earth fell away from beneath her feet, exposing coffins, the lids of which sprang open to reveal dessicated Margie Packer after dessicated Margie Packer rising, specterlike, to dance grotesquely in the air, until infinity was crowded with gyrating, shrunken apparitions screaming choked little screams that burned her ears like dry ice.

Carey was trapped for more than a minute between sleeping and waking before she could realize the pathetic, dehydrated sounds were issuing from her own throat. Her ears were searing, one from the sun and the other from bearing the weight of her head upon her right shoulder, humped agonizingly over the starboard gunnel. Painfully, she righted herself on the center thwart. With hands numbed by the cold water, she dragged the milk container out from under the stern thwart and all but drained it before she fully realized, again, where she was.

"Oh, God," she moaned, snatching the container from her mouth and replacing the cap. She hugged it to her body. She was trembling with cold despite the blazing sun of the afternoon. "Oh, God, help me. Help me. Don't let me die. Please, God, please."

Demoralized by her dreams, she made no further attempt to row. She sat hunched over the almost empty milk container, her feet and ankles in the rising, ice-cold water swashing about in the bottom of the dinghy, shivering with chills from her severe sunburn. When God did not answer her, she cried for her mother. She felt utterly abandoned. At one and the same time she could not believe she was going to die like this, out here alone on an endless ocean, frightened and in severe pain, and remained convinced that this could not be happening to her, Carey Hunter, who led such a quiet, uneventful life, and so would all be over any moment.

The sun was sliding into an otherwise empty sea before hunger roused her and drove her to eat two potatoes and an apple, and, with gritted teeth, take hold of the oars again. She rowed, one stroke at a time, throughout most of the night, indifferent to her direction as long as the dinghy was going somewhere, anywhere, not by drift only.

9

"What?" Tilley glared at Orris Perkins, the officer stationed on the ferry dock.

"That's what he says, sir," Perkins replied anxiously. "He's got the boys with him—in his car right there." The youthful officer gestured over his shoulder at the lot where Polly McCannister's car stood smack in the middle, braked in midturn at a hasty angle. McCannister, sweating importantly, paced up and down beside it. "And they're three upset kids if I ever saw upset kids. Scared out of their wits."

"Crowley," Tilley barked, swinging around, "get the unit ready to follow me in two minutes. We may have another one."

He strode off the dock toward the local sheriff. He left Sgt. Crowley, the seven officers who had comprised the second-day search unit, and Archie English in sudden, shocked silence behind him.

"Who's at the scene?" he challenged McCannister as he approached him.

"Well, uh, ain't been there yet, Lieutenant Tilley," the sheriff sputtered. "Came—"

"Jesus Christ!"

"—straight here t' you 'fore anythin' else," McCannister finished defensively.

Tilley yanked open the rear door of the sheriff's car and grabbed the nearest boy by the arm.

"You," he ordered. "You come with me." He hurried the teenager out of the car and snapped at McCannister, "You follow us with the others."

"You know where it happened?" he demanded of the boy as he rushed him across the lot toward his own car, which Crowley, anticipating him, was already starting up. "Can you direct us there?"

"Yes, sir," the boy mumbled. "I think so."

"Don't think. Do it."

Tilley shoved the boy onto the back seat of his car. "Follow us," he shouted to the two squad cars, and leaped into the front seat. "Step on it, Jim," he ordered, and swung around to confront the frightened teenager. "Left or right out of here?" he snapped.

"Left, sir."

"Hit it, Jim."

"You want the siren, Paul?"

"Yeah, what the hell. We're never going to keep this quiet now."

Crowley hit the switch and, siren screaming, the car roared out of Archie's parking lot, followed by the two squad cars and Sheriff McCannister's old blue sedan.

"Look smart, kid," Tilley commanded the teenager as they raced south on the county road. "Don't take your eyes off the road. About how many miles?"

"Gee, I don't know, sir," the boy mumbled after a silence. "I didn't think—"

"Well, you came this way afterward, didn't you?"

"Yes, sir, but . . ." He hesitated a moment. "Well, there's a real snake in the road, a real bad curve, right after where we pulled off. . . ."

"Coming or going?"

"Huh?"

"What'll we pass first? The curve, or the place you boys pulled off with the girl?"

"The curve, sir."

"Sing out the second you spot it."

The four cars roared down the narrow coast road in the gathering dusk. About three miles below Archie's ferry, they passed an old pickup truck which had pulled off the other side of the road, as much as it could with the dense pine woods on either side. Tilley noted that two T-shirted, long-haired young men, one hanging out the driver's window and the other apparently standing and peering over the roof of the cab, watched them go by. About two miles farther on, the road swung sharply to the left and dropped steeply down toward the bay.

"This the curve?" he barked at the boy in the back seat.

"I think so. Yeah. I'm pretty sure . . ."

"Slow down, Jim. Keep your eyes peeled, son, and tell us where you pulled off. Kill that damn horn, will you, Jim?"

In the sudden silence Tilley's ears picked up the tail ends of the squeals made by the other three cars' being suddenly braked. He kept silent and waited for the teenager to speak.

Crowley had swung back around to the right, pulled out of the curve, and gone about three hundred yards when the boy said in a breathless voice, "There. There where some pines're missing. That's where we pulled off."

Before Tilley had to speak, Crowley pulled over onto the shoulder, tooted the horn twice, and stopped the car.

"Run back and collar those other two kids out of McCannister's car, Jim. I'll start on ahead with—what's your name, son?"

"Perley, sir. Perley Worcester."

"With Perley. Catch up with us fast."

Tilley had dragged Perley Worcester off the rear seat and plunged into the woods with him before Crowley reached the first of the squad cars. Once in the woods, the boy became not only confused but obviously too frightened to be of any real help. Tilley's assurances that nothing could possibly happen to him with nine—he did not include McCannister in his count, nor even think to—policeman around him did nothing to the calm the sixteen-year-old's terror. The other two boys, Mitch Schoopee and Willy Guptill, were equally frightened and equally useless. It was, to Tilley's mild surprise, Polly McCannister who stumbled upon Pennell Schencks's body about an hour later, with an "Oh, m' God," first gasped, then shouted in a horrified voice, followed by a panic-stricken "Over here!"

"Those kids are falling asleep out there, Paul." Jim Crowley closed Tilley's office door quietly behind him. "And their parents are fit to be tied. They want to take them home so they can get some sleep. Can't we release them?"

"Uh-uh." Tilley shook his head, then looked up and handed Crowley the copy of the lab report he'd been studying.

"It's two in the morning . . ."

"What do you make of this, Jim?"

Crowley sighed, took the report, and scanned it quickly. Then he looked up.

"Either we've got two brilliant homicidal maniacs loose—"

"We don't." Tilley took the report back and glanced at it again. "It's the same kind of nipple damage in all three deaths. It's got to be the same killer."

"But it was a young girl who killed the Sartsport kid—Schencks. That doesn't—"

"I know, Jim, I know," Tilley said wearily. "I'd have sworn it was a man, too. But, if those other kids from Sartsport are telling the truth—which they aren't, of course. But if they're telling even *part* of the truth . . ." His voice trailed off and his eyes looked inward for a few minutes. "Send the Schoopee kid in here—what's his name? Mitchell. Mitch. He's a smart-ass; he'll break first. There's no character behind that big mouth of his."

"Can I let the others go?"

"No."

"It's not gonna look good when Jack Hoyt and the rest of the hounds interview these families . . ."

"To hell with how it looks. We still don't have the killer, Crowley. For chrissake, man, worry about who's next, not the goddamn news reports."

Mitch Schoopee, with his corn-colored hair tousled and

his china-blue eyes bleary from sleeplessness, slouched his way into Tilley's office a couple of minutes later and slumped onto the chair in front of Tilley's desk.

"Close the door, will you, Mitch," Tilley said pleasantly, disliking the boy more than ever. "This is just between you and me."

"Yeah. Sure." Mitch turned, extended a leg, and kicked the door closed with a sharp slam. "You 'n' me 'n' the whole fuckin' police department."

Tilley smiled at him, his eyes narrow and observant. He would have liked to have stepped out from behind his desk and given the young punk a good belt in the mouth.

"I understand how you feel, Mitch. Police work's a tedious business, for the most part."

"Yeah. While my friend's still dead. 'N' all you can do is keep callin' us in here and askin' us the same fuckin' questions over 'n' over again."

"Bear with us, Mitch, bear with us. You fellas haven't given us much to go on yet."

"We gave ya a fuckin' description. Why aren't ya out lookin' for that freak?"

"Let's just go over your story one more time, Mitch, shall we? You guys were driving up from Sartsport, and—?" Tilley waited.

"Shit," the teenager uttered with disgust. Then, mimicking Tilley's cool, he continued, with heavy sarcasm, "And we saw this girl hitchhikin' so we stopped 'n' picked her up. You know the rest, man," he finished hostilely.

"Tell it to me again, Mitch," Tilley said patiently.

"Whyn't ya just go fuck off, man."

"Tell it to me again, Mitch." Tilley's voice had changed markedly. Still pleasant on the surface, it brooked no more defiance.

After a brief, angry stare, Mitch blew out a big breath and said, "We rode a couple miles, kiddin' around with her, havin' fun, 'n' then she asked how'd we like to do it in the woods with her—all of us, one right after the other. Well, we was out to have some fun, make out if we could, so we all said, 'Sure, you're on, baby.' Penney pulled the car off the road—you know where,'' he interjected contemptuously, '' 'n' we followed her into—''

"You followed her?"

"Yeah, we followed her, man. She led the way. 'N' then she stopped, in that clearin' where . . . in that clearin', you know, 'n' took off her clothes—''

"What clothes?"

"*Her* clothes, man, *her* clothes. Whaddaya—''

"What did she take off first?" Tilley asked quietly.

"Shit, I told ya ten times already. I'm tired. I wanna go home.''

"What did she take off first, Mitch? Tell me again.''

"She took off her top. Her blouse. You know.''

"Blouse?" Tilley looked down at his desk, pretending to read his notes. "Perley Worcester said she was wearing a T-shirt.''

"All right. So it was a T-shirt. So what? I wasn't lookin' at her T-shirt.''

He did not snicker, which Tilley marked carefully. His type of kid would have, at this point, had things happened the way the boys were insisting they had. Tilley knew Mitch Schoopee was trying to outthink him.

"What color was it?" Tilley asked.

"Was what?" Now the teenager smirked broadly.

Tilley had expected the smirk, and it confirmed his certainty that Mitch was lying. Badly.

"Whatever you were looking at," he said blandly.

"What're ya doin'—gettin' off on it? That how ya get your kicks? That why you're makin' me tell it t' ya one more time?"

"We both know better than that, Schoopee." Tilley's voice was very soft and low—and lethal. "In fact, we both know you're lying through your teeth." He yawned. "Well, I've got all the time in the world to sit here and listen to fairy tales. As you said, it's *your* friend lying dead over in Eastern's lab, not mine. So take your time." He observed, from beneath deliberately drooping eyelids, that Mitch was suddenly upset, red-faced and sweating. "We're ready to start a search anytime you've told me the true story. Suit yourself.'' He leaned back in his chair and swung his feet up onto his desk, clasping his hands behind his head.

"I am tellin' ya the truth, ya son-of-a-bitch cop,'' Mitch spit at him.

Tilley yawned again and recrossed his legs comfortably on his desk.

"I am!'' the boy yelled, gripping the sides of the seat of his chair. For an instant he glared at Tilley, his eyes hot with anger and guilt. Then he leaped to his feet. '' 'N' I don't have t' sit here 'n' take shit from no lousy cop. I know my rights. You can't keep me here''—he strode to the door—''so fuck off, man, just fuck off.''

Tilley let him go, reaching for his phone, a thoughtful, small smile on his face. "Bring Mitch Schoopee back in here,'' he said quietly to the officer at the desk. "By force, if necessary.''

The teenager's shouts of protest could be heard throughout the station as two uniformed officers and Jim Crowley marched him back into Tilley's office moments later. Tilley motioned to the men to force the boy down onto the chair again and hold him there until he quieted. Tilley noticed that the officers looked confused and Crowley worried, and he kept a bland, almost bored expression on his face and waited for his opening.

It came, after some time, when Mitch, tiring, growled, "I'm gonna sue all you bastards, ya fuckin' son-of-a-bitches, just you wait. You can't treat me like this less'n you got a charge against me 'n'—''

"I'm thinking of accessory to murder,'' Tilley mused quietly, enjoying the stunned faces of his men. "Aiding and abetting a killer, covering up her identity, refusing to cooperate in an investigation of a homicide.'' He paused, noting with satisfaction that Mitch had fallen silent, his mouth hanging open. "And I'll add resisting arrest if you pull another stunt like this.''

The teenager stared at him in disbelief. Then he sputtered, "You're bluffin', man!''

Tilley swung his feet off his desk and stood up. His attitude was all business now. "Okay, book him.''

"You can't do this t' me—" Mitch looked stricken.

"I'm doing it," Tilley snapped. He caught Crowley's eye. "Book him on—"

"Wait a minute!" the boy begged, gripping the seat of his chair with all his strength and refusing to be lifted off it. "I didn't— You can't— Look, wait a minute, will ya? Pen Schencks was a friend of mine. I didn't have nothin' t' do with . . . what happened to him, honest. I just—"

"You were just there and watched, right?" Tilley snapped. "And then you just ran away and left him to be killed, right? There are more ways to be an accessory than there are to kill someone, Schoopee. Get him off my chair and book the little punk," he ordered his men, letting all the contempt he felt for Mitchell Schoopee color his voice.

"No," the teenager howled, "wait! All right, all right, we lied about what happened. We were scared. I'm sorry. Please. I'll tell ya what really happened. . . ." His voice broke and he began to cry.

"Tell it, Schoopee," Tilley ordered coldly. "Now. Fast." He remained standing, staring icily at the teenager. "Don't waste any more of my time."

"All right, all right," the boy sniveled, wiping his nose on his sleeve and not looking up. "We were just lookin' t' have some fun—pick up some girls, you know. Just t' fool around. We were just cruisin' the coast, hopin' there'd be some girls with nothin' t' do, you know, go have a few beers with us, blow a joint maybe, fool around some. Then we saw this girl—she was crazy, man, crazy. She was runnin' across the road 'n' tearin' at her T-shirt or somethin', whatever, you know, we could see her—Well, Pen, he pulled the car off the road where she ran into the woods, 'n' we kind of looked at each 'n' Pen said, 'That one's a crazy, guys,' 'n' we kinda looked at each other 'n' then Willy—yeah, Willy—he said, 'Nobody'll believe her anyway,' so . . .''

"I'll be corroborating who exactly said what exactly with your friends," Tilley put in dryly.

Mitch glanced up at him, fear and guilt on his face.

Tilley met his glance with ice-blue eyes.

"Okay, okay, I said it," the boy said helplessly after a moment. "I put them up to it. Well, what fuckin' difference would it make to a crazy?" he protested. "She wouldn't know the—"

"Don't use that word again in my office," Tilley said contemptuously.

"I didn't think it would make any difference to her," Mitch went on, stumbling over his words. "I didn't mean t' hurt her—just have a little fun with her. She didn't seem like it would matter to her—like she'd even half know—"

"I'm not interested in your dirty little excuses, Schoopee. Just tell me what happened."

"So, anyway, we . . . chased her into the woods 'n' caught her in that clearin'. She hollered for us t' stay away from her."

"What exactly did she say?" Tilley interrupted him, suddenly very alert.

"Huh? I don't know, man, I don't remember. She—she threatened us, said she'd hurt us or kill us or somethin'. We didn't believe her, figured it was just her way of tryin' t' scare us off her. Pen said as he was the driver 'n' it was his car that got us there, he should go first. So me 'n' Perley 'n' Willy, we wrestled her down 'n' held her for him 'n' Pen, he . . ." The boy stopped. He was crying again.

"You've all told me she was wearing jeans, Schoopee," Tilley said dryly. "What did you do about her jeans?"

"Huh?" The teenager did not look up.

"Did you leave her jeans on her?"

"Uh, well, no, not exactly."

"What exactly did you do with her jeans?"

Mitch's face, neck, ears, and throat were scarlet. "Well, me 'n' Pen, we kinda pulled 'em down a little—enough," he added unwillingly, "so he could, you know. That was weird," he said abruptly in a puzzled voice.

"What was weird?" Tilley was on him.

"She didn't have no hair down there." Mitch looked up at Tilley. "Honest she didn't. Didn't look shaved, neither. All kinda smooth 'n' little, like a . . . like a little kid. Ya couldn't even see no . . ."

"No what?"

"No, uh," the boy's face positively flamed, "no—nothin'. No . . ." He struggled to find a word acceptable to the men surrounding him and finally managed to get out: "crack." He paused, as if waiting to be reprimanded, then went on again. "No, uh, lips or anythin', neither."

"Didn't that give you pause?" Tilley asked, keeping all expression of his feelings out of his voice.

'Whaddaya mean?''

"Didn't that make you stop and reconsider? Think that maybe she was just a little girl and you'd hurt her?"

There was a silence, then Mitch shook his head slightly. "No. We just figured—"

"We?"

"I just figured Pen was in for a real tight squeeze," Mitch muttered, and fell silent.

"Then what happened, Schoopee?" Tilley demanded. "Come on, you're not in the clear yet, so keep talking."

"Ah, shi— darn, man, you know the rest. Don't make me—"

"Talk, Schoopee. And it better be the truth this time."

"That part is true," the boy protested, visibly upset at having to go over it again. "Pen, he got down, well, he unzipped his fly 'n' . . . took himself out 'n' got down 'n' . . . 'n' . . . it was like the second he lay on her he screamed"—Mitch began to cry brokenly, and his next words were barely audible through his sobs—" 'n' screamed an' then he stopped. The screamin' stopped like right in the middle of itself, 'n' he began to blow up, like a, a, a balloon or somethin'. He just started to swell up. 'N' we didn't know what to do. We were scared, we were really scared—"

"You didn't try to help him?"

"We were scared."

"Did you try to help him?"

"No."

"He was your friend, and you didn't try to help him?"

"No."

"What did you do?"

"We ran for help."

"You ran away?"

"We ran for help."

"You left your friend there, blowing up like balloon, as you put it, and the only thought in your mind was to get help?"

Mitch was silent.

"Was getting help the only thought in your mind, Schoopee?"

"I don't know."

"What don't you know?"

"I was scared. I just wanted t' get away."

"And when did you finally decide to go for help?"

"After. After a while. In the car."

"Who was driving?"

After a brief silence, the teenager muttered, "Nobody. We weren't drivin'."

"Why not?"

"Pen had the car keys."

"Tell me exactly what you three did after you ran away. Did you go back to the road? How far did you run?"

"Yeah, we got back on the road. We even got in the car 'n' tried to drive off before we remembered Pen had the keys. Then we got out . . ." He stopped, then after a time went on again: "We didn't get out right away. We were too scared. We locked the doors and rolled up the windows for a while 'n' just sat there."

When he did not continue, Tilley asked, "How long did you all 'just sit there'?"

"I don't know," Mitch mumbled, "I don't know. Awhile."

"Is that when you put your heads together and made up the story about the girl inviting you to have sexual relations with her in the woods?"

After a very long silence the teenager faltered. "Yeah. I guess so."

"And it wasn't until after you all got your story straight amongst you that *you* suddenly remembered you knew how to jump the starter?"

Mitch Schoopee nodded without looking up.

"All right." Tilley ran a hand through his hair. "Let's

back up a bit. Back to when your friend Pen started to 'blow up,' as you put it. What happened to the girl?''

Mitch looked up at him. ''Whaddaya mean?''

''Did she 'blow up' too?''

The boy looked confused, then shook his head. ''No, I don't think so.''

''Well, what did she do?''

The teenager just stared at him.

''You must have noticed something about her, Mitchell,'' Tilley insisted.

''No, no, I didn't. I was too busy watchin' Pen. She just . . . disappeared.''

''What do you mean, 'disappeared'?''

''Well, he was swellin' all up 'n' she—she was like shrinkin' or somethin', maybe. I don't know, mister. I wasn't thinkin' about her—I was worryin' about my friend.''

When Tilley was finished with Mitchell Schoopee, he had the other two boys brought in one at a time. They added little to Mitch's story, mostly confirming it with their own versions, except to make it clear to Tilley that Mitch had played a far more instrumental role in instigating the attempted gang rape than he himself had admitted and had not kept his ''figurings'' about what kind of sexual experience Pennell Schencks was going to have quietly inside his head. Tilley had assumed that already.

What he didn't learn anything further about, to his annoyance, was the girl's genitalia. In fact, neither Perley Worcester nor Wilbur Guptill could even confirm Mitch's puzzling description, beyond that fact that the girl had no pubic hair. The other two boys had been too busy struggling to hold her down to do more than glance at her body. When he knew he had gotten all there was to get from the three of them, Tilley had them brought in, together, to his office.

''Now I've got something to say to you three,'' he began, in a voice filled with contempt, as he perched on the edge of his desk, ''and I advise you to listen very carefully. I can't book you right now for assault and attempted rape, so I have to let you go. But when I catch that girl—and I will, believe that if you believe anything—if she's willing to press charges, I'll have the three of you up on every related count I can come up with. And it may be to her advantage to do just that, so don't let yourselves get too smug about the trouble you think she's in. She's got good cause to plead self-defense. She may even get off. Remember that. And you three aren't going to get any sympathy from me—or anybody else, except maybe yourselves. You're lousy little punks, all of you, and I'll see that you're prosecuted to the letter of the law when the time comes. Bet on it.''

He studied them for a long minute, despising them. "You know what you three are? You're the lowest form of life on this planet. And if I hear even a whisper about any one of you being in any trouble at all, I'll have the three of you back here behind bars so fast it'll make your heads spin.

"Now get this straight. You don't leave Sartsport until I say so. Which won't be until after the trial in this case. If you do, you'll be arrested on sight. That clear?'' He waited for three hung heads to nod. "Good. The other thing you don't do is talk to anybody about this—not your friends, not your families, not each other. And damn well not any newspeople. You keep your mouths shut until after the trial or it'll go very badly for you, I assure you. Have I made myself clear?'' Again he waited for three lowered heads to bob in agreement.

"Now get out of here. I can't stand the sight of you.''

10

Tilley was dozing in his chair, his hand limp over the telephone on his desk, when Crowley knocked on his office door and pushed it open at 8:00 A.M.

"You look like hell, Paul," Crowley grinned at him commiseratingly. "Like I feel."

Tilley grunted and straightened up, yawning and stretching.

"You been here all night?"

"What night?" Tilley growled, rubbing his stubbly chin. "It was already after four when I finally got those little bastards out of here. Still no sightings by the Coast Guard—or those local search parties. Not that I have much faith in the latter," he added glumly. He looked at his watch. "Guess there's no point in calling them again this soon. You get any sleep?"

"Couple hours. I'm okay."

"You better be. We've got a long drive ahead of us."

"Where to?"

"Pine Woods."

"Pine Woods?"

"Ayup, as they say Down East." Tilley did not elaborate, but went on to what was pressing on his mind. "What do you make of it, Jim?"

"Last night? Those kids' story?"

"Yeah. Start with that. What do you think?"

"Not a helluva lot, Paul." Crowley frowned. "A girl, who may or may not have had deformed genitals, who murders by . . ." He paused, searching his mind for some way to conceptualize something that was inconceivable.

176

". . . by—Christ, Paul, what the hell do you call it? Internal drowning? It's much more than that. Cellular flooding of the victim? Through the breasts, the nipples? That's impossible . . ."

"But it's what's happened. At least in one of the deaths."

" 'Deaths'?"

"What do you think?"

"I think it's obvious now we're dealing with cold-blooded murder."

"Maybe. Maybe not." Tilley thought a moment. "What if it—if the deaths, that is—weren't intentional?"

"I don't get you, Paul."

"What if—just what if—they were accidental?"

"Huh?"

"All three of those little punks said the girl screamed at them to stay away from her, said she would hurt them, maybe kill them, if they got too close."

"Yeah?" Crowley prompted him when Tilley fell thoughtful again.

"Well, they interpreted what she said as a threat—an empty threat. What if it wasn't a threat at all? What if she meant it as a warning?"

Crowley shook his head. "Wait a minute, Paul. We've got a girl about to get gang-raped. Maybe beat up, maybe killed, for all she knows. At any rate, she's being chased by four strapping boys, any one of whom would make at least three of her, from their description of her."

"Remember that, Jim," Tilley interjected. " 'Small, skinny little thing.' Keep that in mind."

"All right. But all the more, you think she's going to warn her attackers? Against what, for God's sake?"

"Against what did happen."

Crowley stared at his boss blankly.

"You're saying she knew? Knew she was going to flood somebody to death through the nipples?"

"Not saying it. Speculating on it. What do you think?"

"Well," Crowley sighed, shaking his head, "the whole thing's so impossible, why not that as well?"

"Exactly. The whole thing is impossible. What happened

to Marjory Packer and Margaret Rambeau is impossible. Drained to death through the nipples. What happened to Pennell Schencks is just as impossible—flooded to death through the nipples till his tissues ruptured.''

"It's impossible," Crowley muttered, despite what he'd read in the lab reports. "It's gotta be impossible."

"Sure it does. But it's happened. So it isn't as impossible as we think. Thought," Tilley corrected himself. "Now, before this Schencks kid bought it, we didn't have a clue as to how the dehydration had taken place in the other two victims, other than the nipple involvement. Now we have good reason to believe that whatever physical process took place to drain—or flood—a victim actually took place when there was body contact. One pair of nipples against another pair of nipples, or some part of the chest. Huh?''

"Back to the impossible again. It can't happen, Paul."

"It did. Now recall that we may be dealing with a girl who has something abnormal about her genitals—or even no genitals at all."

"Paul—" Crowley started to protest.

"Jim, open up. Let's go the whole way, be as ridiculous as our imaginations are capable of. Then we'll work backward to the possible, or at least the barely conceivable. If there is such a girl, and she can and did drain two bodies and flood a third just by making chest contact with them— well, what would you say she must be?''

"Be? Some kind of freak," Crowley said uneasily.

"What kind of freak? A human freak?''

"How the hell would I know? What else could she be but human, and a freak of some kind?''

"Okay. So we have the possibility of a birth-defected human. We label her a freak so we can feel safer. How did she grow to be fifteen, sixteen, twelve, whatever, with nobody hearing about her? If your wife gave birth to a child like that, wouldn't you have seen a doctor? Specialists? Had the defect corrected in some way? Wouldn't it be written up somewhere, in some medical journal or computer bank by now?''

"You've already had it checked out?''

"It's being checked out. So far, what's come in has all been negative. Just for argument's sake, let's say, when all the reports are in, still negative. No such child on record. Then what are we dealing with?"

"You want me to say alien? Extra-terrestrial?"

"I don't *want* anything. Except to know what you can imagine if you unlock a little."

"Okay. We've got an alien loose on the coast."

"Maybe. Maybe not. Somehow, I don't think so. Just can't buy the visitor-from-outer-space trip. Probably seen too many movies on the subject."

"Then what do you think we have, Paul?" Crowley frowned at him.

"Christ, I wish I knew." Tilley yawned and stood up. "Frankly, I was hoping you could tell me. Let's get out of town before the church traffic builds up. We can stop for breakfast above Howland. You get the car, I'll go get us some coffee. Cream?"

"Milk, Paul," Crowley said patiently. "Lots of milk. Very light."

"Right. I remember now," Tilley said absently. He grabbed his jacket off the back of his chair and strode past Crowley out of his office.

Jim Crowley shook his head and tramped out after him.

When Tilley climbed wearily into the car, he not only had two containers of coffee but copies of the Maine *Sunday Telegram* and Boston *Herald* as well.

"Anything?" Crowley asked anxiously, shifting into gear.

"Not yet." Tilley let the papers drop from under his arm onto the seat between them and set the coffee containers on the dashboard. "But wait. It'll be on WABI news tonight. And then we're going to have a circus on our hands."

"What makes you so sure?"

"Jack Hoyt isn't hanging around this morning."

"Oh, God," Crowley sighed. "Sorry, Paul."

"So'm I."

Both men knew that when Jack Hoyt stopped hanging around a case, it meant only one thing. He had a story. They drove in silence. Tilley tore a little triangular hole out of the lid of each container, and they sipped at the hot coffee—Crowley's had cream, not milk in it, but it was light—and stared at the Interstate ahead.

A few miles north of the Alton-Argyle exit, Crowley ventured an opener. "What do you make of the case, Paul? Seriously, I mean."

"I make it a mess." Tilley closed his eyes. "That's costing me a lot of sleep. Swing off on eleven at Medway, Jim. Takes us a bit out of the way, but there's a nice little place to eat the other side of Grindstone. Wake me up when we get there." He drained the last of his coffee and set the empty container back on the dashboard.

He was snoring little more than a minute later.

When they left the restaurant, Tilley took the driver's seat.

"I wake up after I eat," he grinned at his assistant. "You fall asleep. So sleep. You haven't got that long. Paved road ends at Shin Pond."

"Oh, God," Crowley groaned despairingly and stretched out as best he could.

Tilley smiled at him parentally, watching him, out of the corner of his eye, trying to find a comfortable position. Crowley stood a full six foot two and wasn't made for cars—at least, not the size cars policemen could afford.

At 9:30 on a Sunday morning, the secondary road was almost empty. He longed to get some speed out of his car, but did not dare. He still hadn't had the carburetor replaced, and the engine was letting him know it. He kept the speedometer at a conservative 45 and let his mind wander through the details of the case, picking up this one, bypassing that, toying with another, trying to fit first this one and that one together, like pieces of a puzzle, then another and yet another. Nothing much seemed to fit.

He tried another tack, separating the pieces of the case instead of attempting to put them together. Suppose he had two—or even three—killers, deliberate or accidental. One of the only two concrete tie-ins, after all, was the nipple damage. Somehow, then, the two or three killers could be—seemed likely to be—related to each other in some way. The other connection was that all three of the deaths had occurred within a few miles of each other, or on near South Bay. It could be coincidence, but Tilley had learned years ago that coincidence was much too important to be left to chance. If there was more than one killer, he felt certain they shared some connection among themselves.

Only one had been seen; of only that one did he have a description. A young girl, small, perhaps even skinny as the Guptill kid had described her, probably in her early or mid-teens, with light brown hair, wearing a T-shirt and faded jeans, "shrinkin' or somethin' " while the Schencks boy was swelling up. He roundly cursed the Sartsport toughs for not having noticed the color of her eyes. What did this all fit with, if anything?

First, it fit with his own impressions of the people in Pine Woods he had encountered the day before. They had all been smallish, slender, and surprisingly young-looking. And each one of them—including the summer students he had addressed in three of the classrooms and their teachers and Principal Lori Noonan—had had dirty-blond to light brown hair and hazel-green eyes. Damn. If only the boys had looked at that girl's eyes. Not that he was surprised they hadn't; he had yet to meet a bully—he grimaced, feeling he had understated the teenagers' intentions rather patly—a bully who spent much time looking his victim directly in the eye. They were all cowards underneath the sadism.

Disliking even the passing thought of the Sartsport boys, he let his mind move on. The description they had each given certainly matched up with what he himself had seen in Pine Woods. And then there was the description Archie English had given him—when Tilley had learned enough to ask—of the four teenagers on the ferry a week ago, even to the T-shirts and faded jeans. Archie, who went about his work exhibiting an utter lack of curios-

ity or interest in anyone he encountered, had observed a
startling amount of detail. Including four pairs of hazel-
green eyes.

Tilley sat forward with a sudden jolt. Four strange
teenagers. Three hideous and bizarre deaths. All in South
Bay, within the space of less than a week. Great God,
where was that fourth teenager? Was he headed in the
wrong direction? Should he turn the car around and
race back to South Bay? Where would he look if he
did? His only hope of getting hold of something firm
enough to go on lay in Pine Woods, of that he was
certain. Sweet Jesus, there was going to be another killing.
He could feel it in his bones. He knew he was helpless
to prevent it.

I can't live anyplace else. Patti Welles's wistful statement came back to him, chilling him to the bone. *My
father won't let me live away from home.* She had said that
too, earlier in their conversation. One other remark of the
local sheriff's daughter shouted at him inside his head:
They're so stupid and secretive about everything here. On
its own, that represented, to Tilley no revelation about an
isolated, inbred rural community. But placed side by side
with everything else in this unnatural case, it took on new
and sinister meaning. Secretive about what? And why?
What was it that Pine Woods had to keep hidden? He
couldn't even begin to guess, but he was determined to
find out.

They were coming into the little town of Patten. The car
left it behind almost upon entering it, and Tilley turned left
onto Route 159. Less than thirty miles to go. Also less
than an hour, even given the unpaved roads after Shin
Pond, in which to devise ways to unearth whatever it was
Pine Woods was determined to keep hidden from the rest of
the world.

He glanced over at his partner. Crowley was sound
asleep, in spite of his cramped position. Tilley had wanted
him that way, so he himself could think. He had also wanted
to say as little as possible about Pine Woods, in order to get

uncolored impressions from Crowley. He no longer had time for that luxury. He took a hand off the wheel, reached over, and shook him hard.

"Wake up, Jim. Wake up. I need you."

11

Dr. Adrian Widdows halted his pacing on the front porch of Mayor Ada Farley's house and squinted down at Patti Welles, who was standing at the end of the walk, near the road.

"Any sign of them yet, Patti?" he called.

"Nope." Patti turned and walked toward him. "You ought to sit down and rest, Adrian. You've been pacing like that all morning. It might be hours yet before they get back."

"I should have gone with them," Dr. Widdows said emphatically, a hint of anger coloring his voice. "Ada shouldn't have insisted I stay behind."

"But you won't be ready to une again until Wednesday," Patti replied, frowning. "We just uned last night."

"Chris Dunphy is beyond uning by now," Widdows snapped.

"Well, but he wasn't yesterday. Maybe—"

"Maybe," Dr. Widdows snorted and resuming his pacing. "A very slim maybe, I assure you. Damn it, I simply can't understand why they allowed themselves to get separated. They were all old enough to know better. There's no excuse for that. None. It's unforgivable."

"I think that's cruel, Adrian," Patti said angrily, tears springing to her eyes. "Naida and Harlie and Roe are dead. And Chris could be dying right now, for all we know!"

"We all may be dying," the doctor replied bitterly. "Dying because of the disobedience and stupidity of four children. You don't understand what it means, Patti. You're too young."

"I'm eighteen." Patti glared at him. "And sick and tired of being talked down to as if I were still eight."

Dr. Widdows stopped pacing again and gazed at her. "All right, then. Do you understand what men will do to us if they find out about us? What we are? Do you understand that they'll kill us—all of us—one way or another?"

"How do you know that?" Patti challenged him. "How can you know that, when they still don't even know we exist?"

"History. Human history, that is."

"But they've never known about us. There's no history to make such a judgment by, Adrian."

"There's thousands of years of it. Man has always killed what he didn't understand. And a great deal he thought he did as well," he added ironically. "He'll never let us survive. We threaten him where he's the most vulnerable. In his sexuality. My God," he exploded abruptly and began to pace again, "he'd find a hundred—a thousand—ways of getting rid of us. All perfectly legal and thoroughly defensible—in his own mind. I shudder to think about it. This is the worst thing that could possibly have happened for us. We're centuries away from being sufficiently strong in number to announce ourselves. We don't stand a chance."

"I don't believe they'll all want to destroy us," Patti said with sudden, intensity. "Maybe some of them, but not all. That Lieutenant Tilley—he wouldn't. I know it. There must be others like him among them."

"Of course there are," Dr. Widdows railed excitedly, "but they're never the ones with the power. Read your history, Patti. Dear God! We're not human—they won't lose even a night's sleep over disposing of us."

"Is that really true, Adrian?" Patti frowned, her voice

serious and bewildered. "Or do we just say that to differentiate ourselves from them? I mean—"

"Look it up in your dictionary," Dr. Widdows interrupted curtly. " 'Human: of, relating to, or characteristic of man.' Apes bear more resemblance to them than we do." He gave a short, unpleasant laugh. "Small wonder, since it's the apes they descended from."

"But that's what I mean, Adrian. Humans are what we descended from."

"No!" Dr. Widdows turned on her fiercely. "We did not descend from them."

"But—"

"We transfigured out of man—well, woman, actually." His voice softened and he smiled a little. "Or were transfigured, if you take a more theological point of view. God created man—humans—out of clay. That is, God transformed clay into a man. I say 'transformed,' because that means a major change in the nature, form, and function of something—which is certainly what happened to the clay. Do you follow me?"

Patti nodded.

"All right. Then the next thing God did was to take a rib from the man and transmute that into a woman. Why do I say 'transmute'? Because that implies transforming something into a higher thing, and a woman is certainly a higher thing than a man."

"Why?" Patti interrupted him to ask.

Dr. Widdows eyed her, a curious expression on his face. "I could give you a hundred reasons," he answered at last, "why we believe that to be so. But no matter. Let me simply state the most obvious: because she bears the next generation and nourishes it with her own substance, after the birth as well as before. That alone evinces a higher, more complex ongoing purpose than the mere desposition of necessary genetic materials, albeit essential to humans for a beginning. Does that satisfy your question?"

"Yes, I guess so," Patti replied. His scrutinizing stare made her uneasy.

"Very well, then. The next step in evolution, or divine

creation, if you prefer, was us. Scientifically you could term us—or at least Aretta McVicar, our founder—a mutation. But that's a limited, material way of looking at it. A human way. My personal view of it, simply put, is that God observed Its human beings for thousands of years and decided the model had to be improved.''

"You sound like you're talking about cars, Adrian." Patti grinned a little.

"Do I?" Dr. Widdows smiled back at her. "Maybe it's a good analogy. God knows we share humans' fascination with the automobile." He chuckled. "Anyway, if there ever was to be peace on earth, good will toward"—he hesitated a moment, then threw up his hands—"people, beings, God realized some vitally important changes had to be made. And so Aretta McVicar was transfigured out of a human egg—a change that exalted and glorified a previous, and flawed, creation. Just like redesigning an automobile model to get rid of the bugs," he added. "That's what transfiguration is—an exalting, glorifying change. And it didn't take thousands of years of phylogeny to bring it about it, either." Dr. Widdows' face assumed an expression of intense pride. "It happened in one generation, with one gestation. We here in Pine Woods are a God-given miracle." His face poured sweat; his hazel-green eyes blazed with zealotry. "*We* shall inherit the earth. That is our God-appointed destiny."

Patti unconsciously stepped back from him. He made her think of the evangelist preachers she sometimes watched on TV. She thought how strange it was that, just hours before, they had lain together in anastomosis, exchanging not only all their body fluids, but thoughts, memories, dreams, hopes, emotions and experiences as well, in a state beyond rapture. And now she felt real fear of him. She prayed her fear would not show in her face.

"Adrian, there's something I never have understood," she began hesitantly.

"Oh? What's that?" Dr. Widdows pulled a crisp white handkerchief from his pocket and dabbed at his face.

"Well, we have to une," she used the Pine Woods

colloquialism for their act of intercommunicative exchange, "every three or four days or we'll die. So how could we have been founded by Aretta McVicar? Alone, I mean? Mustn't there have been someone else? Or how did she stay alive until she'd budded and had at least her bud to une with?"

Dr. Widdows nodded. "Good question. We've all asked it. Truth is, Patti, we don't know the answer for sure. My theory is—and it's only a theory—Aretta had a twin. Or a special dispensation from God. But my scientific training makes me lean to a twin."

"A twin?" It was not the first time Patti had heard the word, but the concept was unclear to her. Her people never produced more than one bud at a time.

"Her mother gave birth to two babies, Aretta and another. It happens in humans."

"Oh."

"I tend to think that was the case with Aretta. But we've no record of it. Even my great-grandmother, who knew Aretta, said she never heard her mention a sibling. Of course," he added, "things get lost in oral histories. And that's all we have of our beginnings, of the first few generations in Pine Woods. So if there was another besides Aretta, we'll never know what happened to her. Pity Aretta never talked about her early life. All her stories began with the day she stood on this spot, right where this house stands, and knew this was where she was to establish God's supreme creation."

Patti saw that Dr. Widdows' eyes were beginning to burn with a frenzied inner light again. She nodded quickly, then took a few steps to the edge of the porch and looked down the road.

"There's still no sign of them, Adrian," she said carefully. "But I'm sure they'll be back soon. They have to be. Hovey is with them, and it'll be time for church in a couple of hours. Is the meeting right after the service?"

"Yes. That way everybody will be there, including the children." Adrian came and stood beside her and looked down the road. "Even if they do find Chris—dead or alive—and bring him back, it's time every one of us understood the grave danger we're now in. And what to do about it. There are going to be some important changes here as a result of all this,'' he concluded, his voice ominous.

"Like what?" Patti was anxious. She knew she was considered a rebel by the town's elders.

"You'll find out," Dr. Widdows said in a bland voice. "Ada will detail them at the meeting."

They remained silent for some time, staring down the empty road. Patti's anxiety abated slowly as she considered what the Town Council's changes might be. She felt certain everyone except adults with business outside Pine Woods—like the Pulks, who took their produce into Houlton a few times every week—would be restricted to town. And there would probably be a curfew. Maybe even a watch on the road a few miles below the general store.

These things had happened before, however, and didn't rank as important changes. She was burning with curiosity to know what those important changes would be, but knew the doctor would be annoyed if she asked again. She decided to try to find out something else that had puzzled her greatly the last few days.

"Adrian, can I ask you something else?"

"What is it, Patti?" He turned and looked at her.

"Well, how is it Roe and Naida and Harlie were able to une with humans?"

"They weren't. That's why they're dead."

"But, well, I mean something happened. Harlie and Naida were all—bloated, blown up huge. I saw them when Creighton took their bodies over to Dal's to be cremated. He said I should come along and see what trying to mix with humans resulted in."

Dr. Widdows grunted disapprovingly.

"And Roe I couldn't even recognize. He was all shrunken and shriveled and dried up—he didn't even look real."

"So what is it you want to know, Patti?"

"Well, something must have happened between them and the humans, mustn't it? Some kind of uning? I mean, it kind of looked to me like they joined, but the uning only took place in one direction. Is that what happened?''

"I suppose you could look at it that way. I really can't answer you, Patti. There was no time for me to do autopsies; the risk was too great. And I only saw one of the humans, the one Roe was found with. I scarcely had time even to glance at it, let alone examine it. Some degree of rudimentary inosculation does seem to have occurred, but certainly not uning. Don't ever call that uning.''

"But I thought we couldn't join with humans at all.''

"So did we all. Believe me, it's as big a surprise to everyone else as it is to you.'' Dr. Widdows ran a hand through his dirty-blond hair. "Obviously it wasn't something we'd ever intended to try to find out. Nothing like this has ever happened before. All I can tell you is, it's apparent now the potential for some kind of primitive—oh, call it a pre-uning state, is there in humans. But it's not to be. It can only result in death. To both parties. Always remember that. The less contact we have with them, the better.''

"Why were they different, Adrian?'' Patti asked. "Why was Roe all dried out and shrunken, and Naida and Harlie blown up and bloated?'' She shuddered slightly at the memory. "Why didn't the same thing happen to all of them?''

"Well, you're certainly full of questions today, aren't you.'' Dr. Widdows reached out a hand and rumpled her hair. "Questions I don't have the answers to. My best guess is it has something to do with the gender of the humans. The one that killed Roe was a male. I didn't have to look twice to see that,'' he interposed in a voice dark with bitterness. "The other two, the one who killed Harlie and the one who killed Naida, apparently were females, although I can't be sure. I wasn't there. But Ada and Creighton and the others who found them said they thought they were females because of the size of the breasts. And that one on the island where they found Harlie was wearing a dress.'' He sighed deeply. "I'm afraid we'll never know the answer to your question, Patti.''

Something else now occurred to Patti. "About the night they found Harlie—wasn't it Real Tweedie and Jerral and Meda Pulk and Alvah Rook who found her?" When Dr. Widdows nodded, she hurried on. "Well, what's going to be done about that Carey Hunter person they're all searching for down there? Real said she saw him—shined a flashlight right in his face and then bashed him with it before he could get hold of her. If she's found, what's going to happen to her?"

"What do mean?" Dr. Widdows voice was quiet and careful.

Patti didn't notice. She plunged on. "Well, I mean what are you all going to do about her? The Town Council?"

"What do you think we should do about her, Patti?" His voice was even more careful and deliberate now.

"Come on, Adrian, I don't know. I haven't even thought about it until just now. It just came to me that she could identify Real, if they ever find her and if she's alive. I just suddenly wondered what you and Ada and Creighton and the rest of the Council planned on doing about her if she's found alive."

Dr. Widdows gave her sidewise glance, then looked back down the road. "Why, nothing, I don't imagine. What could we do?" he said offhandedly—a touch too offhandedly, it seemed to Patti. "Anyway, I doubt it's going to be an issue. That's a very big ocean out there, and she's in a very small boat. And every day that goes by lessens her chances of being found. It's unfortunate," he turned and smiled, with just a touch of sympathy saddening his lips, "but I don't think Carey Hunter is going to live to be a threat to us."

"But what if she does live? If she is found? What's going to happen to us if she identifies Real?" Patti persisted.

"She'll never identify Real," Dr. Widdows answered after a momentary pause, his voice bland as water. "One way or the other."

12

"Hey, there! Need some help?"

Carey woke slowly, groggily, and tried to sit up on the center thwart. Every muscle in her body screamed with pain. Her sunburned skin warned her it was about to split open here and there. After raising herself a few inches above the oars prodding her uncomfortably in the armpits, she turned her head gingerly against the alarm of her flaming neck and squinted into the early-morning sun.

"Mother of God!" a voice said pityingly.

Carey could make out only a dark form surrounded by a dazzling aura of light. Bewildered and barely awake, she asked simply, "Am I dead, then?"

"Hell, no," the voice reassured her, "you're not even close. Hand me your line."

An arm swept up against the light, gesturing toward the bow of the dinghy. Carey watched it, stupified for a moment.

"Your line," the voice repeated. "Can you hand me your line."

Slowly, wincing with each new movement, Carey freed herself from the oars and inched her legs around, over the center thwart. She hunkered to the forward thwart and eased herself onto it sideways, then inched her legs over it as well. As she leaned down, the odor that struck her nostrils made her gag.

"What in God's name you carrying?" The voice above her asked. "Pee-yewie."

"Sharks," Carey answered after a moment's thought.

"Sharks?"

"I didn't know . . ." Carey mumbled, her voice trailing off. She couldn't remember anymore what it was she didn't know.

"Well, hand me the line and then chuck that stuff overboard whatever it is," the voice ordered her, puzzled and amused at once. "You smell like a garbage scow."

Carey attempted to pick up the line, but her raw hands refused to close in a grip. After a few moments of trying to force them, she half straightened and held her hands up in front of her. She heard a long whistle of surprise.

"I can't," was all she could say.

"Okay, hold on half a minute."

Carey closed her eyes against the blinding sunlight and listened to the sounds of heavy boots thudding and rope scraping on wood. Shortly the voice said, "Heads up, now," and she raised her head obediently. A moment later something clunked against the bottom of the dinghy. She opened her eyes and glanced down. A small anchor lay in the bottom of the dinghy.

"That'll hold her in water this calm," the voice announced. "Now, I'm coming aboard. Behind you. Sit tight."

Carey did as she was told. Seconds later she heard boots strike the bottom of the dinghy, and felt the little rowboat dip deeply and take several rolls. Almost immediately she heard the oars being shipped.

"Now," the voice spoke again, "can you move back on the center thwart? I'll help you. Sorry if it hurts some."

Strong hands gripped her firmly under the arms, and she felt herself being half lifted, half dragged, backward over the forward thwart. She cried out, and heard the voice apologize, "I'm sorry, I'm sorry, girl. Damn." Then she found herself once again seated on the center thwart.

"Coming around you. Just sit tight. I won't turn her over, I promise. Lean to port—to your left—as I come by."

The dinghy rolled sharply and shipped some water over the starboard gunnel as the man stepped over the center thwart on her right, his legs brushing closely against her.

He dropped quickly onto the forward thwart and rocked from one side to the other, against the roll of the dinghy, until it rode on an even keel again.

Carey could now see a man, or the back of a man. As he hunched over the garbage in the bow, commenting wryly on the stench, she made out what appeared to be three layers of colored sweaters, black on top, a ragged band of beige beneath that, and finally an edge of bluish-gray. As he leaned forward, a strip of white skin appeared, separating blue-gray wool from heavy, wide-wale brown corduroy belted with a broad band of cracked black leather.

"Great God," she heard him mutter as sodden packages of stinking food were flung over the side of the dinghy.

He straightened up on the thwart, and Carey was aware of arms moving rapidly. She noticed untrimmed salt-and-pepper curls crawling thickly all over the back of his deeply tanned neck. Then he stood up, seeming very tall against the bright sun, and hurled something over the rail of his trawler. A second later, there was heavy thud.

"Okay," the man said, dropping to the thwart again and swinging his legs over it to face her, "now let's see those hands."

Carey held them out hesitantly.

"I won't touch them. Don't be afraid." He leaned forward and peered at them. "Jesus Christ," he breathed. "How long you been rowing?"

Carey tried to remember. "I left Thursday night, I think," she mumbled, trying not to move her burned, split lips.

"Good Lord."

"What day is this?" she managed to get out.

"It's Sunday morning." He looked up. "You been two days—and three nights—on open sea in a dinghy?"

He was looking directly at her. Carey gazed back at him, about to nod. Slowly her mind registered the color of the eyes into which she was staring. They were hazel-green.

For a moment she sat stupified and continued to stare at them. Then she snatched up the anchor he had dropped aboard, leaped to her feet, and swung it over her shoulder screaming, "Don't come near me!"

"What the hell—look out there!" the man shouted, throwing his weight to port.

He was too late. The dinghy dipped sharply to starboard and rolled over even as he was shouting and trying to counterbalance her frenzied movements. Carey flew backward into the ice-cold North Atlantic, carried as much by the weight of the deceptively small anchor as by the roll of the little boat.

The anchor plunged straight downward, taking Carey with it as if she were no more than a lure on a fishhook. Stunned by the icy water, her mind gave no direction to let go. She was too terrified of the hazel-green eyes, in any case, to part with her only weapon against them. She clung to it, clutching the stock, blocked from feeling the pain in her injured hands by panic and shock. Even when she began gulping great mouthfuls of frigid salt water, choking and gagging in a frantic attempt to draw breath, her hands remained rigid, clenched around the stock of the anchor.

Then everything inside her head went as black as the water around her.

"Where the hell is everybody?" Crowley looked at his watch. "Think they're in church?"

"I don't know. Let's go see." Tilley started back down the steps of the locked general store. "Watch that missing step there."

"Where is the church, Paul?" Crowley asked as he followed Tilley to the car. "I didn't see one on the way in."

"Neither did I. Didn't see one as far out as the high school last time up, either. But if it isn't on the way in, it must be out past the high school somewhere." He started the car.

He drove slowly on out of the town center, crawling past Sheriff Welles's dilapidated house. He allowed the car to roll almost to a stop and peered, frowning, at each of the front windows.

"I don't suppose they could have come back while we were at the store," he mused.

"We were here not five minutes ago," Crowley offered.

"Yeah." Tilley depressed the accelerator a little farther with his foot. "You're right. We'll try them again on the way back, if we haven't found anybody." He looked to his right. "Look for a sign of life at the mayor's over there as we go by. Somebody could have come back on foot in that five minutes."

"Still looks all locked up, Paul," Crowley noted as they inched by the mayor's somewhat more presentable home.

"Damn," Tilley muttered, and stepped on the gas a little. "All right, Jim, look for a steeple. Or anything that might serve as a church. Probably can't afford a steeple in this place."

Tilley drove at twenty miles per hour out of the tiny, run-down town. Near the high school he slowed the car and again peered out at the building.

"See any sign of life, Jim?"

"Nope. Not a thing."

"Well, let's give it a try, anyway." Tilley pulled the car off the road and parked it. "What the hell."

Pine Woods High School was as deserted as the rest of the little town. Tilley and Crowley returned to the car and resumed their search for the church. They had driven less than three miles north of the school when the dirt road ended. A forest of dense pines met the end of the rutted road like a towering wall.

"Damn." Tilley craned his neck around, estimating the open space around the car. "Think I have room enough to turn the car around?"

"Only on a dime, Paul." Crowley was also studying the impenetrable pine trees that hemmed them in on three sides. "Better back up for a ways. There's a driveway about five hundred yards back down the road."

Tilley swore and shifted the gears into reverse. He backed the car as fast as he dared, past the drive Crowley had referred to. Then he shifted the gears again and turned into it.

"We're going to try every one of them until we find the damn church—or somebody who can tell us where everybody else is today," he grumbled.

The driveway bore straight through the forest, barely wide enough for Tilley's '78 Chevy. Pine boughs scraped the sides of the car, and Tilley swore each time, fretting about the paint. After half a mile the woods suddenly opened into perhaps a three-acre clearing. Directly ahead of them was a one-story wooden structure which Tilley judged, from its two sets of large double doors, to be a garage. To the left of it was an ancient trailer. Beyond that, littering the uncultivated acreage, was what could have passed for an automobile graveyard. Old hulks and battered wrecks lay about as if dropped from the sky. The trailer was almost as badly rusted as the abandoned cars.

"Jesus," Crowley uttered as he climbed out of Tilley's car and stretched. "Not exactly the little cottage you'd dream of hurrying home to each night, is it?"

Tilley grunted in disgust and looked around. "Well, let's try the trailer first." He walked over to it, climbed the three cinder-block steps to the door, and knocked loudly. "Anybody home?" he hollered.

When no one answered or came to the door, he tried it. It was locked. He knocked again for a few minutes, with no result. He stepped back down the cinder blocks and viewed the mobile home. Faded, soiled curtains were drawn at every window.

Without a word, he marched over to the garage. Both sets of doors were padlocked. He went around to the side, followed by Crowley. There was no window. In the back of the structure, which, again, had no window, he found a large crack where one of the boards had lost a sizable chunk. He peered in.

"Looks empty," he commented. "Take a look. See if you can see anything."

Crowley bent down and peered into the building. "Nothing," he agreed, straightening up. "Empty."

Tilley grunted again and walked away, around the back of the trailer. He found the rear windows curtained like the

front ones. A few yards behind the trailer was a small
vegetable plot.

"Well, at least they eat something," he muttered, thinking of Patti Welles in her unused kitchen.

He walked around the garden, studying it. Tomatoes
were rotting on their stems, string beans and peas shriveling on the vine. Carrots thrust up through the untended
soil, begging to be gathered and eaten before they began to
rot. The back half of the little plot was given entirely to
potatoes. None appeared to have been harvested. Tilley
frowned. The look of the garden made no sense. Whoever
lived in the seedy-looking trailer obviously didn't have the
money to plant vegetables, and then not pick and eat them.

"Paul?"

He looked up in the direction of Crowley's voice.

"Paul, I swear to God this is a Baker Electric." He
sounded excited and disbelieving at once.

Tilley crossed the backyard to where Jim Crowley was
peering into a windowless, rusted hulk.

"Paul, look at this!" Crowley exclaimed. "It *is* a Baker
Electric! Look at that body—it's wood. Jesus, the last one
of these was made in 1916. 1916. This must be worth a
fortune today. If anybody'd fix it up. These cost over two
thousand by 1910. Why would anybody let it just sit here
and rust away? I can't believe it. They used to upholster
the interiors in red velvet. This was a real luxury car in its
day. What the hell is it doing up here in the woods?"

Tilley stared at the car. He did not share his sergeant's
passion for antique cars. "What the hell is this whole
damn town doing up here in the woods?" he muttered. It
was not a question to which he expected an easy answer.

Some of the homes they examined on their way back
into Pine Woods's center were set within view of the road;
some were even deeper in the woods than the first trailer.
Some were one- or two-story frame houses; many were old
trailers. Most had vegetable gardens of one size or another;
only a few appeared tended and harvested. All of the
homes were badly run-down and locked tight. Paul Tilley
was frustrated—and furious.

"Damn it to hell, I've got to call in and see if they've found that girl," he finally exploded back at Mayor Farley's house again, giving the front door a resounding blow with the heel of his clenched fist.

"Carey Hunter."

Tilley glared at Crowley. He preferred to categorize Carey Hunter as merely "that girl"; it kept her distant from, and as unknown as possible to, himself.

"Where've they hidden their church?" Crowley went on, frowning. "You don't suppose they don't have one?"

"Nothing would surprise me in Pine Woods," Tilley growled. "Come on. We've got to keep looking till we find somebody."

As they approached the car, Tilley snapped his fingers. "Wait a minute. There's something I want to check out." He looked up at the second-story windows of Sheriff Welles's house. Curtains were drawn at each of them, as on the first floor. "Come on, Jim. This is probably the only chance I'll have to do this. Hurry."

He sprinted across the yard and around the house with Crowley at his heels. At the back of the house he stopped and looked up. Just as he'd hoped, there was a small window set in the second story at which the curtain was not drawn. More than he could have hoped for, it was directly above the roofing that sheltered the back stoop.

"Jesus, what a break. Give me a leg up there, Jim." He hurried to one of the posts supporting the little roof as he spoke. "Dimes to dollars says that's the bathroom window."

The roof was not high. Crowley could grab the edge of it easily with his hand.

Crowley squatted down, and Tilley climbed to a crouch on his sergeant's shoulders, gripping the post with his hands. Using the post to pull himself up, Crowley eventually got to a standing position.

"Damn," he huffed. "You weigh a hell of a lot more on top of me than you ever did beside me."

"By gory, don't it get you," Tilley replied in his best imitation of the Down East dialect.

"Any second now, if you don't get off me," Crowley groaned.

Tilley crawled onto the short roof and peered into the uncovered window.

"By God, it is the bathroom," he exulted. He glanced around the fair-sized room. "And by God again, I was right. I was right, Jim."

"Right about what?" Crowley asked, squinting up at him and rubbing his left shoulder gingerly with his right hand.

"There's no toilet. A tub, sink, old Victorian cabinet of some kind—even a table and chair. But no damn toilet." He let himself slide down to the edge of the roof. "I knew it. I knew it. Well, hallelujah."

He took hold of the edge of the roof and eased himself over it, turning his body as he did so. There was the sound of fabric ripping as he dropped his weight. He hung by his hands for a second, then dropped to the ground.

"You tore your sleeve," Crowley commented, gesturing toward his right arm.

Tilley pulled the sleeve around, glanced at the right-angle tear just below the elbow, then released it, and brushed himself off.

"It was worth it, Jim. Come on, let's check out the rest of the town. Sooner or later we'll find somebody home, or somewhere. The whole damn town can't have pulled up stakes and moved away overnight."

"Do you seriously believe these people don't ever go to the bathroom?" Crowley asked him as they hurried back to the car.

"I do now, Jim."

"Because one house doesn't have a toilet? I seem to have noticed a privy out back there."

"I know. I used it yesterday. But I'd bet my life no one else ever has."

"The whole thing is crazy. You're crazy, Paul. Every life form on earth has to excrete waste materials—"

"But they don't all do it the same way. And I'll bet you a year's salary these people here don't do it the way you and I and the rest of the world do it—if I can ever find a way to prove it."

"You never will, Paul," Crowley observed, his face worried. "You think anybody's going to take your cockamamie theory seriously enough to help you? Paul, they're going to lock you up so tight you'll never get out. Who are you going to go to with it—Hoho Skillin? Goodbye and good luck, lieutenant. He'll fire you on the spot. You know what he'll think, Paul. He'll be convinced you're bending your elbow again."

"Probably."

"So?"

"So what?"

"So how the hell—wildly assuming you just might possibly be right—do you intend to prove it?"

"I don't know—yet." Tilley grinned from ear to ear and clapped Crowley on the back. "But I sure as hell am going to find out."

They tried every building in the town's small center and then drove slowly back out of town, continuing to take every side road and driveway off the main road. It was always the same. Whether dilapidated house or shabby old trailer, each was locked and the inhabitants not about.

"It's beginning to give me the creeps, Paul," Crowley commented as they returned to the car from the one three-story house they had come upon. Obviously once a proud Victorian, built before the turn of the century, only shreds of its original gingerbread remained along the peak of the patched roof. Its lone, square tower had long ago lost its upper story; rotting, broken boards, part of a leg from a Queen Anne chair, and a piece of a windowframe littered the front yard. The top of what remained of the tower had been boarded over and covered with tarpaper. "It's worse than a ghost town. I can't believe anybody'd live like this."

"Yeah," Tilley agreed shortly.

"How do you suppose they even manage to pay their taxes?" Crowley asked as they climbed back into the car.

"I wish I knew."

A quarter of a mile beyond the old Victorian house, another side road opened among the trees on their left. Tilley turned into it. They had driven almost a mile into the deep woods when Tilley suddenly stopped the car and switched off the motor.

"What's the matter?"

"Shhhh. Listen."

After a moment or two, in the silence of the windless midday, the faint sounds of a piano became unmistakable. Tilley glanced at Crowley with a grim smile.

"Somebody's home here, by God," he muttered, and started the car again.

It was another several hundred yards before the drive opened into a large clearing. A long, one-story building stood more or less in the center of it; the rest of the clearing served as a dirt parking lot. It was filled with unwashed, dented old vehicles: cars, pickups, vans, several rusty bicycles, and an occasional battered motorcycle.

"There must be more than two hundred cars here, Paul," Crowley said in amazement, standing on the doorsill of Tilley's car as he got out. "Maybe even two hundred fifty." He stepped down and closed the door. "We haven't seen anywhere near that many houses."

"Maybe nobody lets their kids live away from home," Tilley muttered, remembering what Patti Welles had told him about her father. "Maybe they all shack up together and spend whatever money they make on second-hand cars." He closed his door as quietly as possible and started for the building.

The sounds of the piano were loud and clear now. Someone was playing Martin Luther's "Ein' Feste Burg," and playing it very well. Tilley suspected the someone was Patti Welles. Then suddenly the piano was all but overwhelmed by a surge of voices singing. Tilley stopped and put out a hand to stop Crowley.

"Listen a minute," he said quietly.

It took Tilley most of the first stanza to begin to distinguish the words being sung by what sounded to him like hundreds of contralto or boy-soprano voices. Although he had not heard the hymn in years, he knew that what he was hearing in Pine Woods was a bastardized version. His mother, a Lutheran, had loved "Ein' Feste Burg." He had grown up listening to her sing it while she prepared meals and washed dishes and puttered in her garden. Tilley could not have quoted Luther's original lyrics exactly, but he recognized each changed word and phrase as surely as if the congregation inside the church were hitting sour notes.

"And though this world, with humans filled / Should threaten to undo us." Tilley frowned. This wasn't the second stanza, it was the third; he was certain, even though many of the words seemed to have been changed. "We will not fear, for God has willed / Its truth to triumph through us: / Mankind of darkness grim, / We tremble not for him; / His rage we can endure, / For lo! his doom is sure, / Our someday might shall fell him."

Tilley felt a shiver race up his spine. He stood like a statue and gave his full concentration to the next stanza as the congregation of Pine Woods launched into its private version of it.

"That might above all earthly powers, / No thanks to man, abideth; / The Spirit and the gifts are ours / Through It who with us sideth; / Let man his evil do, / God's will is clear and true; / In uning we grow strong; / Till the"—the two words were run together, sung as one: "Tillthe"; Tilley's ears caught the added syllable, as well as the new words and changed meaning, as if it were a sacrilege— "earth to us belong, / God's kingdom is forever."

He waited for the piano to close the hymn, knowing that what he had just heard was, in part at least, the fourth and last stanza. Instead, the singers began another verse which he did not recognize at all, save for the melody.

"Transfigured, from man's sins apart, / To us heaven's might draws nigh; / Lo! We, the dream of God's true heart, / Base man and earth to"—again Tilley heard two words deliberately sung as one, to share one note: "earthto"— "purify. / In number we increase / To bring to earth God's peace, / In uning praise Its name / With Whom we are the same, / God our charge eternify."

Tilley felt chilled to the bone as the piano rendered the closing bars and the last notes faded slowly out. For all his insistence to Crowley, he realized with a shock he was praying that his theory about the killings would not prove out. Yet never in his life had he felt so strongly that he was right.

"Hear anything different or unusual in the words of that hymn?" he asked quietly.

"I don't know, Paul. I don't even know what hymn it was. Was I supposed to?"

"What do you think 'uning' means?" Tilley ignored his question.

"What's 'uning'?" Crowley looked bewildered.

"That's what I'm asking you."

"I never heard of it before. What's it got to do with anything?"

"It was a word in the hymn. I thought I heard them singing 'in uning' something or other."

" 'Union,' " Crowley said. " 'In union'—whatever."

"I don't think so," Tilley said thoughtfully. And I've got a helluva good ear, he added silently to himself.

"Had to be 'union,' " Crowley mused indifferently. "Paul," he went more strongly, "you know, unless these old heaps are parked on top of the graves, there's no cemetery around this church."

Tilley grunted. "I didn't think there would be."

"Huh? Why not?"

"Don't know. Intuition, I guess." Tilley paused, thinking. "Revved up by a lot of little pieces that just don't fit together. Or do, but make a picture I don't understand yet. Want to bet Pine Woods cremates its dead? And maybe scatters the ashes, too?"

"A one-horse dump like this? Come on. Why?"

"I don't know yet."

Crowley shook his head. "Nah. We going in?"

"Haven't decided. What do you think?"

"Well, if anything's going on in there," Crowley said slowly and softly, "it's sure as hell going to stop the minute we open that door."

Tilley nodded.

"But, whatever's going on, we sure can't hear it from here."

Tilley grinned wryly at him.

"And if we find a place where we can hear something, we're going to look awfully suspicious to them when they come pouring out of there."

"So which do you opt for?"

"You stay here and look innocent, and I'll go around to the side and see if I can find an open window or something. They don't know me, and besides, if they get out too fast for me, I can always pretend to be taking a leak and look embarrassed." He grinned.

Tilley thought a moment. "You do just that, Jim," he said, seriously. "I mean it. Only don't pretend—do it. Wait until you're in full view of somebody, then take a leak. And watch their faces closely. Go on, go on. I'll wait right here for them to come out." He leaned with mock casualness against the fender of an old Buick and crossed his arms.

13

Carey came to, vomiting and choking on seawater. For the first several minutes of her return to consciousness, she was barely aware of lying face down on something hard. She did feel a massive weight crushing her ribcage and its abrupt retraction. Her lungs burned as if on fire as she gasped to draw in air through the spurts of salt water her system was spastically ejecting.

"Thank God."

Carey was unsure whether she or someone else had

spoken. Her mind had room for only one thought: Breathe, breathe, breathe.

"You'll be all right in a few minutes." Two hands slid under her waist and lifted her off the hard, wet wood. "Throw up as much of the water as you can," the firm voice ordered. "You'll feel better. That's it, that's it. Good."

With her head dangling downward, Carey had little choice. Spurts of water continued to erupt from her throat for a few moments. Then she began to retch.

"Okay, okay." The hands lowered her gently back down. One of them patted the small of her back. "Just lie there. You'll be all right. I'll be right back."

Carey lay, still gasping for breath and choking a little, and listened numbly to the sounds of heavy boots squishing back and forth, rope slapping and scraping against wood, and heavy breathing. Memories of dark, cold water, an apparent angel who'd turned into a man, and a few seconds of kill-or-be-killed terror flew randomly through her mind. She could not recall why she had felt such terror. She felt confused and not yet absolutely certain she was really alive.

"Afraid we lost your dinghy." Boots thudded close to her face. "How you doing now? Feeling any better?"

"Where am I?" Carey felt her lips painfully form the words, but she didn't hear any sound.

"What's that?"

A drop of water splashed upon her cheek. Carey opened her eyes, blinked, and found herself again gazing into a pair of hazel-green eyes.

"Oh, God!" She choked, then coughed, her eyes wide with panic. "No!" She pushed herself half-erect and backward, away from the terrifying eyes. "Get away from me!"

"Hey, hey, easy does it now. I'm not going to hurt you. You've had a bad shock, that's all. Take it easy. You're going to be all right. You just tried to ride my anchor down to Davy Jones's locker, but you're safe now. I pulled you out."

As the eyes receded, Carey began to distinguish a face, a man's face, surrounding them. "Don't come near me," she gasped, "stay away from me."

"Okay, okay." The man smiled at her. "How about some hot tea?"

He didn't wait for her to answer. She watched him straighten up and walk away from her, forward into the wheelhouse of what she began to recognize as a small boat. Moments later he returned with a plastic cup half-full of steaming, milky tea. He squatted down, not too close to her, and held the cup out to her.

"Here. Drink it. You need something hot in you."

"Who are you?" Carey heard herself demand in a shaky, breathless voice.

"Captain Dinny, Mayor of Parson's Cove. Hell and damnation, will you drink this while it's hot? Take it."

Carey reached out hesitantly, her eyes still wide with fear.

"Christ! You can't hold it with hands like that," the man said, frowning. "Will you let me hold it for you?"

"Don't you touch me!" Carey scrambled backward, farther away from him.

"All right, all right." He held up his free hand. "I won't touch you, I swear it. Here." He set the plastic cup down on the deck between them. "Water's calm enough. It's all yours."

Carey waited until he had backed a couple of steps, then worked her burned, oozing hands around the cup and lifted it to her mouth. She took a small sip and whimpered as the hot liquid ran into the splits of her sunburned lips.

"Milk," she mumbled.

"There's milk in it."

She shook her head and took another sip of the tea, wincing. She couldn't explain that what she had meant was that she'd had milk in the dinghy. She didn't even know why she'd tried to do so.

"What's your name?" he asked her.

Carey glanced up at him, a new surge of panic rushing through her. "Margie Packer!"

"Where you from?"

"California." It was the farthest place that occurred to her partially functioning mind.

"No, no, I mean where'd you come from in that dinghy? Where'd you put out from?"

"Bar Harbor." It was the only place in Maine besides South Bay whose name she was readily familiar with.

"Bar Harbor?" He stared at her thunderstruck.

"Yes."

"You got from Bar Harbor to here since Thursday night—in a dinghy?" He shook his head.

"Where am I?"

"A helluva long way from Bar Harbor." He eyed her for a moment. "We'll talk about it later."

"I did come from Bar Harbor."

"Okay. Okay, Margie Packer. Are you hungry? I've got sandwiches of sorts, in the wheelhouse."

"No." Carey shook her head.

"Well, sing out when you are. Can you get out of those wet clothes by yourself? I'll fetch a blanket from below."

He turned away, went forward to the wheelhouse, and disappeared down an open companionway. Carey huddled on the deck, staring at the dark hole that had swallowed him up, and took another sip of the hot tea. She could hear him pounding around below.

Shortly he reappeared up the companionway with an oil-stained, faded plaid woolen blanket under his arm.

"Here." He set it down within her reach and backed off. "I'm going below again and change myself. You gave both of us a good soaking when you capsized that dinghy—" He broke off and leaned out over the side, frowning. "She's bottoms up out there somewhere, but I doubt we'll sight her. Sorry she's gone, but I didn't have time to go for her with you hellbent for the bottom on that anchor." He straightened up and treated her to a dazzling smile.

He appeared very tall to Carey, standing there beside the rail. She was beginning to take in his face, which, it came to her, her mother would have pronounced aristocratic. He was extraordinarily handsome, with fine, chiseled features and high cheekbones. Even a two-day growth of heavy, dark beard couldn't hide the breeding in his face. With his longish, dark hair, salted here and there with silver, plastered wetly to his head and dripping onto the sodden layers of ancient bulky sweaters covering his upper body, he reminded her of Tyrone Power or Errol Flynn in some swashbuckling sea saga filmed during the '30's or early '40's, before the movies went to war.

This did nothing to allay her fear of him, however. The hazel-green eyes beneath his dark brows still set off tremors of fear in her each time she looked at them.

"You're shivering, Margie Packer," he said. "Get those wet clothes off you and wrap up in that blanket. I'll see if I can rout out something below for you to put on."

He disappeared again into the black hole of the companionway.

Carey finished the tea and set the cup on the deck. She took hold of a corner of the blanket and dragged it around her shoulders. Using her hands made her wince, but she managed to get herself wrapped up. She was freezing cold, even with the sun streaming down onto her back.

"You've still got those soaking clothes on." He was back, near her, in another pair of rumpled heavy trousers and more layers of threadbare sweaters. His boots were gone, however, replaced only by a pair of thick Ragg socks. "Can't you manage alone?" He leaned toward her.

"I'm all right," Carey almost shouted. "I don't need to change."

"Well." He set down a pair of corduroy trousers, a colorless shirt, and a dark blue sweater in a neat pile in front of her on a coil of rope. "They're there for you if you change your mind." He looked skyward. "It's getting to be a scorcher, so I guess you're not in danger of catching your death or anything." He looked down and smiled at her, his expression enigmatic. "Sea does funny things to your head when you're all alone on it. I've been through it myself. Ships I've been on have gone down more times than I can count. Just sing out if you want something." He started to turn away, then frowned at her quizzically. "What're you staring at so intently, Margie Packer?"

Carey blanched under her sunburn and looked down.

"You haven't take your eyes off me since you came to."

"Who are you?"

He smiled. "Captain Dinny of *The Mermaid*, out of Parson's Cove. This morning."

"Where are you from?"

"Parson's Cove—and aboard *The Mermaid*."

"Is that anywhere near . . . Pine Woods?"

"Never heard of it. You know, Margie Packer, you really ought to come into the wheelhouse out of this sun. You've got one helluva sunburn. How about it?"

"No."

He shook his head. "I'm not here to hurt you, Margie Packer. Just trying to help. If you change your mind, you're welcome by the wheel."

Carey watched him step to the wheelhouse and get the small boat underway. The sun rose steadily in a cloudless sky as the engine chugged soothingly away beneath her. She pulled the blanket up over her head to shade her face and looked around. Behind her, what looked to be undersized, slat-sided crates with funnel-shaped nets were stacked haphazardly on the deck. Beyond the stern, the Atlantic stretched away to the horizon, a restless expanse of blue freckled with disappearing and reappearing splashes of gold. She looked up. The sky was bluer than any she could remember ever having seen. A gull appeared from nowhere and swooped down over *The Mermaid*, screaming.

Carey turned her head and stared at Dinny's back. Was he really her rescuer? Or had he come to kill her? If he had, why didn't he just let her drown back there? She felt her fear recede a little. Yes, why didn't he? Maybe she was being . . . She couldn't think of a word to describe her behavior, but knew what her mother would call it: rude. She hadn't even thanked him for saving for her life. And the reflected light from the water was as painful on her face as direct sunlight.

She struggled up and hobbled forward into the wheel-house.

"Thank you for saving my life," she said from underneath the blanket.

"You're entirely welcome, Margie Packer." He glanced at her. "Take a seat on that rope there."

Carey eased herself down onto the coil of rope and stared up at the side of his face. "Where are we?"

"A good ways out in the Atlantic. Lucky for you the weather held." He glanced at his compass. "Luckier still I came out this morning, because we're in for a blow. Looks clear now, but take my word for it, by six tonight we'll be in heavy weather. But we'll be back on land long before then," he added quickly, giving her another of his dazzling smiles, "safe and snug in Parson's Cove."

"What are you doing out here?" Carey asked, unable to keep all suspicion out of her voice.

"Setting my pots." He frowned at the compass and spun the wheel a half-turn. "Figured I better get them out again before the weather changed. Took a few days off last week to . . ." He hesitated, turning his head away so Carey could not see his face. ". . . see a friend," he finished in a closed voice.

Carey felt her inner alarms go off like an explosion. She started on the coil of rope.

"What's the matter?" He turned and looked at her. "You getting a chill?"

"No." Her teeth were chattering.

"You really ought to get out of those clothes. They're soaking."

"I'm all right," she quaked.

"Have it your way, Margie Packer." He was silent for a while. "Helluva good thing for you I did," he said at last.

"Did what?" Her voice came out a squeak.

"Come out this morning to set my pots."

"Pots for what?"

"Lobster." He gestured over his shoulder. "That's them, piled up in the stern."

"Oh." Carey glanced back at the odd off-sized crates with their conical nets, then ahead, through the window of the wheelhouse, at the sea.

She could not look at him, but she seemed to see the gleam of his hazel-green eyes in every rising swell of the sea and every trough that followed. Wherever she looked, his eyes gleamed at her dangerously, hinting at death and dessication.

"Real good speech, Adrian," Creighton Welles said to Dr. Widdows, pumping his hand energetically. "You should have gone into the ministry instead of medicine. And more's the pity you didn't," he added. "Just between you and me, Hovey Moholland couldn't get a twitch out of a jumping bean."

"Well, thank you, Creighton," Dr. Widdows beamed, his eyes still smoldering with the dying coals of the inner fire that had burned brightly during his address to the congregation just before the closing hymn. "Glad you appreciated it."

Patti Welles sat at the piano, looking from one to the other as they stood nearby. She, too, felt a lingering excitement, left over from the frenzied sense of purpose Dr. Widdows' spellbinding oratory had so recently whipped up in her. But now she also felt uneasy—with herself as well as him—and more than a little ashamed.

When he got going, Dr. Widdows was so like the evangelist preachers and other fanatics she saw on television. Especially, she couldn't help reluctantly admitting, Hitler, in the old newsreel footage that was being aired so much of late. She thought his body language bore a striking resemblance to Hitler's, with his forefinger stabbing the air, his closed fist clenched against his diaphragm, and his tight, stingy way of holding himself. Even now, smiling and talking with her father, Dr. Widdows gave Patti the impression of being as near to himself as the bark on a tree.

It shamed her that she was as vulnerable to him, whenever he was delivering one of his speeches, as everyone else in town. No matter how she steeled herself against it, his voice would simply seize her, lashing into a frenzy all her needs, frustrations, and confusions, while simultaneously offering her a passionate, seemingly inspired resolution. When Dr. Widdows spoke, all her pains and problems came together into one: man. And could be resolved by one simple—if sweeping—divine event: man's inevitable extinction. By divine hand, out of divine will, in demonstration of divine justice. All that was required of her was to sustain a passionate sense of purpose as an inheritor of the earth—and the kingdom of heaven as well.

Patti had never been able to sustain that passionate sense of purpose—or even a tepid one—afterward. Nor was she today, even in the face of the very real and imminent threat to her life and the lives of all her people, brought about by the grotesque, misbegotten deaths of her friends and some humans. It was not that she had rejected all the teachings of her eighteen years, not by any means. She found her people—and herself—singularly, marvelously, beautiful, and considered their act of intercommunicative union so superior to what she had learned of the sexual union between human beings as to make the two not comparable. How could it be otherwise?

The act of union between her people was essential to their staying alive; they were literally dependent upon each other for the continuance of their physical existence. Violence was therefore unknown to them. One did not harm or kill another whom, tomorrow, perhaps, one would need to join with if one was not to begin to suffer and die. Patti had known all her life that her people did not love their neighbors merely as themselves. They loved each other because every other was the self.

And our union, she thought, watching her father and the doctor exchange endless compliments, is not just of our bodies, but of our entire beings, even our spirits. And it can never be forced upon us when we're not ready. We can't hurt or frighten each other with uning. Uning is an exchange. None of us can use it just to take.

Unless—she thought with a shock of Naida Skedgell

and Harlie Freve. That was exactly what had happened to them. They had taken everything from the humans and given nothing in return. But that was involuntary, she knew, a result of a joining they could not have known was even possible, not a deliberate choice on their parts. And they were dead from the taking; they could not be held to blame for the failure of the human organisms to receive all that they had to give.

Maybe humans were dying from taking, she mused, and not really from all the diseases and disorders they seemed to contract. After all, one of them had taken everything from poor Roe Gaddas. And as far as she could judge from their television shows and movies and books, they certainly did more taking from than giving to each other. Not all of them, though. She brought her thoughts up short. Not all of them. Their history was studded with exceptional individuals who had devoted their lives to giving everything they had to others. Their Christ was the most outstanding example of that. And there were other examples, many others. Patti instinctively felt certain there were many times many more like that, who had lived and died without ever calling any attention to themselves. Even if there were not, she couldn't understand why God would give up on a species that had produced even one such as Jesus was portrayed as having been. And even if he wasn't quite everything he was said to have been—as Dr. Widdows pointed out at every opportunity—well, so much more to the credit of human beings, then. Every piece of him they created themselves, as an ideal, and attributed to him, Patti felt, only spoke more clearly of their innate goodness and potential. She just couldn't be as sure as she'd been taught to be that her kind was the sole of Its creations God was pleased with.

Patti sensed that buried deep in everything Dr. Widdows said there was some seed of truth. But he twisted every-thing around so, it all came out hatred and suspicion and fear. If her kind were really all that she'd been taught to believe they were, wouldn't the capacity for even such benign violence be impossible to them? If it was benign.

She frowned, trying to follow her thought logically. Dr. Widdows possessed as much of the very qualities he despised in human beings as the worst of men did. And if her kind continued to follow him, or the likes of him, Patti wondered, wouldn't they end up being just the same as the humans they believed it was their destiny to supersede? What in the world would God have accomplished by their creation then?

"Patti," Creighton's voice broke sharply into her thoughts, "Adrian is speaking to you."

She blinked and looked at her father blankly.

Dr. Widdows laughed, but his eyes were cold. "I hope I didn't lose all of our young people as I seem to have lost Patti here. But then, Patti's our dreamer, isn't she? Always off in a world of her own."

"I'm sorry, Creighton," Patti said, confused. "I . . . wasn't listening." She glanced at the doctor. "Did you say something to me? I'm sorry, Adrian, I didn't hear you."

"Nothing of importance," Dr. Widdows said with obviously calculated self-effacement. "Don't give it another thought, Patti."

"Adrian asked you," her father said sternly, "if you enjoyed his speech, Hypatia."

Patti winced. She hated her given name. Creighton knew she hated it, too. It was cruel of him to use it like this, in front of someone else, even if he was annoyed with her.

"Talk, Creighton, talk," Dr. Widdows protested humbly. "My goodness, it was extemporaneous, just off the top of my head. Don't embarrass me by calling it a speech."

"I enjoyed it very much, Adrian," Patti said, despising his insincerity but feeling a little sorry for him for his need to beg compliments so transparently. "So much, in fact, that I was lost in thinking about it just now and didn't hear your question." She smiled at him as nicely as she could and avoided her father's eyes.

"Well," said Dr. Widdows. "Well, well. Well."

He looked enormously pleased with himself.

14

Crowley had barely reached the side of the Pine Woods church building when Tilley heard the scraping of chair legs against flooring and the shuffling and stamping of feet. Crowley glanced back at him, alarm written all over his face. Annoyed, Tilley motioned him away from the building. Crowley lifted his arms and shoulders, tightening his lips and raising his eyebrows as if to say, Well, if you're sure it's really what you want me to do, and hurried off between the cars toward the side of the parking lot.

Tilley resumed his casual posture against the Buick. The double doors of the church opened, and Mayor Farley and a man Tilley had not seen before took up positions on either side of the doorway, shaking hands with the departing congregation and talking quietly with them. Tilley watched the people with keen interest. He could not see the color of their eyes from where he was, but he noted there was not a dark, a red, or a tow head in the lot. Everyone in Pine Woods had hair varying only from dirty-blond to light brown. Then he noticed two other things: almost everyone's hair was curly, and none of the men showed the slightest sign of baldness. As those men who had hats were carrying them in their hands, Tilley knew he was not mistaken about the absence of alopecia in Pine Woods.

He remained half-sitting against the dented fender of the Buick until Mayor Farley glanced out across the parking lot and noticed him—with a small start, he was certain. Then he waved, straightening up, and started toward her, smiling. She smiled stiffly back at him, and looked away to speak to a woman who was pumping her hand.

Tilley sauntered slowly through the labyrinth of old, battered cars, stopping to smile and say "hello" or "good afternoon" or "lovely day, isn't it" to everyone he came within three cars of. All the while his mind was ticking off, Hazel-green eyes, small, slim, curly light brown hair, young, over and over again. Before he reached the steps of the church, he made mental notes of several more things.

No one in Pine Woods was overweight. In a nation obsessed with the need to diet, Tilley found that as implausible as the complete lack of baldness in the men, the more so as the poor—and Pine Woods, he felt certain, would be found to be well below the poverty line if anyone were to conduct a study there—frequently numbered among the overweight, due to the high percentage of cheap starch filler-foods in their diets.

Nor were any of the women large-breasted. In fact, they were, to a woman, as small-breasted as slender preteens. Tilley found it surprising, and notable, that not even a single teenager appeared to be wearing at least a padded bra. Even in so isolated a little pocket as Pine Woods, he puzzled that America's mammary mania could have made no impression, especially on the young.

Not a man wore a beard, or even a mustache. Tilley did not see a face that showed so much as a shadow under the skin, let alone stubble. Diet-induced hormone imbalance? he asked himself, answering almost immediately, But the entire town? Nothing else remotely rational came to his mind, and Tilley remained as unsatisfied on this point as on all the others.

Everyone was short. Everyone. At just under five feet nine inches, Tilley felt, for the first time in his life, a Gulliver among Lilliputians. His best guess was that there wasn't a man or woman in Pine Woods who stood over five foot five, if that. Again poor diet sprang to mind. Stunted? he demanded of himself silently, coming back at himself instantly with, The whole damn town?

There were no old people. This, when he realized it, did more than surprise or puzzle Tilley; it stunned him. Mentally flipping through the roster of faces he had already passed by, he found himself unable to firmly classify even one as actually middle-aged. To be sure, he had nodded and smiled at and spoken to some who, like Mayor Farley, had a streak or two of gray running through their light hair. But their skin, their faces—their hands, when he had been able to catch a glimpse of them—were those of adolescents, if not children. Young, firm, smooth, not a line or a wrinkle visible. No pouches under the eyes, no bulbous drooping of the upper eyelids over the inner canthi. Not a single sagging jowl had he seen, and any one of the cheeks could have modeled for an ad for a skin moisturizer. In a community of dilapidated homes and battered old cars, without business or industry to provide jobs, Tilley found the glow of youthful health in the faces of the population alarmingly incongruous. He and Crowley hadn't seen any food animals, not a cow or a chicken. The small vegetable gardens behind every house or trailer almost all had had an untended look, suggesting the produce was left to rot on the vine or in the earth.

What the hell did these people eat, he wondered, to look so vibrantly healthy? They should have been old and haggard by thirty. Instead, they had no elderly at all. Either they've literally discovered the Fountain of Youth, he thought in irritable frustration, or they're somehow doing away with everybody over thirty-five. A shudder ran through his body. The latter explanation seemed far more likely than the former.

Three exuberant children broke free of their parents on the steps of church and ran shrieking in Tilley's direction. They were upon him before they recognized him as a stranger. They stopped, almost knocking each other down, and stared at him with three pairs of widened hazel-green eyes.

"Hello," Tilley said affably. Two of the children were absolutely identical, save that one who was half a head taller than the other. "You two must be twins."

"We're Hallisseys," the shorter of the two corrected him.

"I didn't mean your name. I meant you must be the Hallissey twins," he said, studying them closely.

"What's 'twins'?" the child asked.

"Shut up, Mahlon," the taller child growled, kicking the youngster in the shin.

The smaller one glared belligerently.

"Wait a minute, hold on there," Tilley put in. "I didn't mean to start an argument between you two." He looked at the smaller child. "Don't you know what twins are?"

"Nope. What are they?"

"Babies born together, at the same time, to the same mother. You and your . . ." Tilley glanced over at the taller child; as with Davey Farley, when he first saw him, he was unable to determine the child's sex. He took a guess. ". . . brother look so exactly alike I thought you must be what people call identical twins."

All three children were now giggling, to Tilley's bewilderment.

"Ida's my sister, mister," Mahlon Hallissey snickered, "not my brother. And she's three years older'n me. So there." The youngster bolted forward and darted by Tilley, shouting at the others, "Last one to the car's a devil man!"

The other two, after a stunned moment, took off past Tilley as fast as their little legs could carry them. He turned to watch them a moment, searching for a connection in his mind. He had been so certain of hearing "a rotten egg" from Mahlon Hallissey that it took him several seconds to race through all the information already in his brain about Pine Woods and find what he was looking for. He did, in the new words and phrases he had heard sung, barely ten minutes earlier, to the melody of "Ein' Feste Burg."

Carey sneaked a quick sideways glance at Captain Dinny. She could see his profile, and once again the fineness of his face struck her incongruously. He simply didn't look like a killer; he looked like a movie star. She looked forward, at the sea again, and felt her fear slowly, cautiously, abate.

Perhaps she was mistaken, perhaps his eyes weren't hazel-green and familiar. Perhaps the dirty, dark green sweater he now had on, or the reflection of the blue-green sea all around them only made them seem that way. Perhaps she was safe after all.

As the worst of her fear subsided, the romance and adventure of her circumstances emerged from beneath it like Neptune rising from the depths. She found herself thinking again of the old movies she had seen at the Regency Theater on Broadway. Distantly, she was astounded that anything so genuinely dramatic was actually happening to her, Carey Hunter from Craigmere, New Jersey.

Such things only happened in the movies, or, at most, to strange faces with unfamiliar names on the eleven-o'clock news. It couldn't possibly be ordinary Carey Hunter, sunburned to a crisp, trembling with the cold in sodden clothing, and wrapped in an oily blanket, who was sitting beside a tall, dark, and handsome stranger on a lobster boat in the middle of the North Atlantic. This Sunday morning was a scene from a vintage swashbuckler. It couldn't be happening to her. To Margie, yes, but not to her.

"Penny for your thoughts, Margie Packer." Dinny's voice seemed to confirm her muddled thoughts. "Or maybe I should make it a quarter. They look like deep ones."

Margie Packer? Her mind raced in bewildered circles. Is this really happening to Margie, not me? Outwardly she blushed under her sunburn and said, "Oh, no. I was just thinking that I feel like Maureen O'Hara or somebody being rescued by Tyrone Power in *The Sea Wolf*."

Dinny burst out laughing. "Well, you sure don't look like Maureen O'Hara," he teased. "You look terrible."

"I bet." Carey found herself laughing with him, carefully, in order not to split her sore lips. "You look a lot grungier than Tyrone Power ever did yourself."

"Well, then, by gory we're a pair, aren't we." He chuckled. "Made for each other." He fell quiet a moment. "Good to hear you laugh," he said, his voice warm and friendly.

Carey smiled a careful little smile. "Could I have another cup of tea?"

"Coming right up."

Dinny bent a knee between the spokes of the wheel and took a huge thermos from behind the compass. He opened it and poured her another half-cup. "Down the hatch, as Hollywood thinks we say at sea."

Carey freed her hands from the blanket and took the plastic cup gingerly between her fingertips. She drained it and handed it back to him.

"Thanks."

"Ready for a sandwich yet?"

She shook her head. "No, thanks. I don't think so."

"Let me know."

He poured himself a half-cup of tea, drank it one gulp, reclosed the thermos, and set it back in place.

"Now, Margie Packer." Again Carey's mind went racing in circles. Why did he keep calling her Margie Packer? She did not remember saying who she was. Was he making some kind of ghoulish joke because he knew Margie was dead? How could he know Margie was dead unless he had killed her? All her terror swept over her anew as he continued speaking. "Feel like telling me what happened to you? How you came to be out here in this condition on a Sunday morning in that walnut shell of a dinghy?"

He turned his head and looked directly at her. His face blurred out of focus around the hazel-green eyes that were all Carey could clearly see of him. Her body shook with spasms of fear. Then his eyes multiplied into infinite numbers of pairs that swept at her from everywhere—the sea, the sky, the deck, his dimming outline—gathering themselves into a hazel-green vortex that trapped her inside its deadly, relentless vacuum and sucked her, spinning, down into oblivion.

Come on, Paul, Tilley chided himself silently as he started toward Mayor Farley once again, don't let this backwater dot on the map make a basket case out of you. Kids pick up on things the rest of us never notice. His trained intuition would not let him rest with that, however, reminding him, But that's just the point, isn't it.

He was just coming back at his intuition with, Well, if they don't have any chickens in Pine Woods, the kids have to think up something terrible nobody wants to be, don't they? when he found himself at the foot of the church steps, smiling up at Mayor Farley.

"Hello again, Mayor Farley," he heard himself say pleasantly. "How are you today?"

"Just fine, thank you, Lieutenant Tilley," she replied, smiling back at him. "Are you here on business again?"

"Yes, ma'am, afraid I am."

"In that case, do you mind waiting a few more minutes? I'll be with you as soon as I can."

"Thank you. Is Sheriff Welles here?"

"He's still inside, I believe."

"Fine. I'll wait for both of you."

Mayor Farley turned back to the few people still waiting to greet her.

Crowley joined Tilley before the last of church's congregation had paid their respects to their mayor and the man on the other side of the doorway whom Tilley judged must be their minister. The sergeant was faintly flushed, his face covered with a fine film of perspiration.

"Well?" Tilley muttered quietly.

"Well what?" Crowley whispered irritably. "They stared at me like I was a bum. What'd you expect?"

"Only a bum?" he demanded in an undertone.

"A bum, a weirdo, a freak—what the hell's the difference?" Crowley growled softly. "It is their churchyard, Paul, even if it's covered with cars. And it is Sunday morning," he added pointedly.

"Afternoon," Tilley corrected him, glancing at his watch. "Any kids see you?"

"Several," Crowley hissed.

"Their reaction?"

"For chrissake, Paul." Crowley's mounting anger was

clear in his muted reply. "What in hell are you looking for anyway?"

"Anything. What about the kids?"

"They looked," Crowley enunciated each syllable emphatically although he kept his voice to a whisper, "as shocked and scared as any kids would look seeing a grown man doing something in a public place their parents had drummed into them must never be done. Christ, I feel like a goddamn flasher. 'S probably what some of them thought, too." His face had darkened with anger.

Humor lightened the disappointment in Tilley's face. His blue eyes twinkled. "I'll do my best to have us out of here before anybody reports you to the sheriff. Who's coming now, by the way," he added, glancing up at the man who appeared in the church doorway. "Good day, Sheriff Welles," he called up to him, nodding his head shortly and touching the brim of his hat.

Tilley watched the sheriff nod back at him, unsmiling. Patti, to his satisfaction, came up beside her father; Davey Farley was at her heels. The girl's face brightened the moment she saw Tilley, which pleased him enormously.

"Patti," he said, smiling broadly at her, "Hi. Nice to see you again."

"Hi, Paul," she called eagerly, then glanced guiltily from her father to to the mayor to the minister. "How are you?" she added stiffly, in a suddenly distant voice.

"Just fine, just fine." Tilley kept up his show of warmth, which was genuine, aware of the abrupt change in the teenager. "And yourself?"

"I'm very well, thank you." Patti looked away from his eyes.

"Hi there, Davey," Tilley managed to catch the little boy's curious eye. "How are you today?"

Davey looked up at his mother before speaking. When she nodded at him, he looked back at the detective.

"Fine," the child answered, and closed his mouth tightly.

Tilley directed himself again to Patti. "I enjoyed your playing, Patti. You're every bit as good as you said you were—better, in fact.'' He was still smiling; he hoped Patti would come down to the steps to talk with him.

She did not. ''Thank you very much,'' she replied, keeping her voice distant, though she could not hide the faint blush of pleasure that colored her face. She remained at her father's side.

''I know that hymn very well,'' Tilley went on. ''It was my mother's favorite. I've never heard it played so well.'' He glanced over at Sheriff Welles. ''You have a very talented daughter, sheriff. You must be very proud of her.''

''Yes,'' Welles nodded at him, smiling a little. ''Patti's very good. Nice of you to notice, lieutenant.''

''Couldn't fail to. It's not every day you hear talent that fine. I look forward to the day we'll all be hearing her in concert. Don't forget to play for us folks in your home state sometimes, Patti, when you're a famous pianist.'' He smiled from one to the other of them, curious to see if her father would correct the expectations he had voiced in a way that might tell him something.

Sheriff Welles said nothing. It was Patti who finally spoke up.

''I'm not going on with my music, Mr. Tilley,'' she said in a tight, angry voice. ''I'm going to be a teacher. But thank you for the compliments anyway. I'm glad you enjoyed hearing me play.''

Her hazel-green eyes had the look of a wounded animal. Tilley knew she felt he had betrayed her, as indeed he had. It was one of those moments when he hated his job—and himself and his stop-at-nothing way of getting his job done. He made up his mind to get the girl alone, one way or another, before he left Pine Woods and do his best to reestablish her trust in him. He felt cut to the quick that she now addressed him as ''Mr. Tilley,'' and wasn't even annoyed with himself for being hurt.

'Well, with all due respect to the teaching profession,'' he said seriously, looking directly into Patti's anguished eyes, ''having heard you play just now, I can't help but say I think that's a waste, in a world where genuine talent is rare. Anyway, thank you for 'Ein' Feste Burg.' It's been a long time since I've heard it, and, as I said, I've never heard it played so beautifully.'' He saw in the girl's eyes that she had not forgiven him and decided, with his habitual slight shrug, to get down to business for the time being. ''Mayor Farley, Sheriff Welles, this is my partner, Sergeant Crowley.'' He climbed the church steps, Crowley beside him, as he continued the introductions. ''Jim, this is Mayor Farley; and her son, Davey; and Patti Welles; and her father, Sheriff Welles.''

Crowley shook hands all around, except for Davey, who stared at his outstretched hand a moment, then turned and bolted back into the church.

''Davey—'' Mayor Farley called after her son, a reprimand clear in her voice.

''I'll go get him, Ada,'' Patti said quickly, already turning and starting into the building.

''I'll come with you,'' Tilley strode forward quickly after her, ''and reassure him Sergeant Crowley doesn't bite, he just looks that way. Jim,'' he tossed over his shoulder, ''make arrangements for us to meet with Mayor Farley and the sheriff''—an idea struck him—''and the minister here as well, at her house when we leave here, if she'll be kind enough to let me use her phone again.'' He disappeared into the church, wondering if he just might be able to get some truth out of a man of the cloth.

He caught up with Patti halfway down the center aisle and took hold of her arm.

''Patti,'' he said earnestly, ''I'm sorry. I'm really sorry. I was only trying to help.''

''Forget it, Mr. Tilley.'' She did not meet his eye.

''No, I won't forget it, not until it's okay for you. Look, I realize now it was a stupid thing to do, but I thought maybe if your father heard somebody else—an outsider— say how good you are, he'd reconsider about your going away to college. Please—''

''It's not just my father,'' Patti interrupted him angrily. Tilley sensed this anger was not directed at himself. ''I

couldn't go anyway. It's not . . . Let's just forget it, okay?
It's all right.''

"But why not? You've got a very special gift, Patti.''

"I don't want to hear that. It's not true anyway. Forget
it, Paul, please. It's okay.''

"Well, at least you're calling me Paul again.'' He
smiled warmly down at her as she looked up into his face.
"Patti, I'm so sorry. I like you. I wouldn't knowingly do
anything to hurt you. I hope you know that.''

After a long pause Patti mumbled, "Yeah. I guess I do.
I just wasn't expecting you to let on we'd talked so much.
But it's all right now. I'm okay.'' She smiled up at him
sadly.

"Can't I help, Patti? Isn't there something I—''

"No. There's nothing anybody can do. You don't
understand, Paul. And you never will.'' She twisted away
from him abruptly. "We'd better find Davey and get out
of here. Davey!'' she called out. "Davey! Where are you?
Come on out now, we've all got to go home, and Reverend Moholland wants to lock up the church. Come on,
Davey, don't be a pest.'' She looked around the empty
church, waiting briefly for the boy to pop up or say
something. "Davey,'' she went on, annoyed, "everybody
wants to go home. Come on now, I mean it.'' She waited
another moment or two, then looked at Tilley apologetically.
"He can be a real pain sometimes. I'm sorry.''

"All kids can,'' Tilley smiled. Then he called out,
"Davey? Sergeant Crowley's okay. He was just saying
hello to you. You might like him if you'd come out and
meet him.''

"Davey!'' Patti yelled suddenly. "Mr. Tilley's here on
business and he's in a hurry. He's very busy, and he's got
a lot of things to do besides wait for you to play games.
Your mother's not going to like this one bit, so you better
get a move on. Right now.'' When silence greeted this
admonition as well, Patti sighed. "We better look in all
the rows.'' She gestured at the folding chairs set in haphaz-
ard banks from the back of the church to near the raised
platform upon which stood an altar, a simple lectern,

and—to Tilley's surprise—a grand piano. "He must be hiding."

"You're the boss on this case. Do you prefer the left or the right side, madame?"

"Oh, no," Patti retorted, a trifle too quickly. "You take the back of the church, and I'll look up this way, from here to the . . . pulpit. We'd better hurry."

Despite her last words, Tilley felt Patti was reluctant to turn her back to him until she saw he was moving away from the front of the church. She stood facing him, blocking the aisle, in a posture almost challenging.

"Well go on and hurry yourself, then," he teased her, masking the deliberateness of his words with humor. "And don't forget to look under the altar." He gestured toward it. It was covered with a white cloth, the fringe of which just grazed the wood flooring of the platform. "That's a good place for a little boy to hide."

"Davey wouldn't do that," Patti said hurriedly, in an anxious voice. "He knows nobody's allowed to touch the altar except Hovey—Reverend Moholland." She watched Tilley's face nervously.

"Well, look under there anyway." He thought it mildly curious that she was on a first-name basis with the minister, at her age, and more curious she didn't want Tilley to know it. Even in as small a town as Pine Woods, where everybody probably knew everything about everybody else, he expected to find the local pastor addressed with respect for his calling. "Little boys have a way of doing exactly what they know they're not supposed to, when nobody's looking. I know. I was one once."

Patti smiled—left-handedly, Tilley could see—jerked her head in a series of tight nods, and mumbled an "okay" before turning away from him. Tilley turned to retrace his steps back up the aisle, glancing from left to right between each row of chairs. He saw at once that the slender folding chairs could scarcely have concealed a baby, let alone a ten-year-old.

He let his eyes sweep over the seats of the chairs as well, hoping to find a hymnal in which he could check the

wording of "Ein' Feste Burg." Before he got to the last
row, he concluded that either the congregation supplied
their own hymn books, carrying them back and forth each
Sunday, or the church could afford none and the people
sang from memory, parents teaching their children the
town's repertory orally from generation to generation.

He could see Mayor Farley, Sheriff Welles, and the man
he assumed to be the Reverend Moholland all watching
him from the doorway, despite Crowley's efforts to keep
them engaged in conversation. Tilley gave the group an
amused smile and shake of the head as he approached the
last few rows.

"I think your son has discovered a secret hiding place in
here none of you know about," he announced, strolling up
to the mayor. He turned back and called out, "Any luck,
Patti?"

He could see that the girl was barely to the third row of
chairs and was not surprised when she called in reply,
"No. He's not here, Ada," and hurried back up the aisle
toward them.

"He probably slipped out the back door and ran off to
play," the Reverend Moholland offered easily, smiling at
Tilley, who found it noteworthy the minister did not address himself to the boy's mother. "He'll come home
when he's . . . hungry."

Tilley detected the minister's split-second pause before
the word "hungry," and once again images of untended,
unharvested gardens and the Welles's unused kitchen and
coffeepot flashed through his mind.

"Did you look under the altar?" he asked Patti as she
joined them in the doorway.

"I could see nothing was there from where I was," she
said quickly, blushing.

Tilley knew she could not have, but he merely nodded.
"Well, what do we do now, Mayor Farley?" he addressed
himself lightly to the woman. "Where do we look next?"

"Davey can get home on his own, Lieutenant Tilley,"
she answered. "He'll just have to walk."

"Bit of a long way, isn't it, for a small boy?"

"Davey's used to it. All our children get around very well on the legs God gave them," the mayor said pleasantly. "Now, I know you're in a hurry, Lieutenant Tilley, and have much important things to do than wait around in our little town for a mischievous child, so I suggest we leave and meet up at my house, if that suits you."

"Yes. Thank you, Mayor Farley. Sergeant Crowley and I will follow you in my car. Oh," he added, as if it were an afterthought, "I'd like Patti and the Reverend to join us, also, if they're free. Would that be possible, Reverend? You are the Reverend Moholland? I'm Lieutenant Tilley of the Bangor Police." He held out his hand.

"Yes, I am." The minister smiled and took his hand. "How do you do, Lieutenant Tilley."

Tilley was surprised, in spite of himself, at the soft, small, feminine hand he held in his own.

"Patti has work to do," Sheriff Welles spoke up. "I'm sorry, Lieutenant Tilley. But I fail to see she's needed, in any event. I assume you're still looking for those four young people you said were reported as having been on the South Bay ferry a week or so ago, despite the fact that you already know that, whoever they were, they weren't from Pine Woods. We're sorry about that missing young woman—"

"I'm afraid it's much more than one missing young woman now, sheriff," Tilley interrupted him. "I'll explain when we get to the mayor's. And I must insist on questioning your daughter—and perhaps every other teenager in town."

"More than ever, then, Lieutenant Tilley, I refuse to let Patti be present at your meeting." The sheriff's hazel eyes flashed an angry green.

"Then I'll have to question her afterward." Tilley turned to Patti. "Will you be home later, in an hour or so?"

Patti glanced at her father before speaking. "Yes, I guess so. If my father says it's all right."

"He'll have to," Tilley said in a voice that closed the subject. He turned to the minister. "Reverend, will you join us as soon as possible at Mayor Farley's home?"

"Certainly. I'll come as soon as I've locked up here."

"Thank you. Sergeant Crowley and I will see the three of you in a few minutes, then. Patti, I'll see you in about an hour. At your house."

Tilley strode past the little group, down the steps, and across the parking lot to his car. Crowley followed him. In the driver's seat, Crowley started the car, then turned to his superior.

"You going to tell them about the murders?" he asked.

"Haven't decided yet," Tilley said shortly. "Maybe. One of them's going to be on the news tonight, of that I'm sure. So probably."

"But—"

"I think they already know. About all three murders. I doubt if I'm going to be telling them anything that'll come as a surprise to them, Jim."

"How in hell—?"

"I don't know. Exactly. Except that I'll bet money Pine Woods has cremated three teenagers this week—or whatever they do with their dead. I'm just praying it's not four."

"Paul, I don't get it. Even if they—"

"Neither do I. Not yet. But I sense it, damn it. Turn on the radio." Tilley looked at his watch. "See if we can catch a news report. I doubt if we're going to get them to admit it, though."

"Admit what?" Crowley was twisting the dial of the car's radio, listening for a newsbreak.

"The funerals. That's why we've got to question Patti Welles, and maybe every other teenager in town. Maybe the children as well. There's got to be somebody in this dump I can break."

Crowley shook his head. "What would three dead teenagers tell us about one freaked-out, homicidal maniac?"

"That we're looking for somebody who doesn't exist." Tilley glanced across the almost deserted lot. Two cars, one newer and in better condition than the other, were backing around. "Okay, there go the mayor and the sheriff. Follow them."

"There's no news, Paul," Crowley said, leaving the dial set on WABI as he shifted into first and swung the wheel to turn the car around. "Not till the hour—about twenty-two minutes."

"Okay," Tilley replied slowly. "We'll just have Mayor Farley turn on her radio and we'll all wait for the news. I'll call the station first thing. If I hear what I'm afraid I'm liable to hear, we'll all listen to the news before we get down to business."

As soon as they arrived at Mayor Farley's house, Tilley asked to use the phone in her office. He knew from the reaction of the officer who picked up at the Bangor station that his worst fears had come true.

"Lieutenant!" the voice on the other end of the line exclaimed anxiously, "Where the hell have you been? You haven't called in for hours—the chief's fit to be tied. Hold on, I'll put you through to him. Hang on, and I hope to God you're sitting down."

"Tilley," Ho Skillin barked at him seconds later, "where in hell are you? Why haven't you called in since this morning? Do you have any idea what's happened?"

"Yes, unfortunately—"

"Then you've heard the news?"

"No, but I can guess. We've got another victim on our hands." Tilley meant what he said in the most moral sense. He felt himself—and, as an extension of himself, albeit to a lesser degree, the entire police unit working on the case—responsible for this fourth tragedy. His voice was heavy with culpability. "A man or a woman, chief?"

"A man. How the hell did you know? If you haven't heard the news?"

"Call it an educated guess. He in the same condition as Schencks—the Startsport kid?"

"Yes, and—"

"Where was he found?"

"Look here, Tilley, I'm the one asking the—"

"Damn it, chief, where was he found?" Tilley was in no mood to knuckle under to his superior's power games.

"Between Potawket and Bedenbunkport," Chief Skillin

sputtered angrily. "On the beach. His car was parked on the shore road, a few miles off 187—"

"That's just below South Bay. . . . Has he been identified?"

"He has. And if you were here where you should be, instead of—"

"Who is he?"

"Another tourist. Some New Yorker. Now I've had about enough—"

"What's his name?"

"Pocetto, Niccolo Pocetto."

"Jesus Christ!" Tilley expelled his breath as if he had been punched in the solar plexus.

"You know him? Who is he?" Skillin became suddenly alert. "Speak up, Tilley, I can't hear you. Who is he?"

"He's . . . a friend of Carey Hunter's. Possibly"—Tilley thought of the letter he had read through a layer of plastic bagging; he was disgruntled at having even to suggest to Hoho Skillin details of the woman's personal life—"her boyfriend." He expelled another breath forcefully. "This makes three victims closely connected to her."

"It could also make her a likely suspect."

"The hell it could," Tilley snapped. "Forget that, chief, or you'll just make an ass of yourself." He heard Skillin protesting angrily on the other end of the line, but overrode him without pausing. "Has she been found? What's the Coast Guard reported?"

"Nothing. No sightings, no reports. Nothing. Wherever she is she's still there. Now—"

"They going to keep on searching?"

"I think. At least another day. But they've dropped a few hints—"

"Not while the weather holds good." Anger erupted out of Tilley like a sheet of flame. "She could survive weeks in a dinghy in calm weather like this. They can't abandon the search, damn it, they can't." He felt himself perspiring.

"May I remind you, lieutenant," Chief Skillin barked caustically into his ear, "that you have much more vital things to do than worry about one missing tourist. And I'd like to know just what in hell you think you're doing up in Pine Woods when every victim in this case has been found within five miles of South Bay? I warn you, Tilley, if one more of these murders occurs down there without you—''

"There won't be any more," Tilley said quietly.

"—having brought in a suspect or at least a solid lead, you're going to be off this case. And out of a job as well." Skillin's voice rang with regained authority.

"There won't be any more," Tilley said again.

"And that's a promise," his chief finished smugly. After a split-second pause he added, "What?"

"I said there won't be another death, victim. Not in this case." Tilley glanced at his watch. It was two minutes before the hour. "I've got to go. Is there anything else I should know? Anybody see the killer this time?"

"No. How in hell do you know the killer won't strike again? Just what are you up to, Tilley? What're you holding back?"

"I don't have time to explain. I'll see you when I get back."

Tilley hung up the phone and hurried out of Mayor Farley's office, down the center hall, and into the front parlor.

"Do you have a radio in here, Mayor Farley?" he asked abruptly.

"Why, yes, Lieutenant Tilley," she replied, looking a little startled. "Over there." She pointed to a table on the far side of the room.

Tilley strode across the room and switched on the radio. He swung the dial quickly to WABI, then looked at his watch as a commercial invaded the still room. He had about forty-five seconds to clear his mind of anxiety for Carey Hunter's safety; compassion for her new grief; bitter, guilty regret at being directly responsible for it; and fury with the Coast Guard, Hoho Skillin, and, especially, the people of Pine Woods. Not since his wife's death had he found it so difficult to push down turmoil inside himself and turn his full concentration to the moment. The commercial ended, the station break came and went, and the newscaster's introduction concluded before Tilley succeeded in getting command of himself. He turned to study the reactions of Mayor Farley, Sheriff Welles, and the Reverend Moholland as the newscaster was already a few words into the story.

". . . man was found brutally murdered early this afternoon on an isolated stretch of beach between Potawket and Bedenbunkport . . ." Tilley paid less attention to the news report than he did to the reactions of the Pine Woods officials. He found most notable a distinct absence of surprise in their expressions. They exchanged no glances with each other, all three keeping their eyes downcast.

You're a cool bunch, he thought. He read their faces as almost resigned. While it did not astonish him, being pretty much what he had expected, it did anger him. ". . . refuse to release the name of the dead man until his family has been notified. . . ." Tilley felt Crowley staring at him. How did I know? he thought in answer to the question he knew, without taking his eyes off the others, was in his sergeant's eyes. You won't believe me when I tell you. ". . . Bangor police have so far refused comment on the exact cause of the victim's death, but the couple who discovered the body described it as"—Tilley's eyes narrowed with concentration; he kept them fastened on the Reverend Moholland in the hope that the nature of his calling might cause the minister to reveal somewhat more than the mayor and sheriff were likely to do—" 'enormously bloated, like a balloon, almost, and covered with blood.' Local authorities speculate the body may have washed ashore . . ." The Reverend Moholland lowered his head. His hands came together, fingertips barely touching his lips, in an attitude of prayer. It told Tilley nothing, and he cursed inwardly. ". . . abandoned car with New York license plates was found less than half a mile from . . . has not yet been positively identified as having belonged to the murdered man. . . ." Something now surprised Tilley. He was certain he saw Mayor Farley brush a tear from her cheek. "Police are refusing to comment on reports that a boy's body was found in a similar condition outside South

Bay yesterday . . .'' Tilley reached behind him and located the radio's off–on dial. ''. . . but eyewitnesses—'' He switched it off.

The sudden silence in the room was deafening. Tilley stood watching the three Pine Woods officials. He knew Crowley would say nothing until he was asked, leaving the direction the meeting was to take entirely in his hands. So he waited, his inner radar on full alert to detect the slightest slip or giveaway on the part of the locals.

It was some time before anyone moved or spoke. Finally Sheriff Welles looked up with darkened eyes and said, in a voice not quite empty of emotion, ''And what does this have to do with your return visit, Lieutenant Tilley? I take it you had a purpose in having us listen to that news?''

''In answer to your first question,'' Tilley said flatly, ''that's what I'd like you to tell me.''

''I'm afraid I don't understand.'' Mayor Farley now looked up. If she had shed tears a moment earlier, Tilley could not now detect any sign of them. The mayor's face was calm and composed, as was her voice. ''Could you explain yourself, Lieutenant Tilley, please? We stand ready to help you in any way we can, if you'll just make it clear what it is you wish from us.''

Tilley studied her face a moment. He felt he was beginning to understand how this woman had come to be elected mayor in a backward little place like Pine Woods, where male dominance would ordinarily be rampant. Mayor Farley had none of the defensive surliness apparent in the local sheriff, and not a trace of the timidity afflicting the Reverend Moholland. She had presence, and Tilley found himself admiring her in spite of everything. It's not you I'll break, lady, he said to himself. He took his time in answering her.

''The first thing you can do, Mayor Farley, is turn over all your death certificates for the past month to Sergeant Crowley here.'' He watched her face closely.

''Certainly, Lieutenant Tilley, if you think it will help

you." Mayor Farley did not bat an eyelash. She looked at him expectantly.

Tilley's respect for her went up another notch when she did not ask what the second thing might be, but waited for him to speak again, as he had waited for one of them just minutes ago. He scored her a worthy adversary.

"How many deaths have occurred in Pine Woods in the past week?" Tilley knew, though the mayor's face revealed nothing, that she and the others knew exactly what he suspected. He felt just as certain that they knew he could not have explained the basis for his suspicions in anything approaching a rational, factual manner. You know what I don't know, as well as what I do, he thought wryly, and you also know nobody outside of here would think I was in my right mind if I tried to explain it. He kept his expression as inscrutable as hers.

"Why, none, lieutenant." Mayor Farley smiled ingenuously at him. "We're a pretty healthy lot. Why do you ask?"

"Is there a doctor in town?" Tilley ignored her question.

"Oh, yes. Dr. Widdows." She gestured vaguely. "He's right next door."

"Hmm. I don't recall seeing his shingle," Tilley mused deliberately.

"There isn't one. We're a very small town, Lieutenant Tilley. We all know where to find him when we need him."

"I see." Tilley paused. He felt frustrated. "Well, I'll want to speak with him later. By the way, Reverend," he looked over at the minister, "I'm curious. Sergeant Crowley and I didn't see a cemetery near your church. Is there another church in town?"

"The Reverend Moholland hesitated briefly, "No. No, there isn't. We've only one, I'm afraid."

I bet you are, Tilley thought caustically. He could almost smell fear emanating from the local pastor. "I see. Where is your cemetery, then?"

The minister hesitated again.

"We don't bury our dead, Mr. Tilley," Mayor Farley spoke up. "We cremate them."

Tilley experienced his first triumph of the day, although he had to acknowledge that it was a very minor one.

"There's a mortician in town?" He pretended surprise.

"Of course." Mayor Farley's eyebrows rose innocently. "Mr. Trickett." She leaned forward a little, her eyes questioning. "You seem surprised, lieutenant."

"Frankly, I am. Pine Woods is a very small town. To have both a doctor and a mortician."

"We believe in taking care of our own here," the mayor said blandly. "We're a small, isolated community, but we're not entirely without education, Lieutenant Tilley. I know how we must seem to outsiders, but there are some of us who are working to bring Pine Woods . . . up to date, shall we say? However, there are still a great many of our people who retain strong suspicions where outsiders are concerned, and they wouldn't seek medical attention if it meant going to a doctor they didn't know. Or place their deceased in the hands of strangers." She smiled wearily. "You don't change an entire town's attitudes overnight, as you must know. Those of us who are able go on with our education, then come back and do what we can. It isn't an easy task, but we do it. We're very close here, and we care about each other. And our little town."

"I'm certain you do." Tilley doubted his real meaning was lost on any of them. He took his notebook and pen from his inside jacket pocket and with deliberate slowness made some notes. "That's Dr. Widdows—with two *d*'s, am I right?"

"You are." Mayor Farley's voice remained mild. "Dr. Adrian Widdows."

"Thank you. And Mr.—?" He glanced up at her.

"Dalbert Trickett. Two *t*'s."

"And where is he located, Mayor Farley? Where is the crematorium?" Tilley looked from his notebook, pen poised, and met her eyes.

"Quite some distance behind our general store." The mayor's face took on an expression of patient seriousness.

"It was the Town Council's decision, at the time, to locate the crematorium as far from any of the houses as was practical."

"Mm-hmm." Tilley looked down again and made a note. "I take it there's a road?" He chided himself for not having found it when he and and Crowley were going from house to house.

"Certainly. Right behind the store."

"Ah," Tilley uttered shortly. *And that just happens to be the one place where you didn't go around to the back,* he took himself to task. *I would have thought you knew by now never to assume anything.* He felt derelict, and did not look up again until he had written a more detailed note on the crematorium than he needed.

"Has any resident here been out of town at any time in the last ten days or so?" he asked abruptly, after his lengthy pause, looking up from one to the other of the three. "Please think carefully. It's important."

Sheriff Welles's eyes narrowed with suspicious caution. "I thought you satisfied yourself on that point the last time you were here, lieutenant."

"Not just teenagers, high-school kids, sheriff. Anybody. Any adults? Children? Older folks?"

"Not that I know of," the sheriff replied quickly.

"Well, I'm sure," Mayor Farley put in, "that the Pulks went over to Houlton two or three times. With their vegetables. They always do this time of year. In fact, I think Kee Sawtelle said something about their having gone over yesterday morning."

"The Pulks?" Tilley asked.

"Jerral and Meda Pulk. They have a fair-sized farm out past the Sawtelles' place, west of town. This time of year they're usually making at least two trips into Houlton a week with produce, if not three. Kee—that's Keerock, Mr. Tilley—" Mayor Farley interrupted herself while Tilley was writing busily, "the Sawtelles' boy, is a friend of Davey's. They were playing together here Saturday, yesterday."

"Al Rook drove Norma down to Millinocket this past

Thursday," the Reverend Moholland put in thoughtfully. "Said she needed new shoes and some clothes for school next month, as I recall." His wide eyes said innocently that he hoped this bit of information about local goings-on was helpful to the detective.

"His full name is Alvah," the mayor offered before Tilley could ask.

"Anybody else?" Tilley went on writing, glancing up sporadically to check their expressions.

"Not that I can think of, right offhand." Mayor Farley pursed her lips. "That doesn't mean positively no one else did go, for one thing or another. We're not East Berlin here, lieutenant." She chuckled softly. "We don't require our neighbors to get passes or have visas stamped to get in or out of town."

Tilley nodded, a wry smile twisting one corner of his mouth. His notes completed for the moment, he was vexing himself for not having found the road leading to the Pulk farm. Another place I didn't look behind? he wondered irritably. Or do they hide their roads like they do everything else around here?

"I see," he said after a pause. "Then four teenagers could have gone down to South Bay last week without your knowing about it?"

"I suppose they could have," Mayor Farley responded. Not quite so smoothly, Tilley thought. He noticed, as she went on speaking, that the pastor looked distinctly uncomfortable and Sheriff Welles possibly a shade surlier than usual. "But if they had, I'm quite sure we would have heard about it by now. We keep a close watch on our youngsters, Lieutenant Tilley. We're very old-fashioned when it comes to raising our children. They don't suffer from the lack of supervision that gets so many of today's young people in trouble. It may seem strange to a city person like yourself, but we really see our children as the future. And that being the case, we don't neglect them."

Tilley felt the woman had responded more adamantly, and explicitly, than his question warranted. He felt almost challenged, but concurred, smiling, "Strange—and welcome. My job would be a lot easier if more parents still felt as you do."

"Our children are us, Mr. Tilley." The mayor's hazel-green eyes flashed with intensity; she spoke energetically, her voice louder than previously. Tilley registered that her entire posture had changed, though she had not moved, to that of one ready to spring to the defense.

He found the mayor's choice of words curious, and thought again of Patti Welles, bitterly disappointed, in spite of her insistence to the contrary, in the choice of careers forced upon her by her father. Perhaps the local sheriff—and all the parents in Pine Woods—forced their children to live out the mayor's odd statement too literally.

"Then it wouldn't be unusual for you to go to any lengths to, say, shield or protect them, if they'd done something wrong?"

"Are you implying, lieutenant," Sheriff Welles spoke up sharply, "that someone in Pine Woods is under suspicion of . . . something?"

Tilley shrugged. "Sheriff, you may take my meaning any way you see fit. Look, you're an officer of the law, just as I am. Mayor Farley, so are you, in a manner of speaking. And the reverend here is, let's say, an officer of an even higher law." He looked each one of them directly in the eye, taking his time, then shrugged again. "I have four violent deaths to solve, deaths everyone else who knows about them considers murders. I happen to think they may well have been accidental deaths, although I can't explain why I think so. I also think all of you—and perhaps everyone in this town—already know about them. Now, I have every reason to believe four of your young-sters were down in South Bay a week ago. Frankly, I don't think they ever returned—alive. I think you—some of you—found their bodies and brought them back and cre-mated them, this past week, probably to keep whatever terrible accidents happened from bringing publicity and notoriety to your town." Tilley paused, studying their faces briefly. "Surely I don't have to tell you three that being involved in an accident is not necessarily a

crime in this state—or country. No one's going to prose-
cute four dead teenagers who died in some kind of horrible
accidents that happened to cause the deaths of four other
people.''

Tilley paused again, feeling he hadn't expressed his
thought as well as he should have, and took a deep breath.
''At this time, all the news media know about are two of
the deaths. If you cooperate with me now, right away, I
may be able to keep this case from being blown up out of
all proportion and save Pine Woods a great deal of un-
wanted publicity. If not . . .'' Again he paused and looked
each one of them in the eye for a several seconds, Then he
shrugged. ''Will you give me your cooperation?'' He waited
a moment. When no one spoke, he added, ''While there's
still time? I promise I'll do everything in my power to
protect the privacy of the families concerned—and your
town—and to keep the media from turning your way of
life up here into a public circus. Will you give me your
cooperation?'' he repeated with intensity.

15

It had been well past one in the afternoon when Carey
Hunter saw land again, stark, sleek rock glistening wetly
in the sunlight as it lifted over the water on the edge of the
horizon ahead of *The Mermaid*. It was after two before she
set foot, unsteadily, on the little wooden dock deep in the
north crook of Parson's Cove.

''Still got your sea legs—or sea seat—I see,'' Dinny
joked, half-carrying her, despite her protests, up the short
dock. ''I don't imagine you got much chance to get any
legs in that dinghy.''

Parson's Cove was a miniscule inlet, the narrow channel of which, after turning sharply almost due east around a tall rock spit, opened into a miniature bay, barely large enough to harbor more than three small lobster boats. Carey had caught a glimpse of a small cabin nestled in the dense growth of pine trees on the northwest shore while Dinny was mooring *The Mermaid*. His own two-room shack stood among the sparse pines on the ocean side of the cove where the rock spit began to widen into the mainland.

The clapboard shack was unpainted, gray and weather-beaten. It looked to Carey as if it had been walled with driftwood. Set on jetty pilings driven into the rocky ground, the shack itself stood some three feet above the land. The bay side—all she could see as Dinny helped her up the steep, short climb from the dock—held a wooden door and a window that had been set horizontally, rather than vertically, into the house wall. Nailed over the door was a large rough board on which had been hand-painted in big, once-black letters: DINNY, and under that: MAYOR OF PARSON'S COVE.

"First thing you need is a hot bath," Dinny announced as he guided her up the back—or front, Carey had a feeling it didn't much matter—steps into his little square kitchen. "And some dry clothes, and something for those hands and that face." He shoved her gently down onto an old wooden chair beside the porcelain-topped kitchen table. "Let me get the water on first. Hot baths don't happen automatically in Parson's Cove."

She watched him as he took two enormous pots from the floor-level compartment of a tier of orange crates stacked against the inside wall of the room and set them in a large disposal sink under a window—this one set vertically. A small, cast-iron, old-fashioned hand pump was set in the rough pine counter to the right of the sink, and he worked the handle until he had filled both pots. He carried them, one at a time, to the tank-fed stove resting on an upended metal sea chest against the back wall and set them on the rear burners.

Then he went back to the orange-crate cabinet and rummaged around in the lower sections until he produced another two pots, not quite as large as the first two. He filled these at the pump also, and set them on the front burners of his stove. He lit all four burners quickly, turning them up high. He turned to Carey.

"Tub's under the house," he offered, looking at her intently. "Can you get out of those wet clothes alone? There's a robe somewhere in the front room."

Carey shook her head quickly, the expression of fear on her face as readable as an open book. "They're not wet anymore," she said, her voice a little shrill. "They're almost dry. They dried on me. I don't want a bath."

Her navy sweater was almost dry. She had spent the hours aboard *The Mermaid*, after coming to from her faint, sitting huddled under the blanket out on the deck, as far away from Dinny as she could find a clear spot big enough to hold her. After he had set his pots, she had moved all the way astern to keep the length of the small boat between them. Her jeans were still quite damp, but she did not care.

"Sometimes we all need a little help, Margie Packer." He smiled at her comfortingly, but Carey's mind was once again befuddled and alarmed by his use of her friend's name, and she discounted the warmth in his voice and the gentle caring in his expression as deliberate—and false. She shrank from him as he stepped toward her. "I'm not going to do you any harm. I'm concerned about these hands of yours." He lifted her arms by the wrists, ignoring her recoil from him, and turned her hands up to inspect them. "Well, if you can manage by yourself, fine. If not, just give a holler." He placed her forearms gently back down on her thighs. "I'm here if you need me. I'll go bring in the tub, in case you change your mind." He cocked his head and looked at her quizzically. "You sure need a bath, Margie Packer."

Carey's heart beat like a frightened bird against her ribs as he strode out of the kitchen. She was unable to draw a full breath until she heard him clumping down the steps outside. Then she got up stiffly and shuffled to the doorway between the two rooms.

The only furniture in the disordered front room was a double brass bed, two shredded easy chairs that oozed great gobs of dirty-gray stuffing, and a rickety chest of drawers supported by bricks where two front legs had once been. In the far wall was a door leading out onto a narrow, uncovered porch that faced the sea.

The bed was unmade. Its one torn sheet looked clean; the lumpy tangle of blankets not quite, or simply too old and shabby ever to appear clean anymore. Carey saw a worn woolen bathrobe hanging, under three shirts, two sweaters, and a battered old pea jacket, on a nail on the inside wall.

She could hear the great banging and clanging and cursing going on beneath the shack as Dinny retrieved his bathtub from its storage place. She gritted her teeth. Let him struggle. He would not find her such easy prey as he had found Margie and Mrs. Rambeau. She, now, knew what to expect; she was on to him. She didn't need that detective to tell her why Margie wasn't wearing her Lois Nettleton top—not now. Not after seeing what the murderer had done to poor old Mrs. Rambeau. He wasn't going to come back with his damn tub and find her naked and ready for whatever ritual ablutions he wanted to perform to make her ready for death. She shuddered and drew her arms across her breasts, shielding them.

She shuffled back to the table and sat down again on the kitchen chair. She was trembling uncontrollably and forced her mind to think of something else, something happy, some earlier time when she had felt safe and eager for life, believing it held only good for her. She was determined to get control of herself before Dinny returned.

Her mind, however, seemed bent on keeping her from remembering all the good times she had known. When she tried to recall her father, beaming with loving pleasure as she and her sister, Anne, had stood in awe before the lighted trees of their Christmas mornings, she found herself instead seeing the strangely familiar face on Outer Island's dock, brightly glowing in the flashlight's beam, leering down at her. Before she could shut the imagine out, it fused with Dinny's face, and the two became inseparable in her mind's eye. She tried to picture Anne, smiling and giggling at some shared childhood secret, but her sister's face persisted in metamorphosing into Margie's, which then shrank instantly into an unrecognizable death's-head scream of agony. Instead of her mother tucking her in bed years ago, she saw Mrs. Rambeau's mummified grimace bending down to kiss her goodnight.

No matter whom she tried to think about, the people of her life all were transmogrified by her fear into one or another demonic shred torn from the last few days of her life. She bolted to her feet at the crash of Dinny's tub being heaved up onto the back stoop and stood quivering with terror, her useless hands held out before her in a pathetic gesture of defense, as the tub was shoved through the doorway.

"Did you manage okay? Are you ready?"

Dinny's questions were a series of sounds to Carey, empty of meaning. She closed her eyes as he came toward her, certain he, too, was about to alter in form into something more terrifying than death itself, overwhelm, and obliterate her.

It was Mayor Farley who finally replied to Tilley. "We've already told you everything we know, Lieutenant Tilley. Which is nothing." She looked at him with anxious, innocent eyes. "If there's anything else we can do—?"

"Damn it." Tilley spoke in a low voice. "Now you listen to me. I've got lab reports on my desk in Bangor detailing unidentifiable lymph and chyle samples, so low in fibrinogen and leucocytes they won't clot—samples taken from the skin and clothing, and in one instance from inside the body, of three of the victims. And from bedclothes and carpets. I've also got epidermal prickle cells found under the fingernails of one victim that present a fibril density so extreme Eastern Maine Medical Center's lab reported they couldn't positively classify them as human.

"Shall I go on? I have some very interesting, if puzzling, reports on tissue samples taken from the mammary glands of the victims. Puzzling because none of them was nursing an infant—one being a teenage boy and another an elderly woman—yet all three of them displayed breast changes known to occur only during lactation. Enlarged sebaceous glands. Excessive deposition of pigment in the areolae. Fatty degeneration of the cells in the center of the alveolus and granulation of the peripheral cells, which were also found to contain oil globules.'' He looked from one to the other. ''I don't think I need to go on. It must be clear I have sufficient data to obtain a court order for a complete medical examination of whomever I choose in this town.'' Tilley was careful to keep his voice as low and unruffled during his last statement as it had been previously. He was bluffing now; he knew he didn't stand a ghost of a chance of getting such an order, and prayed Pine Woods had not felt it necessary to equip the town with a lawyer as well as a doctor and an undertaker. When Mayor Farley spoke, he felt God had turned a deaf ear to his prayers.

''As an attorney, Lieutenant Tilley,'' she said carefully, ''I think that highly unlikely, to say the least.''

Tilley cursed silently. He had gambled before and lost, but never had he experienced the loss so keenly. Always before, he had found another move to make, kept yet another ace up his sleeve. But here in Pine Woods he had played his whole hand and discovered his sleeve was rolled up. For the moment at least, his mind not only refused to come up with a new move but taunted him with his inept, precipitous playing out of his hand as well. He was furious with himself and found his concentration divided by the need to use a considerable portion of it to keep his anger from showing. And he would given his eye teeth for just one cup of coffee.

His casually delivered ''Well, we'll have to see about that, won't we,'' fell on deaf ears as had his earlier prayers. Mayor Farley coolly ignored it, noting, unheatedly and with some amusement, the lack of any link to Pine Woods in any of the lab findings and professing a complete inability to comprehend his speculations on the nature of the deaths, or how, even if he was right, such deaths could have anything to do with her little town. She shook her head enough, but not too much; she smiled with bewilderment in all the right places and never in the wrong ones; she proffered all the help at her command without ever, in tone or choice of words, patronizing him. To Tilley's mind, she was too perfect. He gave her credit for a flawless performance and conceded the day to her with concealed bitterness.

But only the day. Tilley had survived too much in life ever to accept losing. His determination to crack Pine Woods and lay bare whatever the town was hiding simply grew stronger as he encountered each new stone wall. The death certificates he asked for turned out to be one—of a reportedly seventy-three-year-old who had succumbed to a heart attack three weeks earlier. Tilley could tell at first glance there was nothing in it that would help him, and he did not reiterate his request that the mayor turn it over to Sgt. Crowley. Without a subpoena she could have refused him, though he felt certain she would not have done so.

His meeting with Dr. Widdows was equally unrewarding. He found only a typical country doctor, in a typical country doctor's home–office, whose recent files revealed nothing more than the usual rural ailments and accidents—the setting of an arm broken in a fall from a barn roof, a tetanus shot given to a child who had stepped on a rusty nail, the taping of a couple of sprained ankles, the delivery of two baby girls and one baby boy, heat applications and rest advised for a strained shoulder, and the like. When Tilley expressed curiosity about the lack of serious illnesses among the population of Pine Woods, Dr. Widdows echoed what Mayor Farley had told him earlier.

"Well, we're a pretty healthy lot up here, Mr. Tilley. I speculate it's because we can't afford any processed foods, get lots of exercise, and nobody can afford to overeat."

Tilley smiled. "Does seem odd, even so, in today's America."

"Pine Woods hasn't joined today's America. Not yet." Dr. Widdows cleared his throat. "I'm pessimistic enough to expect to see some pretty unhappy changes in my files once it does, over the next twenty years or so. If I live that long,'' he added good-humoredly.

Tilley raised his eyebrows. Dr. Widdows looked to him to be a very young man. He glanced up at the array of diplomas and certificates dotting the walls of the doctor's office and was astounded, in spite of all he'd already seen to read that Adrian Widdows had been awarded his license to practice in 1952.

"Besides extraordinary good health," he commented wryly, "Pine Woods also seems to have discovered the Fountain of Youth.''

"It does look that way, doesn't it. However, I assure you, Mr. Tilley, that unfortunately we haven't. If we had, we'd be bottling it for international distribution and sale, and wiping Poland Spring off the map. We do, for the most part, seem to stay quite youthful in appearance until relatively late in life. I've wondered about it a lot myself—is it genetic? for example. We are a pretty inbred community, like all small, isolated—what you probably call backward—villages. No doubt you noticed how much we all resemble each other.'' He smiled at Tilley. "But I'm not a scientist, only a backwoods G.P., and I've never come up with any explanation for our delayed aging that seemed reasonable, let alone worth pursuing. The desire to do so, I will confess, sparked my interest in medicine as a boy and carried me through med school and the early years of what has been a pretty uneventful rural practice.'' Dr. Widdows' face took on a pensive, tired expression as he went on speaking. "But, as I said, I never came up anything, really. The years went by without answers, and the flame of my passion to make a name for myself burned lower and lower as they did so. I finally accepted that I wasn't a genius,'' he chuckled, "and would never change the world, or even Pine Woods. Once I did that, any dream I'd ever had about discovering some secret of prolonged youth in little old Pine Woods regretfully lay down and died.''

Tilley smiled at the doctor understandingly. He liked him. Adrian Widdows was only the second person he'd met in Pine Woods for whom he did feel liking. Still, he felt there was much the man was holding back.

Dr. Widdows seemed go on merely for his own benefit. "I used to think if I could have gone to a better—bigger— medical school, interned in Europe somewhere, Vienna maybe . . ."

His voice trailed off. Tilley thought of Patti Welles and how she had spoken with touching regret about the Boston Conservatory of Music. He was moved by Dr. Widdows' private and possibly unintended confession of disappointed hopes, but not so much that he failed to sense an opportunity to get hold of another tiny piece of the puzzle confronting him.

"Why didn't you?" he asked quietly. "Go off somewhere, to a bigger school, to Europe—if that's what you wanted?"

"Oh, I couldn't have." Dr. Widdows shook his head and seemed to wake up. He stared at Tilley a moment before explaining. "I wasn't good enough. That is, I wasn't smart enough. It was my grades that weren't good enough." He smiled broadly. "Well, is there anything else I help you with, Mr. Tilley?"

Tilley now smiled. "Maybe. You can tell me if anyone in Pine Woods *ever* gets old. I'm thinking of putting your town on my list of places to retire to, one of these days."

The doctor laughed heartily. "Well, I wouldn't put us too high on your list, Mr. Tilley. There is one drawback to our prolonged prime, if I may call it that. When our time's about up, aging seems to strike us like a thunderbolt, not exactly all at once, but it comes on very fast up here. Not unlike the ending of poor Dorian Gray, if you've read your Wilde." He smiled as Tilley nodded at him, then suddenly looked alarmed. "Well, I'm exaggerating, of course. It's not that sudden. My weakness for the dramatic, I'm afraid. What I really don't want to tell you is, I don't think you'd find it much to your liking here. For other reasons. I'm sure you've experienced a distinct lack of friendliness from many of my neighbors. The people here don't like or trust strangers. It would be a cold place to spend your last years, if you hadn't been born here.''

"I've noticed," Tilley said lightly. He also noticed that the doctor was flushed and sweating, disconcerted, obviously, by his own revelation. Knowing he would get no more out of the man, Tilley chuckled deliberately. "I had a feeling you were fictionalizing there for my benefit." His feeling was exactly the opposite. He was certain the local doctor had given something away that he would give an arm, and maybe a leg, to get back. "I have to believe you all stay young a long time, because I've seen it. But you'll never convince me you also age in a matter of minutes, doctor." He stood up. "I think that's about it. Thank you, Dr. Widdows. You've been most helpful, and I appreciate your generosity with your time."

He got nothing at all from Dalbert Trickett, Pine Woods's mortician. Trickett was almost as surly as Sheriff Welles, and even more taciturn. His answers were monosyllabic, and given only after a question had been repeated two or three times when, Tilley felt, he emitted a sound simply in order not to have to hear the question yet another time.

His house was situated a good mile and a half behind the general store. The narrow dirt road leading to it appeared little used, overgrown with groundcover in some places and encroached upon by sweeping, low pine boughs in others. At one point the road dipped sharply down. Tilley stopped his car and got out. He walked ahead slowly, peering at the ground. Here it was still muddy from the edges of the recent northeaster, and he detected fresh tire tracks. He was certain they had been made by vehicles traveling in both directions—or the same vehicle. He knew he would have to have casts made to determine with any degree of reliability how many different vehicles had used the road since the storm. He sighed. He might as well forget it. With Ho Skillin looking frantically for a scapegoat in order to save his own face—and job—Tilley knew it would be a cold day in hell before he himself would get back to Pine Woods.

He squatted down to study one small but well-defined

section of a tire impression, then stood up suddenly and turned on his heel. What the hell was he doing? He was wasting time here without a team. All he could say for certain was that the road had been used recently, probably this very day. That told him nothing. Trickett had undoubtedly been in church with the rest of the town a couple of hours ago. The impressed mud proved about as much as his own presence in Pine Woods. Disgusted, he got back in his car and drove on, hoping at least that Crowley would manage to keep the mayor, the minister, and her father away from Patti Welles until after he'd had a chance to talk with her.

Tilley was angry. He was experiencing far more anxiety about Carey Hunter than he wanted to admit. He had feelings other than sympathy for her where Nick Pocetto's death was concerned, and they filled him with shame. He was furious that Mayor Farley had gotten the better of him. He was almost as angry with his chief, Ho Skillin, though this anger was laced with contempt, for all the things he knew the incompetent Hoho was going to hurl at him when he got back to Bangor that night. He felt compassion for Patti and Dr. Widdows, while he simultaneously resented their lying to him. He disliked Sheriff Welles's surliness and contemplated the satisfaction it would give him to punch the man in the mouth—if the two of them weren't wearing badges. He was extremely irritated at himself for having gone out on a limb with the court-order business—and humiliated that the limb had been sawed off so neatly, publicly. He was even angry with Crowley for having been there to witness him make a thorough ass of himself.

His frustration with the case was close to engulfing him. He couldn't believe his mind was letting him down so completely, that he didn't have a ghost of an idea what to do or where to look next for a solution. The only lead he had, and he knew himself it couldn't be flimsier without disintegrating, was Mrs. Mitchell's delayed report of the four teenagers on the South Bay ferry, with Carey Hunter, nine days ago. And his own gut feeling they had been from Pine Woods.

My gut feeling, he mused sarcastically. Christ, the damn mayor is right. I don't have even a hair to connect those kids to this town. Just another small town's local suspicions about outsiders and new faces and a Sherman tank of a shopkeeper's statement that the kids came from Pine Woods. Good God, she didn't even see them. How in hell I'm going to convince that ass Skillin to let me continue investigating this town I don't know. He swung the wheel to avoid a sizable rock cropping up out of the right side of the road and braked the car to crawl past the spot. "And God, what I'd give for a cup of coffee," he muttered aloud.

The trees opened up after another few hundred yards onto a three-acre clearing. Off to the left a little was a bleak, tired-looking Victorian house, grayed from decades of being left unpainted. Beyond it, and well away to the right, on the bank of a fair-sized pond, stood the crematorium, its blackened chimney standing out uninvitingly against the mellow green background of the pines on the far shore of the pond. Tilley felt a shudder run through his body.

"For a guy who's earned his living off him," he growled with irony as he parked his car, "you're not very appreciative of Old Floorer, 'the pale priest of the mute people.' " Browning had always been his favorite poet and it pleased him—the first thing in days that did—that he remembered the quotation accurately.

Dalbert Trickett was as uninviting as his small crematorium. Getting a reply from him was like pulling teeth, maybe harder. Churlishly, and only after repeated insistence followed, finally, by a thinly veiled threat to subpoena his files, the undertaker allowed the detective to look through his records of the past month. One cremation had taken place, that of a Mrs. Daureen Smen Tweedie, age seventy-three. It had been billed to—and already paid for by—one Real McNure Tweedie, son of the deceased.

Tilley ran a hand through his hair and closed the file.

There was nothing here that would help him, and while he had not expected there would be, his frustration took a giant step forward. He looked up at Trickett.

"I'd like to inspect your crematory, Mr. Trickett."

The man eyed him sullenly.

"Now, if you don't mind."

"Do."

"Well, I'm sorry, but I have to inspect it anyway. Shall we go?"

Silence.

"Shall we go, Mr. Trickett? My time is valuable."

Trickett emitted a contemptuous grunt.

"We'll go now, Mr. Trickett."

"Can't."

"Why not?" Pause. "Why not, Mr. Trickett?"

The man shrugged, remaining silent.

"If you've no reason, we'll go right now."

"Where?"

"To inspect your crematorium." Tilley was, by this time, out of patience.

"Why?"

Because I'll knock your block off if I don't get in there, Tilley said to himself. Aloud he replied, "It's part of my job, one of the things I'm up here for."

"Thought you was a detective."

"Detectives have to do a lot of funny things that don't make any sense to other people. Can we go now?"

"Nothin' funny 'bout inspectin' a crematorium. Do it m'self reg'lar-like. Makes good sense t' me."

Tilley was all but bowled over by the mortician's sudden verbosity, but he plunged right on, seizing the small advantage Trickett had inadvertently given him.

"Fine. Then you understand. So we can get right to it and get it over with."

"Right t' what?"

"Mr. Trickett. I tell you frankly I'm losing patience. 'What' is inspecting your crematory." Tilley's jaw was clenched.

"Don't see the need. Jes' did it m'self yestiddy."

"I don't give a damn if you did it an hour ago," Tilley exploded. "You're going to do it again, with me, and right now, or I'll arrest you for resisting an officer of the law and obstruction of justice."

In the small crematorium, the furnace was cold and spotlessly clean. Tilley could detect no sign of recent usage, except that, once again, his intuition nagged him that it was *too* clean. There were only two ovens; when Tilley, flashlight in hand, put his head in the second to examine the interior, a faint but unmistakable whiff of pine-tar soap struck his nostrils.

It was little enough, but it cheered him out of all proportion to any real value it represented in the case. He would have bet all he had in the world, including his life, that the oven had been used, then cleaned thoroughly to disguise the fact, within the past week, probably within the past twenty-four hours. His confidence returned, and his mood swung from sour to almost sunny. When he backed out of the oven and straightened up, he looked a different man than the one who had peered in seconds before.

"You certainly keep the premises spotless, Mr. Trickett," he said jovially, scrutinizing the mortician's face. "I never saw a furnace so clean. You must have scrubbed this oven this morning I can still smell the soap. You always clean it this thoroughly after use?"

"All depends." Trickett's face wore its usual surly expression, except for a barely detectable narrowing of the eyes.

"You must have cleaned it this this morning," Tilley repeated cheerfully, "The smell's still so strong."

Without replying, Trickett stepped forward and stuck his head into the oven, sniffed loudly, then backed out.

"Don't smell it m'self," he muttered in a tone intended to end the discussion once and for all.

"Mmm, must have been yesterday, then. Late. I do have a very good nose." Tilley was still smiling.

"Mighta been." Mr. Trickett eyed him suspiciously.

"You used the oven Thursday or Friday, then?"

Trickett was not fooled into answering, either by voice

or expression. He watched Tilley's face as closely as Tilley was watching his.

"Neither," he growled, then added, uncharacteristically, "She ain't been used since ol' Miz Tweedie went t' her reward three weeks ago t' the day.

Tilley concealed his satisfaction. Trickett might as well have named the day, so certain was he that the man's need to remind him of the specific information in the file he had just read proved he was lying.

"I don't know much about this kind of thing," Tilley said offhandedly, "and I'm curious to know how long it takes a furnace this size to cool down after use. How long does it take, Mr. Trickett?"

The undertaker eyed him a long time before answering, but Tilley did not repeat his question. He gazed back at the man without blinking, until Trickett dropped his eyes.

"Never timed it," he muttered at last. "Got better things t' do with m' time."

"Oh, but you must have some rough idea? A few hours? A day? Two? How long, Mr. Trickett?" A definite authority now appropriated Tilley's voice. His last question came out more of a demand than a query.

"Told ya, I don't rightly know. Never timed it." He closed the oven door and started across the room, away from Tilley, not looking at him. "Never even thought about it. Coupla days, mebbe, mebbe more. Mebbe less. Don't see what blasted difference it makes, one way or t'other." He stopped at the door and glanced back at the detective. "You finished in here?" He turned and walked through the doorway without waiting for Tilley's reply.

Tilley's next stop was at Sheriff Welles's house. He found Patti in a subdued, uncommunicative mood. She refused to talk about herself or her plans for college in September, and her answers to his deliberately offhand questions about the activities of the other inhabitants of Pine Woods were limited to phrases like "Not that I know of," "I don't know," "Better ask my father," and, where recent deaths were concerned, "Old Mrs. Tweedie

died three weeks ago.'' Patti did not hasten to add that
there had been no other deaths since that one, and Tilley
rather admired her sense for not answering more than had
been asked.

''Well, then,'' he said, ''if that's really all you've got to
say to me, Patti, I guess I'd better get on with my business
here.'' He gazed into her hazel-green eyes, frowning.
He'd thought he had a potential ally in young Patti Welles.
Now he had no choice but to tell himself he'd been wrong.
His supposed ally could no longer be counted on—or
perhaps never existed, except in his own mind. His glee at
scenting pine-tar soap in Dalbert Trickett's crematorium
was rapidly dissipating, overwhelmed by a fresh wave of
frustration. His frown deepened into a scowl. Patti had not
even offered him a cup of coffee. She'd stood the whole
time in her front doorway, making it obvious he was not
welcome, a second time, in her home. ''Is it all?'' he
reiterated in a growl.

''Yes,'' she mumbled, not meeting his eye.

''I see. Well that's that, then, isn't it, Patti.'' He paused,
then shrugged. ''I still think you're a decent person, Patti.
I just hope you can live with your conscience.'' He turned
to leave the porch.

''Paul—?''

''Yes?'' He turned back to her.

Her face was flushed; there were tears in her eyes. ''I
hope you can find that Carey Hunter soon,'' she stammered.
''I really hope you do.''

''Why?'' Tilley challenged her. ''What's it to you one
way or the other, Patti? You've chosen to refuse to help
me—when we both know you know something. What can
it possibly matter to you what becomes of Carey Hunter?''

Her lips trembled as she fought back tears. ''Just please
find her before . . . before something happens to her, Paul.
Please.'' She looked at him with haunted, pleading eyes.

Tilley took a sudden step toward her. ''Before what?
What were you about to say? Before what happens to
her?'' As Patti backed away from him, inside the house,
he stepped forward again. ''Patti, for God's sake, tell me

what you know. Now. While there's still time—not just for Carey Hunter, but for you, too.''

"Feeling better?"

Carey opened her eyes and blinked. A dark form was bending over her; the light from the window behind it blinded her to the features. It took her several seconds to orient herself and recognize Dinny.

"Yes. What happened?"

"You fainted. Again. I think you need some hot food in your belly. How about that bath and then some supper? Feel up to it now?"

He slipped his hands under her upper back and raised her to a sitting position. "Dizzy?" he asked.

"A little." Carey sat still, feeling her lightheadedness slowly subside. She became aware that she was on the rumpled, unmade bed she had seen earlier in the front room, and that her arms were encased in the big sleeves of the tired-plaid bathrobe she had noticed hanging on the wall. "Where are my clothes?" she squeaked, her voice panicky.

"Take it easy, take it easy, Margie Packer." Carey's mind blinked with shock once again at being called by her friend's name. "I took half of them off you while you were out. Figured it would be easier for you that way, with your hands and face in that condition. Now if you'll just stand up," he eased his hands under her arms, and lifted her up and forward, off the bed, "I'll get you out of those jeans and into a warm tub."

"No, no—" Carey started to protest shrilly.

"Now you just look at this as medical." She felt his hands fumbling under the bathrobe for the waistband of her jeans and her breath caught in her throat. "I've worked many a sick bay on many a ship. Passenger ships, too"— she heard the rasp of her zipper—"and it's neither here nor there to me." The damp denim and cool, slippery nylon of her bikinis inched reluctantly down over her hips. "A sick person's a sick person"—her jeans and underwear ganged up at her quivering knees—"and you're going to be a very

sick person if somebody doesn't take care of you. Somebody being me, as I'm the only other somebody here.
There.'' The denim, stiff with salt, grudgingly gave way
and bunched below her kneecaps. ''Sit down now—bed's
right behind you—atta girl—and I'll get these clean off
you.''

Numbly Carey sat and watched him ease off her soaked
topsiders, drop them on the floor, and drag the damp,
unwieldly denim down her calves and over her feet. He
dropped her jeans on the floor and quickly drew off her
bikinis. Her whole body stuttered with anxiety, but she
could think of no way to stop him.

''There.'' He slid his hands under her arms again and
lifted her to her feet. ''Come on. It's warmer in the
kitchen with the fires on, and I'll light the woodstove. By
the time the water's hot, it'll be warm as toast in there.''

He supported her into the kitchen and set her carefully
down on one of the three wooden chairs. Carey found her
body obeyed him like a child, while her mind screamed at
her to run, run, get away from him while she still could.
She felt helpless as she watched him move around the
small, cluttered kitchen with the grace of a dancer, now
checking the huge pots on his stove, now dragging the
old-fashioned, high-backed tin tub into position beside the
sink, now pushing the table a little aside to make more
room for it. Then he crossed the floor to a small, potbel-
lied black stove standing against the wall opposite the sink
and opened the door of it. Carey could see wood already
carefully laid for a fire inside.

''Don't like to have to fuss with it after a day out,''
Dinny said indifferently, not glancing at her, as he lit the
kindling and watched the flames take hold. ''Gets damn
cold here at night, even in summer.'' He closed the small
door and dropped the latch into place. ''I like to come
home and just light her up.''

He stood up, smiling at her. ''You'll be okay after a
bath and some hot soup.'' He patted the top of her head
lightly and went back to the cookstove and stuck a finger

in each of the four pots. "Pretty soon now. Just hang in there, Margie."

He stepped to the sink and rummaged around, his back to Carey. After a moment or so he worked the pump briefly, then turned around. A big, coarse, natural sponge dripped in his hand. He squatted down beside the tub and scrubbed it clean. Carey watched him in alarmed silence. When he had finished, to his opparent satisfaction, he rinsed the sponge under the pump and returned to the stove to test the pots again.

"It's getting here," he assured her. "While you're in the tub, I'll fix you some hot soup."

From his orange-crate cabinet he procured a box of dried soup mix and a couple of large mugs, and set them on the wooden sink counter. He tested the water in the pots another time, then turned to face Carey.

"I should have thought of this before," he said apologetically. "You must need to use the head. You never budged from the deck all day on *The Mermaid*. How about it? Before you get in the tub?"

Carey nodded. Now that Dinny had mentioned it, she felt suddenly as if her bladder were about to burst.

"Good." He came over to her and helped her up off the chair. "There's a chamber pot under the bed—for heavy weather. I'll haul it out for you."

He led her into the front room and dragged a stained china chamber pot out from under the bed. Then, like a father, he eased her down onto it, carefully guiding the long bathrobe over its sides.

"I'll be in the kitchen if you need help getting back up," he said, and left her alone.

Carey did need help, and she called for it out of fear of overturning the chamber pot, which struck her as even more embarrassing then being lifted off it. Dinny walked her, half-supporting her weight, back into the kitchen and over to the old-fashioned tub. It was almost three-quarters full of water, from which a delicious steam curled gently upward into the air.

"Stick a toe in and try it. Felt just about right to my elbow, but even my elbows are old and tough."

He steadied her on one leg while she tested the water.

"If it's okay, just step right in, ma'am," he said with mock politeness.

Carey could think of nothing to do but obey him, for the moment. She dipped a toe in the water and nodded. "It's fine."

"In you go, then."

When Carey was standing with both feet in the tub, Dinny stepped behind the high back of it and placed a hand lightly on each of her upper arms.

"Now, can I take this robe from you before I help you sit down? Room's really warming up. I don't think you'll be cold. And it'll be the easiest thing for you to slip into after you're done, if you let me keep it dry."

Carey remained still for a few moments, crossing her arms over her breasts and closing her mind to what was happening, then slowly brought her hands down to her waist and fumbled at the knotted belt with her fingertips. She did not ask the lobsterman to help her, and he did not try to, but stayed silently behind her, his hands lightly on her arms. When at last the two ends of the woolen belt dropped to her sides, she felt him start to slip the robe gently from her shoulders.

"Okay, easy does it now. Watch those hands, I don't want to hurt them."

With the gentleness of a mother with her child, Dinny eased first one sleeve and then the other down over her raw hands. Not so much as a thread brushed her palms, though the old wool did graze quite painfully the sun-burned backs of her hands. Then the robe landed in a lump on the kitchen table, and she felt Dinny's hands slip carefully under her arms from behind.

"Here we go, now. Take it slow. Don't worry about slipping, I've got you." After she was seated in the hot water, he added, "We won't try to wash your back. It took quite a burn right through your sweater. I'll just rinse it off for you when we're done."

He came around the side of the tub, took hold of her

wrists, and studied her hands again, then shook his head.
"You can't wash yourself with these. The soap'll kill
you."

Carey blanched beneath her sunburn and a shudder ran
through her. He looked up quickly at her face.

"Are you chilled?" he asked. "Damn. Hold on a
moment, I'll stoke up the stove."

He released her wrists and strode to the woodstove.
Grabbing a poker that rested against the wall, he yanked
open the stove door and jabbed at the fire several times,
then tossed in several large pieces of wood from a lidless
metal footlocker nearby. He watched the fire for a second,
then closed the door and replaced the poker.

"That ought to do it," he commented and hurried back
to her. "I'll be as quick about this as I can, Margie
Packer. And you just forget that you don't know me." He
reached into the sink, and a washrag and cake of soap
appeared in his hand. "Pretend there's a war on, and I'm a
medic cleaning you up to treat your battle wounds. I've
been in a couple of wars," he rambled on, soaping the
washrag and gently wiping her sunburned neck with it, "in
my time—I'm skipping your face, I'll just rinse it—mostly
doing just what I'm doing now, cleaning up the wounded."
The washrag moved lightly down one of her arms. "Keep
your hands up, hold them out so the soap doesn't run
down into those sores. Never did carry a gun. And never
fired a shot. Just cleaned up those who did." He soaped
her wrist carefully, then bent her arm at the elbow so her
hand pointed straight up. "Keep your arm bent, the soap'll
run off your elbow that way. Yes, ma'am," he reached
across the tub and began to wash her other arm, "that was
about my part in it, except for once—" He raised her other
hand as he had done the first. "Keep that one up the
same—off Makatea, back in, oh, sixty-eight I think it was
. . ." Delicately, so delicately Carey could scarcely feel
his hand beneath the cloth, he washed her chest and stroked
the thick suds down over her breasts; she went rigid and
held her breath. ". . . or sixty-seven, maybe, can't remember
which, doesn't matter anymore anyway, and it wasn't really

a war—well, it was to them, but it wouldn't be to us. The Kaukuras''—his hands slipped lower, soaping and rubbing her midriff and waist; she relaxed a little, and breathed out—''the Makemos, and the Takumes had joined forces to invade Makatea. I was first mate on a sloop out of Papeete. We ran some things, supplies and all, back and forth between the islands, and there we are coming up on Makatea''— Carey tensed again, momentarily, as the cloth swept quickly over her abdomen, then slipped down one thigh—''when suddenly the lookout yells, 'Boats dead ahead,' and what do you think, Margie Packer?'' He scrubbed at the calf of her leg briskly, then took hold of her ankle and washed her foot. ''Damned if we didn't sail right into three hundred or more war canoes, outriggers they were—with sails, too— and crammed full of spear-toting islanders. Damnedest thing you ever saw, I swear to God.'' He dropped her foot, hunkered around the tub, and began to wash her other leg. ''Well, there we were, smack dab in the middle of a native war. Old style.'' He lifted her right foot out of the water, scrubbed it, studied it, then glanced at her, grinning. ''Scrubs up good, don't she? That's Down East for: looks pretty clean to me.'' He laughed, looked at her, and tilted his head. ''Come on, Margie Packer, give us a smile, just a small one. You've shed about ten pounds of salt—must feel good now, doesn't it?''

Carey stared at him, feeling her face grow hot with shame or anxiety or both—she couldn't separate her reactions to him here, naked in his bathtub.

''Okay, never mind.'' He looked away from her. ''Later, maybe.'' He placed her foot back in the sudsy water. ''Well, that about does your front. How about a shampoo? It just so happens I served once as ship's barber on a ship—can't remember her name—out of Hong Kong bound for San Francisco.''

Carey smiled a little in spite of herself. ''You said that about sick bays, too. Is there anything you haven't done?''

''Not much, Margie Packer, not much.'' He slapped the washrag over the edge of the sink and stood up. ''Would you like me to give you a sailor's shampoo?''

"What is it?" She took him seriously.

"That, my girl," he answered, reaching to test the temperature in one of the two pots of fresh water he had put on the stove to heat after filling the tub, "is one hell of a sudsing with bar soap and, if you're lucky, a big-enough bucket of water poured over your head to get about half the soap rinsed out. Care to try one?"

"Anything would feel better than all this salt," Carey replied, still taking him at his word. "If it's not too much trouble."

"Not a bit. I know the feeling."

He retrieved a small saucepan from his orange crates and used it to wet her hair with the sudsy water from the tub. Then he lathered her hair thoroughly with the cake of soap, dropped it with a clatter into the metal sink, and rinsed his hands under the pump.

"Now to see how much of those suds we can get out." He tested both the pots on the stove and turned off the burners. "It's lukewarm, but that's about all your face and back will bear comfortably. First potful you take sitting down. Close your eyes. This may sting your lips a bit, but it'll be over in a flash."

A moment later Carey felt herself deluged with tepid water. Mounds of lather cascaded over her face and shoulders, slid down her breasts and upper arms, then mounted, in peaks, on the surface of the tub water around her waist.

"That hurt?" Dinny asked as the pot clattered back on the stove.

"Not much. It was worth it."

"Good. Now this one you stand up for, or the tub'll overflow."

She felt his hands under her arm again, from behind, and found herself being raised to her feet.

"Here we go. Eyes closed, and keep your hands up, Margie."

The second potful was poured more slowly and washed most of the suds down to her calves, where they were met by the mountains of lather now built up in the tub. The pot banged onto the stove behind her, and a second later she was gently wrapped in an enormous towel.

"There we go. Clean as a bos'n's pipe. Feel okay?"

"Yes. I'm okay. Thanks."

"Good. Let's step out now, shall we? There's another towel on the floor there. I'll see you don't slip."

Carey looked down and stepped carefully out of the tub, with Dinny steadying her. A path of towels led around the table to where he'd placed one of the kitchen chairs near the stove.

"You'll be dry in no time by the stove," he said, leading her along the towels. "In fact, your face'll be cooked, so keep it turned away."

The chair was placed sideways to the stove, and he seated her with her right side to it. Then he gathered up the towels from the floor, retained one, and threw the others in a lump on another of the chairs. He returned and toweled her hair briskly.

"It's natural," he said complimentarily.

"Yes."

"Curls and color."

"Yes."

"Pretty."

"Thank you."

"Can see you are, too, when you're not burned to a crisp."

"Only just. You should see my roommate—" the moment the words came out, Carey lost her breath.

"Mmm. I'd like to. Where is she?"

Carey did not reply.

"She here in Maine with you?" Dinny tossed the towel aside and fluffed her blond curls with his hands.

"You never finished telling me what happened to you in—Makatea or wherever," Carey said nervously.

"*Off* Makatea," Dinney said easily, from behind her, leaving his hands resting motionless on her hair. "We never did get into Makatea—finally had to turn tail and run, or limp, I should say, back to Rarotonga—"

"I thought you said Papeete?" Carey interrupted, no longer quite completely innocently.

"For a fact. Papeete it was. So many islands out there, I

never could keep them all straight." He squeezed her head lightly with his fingertips. "You've got too good a memory for names, Margie Packer."

For an instant Carey was flooded with fear; her nerves responded as if she had been plugged into an electrical outlet. But Dinny went on with his story in the same voice.

"All we had left was the staysail to run under. You never saw anything in your life like a few thousand native spears coming at you. Took every sail we had, except the staysail, which wasn't set. They must have thought we were coming to help the Makateas." He chuckled, gave her hair a last fluffing, and stepped around the chair to grin at her. "There never was a war, though. We heard later the Makemos and Kaukuras and Takumes didn't have enough spears left to fight one, so they just turned around and sailed home again. Probably thought the gods didn't favor what they were up to. And that's my story, Margie. The one and only war I was ever caught in the middle of. How about some soup? Feeling hungry?

"I don't know."

"Well, maybe you will when you get a whiff of it. How did that bath feel?" he began to ramble as he moved about the kitchen gathering a clean pot, the box of soup mix and mugs he had earlier set out, and a big spoon. "Not exactly the Waldorf-Astoria, I know, but not too bad, eh?"

"You're from New York?" Carey asked in amazement.

"I've been there. I've been almost everywhere. Ran away from home at sixteen and went to sea and stayed with it almost twenty years. On and off. Whenever I needed money." He put a small pan of water on to boil and got a fistful of spoons from his orange crates. "I've been in the merchant marine, several navies, the Coast Guard, and on at least a hundred ships belonging to half as many countries. I've shipped out as everything from jack tar to Jimmy Bungs to deckie—even as lascar, once, from Udjung Pandang." He chuckled. "Didn't get far that time. Rotten little ship. Literally fell apart under our feet in only a force four in the Bandia Sea." He opened two foil envelopes and dumped the contents into the mugs. "So many islands there we just swam ashore. With the rats."

"Rats?" Carey's eyes widened.

"Hundreds of them," Dinny went on, sticking a spoon in each mug. "More rats than crew by a long shot. Nasty little bastards—actually tried to climb on our backs and ride us in to shore like surfboards. They were worse than losing the ship." He crossed to the stove and peered into the saucepan. "Almost boiling. Yeah, one of the filthy things not only tried to cop a free ride on me but have dinner as well. See"—he stepped over to her, pulling his three sweaters halfway up his back, and turned around—"up there, just under my right shoulder blade. See that scar?"

Carey did, though she found it of indeterminate configuration.

"That's from him. His one and only bite. I rolled over to drown the son-of-a-bitch, but he dropped off and swam away, I guess. Gave me one hell of an infection. Ever try to find a real doctor on one of the smallest islands in the Malay Archipelago? I had fever for weeks, thought sure I was a goner." He straightened up and pulled his sweaters down. "But, I guess only the good die young—" He broke off, staring at the woodstove. "Whew, it's getting hot as hell in here." He separated the top layers of dark green and brown sweaters from the bottom, light-blue one, and hauled them up over his chest and head. "Don't need all these anymore." He stepped behind Carey's chair and tossed the sweaters into the front room. "That's better." He filled the two mugs, stirring furiously as he did so. "Have to cool a few minutes. You about dry?"

"I think so."

"Good. We'll get you out of that towel and into my bathrobe again, so you can use your hands—if you can use them?"

"Enough, I think. But . . ." Her bath over, her body warmed, and her fear and shock, lulled by his tall tales, receding to the back of her mind, Carey felt suddenly terribly embarrassed.

Dinny ignored her embarrassment. He stood her up,

lifted the towel gently off her shoulders, and slipped the sleeves of the robe over her hands and up her arms before she could protest further. He laid the shoulders of the robe lightly down on her burned ones, closed the robe over the front of her body, and belted it securely. Then he rolled each sleeve well up over her wrists.

"There we are. Not as good as new, but much better." He picked up her wrists and looked at her palms again. "We really must put something on these," he said, frowning. "And on your face. I'm not exactly loaded with first aid around here." He thought a moment. "Wait a minute. I may still have some of those capsules Maria brought me."

He went over to ransack his orange crates again. He came back with a small, stoppered plastic bottle in his hand.

"Still more than half-full," he announced in a pleased voice. "This ought to do it. Seems to be good for just about everything you can do to yourself."

"What is it?" Carey asked.

Dinny read the label aloud: "E-clip caps. Vitamin E for the skin. Four hundred I.U. Vitamin E per capsule. Contains fifty 'clip-tip' capsules. Somebody she waited on put her on to it." He poured several capsules out into his hand.

"Who's Maria?" Carey asked as he hunted once again through the orange crates for a pair of scissors.

"My girlfriend. One of my girlfriends." He flashed her a quick grin over his shoulder. "Maria Consuela Romersa— or something. She's waiting tables in Boothbay Harbor this summer. Works winters in Boston and goes to school. About your age, I'd say, now that I've got you cleaned up. Dead set on being a doctor. Into health foods and natural healing. She's always bringing me something she's found that's supposed to be good for me. Here they are," he interrupted himself and waved a pair of scissors in the air. "She's a nice kid." He came back around the table, smiling to himself. "Most of what she turns up with tastes like straw and doesn't do a thing, far as I can tell. But these," he shook his handful of capsules at Carey, "really work." He laughed. "I take it all, though, to make her happy."

He dropped the capsules on the table, selected one, and cut the tip off it.

"Give me one of your hands."

Dinny squeezed the capsule over her hand until it was empty, leaving a film of golden oil covering the worst of her open blisters. He used four capsules on each of her hands, palms and backs, and two on her face.

"Okay," he said, pleased. "That's enough until after we eat. I'll put some on your back after you're in bed. You're going to have to see a doctor about those splinters—they're in deep. See you get them taken out before they fester. Here, stand up now, and I'll bring your chair to the table."

After he had Carey ensconced at the table, Dinny brought a loaf of bread on a slab of wood and a knife to the table, and sat down.

"Just keep those hands up," he reminded her. "I'll feed you. Want bread?"

"Yes, please."

He cut two slabs from the round, dark loaf and laid the knife down.

"This is another of Maria's 'finds,' " he explained, breaking off a piece of bread. "I have to admit this is pretty good. Made from sprouted grain, or so she claims. Whatever, it's real bread and you know you've eaten something." He popped the piece into Carey's open mouth. "No butter. Sorry. No refrigerator. In the winter it doesn't matter. I use the windowsills or leave stuff on the stoop out there in a covered pot. But in summer I do without. Like Maria's bread?"

Carey nodded, still chewing. "It's delicious," she said, after swallowing. "You really do know you've got something in your mouth."

"And your stomach. Wait and see. It's hearty. Want some soup to wash it down?"

"Yes, please."

Dinny held the mug to her mouth. Carey blew on the

surface of the contents as best she could without hurting her lips, then sipped, tentatively.

"Ow," she said, wincing. "It's too hot. I better wait. You eat first."

Dinny ate rapidly. He consumed three slabs of bread and drank his soup down as if it were cold consommé. Then he set about feeding Carey, a bite of bread followed by a spoonful of soup, until her mug was empty and her bread gone. He offered her more bread, but she declined.

"Well, it's here whenever you want it. And there're some apples on the windowsill over the sink, and plenty of cans of tuna fish in the crates there," he jerked a thumb in the direction of his cabinet, "and cereal. I've got dried milk I can make up if you want cereal later. Not a wide selection, but plenty of what there is. I load up whenever I get into town so I don't have to make the trip too often."

"How far is it—to the nearest town?" Carey asked.

"Too far to go very often. Between five and six miles."

"Do you have a car?"

"I have two good feet."

"Is there a telephone anywhere here?"

"In Parson's Cove?" He threw back his head and laughed. "Not unless somebody's rigged up two tin cans and a length of waxed string. There's only four of us out here—myself, Clos Ackley and his wife, Kate, and Eppie Babeau. It's pretty primitive. Eppie's got the only refrigerator. Gas, tank-fed. Brings the tanks back from town in her wagon."

"Do they all . . . do what you do? Go out, for lobsters?" Carey didn't know exactly how to say what she meant; she had a feeling one didn't say "fish for" lobsters, and was equally unsure of simply "lobster" or "go lobstering." Dinny did not seem to notice.

"Clos does. And Kate goes out with him a lot. Probably could do it herself if she took it into her head. She's one hell of a woman. Eppie paints." He was quiet a moment, then apparently decided Eppie Babeau's circumstances and choice of occupation deserved some explanation. "Eppie has money, family money. She doesn't have to do anything she doesn't want to." He said it, matter-of-factly, his voice free from envy or criticism. "She's all right, Eppie is. Hell of a painter, too. Works all the time."

"Does she sell her work?"

"Sometimes. To tourists. If they take a wrong turn and find themselves somewhere where's she painting." He chuckled. "Then they always end up coming back here and buying one or two. But Eppie never tries to sell her work. Just does it. Seems to be enough for her."

"Is that her cabin across the bay, the one I saw when we came in?"

Dinny shook his head. "That's Clos and Kate's place. Eppie's is down to the south end of the Cove—she has a real house. Nice old Victorian. Used to belong to her family, till they all passed on. They owned the whole Cove. Now Eppie does. She won't rent out to more than Clos and me, thank God. Keeps it the way I like it—empty. No people, no tourists, no crowds. Just the sea and the pines and *The Mermaid* and me—most of the time."

"What is the nearest town?" Carey asked. "I really should make a phone call."

"West Lubec," Dinny replied. "But you're not going up there tonight. And neither am I." He yawned. "What phone call? You think somebody's out searching for you?"

Carey avoided his gaze and tried to think. Why did he want to know if someone was searching for her? What could it matter to him unless— A stab of fear shot through her. She had not forgotten the color of his eyes and knew, if she looked at them, her fear would mount to panic and she would cease to be able to think clearly. If only there were some way to tell if he was her savior or some demonic murderer—*the* demonic murderer. She shivered.

"You cold?"

"No, no," Carey answered hurriedly. Maybe if she told him just a little bit, maybe then he would give himself away and she would know for certain not to trust him in spite of his seeming concern for her. "I'm fine. And I don't think anybody's looking for me because I don't think anybody knows I'm gone. There was only me and Mrs. Rambeau on Outer Island—"

"Outer Island?" Dinny's eyebrows shot up. "You said you came out of Bar Harbor."

She started and stared at him in spite of herself. All she could see was the hazel-green of his eyes.

"Outer Island's in South Bay, Margie Packer."

He was accusing her, she was certain. "I was—I was—sightseeing," she managed to stammer.

Dinny fell silent. Carey looked away from him, but she could feel him studying her face. She could think of nothing else to say. She had made a terrible mistake in trying to get him to give himself away. All she had succeeded in doing was giving herself away. Had she told him she was from Bar Harbor? She couldn't remember. Maybe she had. Maybe she'd also told him she was Margie Packer. She must have; he kept calling her that. Her heart pounded so loudly she felt certain he could hear it. What should she do now? Try to run away? Yes, that was it—she should run away, at the first opportunity. But run where? She must get to a phone. To call whom? Oh, God, what was going to happen to her?

"Is there anything you want to tell me, Margie?" Dinny asked quietly.

"No!" She hadn't meant to shout, and the blast of her own voice startled her. Irrationally, her mind jumped back to Peggy Rambeau. What had the poor woman thought when she and Margie never showed up with their dinner? That it was all she could expect from city folk, probably. If they'd gotten back there when they should have, Mrs. Rambeau would still be alive. Carey felt suddenly terribly guilty. Was she going to be made to pay for that fatal lateness now, here in this isolated little shack, by this strange, inscrutable man with the terrifying hazel-green eyes?

"Well." Dinny cleared his throat. "Suit yourself. How about a beer? It'll be warm but—or would you rather have some wine? Might help you sleep tonight."

Carey nodded her head quickly. "Thank you." Her words rang absurd in her ears. What a stupid thing to say to a man who was going to kill her. God, how he must be laughing at her. About everything. She had let him bathe her and feed her and make her ready for the slaughter like a helpless child. He must think her a fool. She was a fool. What could she do? There had to be something she could do, there had to be. She must keep calm and try to think. Think.

"Which'll it be then, Margie Packer?"

Margie would know what to do. Margie would think of something. Yes, that was it. If she were Margie Packer—and he kept calling her that—she could think of something to do. Whatever happened to Margie Packer, it didn't happen because she sat around knowing it was going to happen and just waited for it. And she wouldn't do it this time either. Carey glanced up at him warily.

"Wine." He'd gotten the last please and thank you he was ever going to get from her.

Dinny produced a bottle of wine and a can of beer from under the sink. He cleared the empty mugs and bread from the table, gave it a quick swipe with with the sponge, and set a thick glass down in front of her. He filled it, then set the wine bottle down. He popped the tab from the top of the beer can with a snap and sat down again. He lifted the glass of wine to Carey's lips with one hand, and raised his beer with the other.

"Eat, drink, and be merry, Margie Packer."

A fresh stab of fear shot through her. She had to wait a moment, breathless, before being able to take a sip of the wine. Of all the toasts he could have made, he chose that one, of which everybody knew the last phrase, the phrase he hadn't spoken. He *was* going to try to kill her. And he was getting a kick out of setting her up for it, besides. She watched him toss back his fine head and drain the can of beer. Think. Think. There had to be a way to get out of here, to get away from him. Think.

"I need something stronger than beer." Dinny tossed the empty can into the sink, where it rattled around noisily before coming to rest in the drain. He went into the front room, and came back with a bottle of Scotch. He took another glass from the orange crates and sat back down.

"No strong spirits for you, Margie Packer," he explained as he poured himself a glassful. "Alcohol is a shock to the system, and you're already in shock." he drank half the glass in one swallow and smacked his lips. "That's wicked strong. Wicked strong." He grinned. "Now, Have I told you about the time I shipped out of Rangoon for Karikal on an honest-to-God Chinese junk? Want some more wine? Well, give me a nod when you do. Wasn't a straight shot across the Bay of Bengal." He took another enormous swallow of Scotch and refilled his glass. "We had stops to make in the Andaman and Nicobar islands, which, for all intents and purposes, took us out into the Indian Ocean. And it was August—hot as a son-of-a-bitch. I was the only white man aboard, the rest of the crew was Oriental or Indian or whatever. Not a damn one of them spoke a word of English except the captain. Can't remember his name. Hardly ever saw him. I think he was drunk in his cabin most of the voyage." He drained his glass and poured himself a third. "Little Burmese guy. Wore glasses and had a mustache. Ready for some more wine?" He reached out and lifted her wine to her mouth.

Carey pretended to sip at it. He wasn't going to get her drunk and make things even easier for himself than they already were. With her head lowered over the glass, she glanced at her hands. She couldn't think of one single thing to do, but, by God, there had to be something. Now think. Think what that something could be.

"Margie Packer, I can tell you stories from now until the year two thousand and two." He set her glass down and drained his own. "And I just might, tonight. At least until you fall asleep on me." He laughed—Carey was certain unpleasantly, threateningly. "At least until then."

Margie Packer isn't going to fall asleep, she said to him silently. That's the first thing Margie Packer isn't going to do. And the second thing is—

Her mind went blank. Her heart began to pound again. Her breath caught in her throat in hurried, shallow gasps. The harder she ordered her mind to think, the less it seemed able to do so. Was there no hope, then? Was she really going to sit here and just wait for him to decide to kill her?

"Yes sir," Dinny chortled, as if in answer to her silent question. His face was flushed under his tan, his eyes bright with his own thoughts, his mouth a little slack, sloppy. He poured himself another glass of Scotch and downed it. "At least till then. And maybe, even after."

The door slammed shut in his face. It took Tilley a split-second to collect himself; then he struck the door a resounding blow with his fist.

"For God's sake, Patti—" he shouted.

"Go away! Please go away, Paul," he heard her hiss at him through the wood. "Leave me alone!"

The latch clicked and he heard her footsteps pounding up the stairs. He cursed aloud and kicked the door savagely. Goddamn it! If ever there was going to be a time when he could get through to Patti Welles, break her down, make her tell him whatever it was she knew about the killings— and her town—this was it. He kicked the door again, furious. Here he was, some two hundred miles from Bangor, without even a search warrant to enable him to get inside the house and go after her. Oh, God, what he'd give to have Patti back in his office, away from here, right now.

He paced up and down the length of the porch, thinking. Dare he take her back to Bangor for questioning? On what grounds? His intuition? Christ, if he only had a chief who would back him up. Even Crowley he couldn't count on this time. Despite all he'd told him of his suspicions, Jim hadn't really picked up on what was wrong in this town. He hadn't been able to grasp what Tilly was after. Damn it—and double-damn it. If only there were just one small shred of something he could use as an excuse to take Patti in. Anything except his own gut feeling that here, in Pine Woods, was where the answers lay hidden.

If he took her in without some kind of grounds and she stuck to her guns—well, at the least he'd be off the case, and at the most he'd be out of a job. More important, he still wouldn't know what it was Patti knew about Carey Hunter, and the case would remain unsolved. He stopped his pacing and leaned against the porch railing. What in God's name was he doing up here, anyway? Nothing he was going on made any sense at all; none of it was even remotely possible. People who didn't eat, didn't eliminate, didn't possess genitals or gender? He must be as crazy as Crowley was beginning to think he was. Maybe old Skillin was right—he should be back in South Bay looking for a maniac. All his suspicions seemed suddenly preposterous to him. Untenable. Absurd.

Even he couldn't conceive of what it was he was trying to find out. How could he take Patti to Bangor if he couldn't even explain his own theory rationally to himself? What would he put in his report? That he brought her in because he suspected she had no sex organs? Jesus Christ. He must be losing his marbles. Maybe he needed a vacation. Or a new career. Maybe he was getting too old to take on a case where there just weren't any clues. And maybe he ought to get the hell out of Pine Woods and back to South Bay.

He strode off the porch and across the street to Mayor Farley's house. His check with the station in Bangor told him again that Carey Hunter was still missing without a trace—of her or the dinghy—and that Ho Skillin was still boiling mad over his handling of the case. Mayor Farley remained verbally helpful while hindering him at every turn. Sheriff Welles became a notch surlier to him upon learning he'd already questioned his daughter. The Reverend Moholland stayed even farther in the background than he had earlier. Davey Farley came home, with his friend Keerock Sawtelle in tow, but Tilley's attempted questioning of them in the Farley backyard gained him nothing but ten-year-old skepticism—and contempt.

"How come you don't have a lollipop?" Kee challenged him when he informed the child he was a detective.

"Because I'm a real-life detective, not a television actor," did not convince Kee. He refused to answer any questions put to him by anyone minus the familiar trademark, implying in no uncertain terms he considered Paul Tilley a fraud.

Tilley's display of his badge provoked a momentary curiosity, but established no base of trust. The end results of his attempts to eke some information out of the boys was that Kee decided he had better go home before his father came looking for him, and ran off; and Davey, taking his cue from his friend, darted up the back steps of his own house and disappeared inside.

Tilley was left standing in the yard alone.

"Drive like hell for Patten," Tilley growled as Sergeant Crowley started the car a short time later. "It's"—he looked at his watch—"almost seven already. If I have to wait till we get all the way down to Lincoln for a lousy cup of coffee, I won't be fit company for a bear." He flipped through the pages of his notebook. "Did you get everything I asked you to? Including the names of the Pulks' outlets in Houlton for their produce? Did you question both of them? Did you question some of the teenagers— and the kids?"

"Yeah." Crowley took a hand off the wheel and fished his own notebook out of his jacket pocket. He handed it to Tilley. "It's all here. Take a look."

Tilly read quickly through his partner's notes, then handed the small notebook back to him.

"Christ, we don't have a thing. Not a goddamn thing," he said sourly. "And old Hoho's just sitting back in Bangor waiting to kick my ass right out the door." He leaned back against the seat and yawned. "Some waste of a day, huh? How does it feel to get skinned by a bunch of bumpkins? Aah, the hell with it. I'm too hungry to give a damn right now."

"Paul," Crowley said quietly after they had driven in silence for several miles, "where'd you get all that stuff about the lab reports? About, uh, prickle cells and leuco-cytes and all that? Was that all in the reports?"

Tilley grunted noncommittally.

"Was it?" Crowley persisted, a frown knitting his brow.

"Some of it," Tilley muttered after a long pause.

Crowley turned his head and stared at him, an expression of sheer awe on his face. "You mean you made all that up?"

"Let's just say I enlarged upon the reports a little. Deduced a thing or two here and there, put them all together, and came up with a working premise." A sardonic smile played with the corners of Tilley's mouth.

"Jesus."

"Just drive, Jim, don't try to think. Neither of us has had a bite since early this mornning. Even if it made sense, I won't be able to tell it right now. We'll talk after we eat." Tilley stared straight ahead through the dirty, insect-spattered windshield.

They drove the length of the unpaved road between Pine Woods and Shin Pond without speaking, Tilley slouched in his seat, his eyes half-closed. The rear wheels of the car had barely rolled onto the paved surface of Route 159 when he jerked upright and struck the dashboard with his fist.

"Goddamn it, Jim," he hissed through clenched teeth, "I know that lying little one-horse falling-apart sleazy junkpile of a town is guilty. I know it. They're all covering up to protect somebody—*four* somebodies, I'll lay you dimes to dollars. That don't even need it because they're as dead as their victims. I know it, I tell you. I damn well do know it." He stared at the road ahead for a moment, then sank back against the seat again with a groan. "What I don't know is how in the hell to prove it." After a moment, in an even more irritable voice, he added, "I don't know how to protect Carey Hunter from them, either. I don't even know for sure one of them hasn't already killed her."

16

Carey watched him as he slept on the procelain-topped kitchen table, his mouth slack and drooling a string-thin pencil of saliva onto his dirty sweater sleeve. He did not snore, but his breathing was deep and wheezed slightly in his throat. A half-empty glass of Scotch was still clutched in his hand. He looked a far cry from a swashbuckling movie star now.

Her anxiety gave her no relief, however, even with Dinny out cold where he sat. Had he really passed out? Or was he just pretending, waiting to leap up and grab her at the first move she made? Despite exhaustion, hunger, fear, and pain, she had fought off sleep and outlasted him at the table. But having done that, she now found herself paralyzed by terror, unable to make a move toward her escape.

She sat and watched him with a horrified fascination for what seemed hours, hearing his unpleasant wheezing against the muted pounding of the surf outside. The interior of the shack was diffused with a soft, pearl-gray light that chastened the harshness of its unfinished, unpainted walls, decrepit furniture, bare floors, and sordid, unconscious owner before her fear of waiting too long superseded that of moving too soon.

Stiffly and cautiously, Carey stood up; the floor beneath her feet squeaked deafeningly in the otherwise quiet room. She stayed still, holding her breath, but there was no movement from the apparently drunken lobsterman across the table. She made her way into the front room on tiptoe, a step at a time, freezing to the spot each time the floor creaked, not daring to breathe again until she was certain

Dinny had not stirred. Once there, she disregarded her injured hands' protests, flung off his bathrobe and all but leaped into her sweater, bikinis, and still-damp jeans. A third of the way closed was as far as she could force the zipper before her thumb started to bleed; she left it there and pulled her sweater down as far as it would go. She rammed her feet into her wet topsiders; they felt as if they had not dried at all. Her fingers could neither tie the laces nor remove them, so she merely shoved the ends between the tongues and lacings.

Before she could leave, she felt compelled, almost obsessed, to tiptoe to the doorway and reassure herself Dinny was not conscious and preparing to pounce upon her. She had taken but a step toward the kitchen when a deep groan, followed by a clunk, a brief series of crashes, the scraping of heavy boots against wood came from the kitchen.

Carey froze against the inside wall. Her breath caught in her throat; her diaphragm was paralyzed. Her heart skipped a few beats, then slammed against her ribs with the thunder of a kettledrum. Many long minutes ticked by before she could dredge up the courage to peer around the doorless jamb.

Dinny seemed to be still asleep at the table, one arm now flung clear across it. The glass was gone from his hand, which lay limply in the spreading darkness of spilled Scotch. Both glasses and the empty Scotch bottle were on the floor. It was several minutes more before Carey made for the seaside door of the bedroom as fast as she could on tiptoe.

At the foot of the wooden steps leading off the narrow open porch, she found herself on the beach.

A thick, patchy fog lay over the sea and the land like great rolls of mist-colored carpeting. Carey had seen such a fog her first morning on Outer Island, and had arisen before dawn almost every morning thereafter in hopes of being able again to watch the way the enormous whorls of fog would start to uncoil, roll out, shortly after daybreak, until they brushed edges with each other, melded together, and eventually became one soft blanket of thin mist that drifted upward as it burned off or, on cloudy days, simply melted into the air and disappeared. This morning, however, she took no notice of it.

The surf was louder now, but not so loud as the frantic beating of her heart. She tried to listen for any sound from inside the shack, but could distinguish no external sounds from those made by her own heartbeat and labored, rasping breath. She crept around the side of the shack and stopped beside the kitchen wall. Still all she could hear was herself, and that self seemed to have grown deafening now. She broke and ran up the spit and disappeared into the dense pine wood that bordered it.

The jarring ring of his office phone woke Tilley from a dreamless, exhausted sleep. He blinked his eyes, momentarily disoriented, wondering what in the world he was doing on the battered brown-leather couch behind his desk instead of comfortably in his bed at home. Then it all came back to him in an unpleasant rush.

He got up and reached for the phone, remembering his long and frustrating day in Pine Woods and his blistering confrontation with his chief late last night. As he had anticipated, Skillin had shouted down his carefully worded suspicions regarding the backward little community's probable connection to the recent bizarre deaths, accused him of dereliction of duty, intimated he was suffering from mental derangement, threatened to fire him, and demanded instant action that would satisfy the press—and the public—with a speedy wrap-up of the case. When Tilley had pointed out that he had no leads to follow other than the report of the four unknown teenagers on Archie's ferry a week earlier, Skillin had become apoplectic and ordered him to find one if he expected to stay on the force.

He had spent most of the night restudying every note, written report, and the lengthy autopsy reports from Eastern Marine Medical Center. He had even called MacKay Logan around three in the morning, waking him up out of a sound sleep to bombard him with questions and speculations. It proved as fruitless as everything else he had done so far; he learned nothing new and had, finally, to hang up without the slimmest lead to follow up on. He couldn't remember, or didn't know, when it was he had finally given up for the night and stretched out on his couch, hoping to get either a new idea or a little sleep. The thick, gray, predawn light of what was obviously going to be a dismal day told him it couldn't have been more than an hour ago.

He picked up the phone and muttered huskily, "Tilley here. What's up?"

As he listened he came fully awake, his face darkening with anger. "What?" he barked. "Oh, for Christ's sake." He slammed the receiver back down on its cradle.

Patti Welles stirred restlessly in her bed, watching the gun-metal light of the coming cloudy day sneak up against the windowpanes of her bedroom. She felt a tiredness she had not yet known in her entire life; she had never spent a sleepless night before. She stared at the heavy sky, feeling the chill damp in the air that always preceded rain in the mountains.

God, she prayed silently, please don't let it rain until they find that Carey Hunter. And please, God, let them find her before we do.

She shivered, suddenly cold in spite of her heavy wool blankets and thick quilt. The house seemed colder without her father in his room, and colder yet knowing where he had gone last night. Not that he had told her. He had not. But she would have known even if she hadn't overheard Real Tweedie's hurried instructions when he came to the door after she'd gone to bed.

"It's on, Creighton," Real had announced in an urgent, low voice. "Ada's decided. Hovey objected, but she and Adrian overruled him. Adrian's been charting the current and probable drift all along, as you know, and he's got search areas all mapped out for us from Cutler to Quoddy Head and up the east coast of Campobello. Ada wants sixty cars out—so far we've got twenty. You're to take

Lori Noonan in your car—hers wouldn't start, and there's no time to try and find out what's wrong with it. She's over to Ada's now, getting instructions on your search area from Adrian. I think he wants you to stop by the Pulks' on your way out of town and get them going. You better check with him when you collect Lori, and find out if they're to check in with him and Ada first, or if he's giving you and Lori a map and instructions for them.''

Her parent had muttered something in response; she had not been able to make out his words.

"Ada and Adrian—and Dal, of course—are staying here. And Hovey—nobody feels he'd be much use since he's against it. But he's helping Dal and me round up everybody we need. Get over to Ada's as fast as you can.''

Again her parent had muttered words too low for her to understand. But she could guess at what they were as soon as Real answered.

"You better believe I'm going. Just as soon as I've finished my calls. Vangie Alamady's my last one, and I'll be taking Vangie with me. Don't forget, Creighton,'' Real's voice had changed here, taking on dark and threatening overtones, "it was my face she shone that searchlight on Thursday night. I'll find that woman if I have to tear the whole coast apart to do it.''

"What do Lori and me do with her if we're the ones who find her?'' Patti had no difficulty hearing her parent's anxious question.

"Adrian'll instruct you. He's got packets for everybody all ready to go. Now get over there right away. If she's put to shore someplace, this whole town's in real trouble if we don't find her first. And once you're there, stay on your radio. We've got to be in touch with each other at all times.''

"I'll just run up and tell Patti I'm going to be out for the night,'' she'd heard her parent agree. "She's already in bed''

Patti had closed her door and jumped hurriedly into bed, pulling the covers up around her ears. She'd realized that no one who wasn't considered an adult was being told

what was under way. So she'd feigned sleepiness, kissed
her parent good night, and mumbled that she'd see him in
the morning. But after he'd left the house she had gotten
up and watched him hurry across the road to Ada's house
and disappear inside. Ten minutes later she'd seen him
hurry out again, with Lori Noonan, and the two of them
race south out of town in his battered old Ford. For the
next two hours she had watched cars drive up and cluster
on both sides of the road, and her adult neighbors hurry in
and out of Ada Farley's house and drive off again, always
south out of Pine Woods. The main street wasn't quite
empty of cars and people when she'd finally left the
window, chilled to the bone, and crawled back into bed,
where guilt had overwhelmed her.

It still engulfed her in the moleskin quarter-hour before
an invisible dawn. She pulled the covers closer around her
body thinking, Sometimes I wish I could eat and drink.
Humans seem to decide everything with a cup of coffee. I
wish I could drink one now, so I'd know what to do.

She thought of Lt. Tilley's phone number, hidden between the cardboard backing and the picture of Franz Liszt
she'd cut out from a magazine and framed, years ago, in a
cheap Woolworth's frame. That still hung on the wall over
her bed. By twisting around in her tangle of blankets and
quilts, she could see the bottom of the black wood frame.

She stared at it a second, then buried her face in her
pillow. She couldn't call Paul. She couldn't tell on her
own kind. Besides, her parent didn't have a phone, and
she certainly did not dare ask to use one of the few that
existed in Pine Woods. She was in trouble enough already
for just talking to Tilley—that would really be the finish of
her. Anyway, she didn't owe anything to some human
she'd never met. She felt sorry for her, sure—and would
pray she'd get away, get found by her own kind and
protected till she got out of Maine. The TV news said she
was a tourist. She surely wouldn't want to stay on here
after everything that had happened to her and her friends.
She'd leave, and everything would be okay. Not even

Adrian Widdows, Patti felt certain, would recommend following her out of state. It would be too dangerous.

Regardless, Carey Hunter wasn't her responsibility. Carey Hunter had a lot more of her own kind to look out for her than Patti did. There were millions of human beings and less than a thousand of her kind. Oh, sure, Cony Grotton taught in future class in high school that there had to be other communities of their kind all over the country—all over every industrialized country in the whole world—living just as Pine Woods was, and waiting for the Time of the Sign, when they would know to rise up and join forces and announce themselves. Then they would take over the world and bring peace on earth. Patti treasured this promise like a jewel in her heart, but it bothered her that no one seemed to know when that time was, or what the sign of its arrival would be. "We will know it when it comes" struck her as questionably open to individual interpretation by anyone who felt like believing he or she had been chosen by God and given the grace to know and tell. Probably someone like Adrian. The thought was not reassuring to her.

Well, that didn't have anything to do with right now. Right now she still had only a relative handful of her kind to protect her, in comparison to the Hunter woman, and the whole thing was none of her business. Even if it were—Patti could not put her conscience to rest on this point—there was nothing she could do. She'd be found out; there was no way to keep a secret among her kind. Even if nobody caught her calling Tilley, the next time she uned her partner would receive all her thoughts and memories, experiences and emotions, along with her body fluids. The thought of that frightened her. She shouldn't even be considering calling that detective or having any doubts at all. She had to start right now putting all this out of her mind, and refuse to think any thought other than that her kind were right in anything they chose to do.

Yes, if she started immediately, she could weaken these dangerous ideas to the point where they would pass unnoticed amid all else she would be sharing with her uning partner. She had to. Otherwise, she would be punished.

Patti shuddered and curled into a ball beneath her covers. Like every other Pine Woods child who had budded into the world in the last hundred years, she was well aware of the town's one and only punishment for wrongdoing—or wrongthinking—that jeopardized the community. That was being shut up alone forever in the mysterious room somewhere in the cellar, or so the children whispered to each other, of Real Tweedie's house.

Nobody ever admitted to knowing for certain where the room actually was; Patti sometimes wondered if it did, in fact, exist. It struck her as too great a cruelty for a people sworn to bring peace and love to the world to really ever use. Every once in a while each of them had, for one reason or another, experienced a delay in being able to une when they needed to. The pain and suffering at such times was terrible, and grew more agonizing with each passing hour. She couldn't believe her people could bear knowingly, deliberately, to inflict such suffering on one of their own. Just suspecting what that one was going through would haunt their minds forever.

The room had been used once in Pine Woods hundred-year history, though—or so she had been taught—back in 1935 when one Zita Plourde tried to talk Vonalee Keezer into running off to Hollywood with her to become movie stars. Vonalee, so the lesson went, had reported Zita to the Town Council, which called Zita to appear before it. Zita was never seen again. A week later, in the middle of the night, Vonalee had hung herself from a rafter in the church, leaving a note on the altar. It rested there to this day, sealed between two sheets of glass, along with Vonalee's ashes in a silver box that bore the engraved inscription: "Lest We Forget." The note itself read: "I know I did the right thing, but the knowledge of Zita's agony is more than I can bear. Never let this happen again. Vonalee."

Vonalee Keezer was Pine Woods's sole martyr and saint, and every year the anniversary of her suicide was celebrated as a holy day. The church was open for twenty-four hours, and Hovey Moholland conducted services from midnight to midnight. During that time every single person in Pine Woods came to file past the altar, pause to read her words, kiss the urn holding her ashes, and pray for the coming of the Time of the Sign, when they would inherit the earth.

At home and in school, children were warned from their earliest days not only never to end up as Zita Plourde had done, but also never to be the cause of one of their own having to depart life as Vonalee Keezer had been forced to do. Despite Vonalee's elevation to martyred sainthood, the town elders made it clear they neither wanted nor needed to so exalt another.

The only people who had ever left Pine Woods success-fully, never to return, had been three families back in 1906, known collectively as the Smickles, the head of the Smickle household having been considered the instigator of their defection. The town was young then, and very small, and lacked the sheer numbers necessary to stop eleven adults and two-and-a-half times as many children from doing as they pleased. In fact, it was only after the Smickles had packed up and gone west—which was as much as anybody knew about their destination—that Pine Woods had decided it needed to exercise more control over the lives of its people, and elected a Town Council to draw up a charter and a set of ordinances that would prevent future desertions of the little community by any of its members.

That done, it had elected its first mayor and sheriff, and built a church. Having no minister, the town asked its then oldest inhabitant and founder, Aretta McVicar, to lead the services each Sunday. Patti grinned, thinking about it. She suspected the first minister had been chosen as much for her name as her age and status as founding mother, and had always found it funny that the older residents—her own grandparent, for one, when she was alive—could tell the story with absolutely straight faces.

Where the idea for the isolation room had come from, or when it had been built, or where it really was—if it existed—Patti had no idea. She had sensed as she grew older that it was purposely left a little mysterious, to add an extra note of terror to the warnings.

That must be it, she decided. It didn't exist, except as a means of teaching them all that it was essential they do nothing that might force premature human attention to their existence. And even if the room did exist, she couldn't believe her people had ever actually consigned anyone to it. The story about Zita and Vonalee had to be an allegory. There wasn't a person in town, except the very newest buds, who hadn't uned, at one time or another, with every other. One couldn't hurt anyone with whom one had uned. That was the whole point of being what they were, wasn't it? Otherwise, they might just as well be like the rest of the people in the world. Besides, one never knew when some particular individual or other might be the only person around when one simply had to une, or start to hurt and die. No, no one could injure someone on whom his life might depend at any time.

She had been foolish to get herself so worked up remembering that old, dark, threatening tale. She could undoubtedly phone Tilley, and the worst that would happen to her would be that she'd be forbidden to leave town for a while. Still—she threw back the covers and sat up, shivering in the cold air of the room—it would be better to decide once and for all *not* to make such a call, to start putting the whole thing out of her mind and concentrate on good, simple thoughts about her own kind. Just in case.

The patchy coastal fog added a further element of terror to the deep woods above the rocky spit. Yet barely illumined by the gray morning light, the darkness beneath the pines was fraught with ominous smoke and lead and taupe shadows everywhere Carey ran. She started at the sight of each one and veered, heart pounding, away in another direction. She soon lost the worn footpath that had led her into the densely grown trees. When she finally had to stop to rest and catch her breath, she had no idea where she was.

No sun had penetrated the low, dark-gray cloud layers

obscuring the sky to give her a clue in which direction lay safety and in which terror and death. The storm Dinny had predicted for the previous evening had not yet struck, but it was coming. Carey knew there would be no sun by which to direct herself that day.

When her breathing had quieted, she tried to listen for the sound of the surf. If she could determine where that was coming from, and keep it on her right side, she would be heading away from Parson's Cove and Dinny and his dangerous eyes. She could hear it—or was what she heard the wind now springing up, soughing through the pines?— but it seemed to be coming from all around her.

Several times she picked an arbitrary direction and took a step or two forward, but each time panic overwhelmed her, stopping her in her tracks. What if she was heading back toward Dinny—even walking right into his arms? She made several false starts before she got hold of herself and hurried off again.

The woods grew slowly lighter, and the patches of fog thinner and less frequent as she pushed her way through the low branches of the dense pines. The earth, seldom if ever touched by sunlight here, was still muddy from the past week's northeaster. Carey was soon thoroughly muddied halfway to her knees, and her topsiders, untied and filled with mud, slapped and sloshed off her heels with each step she took. Her hands were bleeding all over, palms and backs and fingers, from pushing aside sharply needled pine boughs. Initially she had been oblivious to them, but as the morning wore on she felt their pain more and more acutely, until it was all she could do simply to reach toward the next bough blocking her way.

When the trees and underbrush began to thin out ahead of her and the darkness of the woods lighten noticeably, Carey felt hopeful and alarmed at once. She was coming out of the trees somewhere, but where? Back on Dinny's isolated, miniature headland she had first seen off *The Mermaid's* starboard bow? It had started as impenetrable rock, but in due time had parted, to her surprise, as if someone had said, "Open, Sesame," and admitted the little boat into the narrow inlet that made an almost 180-degree turn around the towering rock spit and opened into a Lilliputian bay.

The recall of her first perceptions of Parson's Cove acted as a key to the door of her memory. Random impressions of the last twenty-four hours flooded her mind and rushed her emotions. They all involved Dinny. Every face and feature and aspect she had seen or imagined of the movie-star–handsome lobsterman, the hazel-green–eyed murderer, and the slobbering drunk flashed through her head willy-nilly, leaving her breathless, awed, terrified, repelled, a little guilty, and very baffled. In the alabastrine light of midmorning, as she approached the edge of the wood, Dinny remained as much an utter mystery as ever to Carey.

She was not back on the spit sheltering Parson's Cove she saw with relief as she peered cautiously through a screen of branches. Though she had been completely unaware of the increasing volume of the Atlantic breaking against sand and stone, the sea swelled endlessly ahead of her, beyond and below a rock cliff that stretched as far as she could see in either direction.

She looked warily back and forth along the cliff, then pushed aside the last of the pine boughs and stepped out of the shelter of the wood. At the edge of the cliff, she stared down at the rocky beach below. It was not more than twenty or thirty feet below her, but the water-worn face of the cliff was perpendicular, even overhanging in places. There was no way to climb down it to the beach below. She turned and hurried off, the gray sea on her right and the fragrant pines on her left.

Every few steps she glanced back anxiously over her shoulder. She kept close to the pines in order to be able to dart into them if she saw anyone suspicious-looking. Sooner or later, she told herself, she would come to a house, or see some tourists strolling along the cliff to look at the sea. Or the coast road would surely touch the shore at some point where the view was particularly impressive. Then either a car would come along, or she could follow the road until it led her to a town.

"There has to be a town up here somewhere," she mumbled aloud, "there has to be. This"— she was barely conscious that by 'this' she meant not just the cliff and the sea and the pines, nor even her blind escape race, but the whole grotesque and terrifying nightbare of the past four days of her life—"can't go on forever."

It was nearly noon when Tilley's office phone rang for the eighth time that morning. He looked up, irritated, from the notes he had taken in the course of his phone call with MacKay Logan during the night.

"Not another goddamn crank call," he growled.

He got up and stomped out of his office and down the hall to the front desk. He groaned when he saw young O'Malley behind it.

"O'Malley," he said testily, "No more crank calls. Will you for God's sake screen my calls before you put them through to me? Please."

O'Mally looked petrified. "He said he was your brother, sir."

"I haven't got a brother. Or a mother or a father or a sister or aunts or uncles or cousins or even woodpile relations. Do you understand that?"

"Yes, sir."

"I'm an orphan, O'Malley. I'm a goddamn frigging orphan. Is that clear? Until this case is solved, I am an orphan." He glared at him.

"Yes, sir." O'Malley's face was crimson.

Tilley jerked his thumb toward the desk phone. "Now, who does this caller claim to be?"

"The Coast Guard, sir. Jonesport station."

"Jesus Christ! Why didn't you say so?" Tilley took off back down the hall, hollering over his shoulder, "Tell him I'm coming!"

He snatched up his phone. "Tilley here."

His face brightened as he listened. He wrote rapidly on the note pad lying on his desk blotter. "What's his full name?'' he demanded suddenly, his pen poised above the paper. Then, after a moment, yelled, ''What do you mean, that's it? What's his last name—or first?'' He swore under his breath as he heard the reply at the other end of the line. ''All right, all right, what did he say?'' He listened, then shouted, ''Margie Packer? For chrissake,'' he went on after a second, ''Margie Packer's—never mind, never mind. Just give me his report.'' He wrote furiously, then quickly read what he had written back to the caller. ''That it? Have I got it all? Right. Is there anything else? Well, what time did he radio you?'' He noted the time on his pad. ''Got it. Thanks. What towns are near there? I haven't got a map handy. Good. Call them all. Get every sheriff in every one of them out looking for her. Captain Dinny had no idea when she'd left? Damn. Well, she can't have gotten far on foot. Machias, Machias—that's a county seat, isn't it? They must have a police force—get them on it. And tell everybody you talk to they're probably looking for Carey Hunter, not Margie Packer, whatever name she gives. She may be confused, or frightened. The description fits Carey Hunter,'' he added, glancing at his notes. ''Tell them we're on our way.''

He slammed down the phone, tore the sheet of paper off the pad, and raced out of his office. At the front desk he stopped and demanded, ''Where's Sergeant Crowley?''

''Stepped out for a minute, sir,'' the young officer said.

''Where's the chief?''

''He's out, too, lieutenant—''

''Well, tell them both I've gone to Parson's Cove. There's a report Carey Hunter—calling herself Margie Packer—was picked up yesterday by a small boat owned by a Captain Dinny. If it's her—or whoever it is—she was missing again this morning. Ran away during the night sometime. When's Crowley due back?''

''Any minute, sir. He said—''

''I can't wait. Tell him to get every available car up there as fast as he can. When's the chief coming back?''

''In a couple of hours, he said, sir.''

''Good. Tell Crowley to get those cars out on my

authority. And if Chief Skillin raises a ruckus about it when he gets back, remind him Carey Hunter is the only possible eyewitness we've got to the Rambeau murder, and we've got to find her before they do.''

'' 'They,' sir?''

"The killer—or killers. Unless they're a lot dumber than I think they are, they knew before I did she'd been picked up and brought ashore. Tell Skillin I'll phone in as soon as I know something.''

Tilley was out the door and down the steps of the station house before the desk officer had fully opened his mouth to reply.

He crossed the Penobscot into Brewer and took Route 1A out of Bangor. At East Holden he decided he might make better time if he stayed away from the coast, and switched to Route 46 in order to pick up Route 9 in East Eddington. Once on 9, he settled down for the long stretch to Wesley, listening unhappily to the protests the car's carburetor was still making. Even so, he pushed the car beyond what he knew was wise, and soon mostly forgot about the ailing carburetor.

His mind was totally taken up with Carey Hunter, and the possibility she was alive and all right. He reread his notes from the Coast Guard piecemeal as he sped along. The description certainly fit her: blond, short, curly hair; brown eyes; slender; 'not too tall.' He snorted and spread the piece of paper on the seat of the car, where he continue to glance back and forth from the road ahead at it.

Margie Packer? Why in hell had she identified herself as Margie Packer? The two days—and three nights—at sea in a dinghy? 'Badly sunburned, hands too blistered and raw to use,' his notes read. Well, maybe. She'd be in shock. Maybe she did think she was her friend, after all she'd been through.

It didn't satisy Tilley. He'd found Carey Hunter a strong, self-possessed young woman. More likely something else had happened to frighten her, and she'd felt it necessary to try to hide her identity. But what? His heart beat a little faster. He felt certain it had to have been something fairly substantial to cause Carey to lie about who she was. So what about this Captain Dinny—what had he done, or tried to do, to her that frightened her that badly?

Tilley felt his blood begin to boil. The son-of-a-bitch. Just wait till he got his hands on him. He'd done something to her all right. Why else would she have run away while he was sleeping? *If* it was sleeping he'd been really doing. He punched the steering wheel, scarcely realizing he did so.

"Goddamn him," he yelled.

The car swerved sharply in response to his blow to the wheel, and his attention went, for a few moments, to straightening it out on the road. He glanced up at the sky. It was going to storm again, probably before evening. The Coast Guard would call off the search at that point, and Tilley knew the likelihood of their resuming it again afterward, when the weather cleared, was remote. He scowled and stared ahead at the road.

This lobsterman's report had to be about Carey Hunter. Who else in Maine knew there was—had been—a Margie Packer besides a few police, a couple of undertakers and sheriffs, and Carey Hunter? She was all right. Would be all right. And his concern about her was strictly professional, he told himself, strictly professional. After all, she was his only possible witness to Margaret Rambeau's murder—in spite of himself, he prayed she hadn't been. But still, she might be able to tell him something he didn't already know. There'd been signs on the dock at Outer Island that she'd cast off that dinghy in one hell of a hurry. She must have seen something. Probably the old lady's body—what had been left of it. But she just might have seen the killer. And that was the reason he was in such a hurry to find her. The only reason.

The killer. He suddenly thought of the look-alike population of Pine Woods. Jesus. What he'd said to the desk officer was right—if that secretive little backwater hadn't already possessed the radio equipment to monitor the Coast Guard and ship-to-shore and 2182, he'd bet ten years' salary they did by now. They'd heard Captain Dinny's radio call to the Coast Guard before the Coast Guard called him. He felt in his bones they were already on their way to Parson's Cove, and pressed a little harder on his gas pedal.

"But I've still got a two-hour jump on them," he muttered aloud. "I'll get there long before they do. And by God I'll find her."

Unless. His mind reeled for an instant. Goddamn it, why hadn't he thought of this before? What the hell was the matter with him? He hadn't ordered a land-search party north of Starboard and Bucks Harbor, figuring, if she were on foot, there was no way she could get across Machias Bay. If Pine Woods had as much to hide as he felt certain it did, and if Carey Hunter *had* seen the killer—or whoever removed his body, Tilley reminded himself—then it could have had its own search parties out all along, moving up the coast as they estimated and reestimated drift and currents. Jesus Christ, they were undoubtedly already there—they'd be fools if they weren't. Tilley knew the people in Pine Woods, whatever they were, were not fools.

He stepped on the gas even harder, threatening his carburetor as it loudly objected. At Wesley he turned onto 192 and made the twenty miles down to Machias in less than the same number of minutes. He picked up Route 1, without even thinking, for once, to stop for a container of coffee, and took it as far as East Machias, where he turned onto 191 and headed along the coast toward North Cutler.

He'd find Carey Hunter before they did, or he'd raze Pine Woods to the ground and find a way to put every man, woman, and child in it behind bars. For strictly professional reasons, of course.

Carey held her breath and peered through the pine boughs at the two people—they were too far away to tell if they were men or women; both wore pants—far up ahead of her on the cliff. They didn't look like tourists—why, she wasn't sure, but they didn't. Maybe it was that black thing with an antenna that looked like a walkie-talkie one of them was carrying.

Not that tourists couldn't be toting a walkie-talkie. They

might be kids, out just fooling around. Maybe she should step out and signal them; they might be able to help her. At least tell her where the nearest town was. They might even have a car parked somewhere nearby and be willing to drive her there. She really shouldn't let the chance go by—after all, they were the first people she'd seen all day. She might not see anyone else for hours, maybe not until tomorrow. She couldn't stay hidden in the woods forever, she'd starve. She was starving now, and desperately thirsty. She'd go out and yell and wave to them.

But she didn't move. She stayed huddled in a clump of blackberry bushes and watched them walk slowly along the edge of the cliff, one of them alternately talking and listening to the walkie-talkie, the other stopping here and there briefly to look down at the beach below. Something about them, even at a distance, bothered her. She felt something wasn't right about them, and she couldn't override the feeling. Something about them reminded her of somebody—she couldn't think who. But she couldn't bring herself to reveal herself to them.

She stayed hidden until the two were mere specks on the cliff far ahead of her, trying to decide what to do next. She dared not go back on the cliff again, in the open. She'd have to stay in the woods. She was afraid of losing her way again, though, if she went too far from shore. And she should stay near the cliff to watch for them in case they turned around and came back—or in case somebody else came along, somebody she might be able to risk trusting. She stood up and began to pick her way carefully along under the cover of the pines.

God, she was thirsty. And hungry. She should have taken the rest of that loaf of bread with her from Dinny's. Dinny. He really hadn't done anything, except to take care of her as if she were a child or an invalid. In fact, he'd been awfully nice, except for getting drunk and a little crude, and making a few clumsy passes at her shortly before he passed out. Maybe she'd made a terrible mistake in running away from him. After all, if he'd intended to murder her, why would he have gotten so drunk? In retrospect he appeared less frightening to her than the two people with the walkie-talkie she'd just been watching.

Why had she told him she was Margie? She couldn't remember telling him that, but she must have. He kept calling her Margie Packer. Margie. Her heart constricted a little. Warm, funny, wonderful Margie. Ever since she had met her, Carey knew she had been affectionately envious of her. She would have given a great deal to be like Margie . . . had been. Tears sprang to her eyes. Margie . . . wasn't, anymore. Margie was dead. And not just ordinarily dead, but—The tears spilled over her lashes and dripped down her sunburned cheeks. Because of her, because of her insistence on their spending their vacations in Maine. If she had let Margie have her own way, Margie would still be alive. Margie had been the best friend she'd ever had. Ever would have. No one could ever replace Margie. Carey felt utterly bereft.

She wondered suddenly if Jeff knew—if that detective who had questioned her and helped her get through identifying Margie had notified him—then realized that could only have happened if Margie had been carrying Jeff's address with her. Knowing Margie, she thought that was unlikely. When Margie so much as went three blocks away to the supermarket she left everything behind.

"You never know, Hunter," she would grin whenever Carey tried to delve into her reasoning processes. "Life is a great adventure. I may turn the corner on Broadway and fall through a time warp into another dimension. How do I know? And what would I do with a grocery list there? Anyway, I know what we need—and if I forget I'll surprise you."

A sob caught in Carey's throat. How was she going to tell all their friends about Margie? Well, maybe that detective had notified someone, and they all would know before she got back. With a fresh rush of grief, she remembered there was no one to notify, really, besides herself. It was her name Margie had written in on everything that read "in case of accident or illness notify."

Margie had been an only child, and her parents were both dead. Margie's mother had died a few weeks before she'd graduated from college—Margie never would say how—and her father, Carey knew, had died of a heart attack when Margie was eight.

Carey pushed a pine bough aside with her forearm, remembering a conversation she'd once had with Margie after one of her temper tantrums. Margie's tantrums had always puzzled Carey, because no matter how voluble they became, or how silly and childish, they, like Margie herself, always managed somehow to be funny and charming at the same time.

"You know, Packer," she'd said to her, "if I exploded all over the place over everything the way you do, I wouldn't have a friend in the world. Including you. But you do it at the drop of a hat, and everybody loves you for it. I just can't figure that out, darn you."

"It's because I love me for it," Margie had responded, grinning like a mischievous child. "Anyway, you know it'll all be over in a minute."

"More like four or five, at least, Packer," Carey had teased her.

"Five, ten, fifty—I don't give a damn," Margie had come back at her, green eyes flashing. "Heart attacks suck." She'd been been silent then for a moment, and added, "Do you have any idea how many thorns there are on the stem of a rose, Hunter? If you don't yell every time you prick yourself, you won't live long enough to pick many roses, that's my philosophy."

What had it been that made Margie so appealing to so many people? Carey wondered sadly. Now that Margie was . . . gone . . . she ought to figure it out and be able to tell people, not just that she'd been a special person, but what it was that had made her special. Well, there was her energy, that was one thing. No matter how down you felt, when Margie walked in you always began to feel like you could pick yourself up and start again. And her humor—God, she was funny. She was just so funny. And the best part of that was, she was always quick to laugh at herself first. As for her tantrums, well, maybe it was because they were funny, too; Margie was one of those people who could say anything and get away with it. There was so much of the little girl in her. But it was more. It was that she never stored up any anger or held a grudge. She never, as Carey thought of it, let herself get full of unsaid things. So she never had to try and get them said later, in sneaky, hurtful ways. Everything was out and over with as soon as it happened, and Margie forgot about it. She let go of things—that was it. Margie knew how to let go of things. And when she liked someone—and Margie liked almost everyone she met—there was nothing she wouldn't do for them. What was it Jeff had said about her, that weekend she and Nick spent with them in Connecticut? After Margie had jumped all over him for something he said, and which she'd found offensive? And ended by announcing, "I hate what you said, but I love you," and kissing him? Oh, yes: "The great thing about Margie is, she never takes one thing you say or do and makes it into all there is of you. She sure doesn't hold anything back, but you never have to worry she's secretly starting to hate you because she didn't say exactly what she was feeling. Margie is always Margie, and she never has to stop loving you to try to find herself again."

Carey sighed, trudging along. Was that what had gone wrong between her and Nick? Had they both held back so many of the little things that they'd lost themselves, and had to separate to try and find those selves again? She didn't know, and ached for Margie to be there so she could ask her what she thought.

But Margie would never be there again. Margie, who had been so determined to live, was already dead. Carey could think the words, but she could not yet accept the fact. Margie's death remained both real and unreal for her, as if she were two separate people who were each demanding her truth be acknowledged as *the* truth.

Both, however, agreed without defense on one thing: the guilty responsibility she bore for Margie's death. Margie is dead and it's my fault, one part of her brain reminded her, over and over again. Margie isn't dead, she can't be dead, she mustn't be dead, another part replied, but it's my fault if she is, even though she isn't.

As the afternoon wore on, Carey found herself surprised that she herself was going on living—and wanting to go on living—that her body's needs and functions could still command her attention when she felt so desolate. Aside from a grandmother who had died when she was seven, and a classmate, with whom she had not been close friends, killed in a car accident during their junior year in high school, this was her first experience of death. She found her body's demands infuriating, almost obscene.

"Damn it," she snuffled aloud, wiping her sunburned nose carefully on her sweater sleeve, "why can't I just stop and stand here and cry? Why doesn't everything come to an end, as I feel like it's done inside me? How can I keep on trying to save myself, and feel hungry and thirsty, and have to pee, and wish my hands didn't hurt so much and I wasn't so tired? I'm sorry, Margie, I'm sorry. I just don't understand. I don't understand anything anymore."

It was all true, though; she did feel all those things as sharply as she felt her grief for Margie. And her legs continued to move her forward, step by step, no matter how she castigated herself for a shameful and unforgivable lack of feeling for her friend.

In a little while, the pines bordering the cliff began to thin out. She crept up behind the trunk of an enormous pine and peered out warily, up and down the cliff. There was no one there. She leaned against the tree trunk and stared out at the rock and water and trees, becoming half-mesmerized by the quality of the afternoon light. Sun and sky were still obscured by thick layers of clouds that appeared lit from above and below at once, so varied were the streaks and shadings, tones and shiftings of light and less light. The ocean shimmered silvery-gray with hints, here and there, of transient blue, green, pearl, and acier that left a lingering opalescence hanging in the air between the sea and heavy sky. It seemed to Carey she could see the air itself; she found it beautiful, but also disturbingly phantasmagorical.

The illusion heightened her already strong sense of unreality. What was she doing, wherever she was? Was it anywhere? Was she actually there? Or was it all a dream? Were the last few days a dream from which she would wake up, to trek up the hill to Sternfirst and get Mrs. Rambeau's shopping list, row the dinghy across South Bay to Fustin's, and beard Mrs. Mitchell in her den of a general store, see Archie's ferry approaching the dock and—oh, God, yes— Margie waving wildly from the stern?

Margie. She blinked her eyes, and turned away into the woods, and began to walk again, trying not to know that the only dream was her own clinging to the hope of a dream. Still the iridescent, almost visible air continued to play tricks with her vision, diffusing the light, with its soap-bubble play of hints of colors, so that she could not clearly distinguish the tree trunks from the spaces between them. She glanced out at the sea again. The water rose and fell away without warning or regularity. She looked ahead, along the cliff. The pine trees bordering it moved toward her, then back, giving the impression that the cliff itself was contracting and expanding erratically. She blinked and looked up to where the topmost boughs seemed to touch the clouds. The spired tops of the distant pines shot taller, then shrank against the nacreous sky as her eyes searched for one stable, steady thing to fasten on.

There was nothing so. Everything changed as soon as her eye beheld it; nothing stayed still or the same. She felt bewitched and drained of energy. Slowly she sank to her knees, then squatted, then sat for a few minutes. Her eyelids felt weighted with lead. Well, she could rest for a few minutes, she was nowhere anyway. She shouldn't rest here, though, she was right out in the open under the pine trees. She had to rest. What did it matter anyway, Margie was dead. But she wasn't, and she should find a safer place, some bushes or branches to crawl under. She would, in a minute. Right now she couldn't move.

A moment later she almost fell down sideways on the thick bed of pine needles. She opened her eyes once and stared into the rainbow light of the opaline afternoon. She really would find a better place in a minute. Then her eyes closed again and she drifted off.

Outside of South Trescott, Tilley left 191, turning onto the coast road leading to Quoddy Head State Park. He prayed Parson's Cove would be marked by a road sign but felt fairly certain it would not be; it wasn't on the map he kept in the glove compartment. He drove slowly now, keeping a sharp lookout for an unpaved road leading off to the right. About four and a half miles past South Trescott, he spotted it and turned onto it.

After a short distance it forked. Tilley stopped the car and stared briefly to his left and right. The road to his right appeared distinctly more heavily used, so he took it. If it didn't lead to Captain Dinny's place, at least it seemed the more likely to lead someplace where there would be somebody to direct him to Captain Dinny's.

An enormous towered and turreted, gingerbreaded and widow's-walked Victorian house came into his view without warning, around a sharp, double-S curve in the unpaved road. Aside from being in need of a fresh coat of paint, the house looked to be well kept up, with neat flower beds bordering either side of the flagstone walk that led from the end of the drive to the front door. Tilley parked his car beside an ancient Ford station wagon and hurried onto the porch. He called through the screen door— the front door stood open—''Hello? Anybody home? Anyone here?''

''Who wants to know?'' a woman's voice nearby came back at him, and a moment later footsteps sounded on the floorboards of the porch to Tilley's left.

They were followed by the appearance of a tall, handsome woman around the curve of one of the house's many towers which bellied into the wide porch. Her gray hair was pulled severely back from her face in a French twist; she was dressed in a pair of faded overalls and a plaid

flannel shirt. Tools protruded from every pocket and strap
of her overalls, and in her right hand she carried a
screwdriver.

"Been rehanging one of the shutters. Took a branch in
last week's nor'easter that skewed it a bit on the hinge,"
she said, not smiling. "Didn't like the look of it with a
fresh blow coming. What can I do for you?"

"I'm Lieutenant Paul Tilley, Bangor Police," he offered,
reaching to take off his hat. He discovered he wasn't
wearing it, that in his rush he had left it behind in his
office, so ran his fingers through his hair instead.

"Believe you forgot it." The woman smiled a little
now.

"I think you're right." Tilley smiled back at her. "I
was in a hurry. I'm looking for the home of a"—he pulled
out the piece of notepaper and glanced at it—"Captain
Dinny. Is this Parson's Cove?"

"It is. And I'm Eppie Babeau. I own it. What do you
want with Captain Dinny?" Her eyes narrowed warily.

"He radioed the Coast Guard earlier today that he had
picked up a young woman yesterday at sea. We've been
searching for her since she disappeared, sometime last
Thursday night or early Friday morning, from Outer Island
down in South Bay. We didn't know for certain, but we
had reason to believe she'd left the island hurriedly, in a
dinghy. Captain Dinny reported he'd brought her back to
his house in Parson's Cove. I'm here to confirm the report
and take her back with me."

"Hmm." Eppie Babeau eyed him a few moments, obviously weighing his words before answering. "Well, I
haven't laid eyes on Captain Dinny for more'n two weeks.
He could have rescued somebody, and I wouldn't know
about it yet. I suppose you want directions to his place."

"Yes, I do. Thank you."

She motioned him to follow her. "You can see it from
the back of the house, if you know what you're looking
for."

Tilley followed the woman along the porch to the side
steps, where it ended against the wall of a short, wide

turret. They descended and continued along another flag-stone walk that right-angled this way and that with every bulge and setback in the side wall of the ornate old house. At the end of the long side wall, there was another short flight of steps leading up to a back porch almost as deep and long as the front one.

"That's the Cove," Eppie Babeau announced, a touch of pride in her voice. She leaned on the porch railing with one hand and pointed to patches of water glistening darkly, between the green-needled boughs of the pine trees, in the milky light of the afternoon. "Been owned by Babeaus for three hundred years, ever since Enoil Babeau came down from New Brunswick to try to Christianize the Algonquins." She laughed. "Family legend has it he came as a soldier during the French and Indians Wars, and stayed as a preacher after being visited by an archangel of the Lord who warned him he'd burn in hell if he continued to side with savages. The archangel offered him a last chance to save his soul if he'd put off his uniform and put on the cloth, so to speak, and convert his heathen allies. Enoil took his chance and made the best of it—and here I am." She paused a moment, smiling to herself, then added, "Thank God. Well, if you look over there," she moved her hand a little to the right, "just east a bit, past the water, you'll see the spit. Maybe. Where it looks like a hole in the trees. Can you pick it out? Well, Dinny's place is out there, on the spit. You can't miss it when you get there."

"As you said, Mrs. Babeau, 'if you know where to look.' How do I—"

"Ms., Lieutenant Tilley, Ms. Babeau," she corrected him energetically. "I like to keep up with the times. I didn't marry into the Babeaus. I *am* a Babeau," she finished proudly, standing erect to her full height.

Tilley realized with some discomfort that Eppie Babeau stood at least three inches taller than he did. He had to look up to look her directly in the eye while apologizing.

"I'm sorry, Ms. Babeau. I didn't know."

"Oh, pshaw," she said, relaxing again, "that's all right. I just like to hear it. And everyone around here calls me plain Eppie, so I've got nobody to go after 'cept strangers like yourself. Now you're wanting to know if you have to row across the Cove, eh?''

Tilley grinned. ''Do I?''

''Lord, no,'' she grinned back at him. ''Go back the way you came and take the north fork. That'll take you 'round the Cove to the spit. You took the south fork.''

''It looked better traveled.''

'' 'Tis. I've got the only automobile in Parson's Cove.''

''Does anybody else live here, in the Cove?'' Tilley asked.

''Just the four of us. Myself and Dinny and the Ackleys, Clos and Kate. And I intend to keep it that way. Don't like crowds.''

''By the way, what is Captain Dinny's full name, Ms. Babeau?''

She looked surprised. ''Don't know as he's got one. If he has, he doesn't use it. Dinny is all I've ever known him by. It's enough,'' she added pointedly, letting him know she was not going to tell tales on her tenants. ''You'll have to ask him if you want to know.''

''It's not important,'' Tilley murmured. ''Thank you. I'll be on my way again now. Appreciate your help.''

''Any time. And if you find Captain Dinny to home, Lieutenant Tilley, I'd much appreciate your telling him I'm going into Lubec tomorrow, if he needs anything.''

''Be glad to. Thanks again. Good day.''

''Good day to you.'' Eppie Babeau nodded her gray head. ''Believe you can find your way around the house by yourself this time.''

''I think so.'' Tilley retraced his steps around the house and across the front yard to his car.

At the fork in the unpaved road he bore north, and drove as far as the road went, about a mile. He stopped the car and got out. He was still in a dense pine wood, and it took him a few minutes to find the footpath leading off, through the tall, fragant trees, toward the southwest. The energy he'd felt for so much of the long ride had waned, and Eppie's casual remark that her tenant could have rescued

Carey without her yet knowing about it had not encouraged him. He felt hungry and tired, and recalled with irritation his missed opportunities for coffee in Machias and Cutler and South Trescott.

He was totally disgruntled by the time he came to a fork in the path. "Damn it to hell," he muttered aloud, "why didn't the dratted *Ms*. Babeau tell me about this?" He stopped and tried to orient himself. Eppie's Victorian monstrosity of a house must be approximately straight ahead of him, on the far side of the Cove. From her back porch, Dinny's house had been pointed out to the right. Therefore, from where he stood now, deep in the woods, he judged that Dinny's house was somewhere along the left fork, and her other tenants, the Ackleys, must be to the right. He strode forward onto the left fork of the path, hoping irritably that he'd been given the right directions.

"She was pretty royally cagey," he grumbled as he walked rapidly along. "Not exactly eager to lead anybody to her subjects."

After half a mile, he saw a ramshackle wood outhouse, with a rough anchor cut out of the top of one of the planks in the door, standing in a small hollow about a hundred yards to his left. Automatically he left the footpath and tramped down to it, opened the door, and looked inside.

"Well," he muttered as he climbed back up to the path, "where there's a privy, a house can't be too far away."

The trees began to thin out, and in a short time he saw the narrow rock spit, the side wall of a stilted shack, and the dark gleam of the waters of the Cove. To his confoundment, his heart started to beat faster and his mouth went suddenly dry. He hurried forward, almost running out of the woods along the rocky spit.

"Halloo?" he hollered. "Anybody here? Captain Dinny? I'm looking for Captain Dinny—is he here? Halloo?"

He reached the back steps of the shack and bounded up them. The door stood open, and Tilley stuck his head inside and looked around.

"Captain Dinny?" he called out.

When there was no answer, he turned around and looked

down at Parson's Cove. Two small trawlers rode at red-and-white buoys; three short docks, like the points of a scalene triangle, extended into the little bay. A dinghy was moored at each; at the one to his left, across the Cove, there was a half-decked motor launch as well. On the dock closest to him stood a tall, dark-haired man in rumpled clothes, who was watching him. Tilley went back down the steps and strode across the spit to where a steep, rocky climb led down to the dock.

"Are you Captain Dinny?" he called out.

The man nodded.

"Lieutenant Paul Tilley." He flashed his badge quickly. "Bangor Police. I need to talk to you."

Dinny nodded again. "Be right up," he called back.

Tilley watched him as he strode up the dock and scrambled agilely up the steep rock. Dinny's face and form did nothing to cheer him up. So this was the man who'd rescued Carey Hunter. Well, the one-name captain was entirely too good-looking, too tall, and too athletic to suit Tilley. He was scowling by the time Dinny reached the top of the spit.

"You're Captain Dinny?" he growled.

"Right." Dinny took his hand and pumped it once. "Pleased to meet you. Police, you say? Then you've come about Margie Packer?"

"That's right—"

"She isn't here anymore. Was gone this morning when I woke up." Dinny looked a little sheepish, Tilley thought.

"Do you have any idea what time she left?"

"Nope. I was out like a light."

I'll bet you were, Tilley said to himself, noting Dinny's puffy, bloodshot eyes and the pallor, in spite of his deep tan, of his facial skin. He knew the look all too well. He'd seen it too many times in his own mirror. "Any idea where she might have been heading?" he asked.

"Not a clue."

"Why did she leave?"

Dinny stared at him a moment. Tilley saw his eyes darken with resentment. "You'll have to ask Margie that, lieutenant. Afraid she didn't bother to tell me."

By God, his feelings are hurt. Tilley watched him closely. "You had no idea when you . . . fell asleep that she was planning on running away?"

"None."

"You hadn't noticed anything, oh, strange, or a little off, say, in her behavior that might have tipped you off?"

"Tipped me off to what?" Dinny asked sourly.

"That she . . . didn't feel safe here, was frightened of something, maybe—anything about her out of the ordinary?"

"Of course I noticed that. All of it. Every so often she'd look at me and jump clean out of her skin."

"Well, didn't you think anything of that?"

"What I thought, lieutenant," Dinny replied, sarcasm tinging his voice, "was that she'd been through a hell of an ordeal. Three nights and two days at sea, in a dinghy. Sunburned red as a lobster, and her hands raw to the bone from rowing. No food or water, as far as I could tell, except some kind of rotten meat—I threw it overboard. She was scared out of her wits. I don't even think she gave me her real name—she kind of started and looked a little wild-eyed every time I called her Margie Packer."

"She didn't," Tilley said flatly. "Her name is Carey Hunter. There's been a sea-and-land search on for her since last Friday. You probably heard it on your radio." He gestured toward the trawlers bobbing gently in the little bay.

Dinny shook his head. "Haven't been here. Hadn't taken *The Mermaid* out for a week until yesterday."

"Where were you?" Tilley asked.

Dinny eyed him a moment, then an expression of resignation crossed his face. "Boothbay Harbor. Visiting."

"Is there someone who'll corroborate that, captain?"

"Maria Consuela Romersa. Want her address?"

Tilley shook his head. "I'll find her if I need to. What happened between you and Carey Hunter after you picked her up out there?"

"What happened?" Again Tilley saw anger and hurt darken Dinny's eyes. "What happened? Let's see. First she tried to drown herself and I damn near drowned with her trying to save her. Then—oh, yeah, then she fainted, and when she came to, she sat all the way in the stern like I had the plague. What next? Well, we got back here and I carried her ashore, with her acting like I'm Quasimodo, mind you. Then what happened?" He paused a moment, rubbing his bloodshot eyes. "I brought in the tub and undressed her—"

"You what?" Tilley snapped.

"I undressed her and gave her a bath, lieutenant." Dinny gave him a long look, the corners of his mouth twitching ever so slightly. "She was dirty and salty and cold, and her hands"—he winced—"they hurt you just to look at them. She must have rowed near the whole time she was out there. I've seen a lot of injured hands at sea—rope burn, for one, can tear the flesh right off your bones—but I've never seen any look any worse than Margie's. What did you say her real name is?"

Tilley stared at him, scarcely aware of his question. Images he could not control raced through his mind, each more disturbing than the one before.

"What did you say her name is, lieutenant?"

Tilley started slightly, and blinked. "Carey Hunter," he finally managed to almost snarl.

"Right." Dinny smiled—smirked, Tilley thought. "Carey Hunter. Anyway, she couldn't use those hands for anything, so I took care of her. I did everything for her. Undressed her"—Tilley began to see red; he was certain Captain Dinny was enjoying repeating it all, rubbing it in—"put her in the tub, and washed her up, nice and gentle, being real careful of her sunburn. She was sunburned—face, backs of her hands, even her shoulders and back, right through her clothes. I even had to help her on and off the pot, lieutenant. Be surprised what somebody can't do for herself when she's got no hands."

Tilley felt more than an impulse to hit him. For an instant he considered throwing away his badge and breaking the handsome, gloating face before him. Then he got control of himself and, to keep his hands busy, reached for his notebook and pen.

"I'm sure," he said, neither as lightly nor as evenly as he tried for. "So, by and large, you say you just took care of her, is that it? You did nothing to alarm her in any way?"

"Not a thing."

"Yet she reacted sometimes as if you had."

"Sometimes. Less and less as the night wore on." Dinny grinned.

Tilley dropped his eyes and kept them on what he was writing. "What happened then—as the night wore on, as you put it?"

"Nothing happened. I fed her and gave her some wine."

"You were drinking?"

"I gave her some wine."

"And did you have wine yourself?"

"I had some Scotch."

"And?"

"And what?"

"And then what happened?"

"I fell asleep."

"Had you made a pass at her, while you were having 'some Scotch'?"

"Is there a law against it?"

"Are you saying you did make a pass at her?"

"I really don't remember, lieutenant. 'Some' Scotch was actually about a quart."

"I see." Tilley could not take pleasure in the surliness now coloring Dinny's voice. He still raged with jealousy and ached to punch him out. "So you could have done most anything, am I right? And frightened her into running away in the process?"

"I don't get my kicks frightening women, lieutenant. Or forcing myself on them." Dinny rammed his hands deep in his trouser pockets, and Tilley knew the man wanted to land a few punches as badly as he himself did. "I'm actually a pretty nice fellow. I liked her. She's a pretty little thing, under that mean sunburn. I'm human. I would have taken her if she'd wanted it. She didn't. She was hurt and real upset. Any fool could've seen that. And something about me seemed to scare her out of her wits. I don't know what. But I knew it did. I treated her like she was my kid or something. Tried to reassure her. Seems I blew it all by getting drunk. She was getting to like me, I remember thinking." He was quiet a moment, scuffing the toe of his boot in the sand. "Afraid that's about the last thing I do remember." Again he was quiet awhile, then looked up. "I'm sorry. Probably it is my fault. I hope you find her. Soon. I hope she's all right."

"I need some information from you, captain, quickly, before I go. What time was it when you picked her up yesterday?"

Dinny shook his head. "Haven't the faintest idea. Never thought to check. Morning. That's all I can tell you."

"I see. What was the position of your boat at the time?"

"Don't know, lieutenant. Sorry. I don't keep a log on *The Mermaid*. Just give her her head and let her take me to my pots."

"Well, just something approximate then."

Dinny shook his head. "Like I said, I don't know. And I won't guess."

"I'm not going to make your information public knowledge, captain," Tilley said, suspecting that rivalry among the lobstermen made the locations of their pots jealously guarded secrets. "This is only for my report."

Dinny smiled at him blandly. "If I knew, I'd certainly tell you."

"Very well, captain." He wrote in his notebook. "We'll let it go at 'doesn't know.' " He looked up at him. "The Coast Guard, however, may insist on more specific information. So you might try to come up with some, in case they contact you."

"Fail to see what difference it makes, lieutenant. Won't help find Margie again, will it."

Tilley grunted. "I need your full name, captain. The name of your boat, I take it, is *The Mermaid?*"

Dinny nodded. "And I'm Captain Dinny."

"Is that your first name, or your last?"

"My only name. Dinny's all there is, lieutenant. There isn't any more."

"Come, come, now, captain. Surely you have both a given name and surname?"

"If I do, I've forgotten one of them. Been just Dinny for so long I don't recall ever being anything more."

"I see." Tilley pocketed his pen and notebook. "Well, again, the Coast Guard may want more, captain."

"Want away. I can't give what doesn't exist."

"Oh, yes, captain, I have a message for you from Ms. Babeau, your landlady. She asked me to tell you she'll be going into Lubec tomorrow. In case you need anything."

"Thanks very much. Would you hold on half a minute, lieutenant, please? I have something I'd like you to give to Margie Packer when you see her. Be right back."

He walked away and disappeared into the shack. A moment later he came back.

"Here. Give her these." He handed Tilley a bottle of vitamin E capsules. "Tell her . . . tell her Maria will be bringing me more when she comes up next week. And tell her I said it was nice knowing her. And I'm damn sorry if I did something stupid that frightened her away." He looked directly into Tilley's eyes.

Tilley looked back, not into but at his eyes. "I'll tell her. But I don't think it was anything you did, captain. You can relax about that. I think I know now why she ran away. Thank you for your time, captain. Good luck to you."

He left Dinny standing there, an expression of bewilderment on his face, as he turned and hurried back up the spit and into the woods. His energy was surging more strongly than if he'd drunk three cups of coffee. Carey Hunter *had* seen someone on Outer Island. Seen someone closely enough to determine the color of the person's eyes. Which meant that someone knew he or she had been seen—because they must have looked right at each other. A wave of uneasiness washed over him. Pine Woods search parties—? They were up there all right, searching for her. Determined to find her. Well, he was more determined. They weren't going to find her. Because he was going to find her first. Pray God.

17

The air of augmented secrecy pervading Pine Woods that day depressed Patti Welles. It was thickest directly across the street, where Ada Farley's house stood. Not a single car she'd seen or heard leave the night before had returned. Ada had not left her house, at least not by the front door. Nor had Adrian Widdows.

They're still up there, she told herself, thinking of Ada's attic, filled with the most up-to-date, sophisticated communications equipment money could buy, and with which she or some member of the Town Council always kept in periodic contact with everyone who went out of town for whatever reason. Patti could visualize the activity that had been in progress across the street since the previous night, as her people desperately tried to get to Carey Hunter before the Bangor police did. She could feel the tension and fear emanating from that attic window and spreading over the town like a deadly mist.

She knew, too, that all the people who had ridden out of Pine Woods last night had carried the same fear and tension with them.

"But Carey Hunter hasn't done anything to hurt us,

God,'' she prayed aloud. ''Please, let there be another way. Don't let my people do this. Show them another way.''

Carey woke with a start, disoriented. The afternoon light was fading; under the pines it was already almost night.

She got stiffly to her feet and struggled toward the pounding of the surf. ''It must be late,'' she said to no one as she peered out between the pine boughs, and looked up and down. All the magical tints of the day were gone from the salt air; it hung, sullen and invisible, between the sea and the darkening cloud layers, like a threat. Carey shivered.

''I must find somebody.'' She heard the sound of her words and, as if they had been spoken by someone else, replied, ''Yes, you're right. I must.''

She trudged along, just inside the pines, for about a mile before hearing the sound of a car going by, somewhere off to her left. Her heart seemed to turn over with excitement.

''I'm near a road,'' she cried out loud.

With a burst of energy she plunged into the thinning wood, away from the sea, toward the sound she had just heard, careless now of her hands and face as she thrust aside the needled boughs and prickly underbrush in her way. She did not have far to go. In a matter of minutes she stumbled out of the wood onto the dirt shoulder of a road.

''Thank God!''

She looked quickly up and down the road. About five hundred yards to her right, just before a turn, a battered Dodge van was parked. The passenger door was open; a denim leg and work-booted foot hung outside the vehicle. Standing over them, hands on the curve of the roof of the vehicle, was a second person who was leaning down, looking inside. Carey's heart jumped with joy.

''Hey!'' she screamed, breaking into an uneven run. ''Hey! Help me! Please help me!''

The person outside the van straightened up and looked around. Carey ran faster, and waved.

"I need help! Wait for me—don't drive off! Will you help me, please? I'm in trouble!"

The figure stepped away from the side of the van, and the denim leg became two as a second figure emerged. Carey's heart was pounding and her breath coming in short gasps now.

The two figures looked at each other and started toward her, motioning her to come on.

"Sure, we'll help you. Come on," a husky contralto voice called out. "What seems to be the trouble, lady?"

Once back on the coast road, Tilley drove northeast toward Quoddy Head. His intellect nagged him to stop the car, get out, and go on foot into the woods between the road and the shoreline. He had hesitated for an instant, with the car door open, back at Parson's Cove over the same thing. But some gut feeling had compelled him to get back on the coast road. It now urged him to stay there.

Carey Hunter, he reasoned, had been running since early morning, probably since before daylight. There'd been only one way off the spit: northeast. She could have been going around in circles, it was true, and still be in the vicinity of the little cove. But Tilley gave her more credit than that. He felt strongly that, once over any initial fright, she would have found the ocean and used it as a compass. Probably she wouldn't have made very good time. No doubt she'd stopped to rest, perhaps frequently. But he felt half-confident she must be close to the state park by this time.

He ought to be running into Crowley and however many squad cars Jim had been able to round up soon. With all the time he'd spent at Eppie Babeau's and Dinny's, they should be catching up to him any time, if they weren't already ahead of him. And he sure as hell ought to be passing one of the old wrecks from Pine Woods up here; in fact, he should have spotted a couple of them already. Unless—

He forced the thought from his mind. He simply wouldn't

consider that possibility. Probably they just sent out one car—or a VW bus or a truck, more likely, with a ınch of them packed into it, and it was pulled off the road someplace, and they were out there in the woods on foot. They wouldn't get by him if they came back down the coast road.

Of course, they didn't have to come back this way, he couldn't stop himself from thinking anxiously. They could always head up toward Lubec to 189 and pick up Route 1. They could even take it north up to Houlton before cutting over to Pine Woods. Or just up as far as Topsfield to pick up 6 over to 170. He punched the glove compartment open and snatched his map. Yeah. That's what he'd do if he were them, goddamn it. He threw the map on the seat and stared ahead at the twisting road.

Where the hell were the Machias police? And all the local sheriffs from these parts? Surely that jackass at the Jonesport Coast Guard station had notified them as he'd told him to. But, Jesus, he ought to be seeing somebody by now. He'd be on Quoddy Head in another few minutes.

Maybe he'd better put out a call. One of the Machias cars or one of his own—Crowley, he hoped—was sure to answer. He reached for his radio mike. They all ought to get organized. And goddamn fast. It was going to be dark soon. And probably storm. He was sure as hell going to burn somebody's ass about this radio silence when this was over and he had Carey Hunter safe and sound under his wing.

Carey felt like she was running on a treadmill. No matter how fast her legs pumped, the distance between herself and the two figures—were they coming toward her or were they still way up the road by their van?—appeared to remain the same. The phrase "the endless mile" flew to her mind and stuck there—was it the title of a film she'd seen? Or a book? It didn't matter; it was certainly what she seemed to be running. Now that help and safety were just ahead of her, in plain view, she seemed to be unable to reach them, no matter how hard she tried.

She grew lightheaded. She seemed to have been running for days, or years—even all her life. Despite the cold air, she was sweating profusely. Streams of perspiration blinded her. She blinked and blinked but could no longer make out clearly whom or what she was running to. Or from.

She began to feel afraid. Her fear mounted rapidly into panic. She must reach those people. Now. The very air sweeping past her was charged with danger. Something terrible was coming at her; did she hear feet other than her own pounding up behind her? She dared not slow her pace to look back. She must run. Those people ahead—where were they? Why couldn't she see them? They would save her if she could just get to them. God! Was that a hand on her arm? Yell, scream—why couldn't she hear herself screaming? It was a hand—hands! Fight! Hit, kick, bite, scratch! Scream! Where were those people? Why didn't they help her? God, somebody, help her!

The trees and the dirt and the pavement spun around as Carey felt herself being hurled to the ground and held down. She heard a throaty, catchy voice clamor at her ears, "It's all right, lady, it's all right—everything's all right now. We've got you," but the words were just a string of sounds and made no sense to her. She fought and kicked and struck out wildly, with adrenalin strength she was unaware of. To her, her muscles felt as weak as a kitten's and her motions as slow as if under water.

"Go get the stuff—quick," the same distinctive husky voice dinned at her hearing meaninglessly, "we'll never get her to the van like this. I'll hold her. Hurry!"

Carey shook her head and frantically rolled her eyes around to locate the speaker. There—there was a face. She stared at it as it came into focus—directly into a pair of hazel-green eyes.

Patti glanced at the clock on her chest of drawers, stared at the hands for a moment, then jumped to her feet. The book on her lap hit the floor with a bang. She ignored it, darted across the bedroom, snatched the picture of Franz Liszt off the wall behind her bed, and fumbled at the metal tabs holding the backing in place.

The cardboard tore on one of the tabs as she yanked it out; she didn't care. She snatched the piece of paper from Tilley's notebook and stuffed it into a pocket of her jeans. She had to do something before everyone came back with Carey Hunter—and there was nothing else she could do except call Paul Tilley. If her people killed deliberately, how could they ever expect to inherit the earth as peacemakers?

As Patti peered out across the street at Ada Farley's house to make sure no cars were starting to come back, it occurred to her that maybe there were kernels of truth in the things about which Adrian Widdows spoke so passionately. It did seem to her that her kind had been created as an improvement on the violent configuration of humanity in order that real peace, born of conscious interdependency, might be established in the world. But he had it all twisted, she thought, as she raced downstairs. Adrian had infected their truth with his own disease.

She headed for the back door of the house. She was frightened at what she intended to do, but never had she seen so clearly that the flower of their future pictured by Adrian's words was an amaranth. How could it be otherwise, if it grew from the seed of hatred and murder? Her people would reap illusion and despair—reap hell—if somebody didn't stop them. And there was nobody but herself to do it.

She slipped outside, glanced around to see if anyone was watching her, then hurried across the backyard to the woods. If she cut through the woods, she could be at Lori Noonan's house in less than twenty minutes. Lori had a phone—and Lori was with her parent. If she couldn't find a way to get into Lori's house, Real's house was just a short walk beyond it, and he, too, had a phone. She prayed Lori had left a door or a window unlocked; she would be terrified to sneak into Real's house. There was something to intense and all-knowing about Real. She always felt he could see right through her.

Not that that mattered much, since she shared everything there was of her when she uned anyway. But she still felt uncomfortable around Real. She didn't even like to une with him. Somehow his presence made every bad thought she ever had come flying to the front of her mind. Of course, the instant their nipples conjoined the feeling was gone, lost in the rapture of interchange. Still, she never sought Real out when she needed to une unless she could find no one else who was ready.

She found Lori Noonan's one-story, four-room house locked up tight when she got there. She was grateful Lori liked living out in the woods and had no close neighbors as she prowled around the small house, trying windows and doors. If anybody should see her doing this. . . .

Patti left the thought unfinished and confronted the fact that she would have to try Real's house. And fast. They could be coming back at any time; they could be pulling up in front of Ada's right now. She had no way of knowing. She screwed up all her courage and hurried out of the yard onto the dirt road, little more than a two-rutted track wide enough for a small car, leading on to Real's property.

Real Tweedie's house was even deeper in the woods than Lori Noonan's. Patti approached it apprehensively. Certain as she was Real was out of town, searching for Carey Hunter, she couldn't shake the feeling he was watching her every move. She climbed the front steps on unsteady legs and knocked at the front door. The clang of the brass knocker—curiously cast in the form of a lamb and a lion clasping each other, with beautifully detailed front legs, in what appeared to be anastomosis; she wondered where he could have gotten it—echoed ominously through the big Victorian house. Patti shivered.

Maybe she should forget the whole thing. Maybe Ada and Dal and her parent and Real and Lori and all the rest were right in doing what they were doing. They were older and wiser than she was; surely they knew better than she what course of action to take. Maybe they didn't intend to kill Carey Hunter, just to—what? What else could they possibly be planning to do with a hostage human being? They couldn't keep her there in Pine Woods; that would be impossible. And dangerous.

Well, maybe God would take care of Carey Hunter—if It wanted her to be all right. Maybe Patti should leave the whole business in God's hands. But then, Real had said Hovey objected to their plan, and Hovey was the minister, the man of God. If Hovey felt what they were doing was wrong, surely God did, too. And Tilley hadn't given his phone number to Hovey; he'd given it to her.

"God," she said aloud as she reluctantly tried the door, "I wish You'd chosen somebody else for this. I really do."

The door was securely locked. So, she discovered with growing relief, were all the windows facing onto the long front porch. She made her way around the first floor of the house, trying every window.

If nothing is open, I can't do it, she comforted herself as she went. I'll have to give up and go home. No matter what God wants. This made her feel better, and she hurried along, newly relieved by every window she found locked.

The back door was also locked. Patti was feeling better and better. She was no longer concerned with the purpose and future of her kind; she was doing all she could do, and that was the extent of her responsibility in the matter. Even God could expect no more of her than that. There was no way she could get to the second- or third-story windows, so as soon as she'd checked the other side of the house she could go back home. She'd be safe. And she wouldn't have to feel guilty about this ever again.

Then she noticed the cellar door. She tried to ignore it, to walk past it, but it reached after her like the tentacles of an octopus, from which she was unable to disentangle herself, and pulled her back each time she tried to take a step away. Finally, with a pounding heart, she gave in and tried it.

The wooden outer doors were unlocked. She raised one, laid it back, and went hesitantly down the seven concrete steps leading to the house door. She stood before it a few moments, then reached out and took the knob in her hand. After a few more moments she tried it. It turned with her hand, and the door creaked open.

Patti's heart sank. She had really to go through with this awful task. No, wait. The door at the top of the stairs leading to Real's kitchen might be locked—would be locked, surely. Else why would Real have left the outside doors open? He was terribly careful about this kind of thing, especially in summer when vacationers were all over the place. He was always reminding everybody to double-check their doors and windows whenever they went out, so no humans could wander into their homes and see how they lived.

Sure, they all had kitchens, but there was never any food in them except for a few canned goods, maybe, for appearance' sake. A few people, like her parent, had bathrooms for bathing, but Ada had the only bathroom in all Pine Woods with a toilet. That was why outsiders were always directed to the mayor's house if they stumbled into town, so she could let them use it if they asked. Everybody had a privy, true; that was the law, so the humans who occasionally came there by accident wouldn't think anything. It was all, again, for appearance' sake in emergencies. And Real Tweedie was the most vocal person in town about preventing those emergencies. The door to his kitchen would certainly be locked.

Feeling somewhat better, Patti hurried through the cellar toward the stairs. As she put a foot on the bottom step, a right-angled wall jutting out in a far corner of the basement caught her eye.

The breath went out of her; her heart skipped a beat. She stared at the concrete wall and the heavy-looking wood door with three locks, a chain, and a metal slide bolt set into it. Was that the ''room'' she'd heard about since childhood? Her heart began to pound afresh. What else could it be?

Like one in a nightmare, she moved toward it. The chain was hanging loose; the bolt was in the open position.

Apart from any desire of her own, her hand took the knob and turned it. The door was locked, to her enormous relief. She turned and ran up the stairs, grabbed the knob of Real's kitchen door, turned it, and pushed.

This door opened. She no longer had an excuse. Either she did what her conscience insisted she must, or she ran away—right now—and prayed to God not to let her end up like . . . like Vonalee Keezer, but without the glory among her own kind.

Tilley swerved around an S curve in the coast road and saw the battered back of a van parked up ahead.

"Hope to God that's one of the local sheriffs," he muttered. He was still angry that not one of his radio calls had been answered. He felt he had less than a chance in a million of finding Carey Hunter before nightfall, which was rapidly approaching.

He switched on his headlights and saw something else.

"What the hell?" It looked to him like a young man trying to hold down someone who was having an epileptic seizure by the side of the road. Or—he thought, and stepped on the gas.

He sped to the two figures struggling on the shoulder, leaped out of the car, and ran forward the last few feet to them.

"What's going on here?" he shouted.

"Nothing!" an alarmed contralto voice yelled. "We're only trying to help her—"

In an instant, Tilley recognized simultaneously the husky tenor of the voice, the inbred similarity of the face to so many others he had recently seen—and Carey Hunter, terror-stricken and struggling, on the ground.

"Police!" he thundered, grabbing the person he knew to be from Pine Woods and flinging him aside like a rag doll. "Get away from her!" He caught one of Carey's wildly flailing arms, yanked her to her feet, and caught her to him. "It's all right, Miss Hunter, it's all right. You're all right now. You're safe. It's Lieutenant Tilley, Bangor Police. Everything's all right now—I'm here. You're safe. Miss Hunter, you're safe. This is the police."

With his free hand he had slipped his gun from his shoulder holster and now aimed it at the young man who was half-lying on the road staring at him. "Don't make a move, buddy," he warned him. A movement by the side of the van caught his eye. "Or you either," he shouted. "I don't want to have to shoot anybody. Come over here, you. Get away from that van and come over here—slowly. Get your hands up and keep them there. You, too," he ordered the man on the road. "Don't either of you try anything—"

At that instant two cars careened around the curve in the road beyond the van, and another roared up behind him. All three swerved into the scene at the roadside, blocking the van, Tilley's car, Tilley, Carey, and the two suspects. They braked to a stop. Car doors screeched open and bodies Tilley could not identify in the glare of all the headlights erupted like shrapnel from inside the three vehicles.

18

"Patti?"

Patti heard her parent's intense call as he opened the front door and stepped into the house.

"I'm upstairs," she called out in a voice that was far from steady, "in my room. Hi, Creighton."

"Stay there."

She heard the front door close and, a moment later, the sound of feet plodding up the stairs and down the hall to her door. Then her door opened.

Creighton stared at her.

"Hi," she said, forcing a smile. "You've been gone a long time. Is everything okay?"

He did not answer her; he simply stood and continued to stare.

"What's the matter, Creighton?" she asked nervously. "Is something wrong?"

"Suppose you tell me," her parent said at last.

Patti stared back at him. He knew. But he couldn't know. She'd left everything exactly as she'd found it. But he knew—she felt in her bones that he knew. She flushed crimson.

"Yes, I know, Patti," her parent said heavily. "So do Ada and Adrian and the rest of the Council. Why did you do it?"

Patti got off her bed and stood up. She felt sick with fear, but also strangely defiant. Since they all knew, she might just as well speak her piece for once in her life.

"Why, Patti?" her parent repeated.

"Because it was right!" The words flew out of her mouth. "If we're really everything I've been taught to believe we are."

"I see."

"It's true, Creighton," she protested, growing excited. "All I've ever heard is, we're the peacemakers. We're going to bring all this love and goodwill on earth. Because we were created without the capacity for violence—that's what you all said. That we had no sex or gender, so we couldn't rape and murder like humans do. And we uned instead of eating to stay alive, so we didn't need territory or crops or food and wouldn't make war to get them. Everything we needed to live and stay healthy we got from the air and each other, so we'd never pollute this planet or hurt each other in any way. Isn't that what you taught me? Isn't it?"

Her parent stared at her grimly.

"We're God's love made flesh—Hovey says that every

Sunday in church," she rushed on. "Everybody says it. Well, if we are, then we can't kill anybody, whether they're one of us or not."

"Why not, Patti?"

"Because that's not love, Creighton. Love doesn't . . . murder. What happened with Roe and Harlie and Naida and Chris wasn't murder; it was an accident. But you all are"—she hesitated, searching her parent's face for some sign of the outcome of their hunt—"are—going to kill that Carey Hunter person."

"Who told you that?"

"Nobody. Nobody had to. I heard what Real said last night when he came to get you."

"You still haven't told me why you did it."

Patti stared him, bewildered. Then it came to her. "To save us. We'll never inherit the earth if you go through with what you're planning to do."

"Why not?"

"Because we'll be just like them."

Her parent was quiet a long time. Patti squirmed under his scrutiny.

Finally he spoke. "You think God will abandon us, is that it?"

"Yes. We'll have been a failure—just like they are—and It'll have to start all over again with some new kind."

"Apparently there's been a fatal gap in your education," Creighton said thoughtfully. "We'll have to remedy that from now on. I thought you understood that humans are only a somewhat more complex form of animal species—however they may choose to convince themselves otherwise. More complex, more violent, more brutal. Other animals don't kill wantonly or for pleasure, as man does. Only when they're hungry. Except for rats," he added. "Rats and humans are the only two species that kill their own kind."

"We killed Zita Plourde, didn't we?" Patti challenged him recklessly.

"That was different," her parent said icily. "The Council at that time didn't do it for gain or pleasure. They did it for survival."

"Oh, that's bull, Creighton," she cried. "You don't believe we have some special right to let the end justify the means—I know you don't."

"You're missing the point, Patti, as you seem to have missed it all your life. For us to kill a human is the same as it is for a human to kill an animal. No more, no less. If a human is attacked by a wild animal, or a vicious dog, they put the animal to death—"

"They haven't attacked us."

"They will. If they find out what we are. It would happen if the Hunter woman identified Real. I'm really surprised you were able to overlook the consequences of your act, Patti. Didn't it occur to you what would happen to Real if he were arrested by them?"

Patti shook her head. "I never thought about it."

"Too bad. Let me run it through for you, then. The first thing he'd be subjected to would be a physical examination." His mouth twisted in an unpleasant smile. "I don't think I have to spell out for you what that would mean—for all of us, aside from what they'd proceed to do to Real. He'd be less than a guinea pig to them, and a lot more fascinating. He—" Creighton snorted, "Real's not a 'he'—none of us is. 'He' or 'she.' You ought to know by now we only dress up and play at their roles, and give one bud a male name and another a female, so nobody will ever slip up around humans and give us all away." He shook his head. "Right now it's very hard for me to remember you're my bud, Patti."

"I'm sorry, Creighton," Patti mumbled, suddenly subdued. "I didn't think. It seemed the right thing to do at the time."

"Right?" her parent shouted. "You think it was right to risk us like that? And Real—what about what would have happened to him in three or four days when he needed to une, sitting in one of their jails or under lock and key in a laboratory? Do you think they'd have released him, or let one of us in to save his life? Did you think that? Right? Don't you ever talk to me about 'right,' Patti Welles.''

After a long silence Patti managed to say, "What are you going to do to me?"

"We haven't decided," Creighton snapped. "Fortunately for all of us, you didn't reach Lieutenant Tilley. And at least you had the good sense not to leave your name. Oh, yes"—he nodded at the stunned look on her face—"Ada recorded your call. And I listened to the tape. All calls in and out of town are monitored—if you'd used your head you might've realized that. You're not stupid, Patti. We didn't spend all that money setting up that expensive equipment in Ada's attic because we think protecting ourselves from humans is a game. I may be able to spare you the worst by reminding the Council you didn't identify yourself. If I decide that's the wise thing to do," he added threateningly. "But I'll tell you one thing, Patti Welles. You can forget about college next month—or ever. You'll never leave this town again. And you'll never teach here, under any circumstances. Nobody would ever trust our youngsters to you." He shifted his weight and reached for the doorknob. "When will you be ready to une again?"

"Tomorrow, or Thursday," Patti said faintly, staring at him with widened eyes.

"Well, you better start praying one of us on the Council will be ready then, too. Or some adult whom we're absolutely certain about. Because you won't be allowed to une with anybody we don't approve of for you—for a very long time, if ever. And you don't leave this room unless I tell you to—understand? You have no privileges anymore, except what, if any, the Council may decide to grant you at some time in the future. The distant future. Until you hear otherwise from me, you just sit here and think about what you tried to do. And beg God for forgiveness, because you're unlikely to get it from anyone else."

Her parent turned and walked out, closing her door behind him. Patti sat, stunned, and stared at the door, unable yet to take in most of what he had said. It would be several hours before she realized he hadn't even told her if they, or the humans, had found Carey Hunter. By then she wouldn't care. She would be absorbed in wondering, with real terror, if the Town Council would decide to shut her up in the room she had seen, and now knew did indeed exist, in Real Tweedie's cellar.

19

The rain held off until Tilley, his car between those of the Machias police and the county sheriff—an arrangement he had requested—was pulling into East Machias. Then it began, lightly, a fine mist saturating the night air. His engine sounded as murky as the weather; he glanced at the fuel indicator. He'd better get gas in Machias and have the carburetor checked before starting the long drive back to Bangor. And get Carey Hunter to the hospital to have her hands taken care of.

He glanced over at her and experienced a rush of such a multiplicity of emotions he could not have sorted them all out if he'd wanted to. He didn't. He wanted to be feeling nothing beyond a professional satisfaction that he'd found her before anything more than the harrowing ordeals she'd already survived could occur.

But he knew now he did, and it put him out of sorts, along with his failure to find a legitimate charge on which to arrest the two young women—he'd made damn sure they weren't men when he'd frisked them—from Pine Woods. He looked in his rearview mirror. Yes, they were still there, following along behind the county sheriff's car.

They wouldn't split at the junction of 1 and 191, and try to get away; they wouldn't give him any excuse to arrest them. Well, maybe he could find some technicality before they finished making the report he'd insisted be made at Machias police headquarters.

He glanced again at Carey. It wasn't real, what he seemed to be feeling for her. He didn't even know her. He was just trying to fill the aching void left inside him by Thea's death. Yet, he was forced to admit to himself, he felt more reconciled to his wife's loss at this moment than he had in all the years since she'd died. The admission brought with it guilt, and anger toward Carey. She was making him betray Thea, just by being there. He swore silently and tried to keep his attention on the rain-slick county road.

You certainly have me all bollixed up, Carey Hunter, he said without speaking.

He did not let himself look at her again until all four vehicles had pulled up outside the Machias station house on Court Street.

When he helped her out of the car, he saw for the first time how badly sunburned her face was. Great God, she looked terrible, poor kid. What kind of rotter was he that he fumed and fretted about his own petty feelings when she was obviously suffering so? He gently took her arm.

"This won't take long, Miss Hunter," he said warmly. "Just a few formalities. Then I'll take you over to the hospital, and we'll have you looked at and get something for your face and hands."

Carey barely responded to the questions Tilley and the sheriff and the Machias police put to her. Tilley almost wished she would not answer anything, as he listened to her mumbled replies. Everything she did manage to say only confirmed that she was in a state of shock and her perceptions of the incident could not be relied upon.

The two young women from Pine Woods were unshakable in their protests of good intentions and innocence of

Carey's identity. Tilley gave them each an A-plus for acting. He knew the police and sheriff were baffled and a little concerned that he kept hammering away at them, making them tell and retell their stories of having pulled off the road to relieve themselves in the woods, seen Carey running and screaming for help, and having tried to give that help.

And you had plenty of time driving over here to work it all out, didn't you, he mused as he listened to one of them for the umpteenth time.

Finally, he had to admit to himself there was nothing he could do but let them go. He'd examined their van up on Quoddy Head after the police had arrived; the only questionable things he'd found were a walkie-talkie and radio equipment sophisticated enough to transmit and receive over at least three hundred miles. Curious, to say the least, but there was no law against owning the latest radio equipment. All he could do, finally, was take their names and addresses—which held no surprise for him—and let them go with a warning that he might want to requestion them in Bangor, and that they would be subject to arrest if they failed to show up at that time. He was furious at his helplessness, and more furious that the two women knew it. He could see it in their hazel-green eyes.

Before leaving the station house, he called Bangor. Jim Crowley took his call.

"Yes, it's her," he growled into the phone. "Where the hell were all you guys?"

"The chief countermanded your order, Paul," Crowley explained at the other end of the line. "I'm sorry. He got back from lunch just as we were leaving. I tried, but he wouldn't listen. He was damn near apoplectic that you'd gone off again. All I could do was phone Machias and Lubec, and tell them to hustle their asses. Did they connect with you?"

"Yeah, yeah—finally," Tilley grumbled. "The Lubec sheriff went home after we straightened things out. I'm in Machias with the police and the county sheriff."

"Well, what happened? Is she all right? What can you tell me?"

"Later," Tilley said. "Jim, can you do me a favor? Can you hang around the station house until I get there? My carburetor's on its last legs, and I may need you to come down and pick us up."

"I'll be here, Paul."

"Thanks."

Tilley got the directions to the Down East Community Hospital from the sheriff. The emergency-room team, after treating her hands, begged Carey to admit herself, overnight at least, for observation, but she refused. Tilley did not press her to change her mind. He much preferred to get her safely back to Bangor, where he could keep a sharp eye on her. And, though he wouldn't acknowledge it, he was looking forward to the long ride back.

"How do those hands feel now?" He smiled at her as he settled into the car beside her. "Any better?"

"Yes, thank you," Carey mumbled.

"You must be hungry, Miss Hunter. How about some dinner? First though, I've got to get some gas," he added without waiting for her reply.

He drove a few blocks, then pulled into the first gas station he saw.

"Better fill her up," he instructed the teenaged boy in an olive-drab slicker jacket who trotted out of the station and over to his side of the car.

"Right, sir." The teenager walked to the rear of the car to uncap its gas tank.

Tilley got out of the car and went back to where the boy was filling the tank, his eyes on the spinning numbers in the face of the pump.

"My carburetor's acting up," he said. "I'd appreciate it if you'd take a look at it, when you're done here, and tell me if you think it'll get us to Bangor."

"Sure, okay." The boy glanced at him. "Want me to check your oil?"

"Might as well," Tilley answered. "I can't remember the last time she took any."

He half turned and looked inside the car at the back of

Carey's head. He had not yet told her Nick Pocetto was dead. He hadn't even decided when he should tell her. He wanted to wait a few days, until she was more recovered from her ordeal, but he was worried that she would hear about Pocetto's death accidentally, now that the case was all over the TV news and headlining the *Globe*, the *Herald*, and the *Sunday Telegram*—and probably every local paper in the state as well.

He bit his lip. God knows, this wasn't the time, when she was burned and blistered and sore all over, and still scared to death by her close call with those two from Pine Woods. But what other time did he have, if she wasn't to hear it, with no preparation, from somewhere else? He blew out his cheeks, then released his breath in a long hiss. He thought once again that he had never known how much he hated his job until this case came along.

"You want to start her up for me, sir?" the attendant called out from under the hood of the car.

Tilley had not even noticed he had finished filling the tank, hung up the hose, and gone to have a look at the carburetor.

"Right." Tilley got back inside the car and started the engine.

He sat, letting the engine idle, and waited for the boy to come and give his verdict, still thinking about the onerous task that lay ahead of him. One thing he knew he wasn't going to do was to tell Carey Hunter about her lover on an empty stomach—hers or his own. They'd have dinner first. Maybe the right moment would come, and he'd recognize it, before he had to take the matter arbitrarily into his own hands. He didn't hold out real hope of that, but he knew they would both feel better with some food inside them. Then, if he could just get her to talk a little, respond to some small degree—well, he realized, he didn't know if what, but he told himself there would be an if something.

"Okay," the attendant yelled, "shut her off."

The boy came around to his open window and bent

down. "I think it's about shot, sir," he said apologetically. "You need a new one."

"What are my chances of getting back to Bangor with it the way it is?" Tilley asked insistently.

"Stranger things have happened, I suppose, but I don't know how you even got here."

"Damn." Tilley bit his lip again. "Well, could you replace it? How long would it take?"

"Sorry, mister." The boy shook his head. "I'm closing in ten minutes."

"All right," Tilley concurred reluctantly, "thanks. Guess I'll just have to hope for one of those stranger things. What do I owe you?"

"Twenty-three seventy, sir. She took a quart of oil."

Tilley pulled out his wallet and handed his American Express card to the boy. He tried to think of something casual to say, but he could not. So he sat in silence until the attendant came back with his card and bill.

"Thanks very much, sir," the teenager said as Tilley rolled up the window. "And good luck. Hope you make it."

"So do I," Tilley agreed.

He started the car up and drove out of the station. He still could think of nothing to say, and Carey remained silent. He would have given anything to know what was going on inside her, but felt too much of an intruder upon her personal feelings to ask. As he turned onto Main Street, he finally spoke.

"You like seafood?" He tried to sound cheerful.

She nodded slowly.

"Good. Helen's is as good as they come," he went on, still trying for a cheery tone and feeling instrusive.

"Had your fill of lobster yet, after your summer up here?" Tilley asked her after they were seated at a table.

Carey shook her head.

"Well, as I said, you can't get better than at Helen's, so what say we have the lobster?" When she merely nodded in reply, he added, "How about the Newburg or thermidor?

That'll be easier for you to manage with your hands all bandaged up. But I'll do the hard part if you want boiled or broiled, so go ahead and get it however you prefer it." He felt foolish, as if he were talking to himself.

"Newburg is fine," Carey said without looking at him.

"All right," he commented, too heartily. "I'll get the thermidor so you can taste it." He would have preferred a broiled lobster, but was reluctant at their first meal together to crack shells and make the mess he always did. He wondered, briefly, if he should have suggested steaks, if the lobster might somehow remind her of Captain Dinny, then abandoned the thought as childish. "How about a bowl of steamers to start?"

"I'm not very hungry," Carey said in a small voice, "but you go ahead."

"You may feel differently when you smell them," Tilley persisted with his false heartiness.

Carey did not feel differently when their dinners arrived. She ate three of the steamers, then refused any more. Tilley, ravenous, finished off the enormous bowl by himself. When the main course was set down in front of them, Carey picked at the Lobster Newburg he tried to feed her, politely tasted a forkful of his thermidor, and left more than half of her own dinner in its chafing dish. She got down a couple of bites of green beans, and a few more of salad, but refused even one forkful of her baked potato. When Tilley had eaten his dishes spanking clean, he sat back, stretched, and eyed her scarcely touched food.

"You've hardly eaten anything, Miss Hunter," he said, concerned. "Won't you try to do a little better than that?"

"I'm not hungry," Carey said again.

He sighed. "Well, then, how about dessert?"

"No, thanks."

"Coffee?"

Carey shook her head. "I'd like some tea, please."

Tilley lingered over his coffee, talking when he could think of something to talk about, as long as he could. He

drank three full cups, which was actually one more than he
wanted, so that he could make tentative stabs at getting
something resembling a conversation going. It proved futile.
Carey drank one cup of tea, white with milk, answered
him in monosyllables occasionally, and mostly remained
silent. She kept her eyes averted from his face and did not
suggest that they leave. As far as Tilley could judge, she
seemed to be unconscious of the time passing, removed
from it as if it no longer existed for her. It occurred to him
midway through his third cup of coffee that this was not so
very odd. She had nowhere to go and no one to go to. He
reached across the table and touched her sleeve lightly.

"Will you consider going to the hospital in Bangor?"
he asked. "A couple of days' rest and care wouldn't be the
worst thing for you right now."

"Yes," she answered dispiritedly.

"Good." Tilley heaved a sigh of relief. "Good. That
makes me feel better." He drained his coffee cup and
smiled at her. "Well, ready to go?"

"Yes."

He signaled for their check. "You can sleep in the car,
if you want. You must be exhausted. It's a long drive to
Bangor."

Carey only nodded.

Tilley took Route 1 out of Machias. It was a little longer
than cutting upstate to 9, but he felt he stood a better
chance of finding an open service station on 1 if his
carburetor conked out completely. It was raining hard
now, and he drove slowly, keeping the speedometer at
thirty-five as much for safety's sake as the preservation of
his complaining engine.

He thought anew of Nick Pocetto. And of Margie Packer.
Not only must he be a reminder to Carey of that recent
trauma, but he had to be the bearer of further tragic news
as well. And he had to question her about Margaret
Rambeau's death, too. He was certain she'd seen somebody that night; the color of Captain Dinny's eyes and the
lobsterman's statement that every time Carey had looked

him she'd jumped out of her skin had confirmed that in his mind. No wonder she'd been fighting that Pine Woods woman like one possessed. She must have gotten a look at her eyes. Yes, it all was beginning to fit into place. He'd have to question her in detail, whether he liked it or not.

But not tonight, he decided abruptly, with a shrug. Not tonight. She wasn't going to see a TV or hear a radio or buy a newspaper tonight. She was going right into Eastern Maine Medical Center the minute they hit Bangor—and he'd see to it the TV was removed from her room and the staff warned not to bring her any papers or discuss the news with her. In a day or two, when she was recovering, that would be time enough.

He heaved a huge sigh of relief and glanced over at her.

"You okay, Miss Hunter?" he asked, unable to think of anything else to say.

"Yes."

He drove a few more miles in silence.

"Wouldn't you like to sleep some?" he asked solicitously. "Feel free to stretch out and use my leg as a pillow."

"All right."

Carey obediently eased herself down on the seat, curled up on her left side, and laid her head gently on his thigh.

"Am I too heavy?" she asked, her voice flat.

"Not a bit. Can hardly tell you're there." He smiled down at the top of her head.

"Thank you," she said simply.

After a few more miles he heard her yawn audibly. Shortly after, her breathing changed. Tilley took his right hand off the steering wheel and placed it, without weight, on her head. His heart contracted with emotion.

Oh, you fool, Paul Tilley, he said to himself, slowing the car down to thirty. You great big overgrown, almost forty-year-old fool. You're asking for it. Really asking for it. You better stop right now, while you've still got a prayer.

But he left his hand lying lightly on the side of her head

as he drove carefully on, and let his fingers fall in love
with the feel of her soft blond curls. In spite of everything—the circumstances under which they'd met and
those that would soon drive them apart, even his frustration with Pine Woods and the entire case—he felt happier
than he had in eight long and tormented years.

20

"The Council's ready to examine you, Patti. Come
along."

Patti slowly sat up on her bed and stared at her parent.
"I'm going to have to une by tonight, Creighton," she
said timidly. "It's Wednesday." Her voice trembled a
little.

"We figured that. Come on."

Patti got up, went to the chest of drawers, and ran a
comb through her hair before the large mirror. She watched
her parent in the glass. "What are you going to do to
me?"

"We haven't decided yet. Hurry up."

"Please daddy"—she hadn't called her parent "Daddy"
in years; it made her very aware of how frightened she
was—"won't you tell me anything? You must know
something!"

"I don't," Creighton said flatly. "And if I did, I wouldn't
tell you. You've done a terrible thing, Patti. A terrible,
terrible thing. Now come on, they're all waiting. Stop
fooling around over there. You look fine."

Patti turned around and looked him straight in the eye.
"Are you going to . . . kill me? Is that it? Are you going

to shut me up in the room in Real's house and let me die?'' She expelled so much air with these few words she had to gasp for breath after she finished.

Her parent's face went ashen. He stared at her a moment, then strode across the room and seized her roughly by the shoulders. He grabbed her to him in a fierce embrace.

"No!" he exclaimed gruffly. "Of course not. Don't be daft, kid.'' He kissed her hair. "We don't know yet what we're going to do with you, but it won't be that. I promise you. It won't be fun, Patti, but it certainly won't be that. Mostly it'll depend on you,'' he added, "on how you conduct yourself and what you say. This isn't the first time you've created problems, you know.''

Patti hung on to him for dear life. "They'll drag up all that old business about the Conservatory, too, won't they?''

Creighton kissed her hair again. "Whether they do or not, it'll be on their minds. It did create quite a stir at the time, you know that. You knew when you did it that it wouldn't go down well with folks—that it couldn't accomplish one thing except to make trouble for you.''

"Nobody ever forgives and forgets in this town.''

"We can't afford to, Patti. It's just the way things are for us.''

"I'll be a pariah. No matter what you decide to do to me, nobody will ever speak to me again. Nobody will want to une with me.'' Patti trembled and clung to her parent.

"You should have thought of that before you went storming off to use Real's telephone in some idealistic fit of passion,'' Creighton said, a little sourly now, pulling back from her. "You're a little late with your regrets, Patti, I have to say that.''

"But I was only doing what I thought was best for us—all of us, Creighton.'' Patti looked up at him with brimming eyes.

"I know that, kid.'' He sighed heavily. "Mad as I've been with you, I know that. But other folks don't. And they wouldn't give a damn even if they did. There's too much else up the spout. Come on now, put on your best face and show them whose bud you are." He grinned at her a little. "It'll all be over within an hour or so. And do yourself—and me—a favor, will you, Patti, and don't go sounding off with any of your highfalutin ideas about how we ought to have faith and announce ourselves and trust in God and all. They're not going to be playing games in there with you—this isn't a mill drill anymore. We're in real trouble. The whole town may be headed out to sea in a sieve—we just don't know yet. But everybody's feeling we're overdue, and I warn you they're not in the mood to put up with one more ounce of tomfoolery from you."

Every nerve in Patti's body leaped up as if electrified. Her parent was afraid for her, really afraid. "But you said—"

"They won't, they won't," he interrupted her hurriedly, "I told you they won't, and they won't. Just—" He broke off, his own face contorted with anxiety, and took hers between his hands with a tenderness that surprised her. "Just don't provoke them, okay, kid? Just take your medicine and smile till this whole ugly business blows over. *If* it blows over. If it doesn't, well, then it won't matter much. The cat'll be out of the bag then. We'll all be doomed."

"You didn't find Carey Hunter," Patti said, more to herself than to her parent. "They did."

"That's right. And any hour now, that Lieutenant Tilley is going to be up here with a fistful of warrants to pull us all in so she can identify one of us."

"Real—"

"Real. Now do you have some idea of the mood everybody's in? Listen to me, Patti. The last thing the Council can afford to make allowances for right now is a damnfool teenage idealist. It's not that they don't understand your feelings. They do. We all do. We all felt the same way when we were your age—that's why we have to be so careful now. We know how tempting it is to believe the world's going to welcome us with open arms and treat us as equals." He laughed bitterly. "But we've lived long enough to know that isn't the way it'll be—when it happens. It'll be them against us. To the frozen limit." He sighed anxiously. "Patti, in the best of times man isn't going to want to share the earth with us. And now, with four of their own dead"—he sighed again, as if trying to dislodge a heavy weight from deep in his chest—"well, from where we stand, it's the very worst timing there could possibly be. So bear in mind that the Council's got the whole town to consider, not just you. Don't expect them to go easy on you. And for God's sake don't give them any lip. Please!"

Patti slipped her arms around him again and moved very close to him, burying her face in his shirt. She felt very young, very helpless, and very, very afraid.

"I won't, Daddy, I promise I won't. Please don't be frightened." She was too frightened herself to realize that what she was really saying was, "Don't let me be frightened," unconsciously attributing to her parent, as she had done as a child, the God-like omnipotence to provide comforting solutions to all her problems.

He hugged her hard, then released her and took her arm. "Come on, now. You know how Ada gets when she's kept waiting."

She hurried along beside him out of the house. They crossed the road and started up Ada's front walk.

"You're late, Creighton. Anything wrong?"

Patti looked up, startled. Mayor Farley was standing on the porch of her house, just outside the door. The slight smile curving her lips was belied by the iciness of her hazel-green eyes, which studied the two of them like an x-ray, seeming to Patti to lay bare the last thought in the last of each of their brain cells. She felt as if she had never seen the woman before, never uned with her, and never known her until this moment. A shudder ran through her body.

"Sorry, Ada. Patti wasn't dressed," her parent lied.

Patti felt his grip tighten warningly on her arm. "I'm sorry, Ada. I hurried as fast as I could." Her mouth had gone dry and sticky.

Ada eyed them a moment longer. "We've been waiting," she said shortly, then turned and stalked into her house.

Creighton gave her an admonishing look and shoved her forward. Patti marched along behind Ada into her office, certain, in spite of what her parent had assured her, that she was walking her next-to-last steps on earth. Her last would be the short walk from Real Tweedie's driveway to the room in the corner of his cellar; she would never leave it alive.

21

"Well, how are you feeling today, Miss Hunter?" Tilley beamed at her. "You sure look a lot better." He stepped into Carey's hospital room holding out a cone of florist's paper. "Brought you these to brighten up your room."

Carey gave him a tight little smile. "Thank you, Lieutenant Tilley." She held up her freshly bandaged hands. "Would you unwrap them for me, please? I don't get rid of these until tomorrow—maybe."

Tilley tore off the paper and held a dozen yellow roses under her nose. "Like them?"

"They're beautiful." Carey inhaled the fragrance deeply. "Thank you very much. Would you put them here, on the pillow, where I can smell them for a while?"

"Sure." He placed them sideways on her pillow, the thorny stems well away from her face. "So, how goes it? You getting better?"

"Yes, thank you. I'm feeling better."

"I've spoken with your mother. Your parents are flying up here to be with you tomorrow."

"I know." Carey looked at him, a hurt, puzzled expression clouding her eyes. "She called me last night and said to expect them Thursday. Is that tomorrow? I seem to have lost track of the time somehow."

Tilley nodded. "It's tomorrow. Today's Wednesday. You slept through most of yesterday."

"Did I? How do you know?"

"I was here several times. You were always asleep."

"Oh." Carey frowned. "Well, thank you for coming." She looked down at the huge white mitts swathing her hands. "I'm sorry you wasted so much of your time."

"Nonsense. I wanted to know how you were. Sleeping was the best thing you could have been doing."

Carey kept her eyes averted from him. "Why did you come, Lieutenant Tilley?"

"Why? To see how you were doing," he repeated himself, trying to smile, although the question set off an alarm inside him.

Carey was silent awhile. Then she said, "My mother said how terrible it was for me—both Margie and Nick." She looked up. "She thought I knew about Nick, Lieutenant Tilley. Why didn't you tell me?"

Tilley felt himself flush, and blew out a long breath. "I'm sorry. I intended to. I just didn't feel it was the right time the other night. You'd been through too much. I thought it would be better if you rested first, and got the treatment you needed. You were in shock, you know."

"You should have told me."

"I'm very sorry."

"You had no right to keep that from me."

"Please forgive me, Miss Hunter. I felt strongly you needed to be spared any more pain until you'd recovered, somewhat, from all the rest. I did what I thought was best for you."

"You don't know what's best for me. You're not . . ." Carey hesitated.

"If I made the wrong decision, I'm sorry. And I'm very, very sorry about Mr. Pocetto."

"Nick. His name is Nick."

"Nick." Tilley paused. "I really am terribly sorry, Miss Hunter."

"I won't identify him!" she exploded, glaring at him.

"No," Tilley assured her, "that won't be necessary. His brother arrived yesterday for that purpose." His heart ached for her. "Don't give it another thought, Miss Hunter."

He watched her. It seemed to take a while for her to realize what he had said. Damn her mother. He had told her her daughter didn't know about Pocetto yet and suggested—insisted would be more like it—she not be told until she was well enough to leave the hospital. Apparently the woman hadn't taken him seriously.

"Frank?" Carey asked at last.

She seemed confused, he thought. "Francis Pocetto, yes," he said quietly. "He's taken care of everything. Don't concern yourself about it."

"Why hasn't he come to see me? If he's here?"

"He's waiting to," Tilley said kindly. "You've been sleeping. I'll tell the doctors you can see him this afternoon, how's that?"

"You make all the decisions about my life, don't you," Carey said in an empty voice.

"It must seem that way to you, I know, Miss Hunter."

"I hate this state," Carey said, in the kind of voice she might have said, "It's three o'clock" or "I'm going to the store."

"That's understandable," he agreed softly, watching her face.

"I wish I'd never come here."

"I can understand that." He wanted to touch her, comfort her, but restrained himself.

"Everybody's dead because of me." Carey turned her head and stared out the window of the hospital room.

"Don't do that to yourself." Tilley said quietly. "It won't help—you or them. Life is . . . life, Miss Hunter.

Things happen to people. It doesn't get us anywhere to blame ourselves for the things we can't control.''

"What happened to Nick?" Carey asked, her voice flat. "Was he killed like Marge was?"

"No." Tilley cleared his throat. "It was entirely different."

"My mother kept saying, "Both Margie and Nick—like *that*." She said it several times.''

"We think there may be a connection between their deaths. But I'm quite certain they were not killed by the same person."

"But how did he die?"

"Not like your friend Margie, Miss Hunter, I assure you."

"But how?"

"We don't really know. If I could explain it to you, I would. All we know is there was an excess of . . . fluid in his body. In his cells. It appears to have been some kind of internal drowning," Tilley finished carefully.

"Not like Margie? He wasn't all—?"

"No," Tilley said quickly, "he wasn't. I promise you."

"I don't understand." Carey's eyes brimmed with tears. "I just don't understand."

Tilley's chest ached. He longed to gather her up like a child and tell her everything would be all right, but all he did was to reach out and put a hand gently on her arm. "Neither do we, Miss Hunter. I'm sorry."

Large tears began to brim over Carey's lower lids and splash down her cheeks. "Mrs. Rambeau—"

"I know." He clenched his teeth. "We found her. I'm sorry."

"Stop saying that!" Her voice broke.

Tilley opened his mouth to say it again, then closed it. He felt helpless. Everything in him hurt with the need to comfort her.

"Oh, God," Carey began to cry, "what am I going to do? What am I going to do?"

Tilley threw his professional caution to the wind, sat

down on the side of the bed, and gathered her into his arms.

"Cry," he told her simply. He felt her resisting him and gently pulled her head against his chest. "There's nothing else you can do." His voice was gruff with the pain he felt for her.

She was so still Tilley wondered if she was holding her breath. He gently rocked her a little and muttered, "It's okay, it's okay," over and over against her hair. After what seemed to him a full minute, a convulsion of pent-up emotion ripped through her body, and a strangled, heartbroken sob escaped from her throat. It was followed by another and another and another, each more terrible than the last, as her reserve broke down and her controls swept away in a flood of tears.

Tilley held her closer and buried his face in her hair. He had not suffered so for another person since he had held Thea in his arms as she'd lain writhing in pain in a bed in this same hospital. His chest felt as if someone had sunk an ax into his breastbone. He could hardly draw breath, and he could feel his heart and every pulse in his body pounding.

He lifted Carey half onto his lap and rocked her like a baby, swaying back and forth. He heard his voice mumbling, over and over, "Oh, God; oh, God," but it seemed to be coming from someplace inside him other than his vocal chords. He didn't know if he was praying or cursing, and didn't give a damn which. All he cared about was doing the one thing he couldn't do: suffer Carey's pain for her.

The door opened, and a nurse hurried in soundlessly in her crepe-soled shoes. "Get out," Tilley growled, motioning with his head for her to leave.

She nodded at him. "Oh, good," she whispered, smiling a little. "We've been waiting for this."

Tilley glared at her and hissed, "Get out!"

A corner of her mouth twisted down, and one of her eyebrows lifted in disdain. She backed from the room and closed the door. Tilley buried his face again in Carey's hair and kissed her head.

"Oh, God," he heard himself groan again. There didn't seem to be anything else to say.

Carey cried a long time. Tilley's left leg was tingling with pins and needles from her weight long before she quieted and lay, at last, limply against his chest. He fumbled in his pockets, then saw the box of tissues on the little chest beside her bed. He took it and stretched around her to set it on her lap. She reached for it with her great mittened paws, and he chuckled softly.

"Better let me do that," he murmured. He pulled out a fistful of tissues, and wiped her face and nose tenderly.

When he'd finished and tossed the soggy mass into the wastebasket, Carey reached up and touched his face. To his surprise, she ran a bandaged hand lightly all over his cheeks and eyes and mouth.

"You've been crying, too," she croaked in a hoarse voice.

"Hmm," he muttered, surprised and not at all surprised at once. He took a tissue from the box, blew his own nose, and wiped his eyes and cheeks. "Well, it wouldn't be the first time, Carey Hunter." He laughed a little, feeling shy as a schoolboy and doubly embarrassed by the feeling. "Maybe I figured you had so much to cry about, you couldn't possibly do it all by yourself."

Carey smiled slightly. She made no move to get off his lap, and Tilley felt idiotically happy just to sit there and hold her and let his leg pin-and-needle itself all it wanted to. They sat quietly for several minutes.

"I've really soaked your clothes," Carey said at last.

"Wouldn't be a first time for that, either." Tilley kissed her hair so lightly he was sure she wouldn't feel it. "Don't worry about it."

After another moment Carey leaned her head back and looked up at him with bewildered eyes. "Did you just kiss me, Lieutenant Tilley?"

"Yes." Tilley felt his throat contract and knew his voice sounded tense. "Do you mind?"

"No." Carey continued to look at him, frowning a little. "I was just curious. Why?"

"Because I felt like it, I imagine. That usually why I kiss someone." Tilley kept his voice light and studied her brown eyes, trying to figure out what she was thinking. But he was too involved in struggling with his own feelings to be able to do so. He could think of nothing to say, and finally just expelled an overbig, overloud, "Well."

"I never thought about detectives kissing anyone," Carey said thoughtfully.

"Oh, we're quite human."

"I didn't mean—oh, I'm sorry, Lieutenant Tilley."

She blushed through her slightly faded sunburn, and Tilley's heart skipped a beat. The thought raced through his mind: Damn, but you're pretty, Carey Hunter, sunburn and blisters and peeling and all.

Aloud he said, "How about calling me Paul? It sounds a lot friendlier than Lieutenant Tilley."

"All right."

"Okay if I call you just Carey?"

"Sure." She twisted against him. "Would you mind if I moved now? My sunburn hurts, and I've made your jacket so wet it's uncomfortable."

Tilley chuckled. "Now that's an ingrate if ever I heard one." He felt ridiculously pleased to see her smile back at him.

He lifted her off his leg and stood up, not daring to put his weight on his left leg.

"Hold on," he said quickly, "I'll plump up those pillows for you."

After he had settled her comfortably against them, he stood looking down at her.

"How do you feel about answering some questions? Think you can handle it?"

Carey stared up at him. "I don't know. I'll try." She grinned suddenly, a little sheepishly. "I must be all cried out for at least a year."

He grinned back. "Well, stop me if you discover you aren't." He took out his notebook and pen. "Sorry I have to do this, but that's the job. First and foremost, did you see anybody on Outer Island last Thursday night besides yourself and Margaret Rambeau?''

''Yes,'' Carey replied after a pause.

Tilley experienced a rush of gratification. By God, he'd solve this abysmal case yet! He could have kissed her.

''Did you recognize this person?''

Carey hesitated. ''Sort of. Not exactly.''

''Can you explain that, Carey?'' He was careful to keep his voice bland.

''It just looked familiar,'' she said helplessly.

'' 'It'? What just looked familiar?''

''The face.''

''Was it a man's or a woman's face?''

''Neither—either. I don't know. I couldn't tell.''

''Would you recognize this face if you saw it again?'' He held his breath and prayed.

''Yes,'' Carey said intensely, ''I'm sure I would.''

Tilley inwardly heaved a sigh of relief. Good girl, he silently complimented her, remembering her courage and sharp eye for detail in George Dobbler's room, I knew I could count on you.

''Was there anything outstanding about the face that you'd recognize—if you saw it again?''

''Yes. The eyes.'' Carey shuddered.

''You okay?'' His concern was plain in his voice and he knew it. But he no longer cared.

''Yes. It just gives me the creeps, remembering. But I'm fine,'' she added quickly. ''I want you to get whoever . . . did what they did to Mrs. Rambeau and Margie . . . and Nick.'' Her voice trailed off sadly.

''Okay. Let's go on.'' Tilley looked at her seriously. ''What about the eyes?''

''The color. They were the same color.''

''The same color as what?''

''Those kids' eyes on the ferry last—'' She frowned. ''Whenever it was. Before the northeaster, before all this happened.''

''A week ago last Saturday?'' Tilley prompted her.

"Yes. When I was coming back from South Bay."

"The four teenagers in T-shirts and jeans?" he asked quietly.

"Yes. How did you know?"

He smiled. "I ask a lot of questions. It's part of my job." His satisfaction was enormous. He had them, he had those weird little sons-of-bitches now, by God. And they'd had their chance; he'd offered it to them. And they'd refused. They'd done their number for his benefit, and they'd refused. Well, he wouldn't need their cooperation now. He had them. Right here in Carey Hunter's eyes. Now he'd go for Pine Woods with no holds barred, with every shred and scrap of evidence he could coax out of her. And he'd get them. He'd get them good. Whatever macabre secret it was they were hiding up there, he wouldn't stop until he'd laid it bare in broad daylight for all the world to see. "What color were their eyes, Carey?" he asked casually.

"Hazel-green. I couldn't miss it, because all they did was stare at me."

"And what color were the eyes of the person you saw on Outer Island?"

"Hazel-green. Exactly the same."

"How could you see the color? I mean, wasn't it night—dark?"

"I had a flashlight, a really strong one. One of those big ones you use for emergencies. It belonged to The Berries. To Mrs. Rambeau, that is," she added wistfully.

"You shone it on him—or her?" he asked quietly.

"Accidentally. I think. I don't think I had it in my hand—I'm not sure. I was trying to get away, and the dinghy rolled, or I slipped. I honestly don't know how it happened, I was too scared. No— Yes, I did! I had it in my hand. I hit him with it. I shone it right up on that face, and then I hit him with it. I could see that face clear as day for a second. I'll never forget it."

Carey Hunter, I could kiss you for that alone, Tilley exulted silently. He pulled up the visitor's chair and sat down beside her bed.

"Okay, Carey, why don't we start at the beginning. Feel up to it?" When she nodded, he smiled. "Let's start with that ferry ride a week ago Saturday, in fact. Just tell me everything you can remember. About everything."

His pen was poised over his notebook. Outwardly he was coolly professional. Inwardly he was beside himself with jubilation.

"There, now," Creighton Welles reached an arm around Patti's shoulders and gave her a reassuring squeeze as they went down Ada's front steps, "that wasn't so bad after all, was it."

"No." Patti felt drained from sheer relief, but bewildered. "They were so nice to me. I expected it was going to be awful and instead—" She glanced up at the side of her parent's face. "I don't understand, Creighton. You're the only one who's been hard on me about it."

"Well, I was upset," he said, his tone defensive. "And with good reason, I might add. Besides, I wanted them to know I'd already come down on you like a ton of bricks. So maybe they'd go a little easier on you—which they did. It was all for your own good, Patti," he added self-righteously.

She still felt confused. It had all been, well, too easy, it seemed to her. "They said they'd even reconsider about my going to college—"

"Next year. Not till next year," he reminded her. "And then only if your attitude has changed, and you've gotten all that spooniness out of your head."

Patti nodded absently. Next year was forever to her. She was still busy digesting the Town Council members' incredible understanding and patient tolerance of her recent behavior. Had it been sincere? Did she dare trust it? "They even said I could go on giving piano lessons. . . ."

"Well, we can't have you sitting around for a year doing nothing." Creighton chuckled expansively. "Now can we?"

Could she even trust her parent? She didn't understand

it, but something just didn't feel right to her. Well, maybe it was just her. Maybe she just hadn't gotten over the fright the entire experience had given her.

"Did I do all right? Did I say the right things and act right and all, Creighton?"

"Well, what do you think?" He gave her shoulders another squeeze. "You did just fine, Patti, just fine. I was real proud of you."

He unlocked their front door and held it open for her. She went in, and stopped in the hall.

"Where was Real, Creighton? How come he wasn't there?"

Her parent hesitated. "Real? Oh, he had some business or other to attend to."

He strode past her down the hall.

"More important than a Council meeting?" she followed him into the kitchen.

"You'll have to ask him. Apparently so." There was a slight edge in Creighton's voice. "Don't you have something else to do besides follow me around? Why don't you go practice or something? You haven't touched the piano in days."

"Well, how could I?" Patti tried to make a joke of it. "You told me I couldn't leave my room."

He didn't take it as she hoped. "I don't want to hear any more about that. It was little enough, considering. You've gotten off mighty easy, Patti, mighty easy. Aside from being restricted to town, we let you off scot-free. So just get on with things, and let bygones be bygones."

"Okay, Creighton. I'm sorry."

"You damn well ought to be," he snorted.

"Can I ask you just one more question?"

"If it only requires a yes or a no for an answer."

"Do you really trust me not to say anything to that Lieutenant Tilley when he comes back?"

"Of course I do." Her parent reached out and patted her cheek, his manner suddenly warm and affectionate. "And so does everybody else. Why?" He winked at her. "Shouldn't we?"

"Yes," Patti said, her voice emphatic. Fleetingly she thought his eyes looked cold and hard, but dismissed the thought, chiding herself for being suspicious, and choosing to respond gratefully to the warmth she so desperately needed right now. "You should. I love you. I love all of you. I'd never do anything that would hurt anybody here—again. And I didn't do what I did before to hurt anybody. I did it to help us. I just didn't think . . . about all the consequences. I know now how stupid it was, Daddy."

"We know that, Patti."

"And I know what a trust you've all placed in me, in spite of what I did."

"A very great trust, Patti," Creighton said. "We're trusting you with our lives, and the life of every one of your people here in Pine Woods."

"I won't let you down, Creighton, I promise." She gazed at him, her heart in her eyes.

"We have faith in you, Patti."

"I won't tell him anything. No matter what he does to me."

Creighton smiled. It seemed to Patti a sad and rather knowing smile, and puzzled her.

"Oh, I don't think he'll do anything to you," her parent said easily. "Seemed like a rather nice fellow to me, for a human."

"Well, even if he does," Patti insisted.

He shook his head, still smiling sadly. "He won't. There isn't going to be anything he can do."

Tilley forced his way through the crowd of reporters jamming the police station parking lot.

"No comment, no comment," he reiterated as question on top of question was shouted at him.

"Is it true you've just questioned Carey Hunter at the medical center?" Jack Hoyt shouted in his ear as he hurried up the steps of the building.

"Now, why in the world would I do that?" He flashed a mean smile at the newsman. "Carey Hunter was lost at sea in a dinghy, Jack. What could she possibly tell us?''

"Only who the murderer is," Hoyt came back sarcastically. "Come on, lieutenant. Everybody knows you were hoping she'd seen the murderer before she left Outer Island. Did she?"

Tilley grinned. He knew he looked like the cat who'd swallowed the canary, and he didn't give a damn. "If you go on the air with that fabrication, you'll never get the egg off your face." He glanced over the anxious throng crowding him. "No comment, people. When I've got something to say, I'll call a press conference."

He opened the door and strode into the station house.

"Where's Crowley?" he bellowed, beaming at the desk officer.

"Inside, sir. Somewhere."

"Where's the chief?"

"Out, sir."

"Crowley!" he roared, loping toward his office. "Jim Crowley! Get your ass in here on the double!"

Sergeant Crowley got to his office door at the same instant Tilley did. Tilley shoved him inside and slammed the door.

"I've got it, Jim, I've got it. She saw somebody. Close up. Face to face. Tried to grab her, in fact. And she's certain she can identify him, or her."

"Him or her?" Crowley echoed, with raised eyebrows. "Doesn't she know which it was?"

"It was night. She can't be sure."

"Can't be sure?" Crowley shook his head. "Then how the hell can she be so sure she can identify . . . whoever it was?"

"She'll be able to. I'm certain she'll be able to." He paced back and forth excitedly.

"Paul"— Crowley frowned and looked uncomfortable— "are you sure this case hasn't . . . gotten to you? I mean, if the only witness you've got doesn't even know if she saw a man or a woman, aren't you maybe just clutching at straws or something?"

"Not anymore. The straw turned into a log—finally."
He clapped his hands together and laughed.

"But if—"

"She knows the face, Jim. She's seen four resembling it
before."

Crowley stared a moment. "Pine Woods?"

"You got it. Those four kids on the ferry that night. She
said whoever it was looked just like them, only older. So
we can be pretty sure whoever she saw is an adult."

"Wait a minute, Paul, wait a minute." Crowley threw
his hands up. "She said this person looked just like *all
four of them?*"

"That's right."

"Mother of God." Crowley dropped onto the nearest
chair.

"Now what?" Tilley eyed him good-humoredly.

"Don't you know what you just said, Paul?"

"Of course I do. According to Carey Hunter—and Archie English—they all looked alike. Probably brothers and
sisters, or whatever. Closely related. Hell, the whole goddamn town's closely related." He stopped. The excitement
began to ooze out of him like pus. He leaned heavily
against his desk, his shoulders sagging.

Crowley waited silently. Finally Tilley straightened up
and looked around at him. Crowley shook his head and
looked down. Tilley stood for a while, staring at him, then
raised his eyes and stared out of his window.

"The whole goddamn miserable town looks alike, doesn't
it?" he said at last in a hollow voice. He glanced back at
his partner.

Crowley looked up and nodded. "*Just* alike, Paul. That's
just it."

Tilley slowly sat down in his chair. He leaned his
elbows on the desk and put his head in his hands.

"We've got to try, Jim," he said wearily. "We've got
to do something. We can't sit and do nothing with this."

"What? It's a whole town."

"We can't just sit on it."

"I know."

"Can we bring them all in?"

"An entire town?"

"Hell, it's not a very big town."

"More'n two hundred cars outside that church," Crowley reminded him. "Even if everybody over eighteen has their own car up there, that's a lotta people."

"Shit." Tilley slammed both fists down on the top of his desk. "What do you think Hoho's going to say to it?"

"Say? He's not going to say anything. He's going to scream. He'll never let you do it, Paul."

"Damn it, he's got to."

"He won't. Think of the field day the media would have with a stunt like that." Crowley gestured wildly. " 'Bangor detective arrests entire town in last-ditch effort to find Mummy Murderer.' Jesus, Paul, you'll be wiped off the map. The chances of Carey Hunter—or anybody— being able to pick one face out of that crowd is less than one in a million."

"She's got to," Tilley erupted savagely. "She's just got to."

"Paul, if I saw that mayor—what's her name? Farley— and their sheriff and the minister in a lineup with their hair all cut the same length, I wouldn't be able to tell one from the other, except by the clothes. And I spent hours with them. How good a look did Carey Hunter get?"

Tilley dug his notebook out of his pocket and read his pertinent notes aloud. Crowley sat silent after he finished.

"All right, all right," Tilley growled. "So it was night. And she only saw the face for an instant, by flashlight. *She* says she can never forget it."

"Her forgetting it isn't the problem, Paul," Crowley said with a sigh. "The problem's going to be her picking it out of a couple hundred or more that look just like it."

"We've still got to try," Tilley repeated.

"Granted. But how?"

"Bring a few of them in at a time. In unmarked cars."

"The media'll get wind of it. The story went national

Monday with Pocetto's murder. You'll never pull it off. And when Carey Hunter can't make a positive identification—''

"She even saw the color of his eyes," Tilley shouted in desperation.

"Or her eyes," Crowley said unhappily. "And so what? The entire town's got hazel-green eyes. Come on."

"Well, we could always take her up there, I suppose," Tilley muttered reluctantly.

"Damn irregular."

"Nobody has to know."

"Skillin does. Because somebody will find out and tell him. Or worse, he'll see it on the news. He'll can you, Paul, I'm telling you."

"Christ. If I only had a clue as to which one of them it was."

"You don't."

"Oh, shut up, Jim, just for a minute, will you. Try and think of something positive we *can* do."

"I suggest you dump it right in Hoho's lap and let him decide. That way at least you're off the hook."

Tilley scowled at him. "I'm not interested in getting off the hook. I'm interested in solving this rotten case and finding out just what it is that lousy little hole in the woods is hiding."

"If you make one more move without letting Skillin know what you're up to, it won't be your case to solve," Crowley observed tersely.

"Oh, all right, all right." Tilley snatched the receiver off his phone and snarled, "Chief back yet?" He listened a second, then snapped, "Ring me soon as he walks in," and slammed the phone back down again. He looked across his desk at his partner. "You better come in with me, Jim. I'm going to need you to help me convince him the whole goddamned town looks exactly alike."

22

"I'm sorry, Paul." Carey stood near the passenger gate at Bangor International Airport, looking into his blue eyes. "I was so sure. . . ."

Tilley shook his head and smiled at her. "Not your fault a whole inbred little community looks just like each other. Nobody could have done it. Wasn't just you—those Sartsport hoodlums couldn't make an i.d. either. You tried. You really tried. I'm grateful for that. It was just hopeless to begin with. Try and forget about it—all of it. I'm just sorry I put you through it."

"No. I wanted to do it. I wanted to get whoever—" She stopped and looked away from him.

"I know." He took her hand between both of his. "So did I. We gave it our best shot, Carey. We'll always know that."

The September sun glinted off the side of a jet outside the terminal. Carey realized she was squinting and looked away, back at Tilley.

"I'm sorry you were taken off the case."

He shrugged. "Maybe it's for the best. Maybe Bill Manship can solve it." He laughed; there was a bitter ring in the sound. "I certainly wasn't doing anything but creating a clambake for the media. Anyway, it's given me time to do some other things. Like get my car fixed, finally."

"I'm so sorry, Paul. I made so much trouble for you."

"Trouble? Hey, now, you gave me three weeks of your time—and your mother's. You have nothing to be sorry about. *I*'m the one who's sorry—sorry I asked you to try and do the impossible. Your father meeting you in New York?''

"No. My mom's going to stay awhile at the apartment with me, so he's going to wait until I'm ready to be there alone again before he comes in to pick her up. He hates the city,'' she added.

"Well, maybe I'll see you there one of these days.''

"In New York?'' Carey was astonished. "Really?''

"Maybe.'' Tilley grinned secretively. "I'm thinking about making some changes in my life.''

"But your whole life is here—'' Carey began.

Tilley placed a finger on her lips. "No, it isn't. My life here ended eight years ago—only I didn't know it. Until I met you.''

"I don't know what you mean, Paul,'' she said, frowning at him.

"I know. And this isn't the right time to try and explain it to you. I've got your address. You'll stay in that apartment?''

"Oh, yes. It's too hard to find a new one these days. I'll get used to it—I guess— in time, without Margie.'' Her eyes filled up, and she looked down.

"And you've got mine. If anything develops on the case, I'll let you know.''

Carey nodded.

"Someday I want to see what you look like when your face is all healed. How are your hands feeling these days?''

She held them up. They were pink with new skin and still slightly swollen. "They're getting there. I never realized I was such a slow healer. I still have to be careful not to grab at anything.''

"Oh, that reminds me,'' Tilley said and reached in his pocket. "I have a present for you.'' He held out a bottle of vitamin E capsules. "From Captain Dinny. He said to tell you Maria was bringing him more the next time she visited him. And that he enjoyed knowing you.''

Carey took the little plastic bottle and stared at it. "I must write to him," she said sadly. "He was so nice to me, and I never even said thank you."

"I think he understood," Tilley said gently.

Carey looked up at him. "Well, I won't make that omission with you. Thank you, Paul—for everything."

"It was little enough, Carey, but, my pleasure."

"Please"—she hesitated, not at all sure what she wanted to say and feeling foolish, but she had to say it—"take care of Margie for me, Paul. I mean . . . I guess I don't know what I mean. But I feel like I'm deserting her, leaving her here with strangers."

"I understand, Carey. Honestly, I do."

"You're the only person I know here at all. I know this sounds silly, but I hate thinking of her all alone where she doesn't know anybody. She never wanted to come here at all. She only did it for me." She looked at him pleadingly. "Don't let them make a freak out of her forever. She was so . . . alive."

"I'll do what I can, Carey." Tilley placed his hands on either side of her face. "I do understand what you're feeling. Please know that."

"Do I sound crazy?" Carey didn't know if she was asking Tilley or herself. Suddenly, she just didn't want to leave him. He seemed to be her last link to Margie. Nick had a big family in Brooklyn. She would remain tied to them, whatever else happened in her life. Mrs. Rambeau belonged to South Bay—Mrs. Mitchell and Archie and the rest—and Carey would have parted from her, as from all of them, when the summer was over. But Margie had had no family but her. This relative stranger was more involved with Margie Packer than anyone but she and Jeff had been since Margie's mother had died. She stared at him with her heart in her eyes.

"Not to me," Tilley said softly. "I understand, Carey. I know. Hang in there. I'll be in touch—soon. And I promise I'll look after her."

As he walked away from her, through the terminal building, Carey had the illogical feeling that the rest of her life walked with him. She hadn't the faintest idea what she would do with herself back in New York; Margie had been part and parcel of every aspect of her life, except her work. And she'd quit that—to come to Maine and decide what it was she really wanted to do with her life. Watching the back of Tilley's head moving away from her, she felt she had no life to do with anymore. If it hadn't died with Margie Packer, it was certainly frozen in a morgue compartment with her somewhere in Bangor, Maine.

Nick's death was not yet real to her. Perhaps it never quite would be. She hadn't had to look at . . . whatever had been left of him. She suspected the day might arrive when it would hit her, and she would cry; begin to miss him and grieve for him for a long time after. But he had been always her lover, never her friend. Margie had been her friend. Nearly ten years of her life had been spent side by side with Margie. Dimly she realized that neither of them had ever seriously thought their life together would ever end, that one might get married or move away for some reason, or that anything or anyone could come along to tear them apart. They hadn't had to own each other. They'd been friends, and so free to love and enjoy each other. They'd managed, out of that freedom and love, both to meet each other's needs and respect each other's separateness without ever having to ask. Each had known instinctively when to be there for the other—and when to leave her alone.

Carey knew Margie was irreplaceable in her life. She felt, as her mother took her arm and led her through the passenger gate, that she was both leaving nothing and going to nothing. She also felt, without focusing on it, that Lieutenant Paul Tilley of the Bangor Police might be the only other person alive who would ever understand her feelings. Vaguely she attributed this to the way his incredibly blue eyes sometimes looked at her—and felt a fresh loss.

Leaving Tilley was, in some indefinable way, like losing Margie a second time. He'd been kind to say so, but she knew she would never hear from him again.

23

Patti felt her nipples separate from Hovey Moholland's. She rolled over on her back, on his big double bed, and stretched luxuriously. Her mind still floated free in other dimensions, beyond prayers and dreams and meditations, reluctant to descend to the mere material. She sighed deeply, savoring the last shreds of rapture and the delicious sensations that always accompanied regenesis. She turned her head and smiled sweetly at Hovey.

"I wish I could stay in anastomosis forever," she murmured.

"Someday you will." Hovey smiled back at her.

"When I'm dead." She made a wry face. "I hope you're right about that, Hovey."

"Death is eternal anastomosis with God," he assured her, a touch of pomposity in his voice.

"I don't see how anybody can really know that," Patti mused, frowning a little, "unless they've died and come back to life again."

"We know it every time we une, Patti. Through being one with each other, we get a small taste of what it will be like, someday, to be one with our Creator."

Patti turned away and stared out of the window of his bedroom. Snow was swirling through the November morning light. Yesterday had been Thanksgiving. In a month it would be Christmas. She was terribly glad her people celebrated Christmas and followed the teachings of Jesus—in spite of Adrian Widdows' rantings against it—though their insistence that he had not been a man at all, but the very first of their kind, puzzled her. Oh, it explained a lot; but still, whom had he uned with, if it was true? She knew the answer Hovey would give her if she asked: God. Perhaps that was true, but it didn't satisfy her. His being one of them would certainly explain his celibacy, though. She turned back to Hovey.

"Do men and women feel that about having sex with each other—that it's a little bit like being one with God?"

"I suppose so," Hovey replied thoughtfully. "Some of them may. I've read something of the sort, in their books, when they're what they call 'in love' with each other." He yawned. "But it's not the same. Their sex act is— well, more of a relief than anything else. Or anything more."

"I wonder what it feels like," Patti mused softly.

"Though I've sometimes wondered," Hovey went on, appearing not to have heard her, "if it wasn't God's first primitive attempt to give Its creations some little glimpse of what it was going to be like to be one with It, when the time came."

Patti reached out and touched his face with a fingertip, slowing tracing the features and bone structure so like her own. "If God had already done that, why did It make us?" she asked.

"Always the question box," Hovey rumpled her hair, smiling, "aren't you. Well, let's see. If I were building a church, and every time I hammered in the last nail it all fell down, wouldn't I, after just so many attempts, sit down and think up a new way to construct it so it wouldn't fall down any more?"

"Oh, Hovey." Patti grimaced at him.

"Well, wouldn't I?"

"It's not the same thing."

"It's not all that different, either. Besides, it's as good as I can come up with off the top of my head. Look, Patti," Hovey's face grew serious, "man believes God *is,* which is the same thing as saying It's finished, total, complete—already perfect. That everything's been all laid out and already done, and whatever goes on here on earth is, well, like another act in a play that's already been written, and they're just playing out their parts in it. We believe God is growing and changing all the time, developing. Just as we are, as the whole world is. Every time It thinks of a better way to do something, things here change. Darwin said more or less the same thing when he came up with his theory of evolution. But nobody seems to have considered that his theory might apply to God as well, until we came along. We believe it because there's no other explanation that makes any sense."

"Have we only existed for the last hundred years?"

"As far as we know." He smiled again. "You know Adrian's theories on that as well as I do. Except for Jesus, the first of us—that we know about. I for one am certain there are other communities of us that came along about a generation after humans started milling their grains with steel instead of stone. Adrian thinks we must have started as an adaptation, caused by the heat removing nutrients from their grains their bodies just had to have. Of course, he's a long way from being able to prove that—if he ever does. We could just as well have sprung spontaneously from the hand of God without material cause, if that was Its will. But Adrian's theory makes a kind of sense, if you consider what they've continued to do to their foods and how God has taken care with us that all that couldn't affect us in any way." He chuckled. "When God made us, It saw to it It rubbed all the corners off."

"I can't imagine what it must be like to eat," Patti reflected curiously. "I used to chew on vegetables in the garden, just to see, and once," she giggled, "I even bought a hamburger when I went over to Houlton with the Pulks and chewed up the whole thing, bite by bite, spitting

it out and trying another bite. I put catsup on one, and
mustard on another—and mayonnaise and onion and relish.
Everything there was, even sugar. But none of it tasted
like anything." She thought a moment. "I can taste the
other person, though, when I'm uning. I could taste you,
before." She gazed at him, her eyes full of questions.
"Do men and women taste what they eat?"

"They say they do. They must." An expression of mild
disdain came over Hovey's face. "They spend most of
their time talking about what they've just eaten—or are just
about to." He snorted.

Patti took a deep breath and blew out her cheeks like a
balloon, then expelled the air in a big huff. "I think it's
much nicer to be able just to breathe in everything I need.
And out everything I don't," she added, wrinkling her
nose. "I remember a woman Creighton and I saw once
over in Millinocket with a baby. She was changing its—
what do you call that thing?"

"Diaper." Hovey's mouth curved in a little smile.

"Diaper. What a funny word—for a funny business."
She didn't laugh. "Creighton and I watched her do it. It
was really nasty."

"Mmm."

Patti sat up abruptly and flung the covers back from
their bodies.

"I'm so glad we're not like that, Hovey." She ran her
hand down his smooth, hairless body. "We're so beautiful,
much more beautiful than they are." She stared down at
the undifferentiated, glabrous skin between her legs, then
looked over at the minister's like inguinal area. "I'd hate my
body to be as vulnerable as theirs are. Anyway," she
smiled sweetly to herself, "I think it's lovely that we're all
alike, that half of us aren't all different. Even if we
pretend we are," she added wistfully.

"We have to, Patti, for now." Hovey pushed her back
down on the bed and pulled the flannel sheet and wool
blankets up over the two of them. "Get back under the
covers. It's much too cold for you to be sitting up uncov-

ered like that." He put his arms around her and drew her body close to his. "We have to appear to be just like them for as long as we possibly can." He kissed the tip of her nose. "We'd never have survived this long if Aretta McVicar hadn't had the wit to start us out living as men and women, husbands and wives, as if we were gendered like them—and all the other animals."

Patti snuggled against him, and they lay quietly for a time. She stroked his small breasts and pictured, in her mind, the snow falling outside, and thought how safe and secure it felt to be in Hovey's arms. She loved Hovey and felt comfortable with him. He never got upset with her questions as everybody else did, and, even better, he always had answers. She didn't always agree with them, but she loved thinking about them. She secretly suspected she and Hovey were the only two people in Pine Woods who really thought about things—important things. Oh, Adrian did, of course, in a way. But Adrian was so convinced he was right about everything. His answers were the only answers. Hovey's answers were often more question than ascertainment.

She gave him a hug. "I love uning with you, Hovey." She kissed his throat. "I love you."

He did not reply, but gathered her closer to him.

"It's too bad about Real," she heard herself say, and wondered why Real Tweedie had suddenly popped into her mind. Probably because he always made me feel so uncomfortable the minute we stopped uning, she told herself, thinking fleetingly how odd it was that her people all looked so much alike and yet were so utterly different from each other underneath.

"Yes." Hovey's voice sounded sad, yet uplifted. "Real Tweedie was a saint."

"Do you mean that, really?" Patti asked with an innocent excitement. "Are you going to make him one officially, in church, and keep his ashes on the altar with Vonalee Keezer's?"

"Yes." Hovey tilted her head back and tapped her

mouth with his finger. "But you mustn't tell anybody. It won't be announced until sometime next year." He sighed. "I shouldn't have told you. I never can keep anything to myself right after I've uned."

"I won't. But why, Hovey?"

She waited for him to answer her, barely able to contain her curiosity. What qualified Real Tweedie for sainthood? He hadn't done anything special—that she knew about. Except accidentally set fire to his toolshed somehow and get himself burned to death last August, right before everybody had to start going down to Bangor to the police station. Boy, that had been something—scary, but exciting, with all the TV cameras and reporters and crowds and police and all. And she'd finally gotten to see a real city. Well, sort of. She hadn't gotten to see much of it, but still. To herself, Patti admitted to preferring the experience in retrospect, because she remembered all too well being terrified at the time. But she was now elated that that much at least had happened to liven up her life.

"Because he gave his life for his kind," Hovey was saying in the same sad, uplifted voice. "There's no greater qualification for sainthood than martyrdom."

"He got killed in that fire."

"He killed himself, Patti," Hovey corrected her solemnly. "He set that fire."

She was stunned. "But why?"

"So that woman couldn't possibly identify him."

"Oh." She was silent awhile, taking in what he had told her. "But he didn't need to do that. She couldn't tell one of us from the other. We all look so much alike, Hovey."

"Not that much alike. Not if you really look at us— which humans don't, of course. They seldom even really look at each other." He sighed. "Anyway, Real wouldn't take that chance. If there'd been even a question in her mind that he was the one, the police might have booked him, and he'd have had to submit to a physical examination. We couldn't risk that."

"We?" Patti felt a shiver run up her spine. She knew she shouldn't have let on she'd noticed his choice of pronoun, but she couldn't help herself.

"Don't read into what I say, Patti," Hovey said, more sharply than he'd ever spoken to her before. "It was entirely Real's decision. Do you understand?"

"Sure." She felt anxious now.

"You believe me?"

"I always believe you, Hovey."

"Then that's an end to it. I never want you to bring this up again." He moved away from her and turned over, putting his back to her. "Now go to sleep. It's much too early to get up."

Patti stared at his back for a while in the dim early-morning light, then turned over and stared at the snow piling up against the panes of the window. She was hurt. It was the first time Hovey had ever gotten angry with her and shut her out. The shattered closeness of just moments ago filled the bed between them, scoring her naked skin.

She felt awful, and wondered if this was what humans felt like when they got sick. She didn't know; she'd never been sick. No one in Pine Woods ever got sick, not really. Anyone feeling a little under the weather immediately sought out someone with whom to une, and got up a few hours later feeling marvelous. Adrian had a theory about that, too, she thought wryly. He claimed the germs and viruses and bacteria that caused illness in men and women to become acute got so widely dispersed among their kind, by their act of anastomosis, that disease never had a chance to get a foothold on any of them.

Well, even so, she felt as terrible right now as she knew how to feel. She wanted Hovey to hold her and kiss her and be affectionate with her. This was a miserable way for things to be, after just uning. She wished with all her heart he hadn't said what he did. If it meant what she couldn't help suspecting it did, she'd rather not have known. So she wouldn't think about it anymore.

But why had Hovey suddenly become so strange and distant and angry—and so defensive? No, she wasn't going to think about it. She'd think about . . . What would she think about? So far, the autumn had been deadly dull. All she had to do was give eleven piano lessons a week and clean the house. She'd asked Creighton if he thought the Council might let her learn how to operate the radio equipment in Ada's attic, and he'd had a fit, an absolute fit, and told her never even to think about it again. After what she'd done, he'd hollered, the Council would consider she'd lost her mind even to speculate they might let her be able to contact the human world outside Pine Woods.

She sighed. There were so many things she was supposed never to think or talk about again. Like Hovey's 'we'—no, that she really wouldn't think about. But what else was there to think about until next fall, when she went to college? *If* she went to college, she corrected herself. If they let her go. If they ever let her go. Aroostook State Teachers College was a far cry from the Boston Conservatory of Music, but at least it was something. A few hours a day, anyway, out of Pine Woods. A chance to learn for herself if humans and their world were really as terrible as she'd been told. It was her last hope. If they didn't let her go. . . .

She curled herself into a ball and continued to stare at the swirling snow. Out there, somewhere beyond Hovey's window and the road and the endless pines and the whole constricted, backward town was an enormous world that she wanted more than anything to know—to shine in with her music, like a star. The quotation she secretly treasured from Winston Churchill came to her mind, and she said it to herself, moving her lips silently, like a prayer: I know we are all worms, but I do believe I am a glowworm.

Oh, God, I do believe I am. Don't let me burn out, unseen, here in this awful, dull little town. Don't let me be wasted. Please. I couldn't bear it. Help me, God, please.

There has to be something more for me than this. I have to be something more. I just have to.

But was there? Could she be? *We couldn't risk that.* Darn it, she would not think about that again. But did the Town Council make Real's decision for him? Did they decide everything about everybody? Would they decide her life too? What was the point in trying not to think about it? No matter what she made herself think about, she kept coming back to that.

She lay, still and miserable, for some time. She was trapped. She couldn't leave Pine Woods alone, without a partner, and she couldn't stay. She groaned softly. Maybe she'd bud this year. That would be something. She ran her hand carefully down her right side, exploring each of her ribs and the side of her diaphragm, then made a long face. There certainly wasn't any sign of it. Anyway, it was stupid to think about. Most didn't bud until they were at least twenty-five, often not until their thirties. "So all their wild oats will have already been sown," her parent had said was the reason. But what wild oats were there to sow in Pine Woods? And where was there to sow them even if anybody could find some. It was so damn dull.

She sighed. There were some definite limitations involved in being one of those destined to inherit the earth someday, as Hovey put it every Sunday morning. Even that wouldn't happen in her lifetime. Okay, humans had a lot of problems and drawbacks, but they also had a lot to do. She didn't have anything to do. If the Council would just decide to announce themselves so she could join the world. She couldn't help but wish, almost, that they had been found out last summer and the whole secret of what they were brought out in the open. God, if only Real hadn't killed himself—if he did kill himself. She was growing too sleepy to push away the thought. And if the Council killed him, what a waste it had been for her to try to call Paul Tilley from Real's house that day. She'd wanted them not to kill a mere human. And they'd turned around and killed one of themselves. Did that mean the earth would never belong to them? Because if it did, then her life was doubly wasted.

She really shouldn't be thinking like this. She yawned. Her thoughts wouldn't be only her own for very long. The next person who lay down in her arms would know them all, well before their nipples parted and their consciousnesses gravitated from the ecstatic to the commonplace. She yawned again. It really wasn't safe to be thinking about such things. Especially for her.

But she wanted—something—so much. If she had to give it up, never know it—maybe never even know exactly what it was—then she first wanted to be sure that her kind really still was heir to the world, and whether or not the world was worth inheriting. She drifted off to sleep with her mind abandoned to this search for answers, so urgent was her inner demand to know at least a taste of freedom and excitement, and to find out whether or not the Town Council had already relinquished, for her, any chance of getting that taste. This search would occupy her thoughts the next day, and the next, and the next. After that, it would no longer matter. Patti would have to lie down in anastomosis with one of her kind by then, or begin to die.

In that case, although she did not know it—never having experienced more than the heightened desire to une caused by a brief wait after her breasts and body, brain and spirit had made known their need to interfuse with the being of another—the sebaceous glands near the base of her nipples and on the surface of her areolae would slowly enlarge until small tubercles would be visible beneath the surface of her skin. By the following morning her ampullae would be painfully swollen with the gathering fluids of her body, and the orifices in the summits of her nipples would be oozing degenerated alveoli cells, and immuno and gamma globulins. Her nipples themselves would be in acute spasm by midafternoon; the pain would be excrutiating. By evening they would be weeping blood.

She would be by then suffering from severe dehydration.

Her skin would be dry and flaking, her tissues shriveling, and her bones beginning to shrink and grow brittle. By the second morning she would be suffering acute vascular spasms, and coagulating, sticky blood would be transuding the skin surface of her entire body. Acute paroxysmal pain would be traversing her nervous system like bolts of lightning; the nerves would rapidly become inflamed, and degenerative lesions would erupt along their lengths until there remained not a single healthy cell.

The pain would be indescribable. And unremitting. Even anastomosis could not save her then. Every cell in her body would be dying its own individual, shrieking death, and the only thing anyone could do for her would be to put a bullet through her brain and spare her the next twenty-four to forty-eight hours that it would take her to shrink to less than pygmy size, mummify, and, finally, die.

24

"I still can't believe you're actually here," Carey smiled at Tilley as she cleared away the remains of the Chinese dinner he'd brought for them and poured him a fresh cup of coffee. "I never really thought I'd see you again. Are you going to stay in New York?"

"For a while, anyway. The rest all depends." He smiled up at her. "I'll have to wait and see."

Carey sat down and leaned on the table, her chin in her hands, and gazed at him. She'd almost forgotten how blue his eyes were. "You really left the police force up there?"

"Uh-huh." He laughed. "It was a mutual decision, believe me."

"What are you going to do now?"

"Promise you won't laugh?"

"Is it funny?" She took him seriously.

"Maybe a little." His face reddened slightly. "For an ex-cop. I'm taking an acting class. I think I'd like to try acting—if acting decides it would like to try me."

"Acting?" Carey sat up, staring at him wide-eyed. Memories of Margie rushed at her from all directions. Her throat constricted and, for an instant, she wished he had not come.

"Yeah. Surprised? Well, truthfully, so am I. But it's an idea I've had batting around in the back of my head for a long time now. I thought I'd give it a try for a few months and see if I have any talent or not." He grinned self-consciously. "I hear tell in class that if you've got a police uniform you can always pick up extra work in TV and films. If that includes a Bangor uniform, at least I won't starve."

"Well, my God." Carey could think of nothing intelligent to say.

"You are surprised," Tilley smiled. "Think I'm barking up the wrong tree?"

"No, uh, no," Carey stumbled, "I . . . don't know what I think. I don't think anything, Paul. I hope you'll be very successful at it."

He looked at her thoughtfully. "I'm sorry. Bad reminder, is that it? I shouldn't have said anything. Forgive me, Carey." He reached across the table and placed a hand over hers.

"No, no, it's all right," she assured him. "I just . . . you just caught me unawares." She took a deep breath. As she'd sensed four months ago, he seemed to understand everything about her. She began to feel better. "I'm the one who's sorry—I didn't mean to put a damper on things for you. I really do wish you lots of luck. It's certainly a complete change for you." She smiled at him again.

He nodded. "That's what I wanted. I've had more than enough of policing. Last summer . . ." He hesitated, watching her face.

"It's okay, Paul," Carey said quietly. "We can't never mention it, as if it didn't happen, or we'll never be able to talk to each other." She looked down at his hand over her own, not fully sure she meant what she was saying. Part of her did. But part of her did not. "I need to talk about it sometimes. Only there's no one who wants to listen."

"There is now." He looked at her tenderly. "Anyway, that all made me stop and think about how much I hated my work. Once I did that, I realized I'd always hated it. So I had to ask myself why I was doing it. I didn't have an answer, so I decided to quit. If acting doesn't work," he went on diffidently, "I'll think of something else to try. Right now I like it. Feel a little foolish every time I have to get up and do something in class, but—well, we'll see."

Carey suddenly realized she wanted his hand off hers, wanted him not to be touching her. She stood up more abruptly than she meant to. "Let's move to the couch, shall we? I think you'll be more comfortable."

"Whatever you say."

"Would you like more coffee?"

"Haven't even touched this yet." He smiled and picked up his cup.

"Well, go make yourself comfortable. I'm going to get myself some more tea." She grabbed her mug from the table and hurried into the kitchen.

She stayed longer than she needed to in the kitchen, holding on to the edge of the counter and telling herself she was behaving badly. It wasn't his fault that he upset her so. It was just that being with him brought back everything she'd begun to be able to forget once in a while. The apartment seemed suddenly full of ghosts— Margie's, Nick's, even Mrs. Rambeau's, somehow. But it wasn't that she didn't like him. She did. She even liked him touching her—a lot. That was what made it so confusing. She felt guilty about liking it. It was—too soon. She shouldn't be feeling anything but grief.

She got control of herself, went back into the living

room with a mugful of milky tea, and settled herself on the far end of the couch. She put her mug down on the coffee table and noticed the little scrimshaw mermaid lying there, beside a magazine. Yes, even Mrs. Rambeau's. She picked up the scrimshaw and held it.

"From Maine?" Tilley asked softly.

"Mrs. Rambeau gave it to me," Carey answered, turning it over in her hand. "I think she said her husband carved it. She had a whole glass cabinet full of scrimshaw. No, it was her great-great-grandfather. It's beautiful, isn't it?"

He took it from her and examined it. "Marvelous. I've never seen one as intricate as this." He squinted at the underside of the tail. There's a name and a date here, worked into the scales of the tail. Look." He held it out.

Carey peered at it. "I can't make it out."

Tilley looked again himself. "Neither can I—not the name. But the date is 1846." He looked up. "This is worth a lot of money."

"I thought so too, when she gave it to me." She took the little mermaid from him and put it back on the coffee table. "I said as much, but she got quite indignant and insisted I take it. I'd admired this one in particular when she showed me her husband's collection. She was so proud of it."

They sat quietly, without speaking. Tilley drank his coffee; Carey sipped at her white tea. She got up, poured him another cup of coffee, and sat down again.

"Is the case closed then, Paul?"

"No. It can't be closed until it's solved. Till then it comes under the heading of 'Unsolved.' Bill Manship's still working on it."

"What about . . . Margie's body? Will they ever release it?"

He shook his head. "I honestly don't know. I think it's unlikely, since she has no family, no one who can force them to, legally. That organ-donation specification she signed on her driver's license doesn't help, either. There's so much curiosity about . . . the manner in which she died, Carey. Labs all over the country are still begging for tissue samples and a chance to examine— Bangor hasn't released anything, though," he interrupted himself quickly. "I know that for a fact. And they won't, as long as the case stays unsolved."

"Will they ever solve it?" Carey realized she was feeling better now, talking about it all and learning what was going on, than during dinner, when she'd almost been holding her breath for fear Tilley would mention it.

"I don't know, Carey." He put down his coffee cup. "My gut feeling is they won't. Not until—or unless—they go upstate and tear Pine Woods apart. I can't explain it; it doesn't make any sense, even to me. But I know the answer's somewhere in that backwoods little town." He turned to her, his face serious. "I wasn't able to tell you this at the time—and I hope it will make you feel better about things—but I'm convinced your friends weren't murdered." He shrugged slightly. "I'm the only one who's convinced of that, but I am. Completely. I'm certain they died accidentally." He stopped, looked down at his hands, then spoke again. "There was somebody murdered, though—two, in fact." He shrugged again. "I can't prove that either." He leaned back against the couch. "Which is partly why I'm glad to be done with the whole business."

"I don't understand," Carey said slowly. "Margie—? And Nick and Mrs. Rambeau—? Accidents? What kind of accidents? Who *was* murdered?"

"Two people from Pine Woods. One of them probably was the man you saw on the dock that night," he answered reluctantly.

"I don't know that it was a man—" Carey began.

"I know. But it probably was. He was killed in a fire the day you got out of the hospital."

Carey stared at him, appalled. "Is that why—?"

"No. That's the idiotic part of it. He undoubtedly looked as much like the rest of them as they all did. You couldn't have identified him even if you'd seen him, I'm certain of it. But apparently they weren't willing to take that chance. Whatever it is they're hiding up in Pine Woods, it must really be something," he mused.

Carey sat stunned. He was right, of course. She couldn't
have identified him. She could still see that startlingly
white face with gleaming hazel-green eyes looming over
her when she closed her eyes, but she'd seen hundreds that
looked just like it. Still, if she just could have looked at
him, just once, surely—surely something would have rung
a bell inside her. And if he'd killed Mrs. Rambeau—and
maybe Margie, too . . . But what did it matter, if he was
dead anyway?

"But he didn't kill Mrs. Rambeau," Tilley's voice
came to her as from a great distance, "or anybody, for that
matter. He was only covering up for whoever did."

It was all more than Carey could take in. "Who was the
other person you think was murdered?" she asked automatically, not caring.

"A girl," Tilley said sadly. "A girl from Pine Woods.
She was just a kid—eighteen. I met her a couple of times
when I went up there, and she was one of the ones we
pulled in for the lineups. I questioned her again that day,
but it was useless. She'd been scared—badly. She wasn't
going to talk." He sighed. "I went up there last month,
before I left, to say goodbye to her. Had a Christmas
present for her. I liked her; she touched me, somehow.
Struck me as lonely, or a loner, anyway. I sensed she had
a hard time with that town. I don't think anybody up there
understood her. She wanted to be a concert pianist. She
was damn talented too, I heard her play. But her father
wouldn't let her leave home. No, it wasn't just her father.
I remember she said more than once, 'I can't live anywhere but Pine Woods.' Struck me as damn odd. I guess I
felt sorry for her. She was so frustrated about her music. I
think—" He broke off. "Well, it doesn't matter now.
She's dead."

"You said she'd been murdered." Carey said numbly.

"I'm sure she was. She was only eighteen, and perfectly healthy. Everybody in that town is perfectly healthy—
that's another thing. I just can't believe she died of
pneumonia, which is what the death certificate said. I
think they killed her."

"Why?" Carey felt he expected her to ask.

He shrugged. "I wish I knew. Knew too much, I guess—or knew something she shouldn't have. I know she did know something. You don't spend your life questioning people and not get to know when they're lying."

He sat still, staring down at his hands. Carey sensed a real sorrow in him. She reached out to touch his hand, then drew back self-consciously, suddenly uncomfortable with his nearness.

"I'm sorry, Paul," she said quietly. "You really liked her, didn't you?"

"Yes, I did."

"Well, if you suspected she'd been . . . I mean, couldn't you have had an autopsy or something done?"

He shook his head. "Body'd been cremated before I learned she was dead. They cremate everybody in Pine Woods. There was nothing I could do. It was just another unprovable part of the whole lousy business. I never even knew her full name till I read the death certificate. She hated it, she said." He sat a moment longer, then straightened up with a shrug. "Well, I didn't mean to rake all that up again for you. I'm sorry. It's over and done with, and best forgotten." He smiled at her. "Tell me about yourself. Are you working? What are you doing? Come on, you haven't told me a thing all evening, and I've blabbered away about myself like I was the only person in the world." He grinned at her sheepishly. "Now we're going to talk about you. Tell me what you've been up to."

Carey felt herself blush slightly. She had so little to tell, she was going to sound awfully dull. "Not much of anything, really. I couldn't take the apartment at first, so I went home with my mother to stay with her and my father for a while." She laughed self-consciously. " 'A while' turned into three and a half months. My father paid the rent for me—I couldn't bear the idea of anybody being here but Margie. I just came back last week, after New Year's. I couldn't let my father go on supporting me forever. So I gave myself a good swift kick in the seat of my pants and came back. It's been okay," she added, a little wistfully. "It's lonely without Margie, but I'm okay."

"Working yet?" he asked her.

"Just temp jobs. I haven't decided yet what I want to do." She laughed. "The only thing I seem to know for sure is that I don't ever want to work in advertising again."

"Well, I'm sure you'll come to it when you're ready," he said in a clumsy voice. "Give it time."

They sat in awkward silence for several minutes.

"Listen, there's a Lois Nettleton film on thirteen tonight," Carey said finally. She looked at the clock. "It's just starting. Would you mind seeing it? I kind of wanted to watch it."

"I'd love to. I'm a great fan of hers."

"So was Margie." Carey got up and turned on the set. "It's *End of Summer*. Margie always said it was one of her greatest performances. Would you like some more coffee?" She adjusted the sound and came back to the couch. "There's still half a pot left."

"No, thanks. I've been trying to cut down since I switched careers."

Carey stood looking down at him a long moment, the television talking away behind her. Then she moved away.

They sat through the film in silence, neither speaking a word throughout the entire showing. Occasionally Tilley uncrossed his legs and recrossed them; once he stretched them out in front of him and leaned back, as if relaxed, against the back of the couch for a few minutes. Carey shifted her position several times; twice she curled a leg up under her, then soon straightened it out and sat upright again. She could not relax. She did not so much as glance at Tilley. During the last scene they both leaned forward and stared intensely at the image of Lois Nettleton.

"Margie always said it was one of her greatest performances," Carey repeated herself, unconsciously, as the credits came on. "She's incredibly beautiful, isn't she?"

"Mm-hmm," Tilley murmured emphatically. "She is that. And a great actress. That was really something. I'd never seen it before."

"I used to watch all her films with Margie," Carey said, feeling sad. "Now I watch them for her. I suppose that sounds silly."

"No it doesn't," Tilley said simply. "Not to me."

"Margie loved her work. She said Lois Nettleton was one of the great talents of all time. Margie called her a lyric actor. It infuriated her that Lois wasn't a superstar and didn't get better roles. She said the business was wasting her."

Tilley nodded. "After that performance, I can see why."

"Well, I'll shut up about it now," Carey blurted out. She felt embarrassed. "Can I get you anything?" She got up and took a few steps toward the kitchen.

"No thanks." Tilley stood up and looked at his watch. "I should be going soon."

He was right in front of her. Close to her. Much too close to her. And his eyes were so—damn blue. She felt half-hypotized by them.

"I'm not going to bed yet," she said. Too loudly, it seemed to her. "I'm going to watch the news. You're welcome to stay and watch it with me." She saw his eyes crinkle slightly at the corners. They were so blue—it was all she seemed to be able to think, and she felt like a broken record. "If you feel like it," she added lamely.

"I'd like to," he said.

His face looked very serious. Carey stepped back from him and banged her heel against a leg of the coffee table. She felt herself blush.

"I'm partial to channel four," she said, moving toward the TV, "now that Roseanne Scamardella's not on the late news anymore. Unless you have a preference?"

"Anyone is okay with me," Tilley said. "I haven't been here long enough to have a preference."

Carey twisted the dial.

"There," she announced, feeling stupid.

The news was already under way. She stepped back

toward the couch, but Tilley seemed to be everywhere in front of her, with his blue, blue eyes fastened upon her. She stood still and made herself look away from him.

"I wish you wouldn't look at me like that," she mumbled.

The eleven-o'clock news jabbered away at them, in back of her.

"I can't help it," Tilley muttered. He reached for her hands. "How are your hands these days?"

He sounded upset, almost helpless. Carey started to pull her hands away, then let him take them.

"Fine." Her voice sounded breathless in her ears. Why couldn't she act normally around him? "They've been fine for months." She couldn't stop herself from looking up at him again.

"Good."

His voice sounded muffled to her. If only he wouldn't keep looking at her like that.

"Yes."

They stood staring at each other. He still held her hands; in fact, was gripping them now.

"You're missing the news," she said faintly.

"You're beautiful." He dropped her hands and reached for her, then pulled his arms back, then reached for her again. "Carey, I think—"

". . . the body was discovered early this morning, by two hikers, a few miles outside of Cerrillos, New Mexico, in an isolated arroyo." It took Carey a moment to realize it wasn't Tilley's voice still speaking. "While local authorities have refused to comment on the cause of death, the two hikers who found the woman's body insisted to reporters it was in the same condition as those of the two women murdered in South Bay, Maine, last August. One of the hikers, Julie Hensen, of Santa Fe, described the body as shrunken and mummified, and said they thought at first they had discovered an ancient Indian burial ground. . . ."

Carey turned in Tilley's uncompleted embrace and stared at the TV set. She couldn't make sense of all the words bombarding her eardrums like gunfire.

". . . The case in Maine has not been solved and is reported to be still under investigation. When asked if there appeared to be any connection between the body found this morning and the deaths last summer in Maine, Santa Fe police refused to comment." The picture changed abruptly, along with voice. "In Brooklyn this afternoon . . ."

Tilley stepped over to the set and switched it off. She watched him, paralyzed.

"I knew it," he growled, punching a fist into the palm of his other hand. "Goddamn it, I knew it. They're all over the place. Pine Woods isn't alone—whether they know it or not. I knew it."

Carey just stared at him. The image of what she had seen in George Dobbler's room rose up, a spectral, unholy obscenity, to haunt her once again. Unconsciously, she moaned.

"Carey!" Tilley stepped forward and took her in his arms. "It's a coincidence, just a coincidence." He kissed her face and eyes and hair, more desperately than passionately. "Forget about it, forget all about it. It isn't the same."

She knew he was kissing her, but she couldn't feel it. She seemed to be anesthetized from head to toe.

"When the police release a report, you'll see there's no connection. That newswoman just wanted her story to go national. I know that's it. I know it. Oh, Carey."

He kissed her on the mouth. She felt his lips moving frantically, trying to stir a response in her. She couldn't seem to move even that small a part of herself. He took her face between his hands and looked at her.

"I'm sorry, Carey, I'm sorry."

She didn't know if he was sorry because Margie had been killed again or because he had kissed her. She didn't even know why he should be sorry at all—about anything. Nothing was real. Not this, not last summer, not the vacant months in between. Nothing at all was real anymore.

Except—*them*. Carey stared at him, her brown eyes ghost-ridden and filled with dread.

"They're everywhere, aren't they?"

"Oh my God." He stared back at her.

"Not just in Pine Woods."

"Carey listen to me—"

"Everywhere. Anywhere. Next door—downsairs . . ."

He took her firmly by the shoulders. "It'll be all right."

Carey shook her head.

Tilley wrapped his arms around her and held her close. "I'll make it all right for you."

"How?" The apparitions in her eyes implored him.

"I will. I swear it. I promise you." His arms tightened around her. "Carey . . . Carey . . ." His mouth sought hers. "Darling . . ."

"I'm afraid, Paul"—she was trembling.

He kissed her. "You're safe with me."

"Nobody's safe!" She clung to him, suddenly as frightened for him as she was for herself. "Nobody will ever be safe again!"